TAKE
ONE LIFE

GRAHAM
DONNELLY

The Book Guild Ltd

First published in Great Britain in 2022 by
The Book Guild
Unit E2, Airfield Business Park
Harrison Road
Market Harborough
Leicsestershire, LE16 7UL
Freephone: 0800 999 2982
www.bookguild.co.uk
Email: info@bookguild.co.uk
Twitter: @bookguild

This work is entirely fictitious and bears no resemblance to any persons living or dead.

Typeset in 12pt Adobe Jenson Pro

Printed and bound by CPI Group (UK) Ltd, Croydon, CR0 4YY

ISBN 978 1914471 032

British Library Cataloguing in Publication Data.
A catalogue record for this book is available from the British Library.

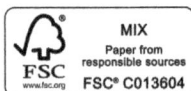

MIX
Paper from
responsible sources
FSC
www.fsc.org
FSC® C013604

For Carolyn

THE UNREMARKABLE MAN LOOKED AT HIS WATCH again and then returned his gaze up the Coast Road, towards the Sailing and Social Club. He was leaning against a railing, his back to the estuary. From here, he could see the house on Coast Road where the great man might be staying, the Sailing and Social Club where he might be eating, and the house used by the army officers which he might visit. He put his hand in his jacket pocket and for yet another time surreptitiously practised releasing the safety catch and holding the trigger for instant firing.

He began thinking about his past life and how it had all conspired to culminate in this moment. The one constant had been the belief, instilled in him by his father, that if there was a moment in his life when he was destined to achieve something of great importance, he would know that moment when it came. He had determined, rightly or wrongly, that this must be that time. But the memory is a dangerous place, full of imaginings, half-truths and delusions. It has evolved an autonomous and brutal filtering system which ensures that treasured memories often fade while those one would rather forget are retained with painful and ominous clarity. We rely

1

on our memory and that of others at our peril. If our life story is drawn from the sum of our remembrances provided by such unreliable sources, is it any wonder we search in vain for our real selves and harbour fictional, sometimes libellous, accounts of the character and history of others? This is why some of us strive to maintain the reliability of our memories through the keeping of a diary or journal. This was the case with William Lyus, who had begun a sporadic journal of sorts in early adulthood, though he doubted it would answer all his questions.

William's first certain memory was of something which happened when he was three. Later, he had a vague awareness of events which happened earlier than this but realised that in all probability, most, if not all, of these were false memories based on events he was told about afterwards or existed only in his imagination. He confidently counted his first true memory as something so significant and joyful that he could remember every moment of this short episode, although it was only later he knew the precise date, the 3rd October 1907.

He was woken by his father in the middle of the night while asleep on a sofa. He felt a gentle shaking while his father whispered, "Billy, would you like to see your new sister?"

Awake almost immediately, William clambered off his makeshift bed to walk behind his father. He didn't really understand what his father was talking about as he had had no idea that he was about to have a sister, nor was he even sure exactly what a sister was. He was just excited that something important was happening and that he was invited to be a part of it.

They went to the bedroom where his old, dark wooden cot, in which he usually slept, stood empty. His mother was sitting up in bed and smiled at him. In her arms she was holding what he assumed to be the 'sister' as he could see nothing other than a blanket. His father picked him up and, as he watched, his mother pulled back the cover and he saw a tiny baby, not much bigger than his rag doll, which appeared to be asleep. He had no memory of having seen a baby before so this was obviously a surprise, and yet, as children often do, he took it in his stride. After a little time silently watching mother and child, in her satin-edged blanket, William was escorted back to his makeshift bed. There he wondered for a moment what having a sister would actually mean, but soon fell asleep.

William's world, at this time, was concentrated on the top two floors of a very large early Victorian house on High Street, Homerton. His parents and he, and now his sister, lived on the top floor in two rooms: one room their bedroom and the other a living room. On the floor below lived his grandparents in a three-roomed apartment, including a kitchen and scullery. Without a means of cooking or running water, his immediate family ate all their meals with his grandparents and such washing facilities as they had centred on his grandmother's sink and an iron bath.

His parents, Jack and Alice, were the linchpins of his entire existence and well-being, so it was his grandparents who were the first people of whom he could take a more detached view. At the age of three, he had no idea where they came from or where precisely they fitted into his life; he didn't even know their names. They were just there, and had always been there, as a second orbiting ring round the centre of his universe, which was him. He didn't think of them as old, as ageing was a concept of which he had no understanding. They were just different to his parents.

Later, his remembered picture of his grandfather was of a man with white hair and moustache and glittering watch chain on his waistcoat. Except on Sundays, or when he went out in the evening, his shirt was collarless. He wore a cloth cap which he would throw onto a peg on the back of the door when he came in. He was nearly always smoking a pipe and William enjoyed watching him sit in his shabby old armchair and going through the rituals of cleaning the pipe, filling it with tobacco and lighting it with one, sometimes two, matches. Ignition completed, he would sit back contentedly puffing away, accompanied by the occasional rumbling cough. He was always giving William old matchboxes so he could collect the labels. William received so many different ones that later he realised that his grandfather must have gone out of his way to get them for him, though he never said as much.

His grandmother was a stout, smiling woman with grey hair, which was still brown in the bun at the back. Like his mother, she wore a dress that went almost to the ground and in some ways he viewed her as an assistant mother as she cooked most of his food and, especially in the first few weeks after his sister was born, she looked after him in other ways too. In later life he remembered her cutting his fingernails and putting his hands in a bowl of warm water first 'to make them softer and more comfortable for you', which his mother never did, before or afterwards. She also gave him sweets sometimes from a jar in the kitchen cupboard.

Whereas he took his parents for granted, he was less presuming of his grandparents' attitude and therefore more able to assess their regard for him. Based on his growing experience of them he judged them to be kind, like his parents, but less likely to scold him or tell him off, especially his grandfather. Perhaps it was their kindness towards him that led to his first act of generosity when, a few days after she was born, he presented his sister with his own rag doll. This left him with only one toy important to him, a little wooden rabbit on wheels that he could pull along on a string, but he didn't mind in the least. He soon learned the baby's name was Katherine, though everyone called her Kitty.

Objectively, his family was poor, but William didn't feel poor. His father sometimes brought home a borrowed children's book which his mother read to him at bedtime. In these books the poor people were pictured with patches in their clothes, gathered wood off the land for the fire and had little to eat. But William's clothes, few though they were, had no patches, even if his mother darned his socks, so he reasoned that he could not possibly be poor. He liked his mother reading to him and sometimes she would tell him stories that were not in a book but that she had learned when she was a girl. She would speak in a different voice for each character, and he enjoyed this aspect of her storytelling very much. There was less time for stories after Kitty was born and though he was disappointed, he felt no resentment. As to food, his grandmother was a good cook and there was always a pot on the range containing stock for the production of meals from the simplest ingredients and cheaper cuts of meat. On most Sundays there was a roast dinner and, until Kitty began eating the same as the rest of the family, he was always fed first and had plenty to eat. The home was clean but shabby. However, the faded and scuffed distemper on the walls, the flaking paint, the old furniture, none of these registered with him then. They were all part of his home and the least important part of it. Nonetheless, his sense of prosperity was heightened a few weeks after Kitty was born when his father assembled a new, or at least new to him, bed in their rather cramped bedroom. Kitty, in due course, took over the cot, which his grandfather sanded down and gave a new coat of varnish.

Despite the limited accommodation, William did not find his world restricted. Although the house had no back garden to speak of, there was what seemed to him a large front garden.

As he got older he sometimes played in this garden with the children of Mr and Mrs Mason, who lived on the floor below his grandparents. There were two boys and a girl, the boys older than him and the girl about his age.

During the week, and on Saturday morning, his father and grandfather went to work. He had only a rudimentary understanding of what work was exactly at this time but he knew it took up most of their day and his grandmother had often lit the lights in the sitting room by the time they arrived home, grandfather first and father later, often after he'd gone to bed. They would have a smell about them at the end of the day, which he liked and thought of as 'the smell of work' and part of what they were. Later, he learned that these smells emanated from oil and coke and the various materials they used where they worked: his grandfather at Berger's paint factory and father at a workshop in Mackintosh Lane.

At the weekend his father would often take him on long walks, sometimes down the hill to Hackney Marshes, where sheep were still set to graze, men and boys played football and other sports, and there were large watercress beds and the River Lea and its canal. Other times they would walk the length of Glyn Road to Millfields and walk back up along Chatsworth Road, or 'Chats', as people called it, and his father would hold his hand as they threaded their way through the crowds of shoppers, especially when the market was busy. Another walk took them to the Wick and Victoria Park with its lake and swings. He so enjoyed these walks as it was virtually the only time his father could spend alone with him. As they strolled along, his father would point out things he thought William would find of interest, such as the birds or animals they saw, or people going about their business. William asked him hundreds of what he realised later must have been tiresome questions, but his father always seemed pleased to answer and strike up a conversation about them. As Kitty got older their mother would join them with Kitty in a pram and he always remembered that time when she was two and they held hands and ran across the fields laughing, while Kitty shouted joyfully and his mother called out to him to be careful. He didn't mind because he took his responsibility as an elder brother seriously and he made sure that Kitty didn't lose her balance as her little legs lurched to and fro in her effort to keep up with him.

One of the Mason boys gave Kitty some old toy bricks and they used to pile them as high as they could or put them in rows and count them. Sometimes they played hide and seek in the garden but not in the house, as they were told to be very quiet when going onto the other floors. They were a little apprehensive when on the ground floor or in the basement, as they didn't really know the people who lived there, only that they were elderly ladies. Kitty liked him scaring her a little when they went past the door of the lady on the ground floor. She knew it was a game because Grandma often took the lady some stew when she had more than her family needed. He was so happy that Kitty was now old enough to join in with his play. She was such a sweet-natured little girl and a source of joy for the whole family; none of them could deny her anything. All in all, he loved the life he had.

It was only when he went to school in Sydney Road that William realised that he was unimportant in the world and had to accept that his status, as the centre of everyone's attention, already vastly diminished by the arrival of Kitty, had finally evaporated. He was now within a milieu of boys and girls from whom he had to find acceptance, seek collaboration and compete with for the favour of their peers and the good opinion of their teacher. The teachers were the usual mixed bag: philanthropists and tyrants, those who inspired learning and those who deadened the interest of their pupils, those who cultivated understanding and those who rammed knowledge into them. While some lessons were periods of joy for William, others were tedious or directed towards the avoidance of punishment.

The challenge of entry into school life was eased by the presence of the Mason children already at the school while their young sister, Lucy, started on the same day as William in Class One. His mother, accompanied by the Mason children, took him to school on the first day and the older Mason boy, Cecil, showed him the ropes at playtime. The teacher, a pleasant elderly lady, told him to sit next to a boy named Amos at a double desk with a bench seat. Amos became his first new friend at the school.

He soon adapted to his new surroundings and enjoyed the experience of learning, even if much of it was by rote. His family had always referred to him as 'Billy' but now he got used to his full name of William Lovett Lyus when practising his writing. The school was opposite the Hackney Workhouse, and Cecil and his brother Stanley, along with their friends, would regale the younger boys and girls with stories of life in the workhouse. They painted lurid pictures of the discipline and hardships experienced by the inmates as well as the frightening goings-on within its confines, especially as it had a 'lunatic block'. Now, not only did William not feel poor, he understood that there were people much worse off than himself. Some of them went to his own school: boys and girls who had patched clothes and wore boots or shoes previously worn by elder brothers or sisters. He was beginning to have a rudimentary understanding that there was a social hierarchy and was relieved not to be at the bottom of it. He realised later that perhaps nobody ever thinks they are at the bottom of it, otherwise they might lose the will to go on.

Once he had started school his mother and grandmother took him to church with them on a Sunday and he wore his best short trousers and long socks, which his grandmother called 'stockings'. Although he didn't understand much of what was going on at the service he liked listening to the singing and the playing of the organ. Later on, he also began to attend Sunday school every Sunday afternoon, where the children would listen to stories from the Bible and then draw pictures based on them. William found many of the stories quite exciting and every bit as good as the fairy tales he listened to at home. All in all, it was so much better to have an hour out the house on a Sunday, rather than having to sit quietly at home, trying to be especially good and to resist the temptation to play hide and seek or tag with Kitty. Nor was he permitted to do any jobs or to go out and play with his friends as he could on other days.

Now that he was at school, there was a noticeable loosening of the apron strings by Alice. He was allowed to accompany the Mason children on their adventures beyond the confines of the garden, at first to the hinterland of the neighbouring streets, and later into an ever-expanding universe in the rest of Homerton, Clapton and Hackney. Just behind their back garden was Nisbet Street with its rows of small terraced houses, their front doors opening directly onto the street. William compared them unfavourably to his own house with its big front steps and large windows. Off Nisbet Street were narrow alleys which contained workshops and other commercial premises. There was even an abattoir in one of these little roads, and once or twice he watched the animals on their way to be killed and butchered. Cecil Mason had a school friend in Nisbet Street named Albert Mutton. Albert's father owned a barrel organ and sometimes Albert would play it in the street while the local children danced round it. The first time he saw this William was too shy to join in, but Lucy Mason took his hands and they danced round and round until they were giddy.

He liked Lucy very much and at this time played with her at least as much as with the Mason boys. Together they learned many of the games the children played in Nisbet Street such as Ring a Ring a Roses, Oranges and Lemons, Hopscotch, and Fivestones, which they called 'Gobs'. These games always took place on the street because it was virtually free of road traffic of any kind. They were only interrupted, and then pleasantly so, by the visit of street vendors: lavender seller, knife sharpener, orange seller and the muffin man with a clanging bell. Without money of his own, he was neither able to purchase any of the items on offer nor usually persuade his mother that she should do so. He was always a little sorry for any vendors who were unable to sell some of their goods on the day because he so enjoyed watching these colourful characters going about their business. Of particular interest was a man dressed in smart clothes with a bowler hat and striped apron. He carried a large basket and written round it was 'Charles Gardiner, Gentleman Purveyor of Cat's Meats'. When he mentioned the man to his mother she explained that he was her Uncle Charles and therefore his granduncle. One day he ran to tell Alice that Granduncle Charles was coming down the road and she introduced them. After that, whenever Charles saw William he would give him a ha'penny, sometimes a penny, and tell him to buy some sweets.

At school William's first friends were Amos and, not surprisingly, the Mason children. But he soon made friends among the boys in his class and four of them, including Amos, tended always to play together and take each other's side in the various squabbles and points of honour which mark that age. Perhaps inevitably, these new friendships led to William seeing less of the Mason children, though there was nothing intentional about it and the change was so slow it was barely perceptible at first. In this first year at school his association with his new classmates would come to an abrupt end with the last bell of the day at four o'clock. Then he would meet the waiting Cecil Mason, at nine years of age entrusted with the task of escorting home his siblings with William, and all four would make their way home. Sometimes they would play together, but he liked to go straight home to play with Kitty, who was not yet old enough to go out to play.

When he had been at school for about eighteen months, William's class was told that the King's coronation would soon be taking place and that they would see the school decorated by the older children in preparation for the event. Soon a rash of bunting and flags spread throughout the school while everywhere there were pictures of the serious-looking King and Queen. Many of the shops in the High Street were also decorated and had royal pictures and flags in the windows. Their teacher told the class a little about what would happen on Coronation Day, but most of it, apart from the wearing of the crown and the procession through London, went over their heads, especially as they would see nothing of the celebrations on the day. They said special prayers in class for the King, as they had done the previous year when he'd ascended the throne. On Coronation Day bands could be heard playing in the distance and there was a military parade and procession which the children watched. The highlight of the day for William was the street party he attended. There was no party organised anywhere in the High Street as it was too busy a road to be closed. Instead, Kitty and William, together with the Mason children, were invited to the party in Nisbet Street and his mother and grandmother helped to serve the food. It was a cloudy day with a chill breeze, but this didn't spoil the party as there was no rain. The children drank tea or diluted cordial and had sandwiches, cakes and buns to eat while some of the adults drank beer and other alcoholic drinks. There was music played by Albert Mutton's father on his barrel organ and some songs were sung. Every child received a mug with the King's picture on it and a big man wearing a top hat suddenly appeared, distributed sweets to the children, toasted the King with a glass of beer and then was gone. Kitty wasn't sure exactly what the party was for, but she clearly still enjoyed it very much. However, she was tired and flushed when they returned home and was put straight to bed.

The next morning, Kitty woke with a sore throat and temperature and her mother kept her in bed, thinking it was either a summer cold or her having had too much excitement the previous day. But it wasn't actually either of these things and the following day she was much worse, with a barking cough and a slight swelling round the neck. The doctor was sent for and William's bed was moved into his grandparents' bedroom. The doctor came that afternoon and his examination revealed a grey patch in her throat and he noticed her breathing was becoming more laboured. His father told William that Kitty was very ill, so he asked if he could see her and perhaps cheer her up, but his father shook his head and said it was not possible. William was allowed to wave to her from the doorway and she smiled her sweet little smile and closed her eyes. Later that day the doctor arranged for her to go into hospital and William was told that she would be well looked after. As the days passed he heard his parents' and grandparents' worried conversations about her progress, but it did not deter William from beginning to make plans and to look forward to Kitty getting better. He never saw her again because she could not be saved; she had come into his life without his expecting it and now she had left it in the same way.

That day when Kitty died was engrained forever on William's mind. It was after supper and he was sitting with his grandparents. He felt there was something odd about the atmosphere in the room because neither of his grandparents said very much. His grandmother was in her rocking chair knitting, and his grandfather and he were playing a game of dominos in which his grandfather kept making mistakes. William stopped playing when he heard his parents' footsteps downstairs in the hall on their return from the hospital. Although he was not anticipating anything momentous, he could feel a rising sense of tension in the room as his parents began to climb the stairs and his anticipation of seeing them was heightened by each successive flight. He was a little perturbed by the slowness of their steps, especially when he saw his grandmother put down her knitting and grandfather puff more energetically on his pipe, his ear cocked towards the door. As they came into the apartment, William looked first at his mother, expecting the smile with which she always greeted him, but she didn't even look at him. Clearly distraught and with swollen eyes, she shook her head and went over to her mother-in-law, her hands raised in supplication. The older woman put her arms round her and it was the first time William saw his mother cry.

Jack, ashen-faced and mouth twisted in grief, managed a faint smile and said, "Hello, Billy. You still up? I think it's time you went to bed." He glanced at his own father, who nodded and, clasping William's hand, took him upstairs.

With a growing sense of realisation and shock William knelt, whispering falteringly as his grandfather recited his prayers with him and said they should say a special prayer for Kitty that God would look after her. William noticed there were tears in the old man's eyes and his voice broke as he spoke. Then he tucked William up in bed and kissed him on the forehead. William hoped his grandfather would stay and talk to him, but the old man couldn't speak, and he closed the door gently while taking a handkerchief from his pocket.

In the Edwardian period it was still all too common to lose a child to illness, but the acute sense of loss was not in any way diminished by a greater familiarity with such events than in later years. Nothing could be further from the truth. As in any other family, now or ever, the loss of a child was devastating for William's parents and hardly any less awful for his grandparents. A terrible pall of grief and despondency lay over the household, and its effect soon rippled out to their wider family. The next morning William's other grandmother, his mother's mother, came round to give her support. He did not know her as well as his father's mother as, her first husband having died some years before, she had since remarried and become more involved in her second husband's family. William had seen her no more than half a dozen times. To him, she seemed much larger than the woman he called Grandma, both physically and in her dominating presence, which he found abrupt and daunting. It made him feel very uncomfortable, especially as she talked over him and barely gave him a glance. Her offer to take him home with her for a few days was refused by his mother, much to his relief. In the next few days lots of other people he barely knew called to give their condolences. He recognised the two men who closely resembled his father as his uncles. There were also several ladies who were his uncles' wives or sisters of one of his parents, and he had seen most of these before too. There were many tears shed and sad embraces exchanged. Granduncle Charles also called and spent quite a long time talking to Alice, and he asked William how he was getting on at school, patted his head and gave him sixpence.

It was his father who undertook the task of explaining to William what had happened to Kitty. Only seven years old, he had yet to cross the threshold of that moment when one grasps the truth of what death actually means. A week or so earlier his schoolteacher had explained that this was the twentieth century and that it would give way to the twenty-first century in due course. After school William asked his father how old he would be when the next century began and was told he would be ninety-six. William knew that ninety-six was a very big number and that he might not reach that age. Yet still he couldn't quite feel any sense of apprehension that he would cease to exist. Now, when his father explained, quietly and calmly, that Kitty was not coming home because she had died and gone to Heaven, he felt a sense of loss but was unable to comprehend that it was any more final or much different to when one of the boys at school had moved with his parents to Old Ford. He knew only that he missed Kitty. He would have to experience the true realisation and grief in subsequent years.

In the following days, the family busied itself with the rituals of mourning as a distraction from the true matter at hand. Alice sewed black material in the shape of a diamond on both her husband's coat and his jacket and also on her father-in-law's overcoat. She borrowed a black dress from Mrs Mason while William's grandmother pulled out of retirement a black dress she had from a family funeral several years before. They decided on the hymns to be sung and chose wreaths suitable for a child. William's grandparents paid for the funeral, a very simple affair at St Barnabas Church, with the proceeds of an insurance policy for an event such as this. William did not attend the funeral, so he did not see the tiny white coffin on the bier, his mother restraining her sobbing at the service or his father weeping silently at the graveside. He spent the morning with the Mason family, hoping that one day soon his family would be happy again and perhaps that he might have a new sister to play with and to make laugh.

These hopes for the future were not to materialise. As the weeks passed, the atmosphere of sadness and hopelessness did not diminish. Jack had removed the cot and packed it away in the roof, and William was now back in the bedroom. There was an air of restlessness in the room and he would be woken at night by the sound of his mother crying and the attempts of his father to comfort her. In the daytime he was at school and was cheered by the companionship and play of his classmates, but in the evening he would return to the quiet flat where everyone would sit in silence. At first Alice went to church more often, nearly every day, but after a while she stopped going even on Sundays and William went only with Grandma. His father came home even later than before and William rarely saw him in the week. Grandfather seemed suddenly older and less full of life. His cough was now much worse so that, whereas once he'd smoked more than he'd coughed, now it was the other way round. Only Grandma seemed more like her old self, always busy at the sink or cooking meals which were rarely eaten with much enthusiasm, except by William.

William would sit and watch his mother, waiting for her to give him a sign that he still mattered to her. He wanted to cry out, "You still have *me*! Can't I make you happy again?" but he said nothing; he just watched and waited. Then, one day she looked up from her reverie and said, "Stop staring at me. What do you want?" He knew then that he could never fill the void left by Kitty and suspected that his mother would rather have lost *him*.

The next day was a Sunday and William went to church with Grandma, as usual. As they walked along she took his hand and said, "Don't take to heart what your mum said yesterday. She doesn't mean it; she is so upset by losing Kitty. The death of her child is the hardest thing for a mother to bear; she'd have felt exactly the same had it been you."

He smiled at her and knew she was being kind to say that. After that he felt closer to Grandma and more able to say things to her that cropped up in his mind. But he didn't believe what she had said about it being the same for his mother if she had lost him instead of Kitty; he just felt better about it.

At church that day the lesson was the story from the Book of Genesis of the brothers Jacob and Esau, and how Jacob had pretended he was Esau to his blind father, Isaac, so that he would receive his father's blessing and steal the birthright due to Esau. William spent the rest of the service puzzling how it could be right for God to give his favour to Jacob so that he became the patriarch of his chosen people when he was such a cheat and a thief. As they left the church he asked his grandmother what she thought of the story and whether it was right what had happened.

Grandma looked down at him with an expression of bemusement. "Goodness me, the questions that go through your mind. It's not for us to judge what God does, Billy," she said, smiling. "God's ways are not our ways, but we must trust Him to know what's best for all of us. In any case, it's in the next world that good people like Esau receive their just desserts."

He was not convinced that Grandma's explanation was a satisfactory excuse for Jacob's behaviour, but he thought Esau was a very good person to forgive his brother at the end of the story. However, the reference to desserts, with its connotations of apple pie and rice pudding, left him stumped for any further comment on the matter and his mind turned to Sunday dinner and what they would have for dessert.

Resigned to the fact that his presence alone would not be enough to win his mother's love, William saw himself as a kind of Esau who would forgive the loss of his mother's favour and seek to make himself useful to her. He offered to help her with the housework and assured her he was old enough to run errands. He happily accepted the task of regularly black-leading the range and fireplaces and polishing the brass fireside tools: the poker, small shovel and tongs. Both jobs he enjoyed doing because it made things look newer and smarter. When his grandfather bought a new pair of hobnail boots, he watched him smooth the toecaps with a heated spoon handle, treat them with leather oil and then polish them to a fine lustre. After that, he let William polish his boots when he came home from work. What he liked most was that Alice now entrusted him with the task of going to the shops on their side of the High Street. He would take the enamel jug each morning to the dairy on the corner of Crozier Terrace for a quart of milk and, with money wrapped in a piece of paper on which was a shopping list, he would often go to the grocers just the other side of the terrace. The grocer had large sacks from which he measured out the correct amounts required of flour, rice and so on, and then wrapped them in neat packages. William liked the smells in the shop and watching the grocer and his wife serving the customers. Best of all was the machine they had for cutting slices of bacon, ham and other meats, which he thought quite magical.

William now believed he was becoming useful to his mother and, most gratifyingly, she praised his efforts when he returned home. By the time he was eight he was allowed to cross the High Street on his own and buy bread from the bakers and get grandfather's pipe tobacco from the tobacconists. This was another shop where he liked the smells and enjoyed watching the tobacconist use his scales to mix up his grandfather's favourite blend. Sometimes, Grandma asked him to buy some sweets from the newsagents when he went to collect the tobacco and she would always give him a couple of the sweets when he handed them over. On one occasion, she asked him to buy a quarter of peppermints for her. As he came out of the shop, he went to run across the road, but he slipped on the stone sets and the peppermints spilled out of the bag and landed in some horse's dung. He wiped the peppermints in his handkerchief until they were clean and took them home. His grandmother didn't notice anything different about them but wondered why for once William refused one, when offered. William was worried for a few days until he was sure she wasn't going to be ill. He was relieved it turned out all right because he was worried that Alice would think him no longer good enough to run errands.

Soon after his ninth birthday, William and his parents moved from their rooms above his grandparents to the bottom half of a house in a road off the High Street, a little nearer to his school. He was sorry to move because he was very fond of his grandparents and enjoyed going out to play with the Mason children, especially Lucy. But Jack said that it wasn't right that they took up some of the rooms that belonged to his grandparents and it was time for them as a family to make their own way in the world. The house was in Daubeney Road, which his grandparents still referred to by its former name of Pincey Road. Though William regarded himself as continuing to live in Homerton, his father later explained that actually they had crossed the border into Clapton. Through the idiosyncrasy of local boundaries, a peninsular of Clapton followed Glyn Road and Daubeney Road right up to the High Street.

The family now had three rooms plus a scullery so that his parents had their own bedroom with a large bay window at the front, while William had a smaller bedroom behind this one. They brought with them the furniture they'd had in their old home and a cart arrived the day they moved in with some second-hand furniture his father had ordered. His mother let him give a lump of sugar to the patient old horse and he watched, fascinated, as the horse gently took the sugar without his big brown teeth even touching William's hand.

In their new home they spent most of the time in the back room with its large fireplace and fitted range and the scullery leading off it. The dining table was the focal point of the household; they not only sat at it for every meal, but his father did his paperwork there and his mother her sewing while William read or listened to his parents' conversation.

The upper floor of the house was occupied by a young married couple, Mr and Mrs Poulter. William didn't see much of Mr Poulter, a thin young man with metal-framed glasses and a drooping moustache, but he often saw Mrs Poulter when he was looking out of the front window and she came up the front path. She always smiled and waved at him, and he thought her very pretty. The two families kept a discreet distance from each other and the only interaction between their lives was that they had to share the toilet and the coal cellar. The former could be accessed by going out the side door of the house rather than through the living room and so any potential embarrassment was avoided. Similarly, the cellar door was in the hall and the Poulters could obtain coal without invading the lives of their co-tenants. William liked the fact that the coal could be delivered via a chute under a small cover in the pavement outside rather than being brought through the house. If he was home and heard the coalman's cart in the street he would go to the front gate and watch the coalman, in his leather overall and strange hat, stop at each house, take a bag on his back and pour it down the coal chute. When the cart reached his house, he would run inside and descend the cellar steps to watch the coal cascade into the coalbunker with a loud whoosh, always standing well clear to avoid the cloud of coal dust. Then he would rush back upstairs and take a piece of sugar for the coalman's horse.

In all aspects of life it appeared to William that his family was richer than it had been before. Now they had their own home his mother allowed him to have friends from school, including the Mason children, come round to play, in his bedroom or in the garden at the back of the house. He received a small amount of pocket money each week and when Christmas came round his parents bought him some toy soldiers and a *Boy's Own* annual. He felt so fortunate because in the past at Christmas he had usually received only an orange, an apple and a large chocolate coin wrapped in gold foil with some real money from his grandfather. This rise in living standards was manifested in other ways. His mother took him shopping in Mare Street to buy him some new clothes and as a family they went on a couple of day trips over the course of the year. One of those was to Thorpe Bay and he lost count of the many things he did that day for the first time. He had sometimes spotted a train pulling into Homerton Station but that day a bus ride to Stratford was followed by his first train journey. When the three of them walked from the station to the front, the sun seemed brighter and the colours lighter than William was used to at home and suddenly he saw the sea for the first time! The tide was in and he stood in awe as the waves rolled and uncurled from the sea, scrambling up the beach to its highest point before receding for another push. His father bought him a bucket and spade from a nearby shop and he had a wonderful time playing in this magical new environment. What made it for him a very happy day was that his mother clearly enjoyed it too. When they were on the beach she filled William's bucket with seawater and playfully teased her husband by acting as if to throw it over him. It was the first time William could recall seeing his mother laugh since before Kitty had died. In the late afternoon they went to a tearoom and had a cup of tea and a cake. William tried very hard to use the shiny silver knife properly and was careful not to spill any tea. He would go to the seaside many times after this, but he would never again experience the wonder of that first day at the sea.

William had no idea how this newfound improvement in their circumstances had come about, but his nine-year-old imagination conjured up its own answer to this conundrum. He fancied that his father had been the fortunate recipient of some kind of magical event, like the heroes and heroines of the fairy stories he read at school, perhaps finding a crock of gold at the end of a rainbow or being given a magic lamp like Aladdin. The truth was rather more prosaic: much of his parents' past frugality had been due to them saving up so that they could afford the move to the new home. In addition, his mother had resumed her former work of taking in sewing and dressmaking. A few months later his father would secure a better-paid job in a bigger firm, after improving his qualifications, and their living standards continued their upward trajectory.

It was now that Jack introduced his son to his own world. William was very pleased because his time spent at home was often dull and without excitement of any kind. When he returned home from school, it was, metaphorically speaking, to a cold, lonely place. His mother was not unkind, but she had never recovered the warmth of personality of the time when Kitty was alive, much as he had wished for it to be so. Disappointingly for him, the happy day in Thorpe Bay had not led to a long-lasting change in her demeanour. She would show little interest in his day at school nor relate to him the activities and events of her life. They ate their tea in relative silence, most conversation limited to requests or directions from mother to son. Afterwards, she would resume her work, sitting in a chair under the gaslight while he played on his own. Now that he was nine, he was much more likely to be up when his father came in. After throwing his cap on the peg behind the door in a way reminiscent of his own father, he would sit down with William and ask him what he'd learned that day. Whatever it was, he would be able to find some little titbit of amusing or interesting knowledge he had of the subject. Then he would spend a little time playing with William or reading a story before sending him off to bed.

One day Jack came home earlier than usual and had tea with his wife and son. Afterwards, while Alice washed up, he sat in his chair and talked about his day for a while. Then he looked at the clock on the mantelpiece and said, "I must go to the library. How would you like to come with me this evening, Billy?"

William was totally surprised by this question and could feel the grin spread across his face at the thought of being offered participation, however limited, in his father's activities. Stunned into silence he could only nod vigorously his acceptance of the offer. He jumped up and went over to the clothes cupboard to get his coat.

"Hang on a minute, son," said Jack, smiling, "I'll just finish my cup of tea."

Ten minutes later they were walking along the High Street on the way to Homerton Library in Brooksby's Walk. Although he knew what a library was, William had never actually been in one. This was a brand-new library and the building of it had taken nearly a year to complete so that he and his father had often stopped to watch the work on the site on one of their walks up Chatsworth Road. It had been finished several months earlier, but whenever he passed the building William was always struck by the grandeur of its Portland stone facade and Doric columns. Today, as they approached the entrance, his father pointed out the foundation stone and William nodded, but his attention was fixed on the large doors while he considered what wonders awaited in this grand, impressive place.

As they walked through the doors William thought that this must be what a palace was like: the large open space with a high ceiling, patterned floor and impressive staircase leading to the upstairs rooms. But of course it was a library and, looking round at the shelves upon shelves of books, he was awestruck by the existence of their number and variety.

Jack had two books to return to the library and went to the counter first before taking William over to the children's fiction. He pointed to the shelves and whispered to William to find a book to read while he went to get a book for himself. William was a good reader but, intimidated by his surroundings and the vast number of books, he suffered a sudden loss of confidence and chose a copy of *Mr Midshipman Easy*, as he presumed from its title that it would not present him with too much of a challenge. He sat down to read it and found that it was actually quite hard to understand but ploughed on with it anyway. After a few minutes his father joined him. He had a couple of books in his hands and, producing a pencil and small notebook from his coat pocket, proceeded to look through one of the books, making the occasional note, sometimes flicking back to an earlier page before making an entry in his notebook.

"What are you reading, son?" he asked, eventually looking up.

William raised the cover towards him so he could read the spine.

"Ah, *Mr Midshipman Easy*. How are you getting on with it?"

"It's all right. It's set in the olden days."

"I can borrow it if you'd like to read it."

"I'm not sure."

Jack smiled. "Give it here; I'll get you something else by the same author which you might enjoy more."

He took the book away and returned a couple of minutes later with *Children of the New Forest*. "I've got it on loan, so you have two weeks to read it. We'll take it home with us. I've got my own books stamped too so we can go when I've finished taking these notes."

"Do you come to the library every day, Dad?" asked William.

"Most weekdays, I suppose," Jack replied, without looking up.

"Why don't you borrow all the books instead of reading them here?"

"Well, some, like this one," William caught a flash of the title but didn't quite see what it was, "can't be taken out on loan. They're for reference only."

"What does 'reference' mean?"

"They are usually books which people use for reading a section of or looking things up, like a dictionary or an atlas. So people know it will always be here when they want to make use of it," Jack said patiently.

"Why do you want books like that?"

"To help me with my studies." Jack ceased looking at the book and smiled at his inquisitive son.

William had heard his father refer to his studies before, when talking to his mother about becoming qualified for a better job, so he nodded. "To help with your job?" he asked.

"Not this time. I'm studying other things I'm interested in. I'll tell you all about it one day, but now I have to put these books back and get you home before we both get into trouble with your mother," he said, wrapping up the subject before it could be taken any further.

After that, William began to go with Jack to the library every two weeks, exchanging a book he'd read for another, usually selected after advice from his father. Some of them he found harder to read than others or only mildly interesting, but he always read them through to the end as his father had taken the trouble to find them for him. Generally, they were adventure stories by authors such as Walter Scott, Anthony Hope and Robert Louis Stevenson. Not only did he enjoy the adventures, but he also learned about other times and other lands; even Scotland seemed a land of alien geography and exotic people. Sometimes the books stretched his understanding so that he had to grow into them, which was challenging but ultimately satisfying.

As the weeks went on he learned a little more about the books that his father was studying and he even had the opportunity to look at them, though the subject matter, politics, philosophy and the law, he found difficult to comprehend and certainly too much to read. Jack tried to explain them all in simple terms, but William was not yet ready even to think about such matters. He was more concerned with his own name.

Before he'd started school he had never thought about his name. It was one of those facts he accepted without question, like where he lived and who his parents were. He knew from the names of the Mason children and of the others he played with in Nisbet Street that there were many first names but that often he would come across other boys with the name William. This was confirmed when he started school and there were three other Williams in his class. As the boys all referred to each other by surnames or diminutives of them there was little confusion: he was called 'Ly' and another 'Smithy' and so on. It created something of a bond, a shared belonging, that they had names in common. Well over half of the boys in the class had John, or its diminutive Jack, as one of their forenames. William was pleased that his first name was common, though not too common. But as time went on he became self-conscious about the uniqueness of his middle name, 'Lovett', especially when some of his schoolmates teased him with the name 'Love' for short. He didn't like standing out so much from the crowd, being the centre of everyone's attention. His surname he was indifferent about since it was neither peculiar nor could it be shortened to something comical or insulting. He raised the subject with his father on one of their walks to the library.

"Dad, how did I get my name?"

His father looked down at him and smiled. "Well, you are named William after your mum's father just like I was named after my grandfather, John."

He was not really thinking about 'William', but this answer triggered another query he had. "But if my name is William why am I called 'Billy' with a 'B'?"

Jack nodded. "It's something people have always done. They shorten a name like William to 'Willy' and then give it a rhyming name like 'Billy'. It's like your uncle Ted's name is Edward but he could be called 'Ted' or 'Ed' or 'Ned'."

"Like, Uncle Bob is really 'Robert'?"

"Exactly, you've got the idea."

William enjoyed this game and they spent the next few minutes going through male and female names looking for rhyming diminutives. But then he returned to his first question. "What about my other name, where does that come from?"

"Lyus? I don't know much about it, except that it's not very common. I suppose it's a name that originally described where we came from; many surnames are like that."

"No, not 'Lyus': 'Lovett.'"

"Ah, 'Lovett'. I named you William Lovett after one of my heroes."

He was pleased that he'd been named after a hero but was surprised not to have heard of this person before. "Who was William Lovett?"

"Well, he was a man who was a carpenter who gave it up to work hard to try to make life for the poor better through peaceful means, as he opposed violence."

"He was like Jesus then?"

Jack nodded. "I suppose in some ways he was, but he didn't claim to be from God or a holy man, just someone who believed that the country should be made a better place for everyone, not just the rich. That is something I believe in too."

William was a little disappointed to be named after a hero who seemed not to have achieved great victories in battle, but he liked the idea of being named after someone whom his father respected, even if it was something to live up to.

Often on these library trips they would call in to see his grandparents. Granddad Lyus was not very well in the winter as his cough was always worse, especially when the fog was very thick. Just before Christmas they went to see him, but he was so unwell that he was in bed. There was lots of chatter about 'bronchitis' and his grandmother seemed very worried. William was allowed to see his grandfather and the old man waved to him and smiled, and it took William's mind back to when he had last seen Kitty. Suddenly he felt the pang of loss when he thought about Kitty and fervently hoped Granddad was not going to die too. He was so pleased when Granddad recovered the week afterwards and was well enough to come over for Christmas dinner. He retired the following April and that seemed to give him what everyone agreed was a 'new lease of life'.

AT THAT TIME, APRIL 1914, WILLIAM HAD NO IDEA what a momentous year would now unfold, but not many grown-ups did either, as he subsequently found out. There had been several crises between the great powers in the previous ten years or so, but they had never come to blows. They had always found a way to defuse the situation and there seemed to be no reason why this latest crisis shouldn't follow a similar pattern. So when the school holidays began in July his mind was focussed solely on planning what he, with his school friends, as a group of nine-year-old boys in search of adventure, would do with the seven weeks that now stretched before them. While they shared a common purpose, they were a mixed bunch. There was Leonard, generally regarded as their unnamed leader, the one who usually came up with suggestions of what to do and the first ideas of how they should put their plans into effect. Cyril was the tallest and burliest of them. He was quiet and unassuming but could usually be relied upon to take a lead in implementing their plans and going the right way about things. His presence in the little band was always enough to deter rival groups from trying to intimidate them. The third member was the first friend he'd made at school, Amos, an impetuous boy who would be the first to say 'yes' to any exciting idea. He was a great lover of practical jokes, though rarely anything that would be regarded as cruel. Finally there was William; by his own admission shyer than Leonard or Amos and more questioning of ideas before agreeing to go along with them. On one of their typical adventures, pretending to be explorers across the fields and down by the river, Leonard would take the lead and decide where they would camp, Cyril would light the fire and look after it, Amos would invent the games or try some stunt or experiment involving fire and water, and William would help out where needed and then tidy up before they left.

As they planned their schedule for the summer, the possibility of war was as far from their minds as it was from that of almost the whole country. Then, Austria's crown prince was assassinated by a Bosnian Serb in Sarajevo. An Austrian declaration of war on Serbia was followed by a series of apparently unstoppable tit for tat declarations of war by all the great powers. Within a week they were divided into two opposing sides lined up against each other. Suddenly, the boys' focus changed. Plans for expeditions in the park or down the marshes, swimming, fishing and playing with model boats on the river, and imitating the gun fights and ambushes of the Wild West, gave way to reconstructing the activities of the armies now engaged in the Great War.

While they might keep it from their parents, William and his friends, at the age of nine or ten, saw nothing but excitement in the prospect of war, especially as it reflected the attitude of most of the male population. Britain was accustomed to nearly a hundred years without a conflict on the scale of the Napoleonic Wars and understandably, if without justification, most people assumed any war would be short-lived. Military experts anticipated a war of rapid movement lasting a few weeks, a view accepted by most of those who volunteered to join the army. If those who would be doing the fighting thought it all so exhilarating how could schoolboys, used to war games in which people who were killed were instantly able to come back to life, be expected to anticipate the reality of what was to come? In any case, they were sure their side was the right one and knew from their own stories and playing at war, it was usually the 'baddies' who got killed. With other groups from school or the neighbourhood, the boys turned parts of Hackney Marshes and Victoria Park into north-west France, at least in their minds, and conducted their own make-believe battles, taking it in turns to be the British and the Germans. Leonard's father stuck a spike from a broken railing on an old coalscuttle to produce a reasonable copy of a German pickelhaube helmet and so Leonard was always elected to command the German troops in their games, an honour he retained even when other boys acquired comparable headgear.

Within weeks of the war starting William and all his friends knew someone who had joined up: a brother, a father, an uncle or a neighbour. In William's case it was Mr Poulter, the young man who lived upstairs in his house. He rather hoped that his father would show some interest, however fleeting, in the possibility of volunteering. But as the weeks went on Jack didn't mention the subject of the war and showed none of the patriotic, sometimes jingoistic support for the British Expeditionary Force of most of the men William knew, including his grandfather. Of course, William was aware that his father was not very young, probably in his late thirties, though he was younger than both his brothers. But he knew lots of people of his father's age, or even older, were joining up; one of their neighbours had tried to enlist but had been rejected on the grounds of age because he was in his late forties. When William went back to school his class was full of excitement about the war and their teacher explained what was going on with the battles in France and Belgium, usually in places which sounded nothing like the way they were spelled on the blackboard. Classmates regaled each other with tales of family members going off to war and the haste with which they had done so for fear of missing out since it would 'all be over by Christmas'. Exasperated by his own lack of any story to tell, William determined to ask his father what he thought of the war and his place in it. So, on their walk to the library one evening in early September he plucked up the courage to raise the topic.

"Are you going to join up, Dad?" he asked, as they walked along.

His father laughed. "I don't think so. Why do you ask, son?"

"Well, lots of my friends' dads or elder brothers have joined up and I just wondered what our family could do."

"You don't want to be left out, so you expect me to go off to fight on your behalf, is that it?"

It was the first time he could recall his father challenging his motives and implicitly questioning his character. He was self-aware enough to realise that his father had a point and, momentarily ashamed, blurted out, "I would go if I was old enough. I'm not afraid." The salt of a tear stung his eye.

Jack put his hand on his son's shoulder. "I know," he said. "I'm not afraid either, but there was no need for this war and I won't fight in it."

William didn't quite understand what he meant by this statement as he had assumed that the war had come about precisely *because* it was necessary. So he didn't answer but put aside that remark for consideration later.

Jack stopped walking and reached into his pocket for his wallet. He took something from it and showed it to William. "Do you know what this is?" he asked.

"It's a white feather."

"It was given to me last week by a lady as a sign of my cowardice for not fighting for my country. Now answer me this, Billy: am I more of a coward by refusing to enlist when it's against my principles or by giving in to the bullying of others who want to shame me into fighting when I think it's wrong?"

William hesitated for just a moment or two. Thinking back to the behaviour of the heroes in the adventure books he had read he knew there was only one answer. "I don't think you are a coward if you do what you believe is right."

"Well said, son." Jack patted him on the shoulder.

The next day at school William's dilemma came to a head. Out of respect and admiration for his father, he wanted to agree with his position regarding the war, but he didn't want to feel isolated among his fellow pupils and their teacher, all of whom were enthusiastically patriotic towards the conduct of the war. William solved the problem by maintaining simultaneously two attitudes: one with his friends of unambiguous support for winning the war and one with his father of quiescent scepticism as to its purpose. In the first case, he was able to join his classmates in playing at soldiers in the playground or the park, being part of a group from class that salvaged metal and other scrap for the war effort and occasionally donating some of his pocket money for war charities. With the whole school, he stood on the pavement waving flags and cheering to the smiling, marching troops as they went off to fight. With his father he avoided bringing the subject up but nodded silently on the rare occasions that Jack spoke sadly or critically about the conduct of the war.

This ambiguous attitude to the war became easier as William's early enthusiasm about it soon faded. Its very existence became oddly normal, a permanent background to most of what remained of his school days. Whatever its national importance, it now had to compete with all the other demands on the growing horizons of a boy in the last few years of childhood. This was especially so as the stalemate on the Western Front ensured there was little to grab the imagination of a young boy inspired by sweeping cavalry charges and 'tales of derring-do', a phrase he'd picked up from reading Walter Scott's *Ivanhoe*. Increasingly, the war only came to the fore of his interests in those momentous or unusual events which remained part of his most enduring memories of that time, and one in particular which occurred in April 1915.

Because the war was expected to be of short duration, life carried on as usual at first and even leisure and sports activities were hardly affected. The football season of 1914–15 was played right through until its completion in April and William's grandfather introduced him to the pleasures and tribulations of watching professional sport by sometimes taking him to see the local Football League team, Clapton Orient. Granddad would collect him from home and they would walk the ten minutes or so to the ground in Millfields Road. There, they would stand on the terrace, Granddad getting William to the front so he could see properly. They always stood in the same place and, on the occasions when he came to the match, Uncle Bob, Granddad's eldest son, would come and stand with them. Afterwards, they would all have a cup of tea and a slice of bread and dripping or a piece of cake in the Orient Café in Chatsworth Road. Then William and his grandfather would stroll up to the High Street, where William would leave him at the tobacconists, running home to relate the result to his father, especially if the O's had won. In April, they went to the last match of the season against Leicester Fosse.

"This is the last match we'll see for a long time, son," said Granddad, as they joined the stream of supporters heading for the turnstiles. "The League won't be able to start next season with so many players joining up. Pretty well our whole team: Parker, McFadden, Jonas, Hugall and the others have enlisted, and they'll be off to train for the front after today."

It was a memorable match. Uncle Bob and his dad's other brother, Uncle Ted, were both there, and they squeezed through the crowd to join them. There were over 20,000 people in the ground, cheering on their team, who won 2-0. At the final whistle the players went off, but the crowd didn't disperse as usual. There remained a buzz around the ground and a few minutes later ten Orient players returned in their army uniforms and paraded round the pitch with other enlisted soldiers from the 'Footballers' Battalion', the 17th Middlesex Regiment. Everybody was cheering and waving their caps and handkerchiefs. Perhaps for the first time, certainly more than ever before, William rejoiced in belonging to something bigger than the narrow world he usually inhabited. As he looked at his uncles and then at the crowd and the players on the pitch, he was enraptured by the knowledge that he was a member of a larger family, one in a community united behind a football team, and of a country fervently supporting its soldiers. But in the elation there was the twinge of disappointment that his father was not, nor would be, with him in this joy.

Above the noise Granddad leaned down and said to him, "You know, Billy, I've supported this team since before they even played in the London League and I've watched them get all this way, but I've never been so proud of them. The first English Football League club to join the war effort, lock, stock and barrel."

William looked up at his granddad, who was smiling and wiping his eye, and his pride was rekindled.

After all the post-match celebrations his uncles went off to the pub and William went back with Granddad to his flat, as he hadn't seen Grandma for a while. He immediately felt at home, sitting in a familiar chair and enjoying a reversion to happy former times watching Grandma making tea and cutting some slices of her fruit cake while Granddad fired up his pipe.

"Granddad," he said, emboldened by a sense of security to raise a difficult question.

"Yes, son?" replied Granddad, holding a matchbox over the pipe bowl as he drew on it.

"Why doesn't Dad like doing the things we do?"

"How d'you mean?" He sat back, satisfied the pipe was doing its job and giving the boy his full attention with his light blue eyes.

"Well," he started hesitatingly, "he doesn't come to the football and he doesn't have the same view of the war that we do."

Granddad glanced over at Grandma, aware, as was William, that she had stopped what she was doing and was listening for his answer. He gave a slight shake of the head. "Your dad's got some funny ideas about things, Billy. He gets his beliefs from books."

"Where do you get your beliefs from, Granddad?"

"Same as you, Billy: from here." He patted his heart.

William merely nodded. He felt a warm glow of affection towards his grandfather and thought how good it was to have him in his life. "Did you know your granddad?" he asked.

Granddad smiled and was quiet for a moment, as if in fond remembrance. "Yes, one of 'em, my mother's father. He died when I was twelve, but I remember him well. He was a rope-maker in Cripplegate and he'd been born in the eighteenth century, so he remembered the last King George, the fat one, and his father who was mad, poor devil. He smoked a clay pipe and had long side whiskers and he was hard of hearing, so he had an ear trumpet." He paused and smiled again. "He told me some marvellous stories when I was about your age, about the war against Napoleon and Lord Nelson's funeral procession, which he watched, standing in the crowds that lined the route, all standing to attention with their hats off. He wasn't even born when the war against the French started, but it went on so long that he was old enough to fight by the Battle of Waterloo. But he didn't join up; he did his bit making ropes for the Navy."

"Do you think this war will go on until I'm old enough to fight?" asked William, his mind alive to the possibility of derring-do but equally filled with the trepidation that came with it.

Granddad's expression changed to a wince as he considered the possibility. "I don't think that's at all likely, Billy. I certainly hope not. In my opinion, it would be a blessing if it were all over very soon."

William walked, half ran, home, full of joy, reflecting that this day had been one of the happiest of his life.

The war did not impact directly upon William very much; especially as he was too young to be called up for any role and none of his close family were directly involved. He was the casual bystander, watching or waving at those who were going off to fight in a foreign country that he would probably never see. However, later on there were Zeppelin air raids and a few bombs fell in the area. He often watched the monstrous Zeppelins flying overhead, though he saw little of the damage they inflicted. He went with his mother to see a burned curtain and singe marks on a tablecloth in a house where the lady who owned it charged a penny a time to view the 'bomb damage'.

At the end of September 1915, Cyril was off school for a couple of days and the class teacher, Miss Nugent, relayed the news that Cyril's father had been killed at the Battle of

Loos. He was the first war casualty that most of the class had known. When Cyril returned his friends had no words to express their condolences. They thought, certainly hoped, he knew how much they cared and after that Leonard never wore his pickelhaube again and they stopped playing games about the war. The rest of the war was punctuated at regular intervals with news of someone William knew, or knew of, being killed, missing presumed dead, wounded or captured. These included three Clapton Orient players who died in the Battle of the Somme in 1916 and whom William felt he knew, even though he didn't really. However, there were lighter notes too. There was great excitement when a Royal Flying Corps airman landed his plane on the marshes. He paraded up Marsh Hill, followed by a crowd of young and not-so-young admirers, on his way to visit a friend in Glyn Road. But such events were few and far between, as opposed to the regular reports of casualties at the Front, and the growing appearance of men retired from the front because of a 'blighty'.

When conscription was introduced in 1916 William was worried for his father in case he had to join up, against his principles. But, although he was just below the upper age limit of forty, Jack was not called up. William had no idea what would have happened had he been conscripted, but he was present when his parents had a heated argument over the subject. Jack told Alice he would not go to war under any circumstances and she responded that his principles appeared to be more important than his family or his reputation. William wasn't sure whether she wanted him to go to war or not, but *he* didn't want him to go. He didn't want him to be a casualty, like Cyril's father.

V

By the spring of 1916, William was eleven years old and revelling in that age when a lad often feels at the height of his boyhood powers, free to do what he wants and with no responsibilities, other than the few chores at home. He saw himself as the master of his admittedly small domain, free to go off when he wished with his friends and looked up to, physically at least, by the younger children at school. He possessed a confidence built on acquired skills and growth in experience that was yet to be ruffled by the onset of adolescence and all the fears of inadequacy that would bring. So, despite the poor summer weather of 1916, he had a wonderful time with his friends in the school holidays that year. He would leave home most days in the morning with his friends and return perhaps at lunchtime or just in time for tea. The days would be spent exploring the local terrain in search of adventure, being a mild nuisance to those forced to endure briefly their high-spirited horseplay or just enjoying each other's company. The high spot was when he went camping for a few days with the Mason brothers and Amos in Epping Forest, Cecil Mason now regarded as grown up enough, at nearly sixteen, to be trusted with leading the expedition. Cecil lived up to the trust placed in him and they had a few days' rambling in the countryside, climbing trees and purposely getting lost for a while in the forest, which for all of them was every bit as exotic as any equatorial jungle. Unlike the heroes of their adventure novels, they could not retire to the officer's mess in the evening, but they could sit on the grass outside a country pub while Cecil went in and bought glasses of ginger beer which, with their boisterous good humour, left them as intoxicated as any of the patrons inside the pub.

Towards the end of August, Leonard, Cyril, Amos and William hired a rowing boat on the river and it began like one of those days where nothing much happens but is enjoyable at the time and is remembered fondly as totally blissful. They settled comfortably into their usual roles: Leonard sitting in the stern, steering and pointing out items of interest, Cyril rowing elegantly and without much effort, Amos leaping too early from the boat as they made for the bank and standing in mud up to his ankles, and William securing the boat while all four of them laughed. Then Cyril lit a fire, not because they were cold but because 'that's what explorers do'. While Leonard and William foraged for firewood, Amos rinsed his socks in the river and dried off his shoes, supervised by Cyril. Then they sat down under the shade of a tree and ate the sandwiches their mothers had made for them while they shared a bottle of cream soda. For the first time they discussed their ambitions for the future when they would leave school and go to work. Cyril was the only one who was sure what he wanted to do: train as an apprentice in engineering of some kind. Leonard thought he might like to follow his father and work in the building trade, while Amos aimed to drive a bus or something similar. Only William hadn't a clue what he wanted to do. Before it came to his turn, he sought to avoid any awkwardness by commenting that the fire was getting low and that he was going off to get some more wood.

He was wandering among the trees, poking about for dead and dry pieces of wood and trying to think of an occupation that would satisfy his friends' curiosity when he heard a commotion some way off. Picking up the wood he'd scavenged in both arms, he walked back towards their little camp but froze when it came into view. A group of five youths, aged about sixteen, was standing by the fire and talking to his friends in loud voices. One of them kicked earth on the fire and when Cyril tried to stop him, another one of them punched him, knocking him to the ground. As he tried to get up a third youth kicked him and put his booted foot on Cyril's stomach. Amos had been holding his wet socks by the fire and as he told the older boys to leave his friend alone, one of them took his shoes and threw them towards the river, followed by his socks, which were grabbed from Amos's hands. As Amos ran barefoot to the river edge, Leonard remonstrated with their antagonists, but he was pushed over by one of them while the others trashed anything of theirs they could find before marching off.

William had watched this brief, tumultuous episode, unable to move. Afterwards, he would rehearse in his mind what he should have done. He envisaged himself dropping the wood and running into the camp to support his friends, whatever the personal danger. It would probably have made no difference to the outcome, but it would have been a noble, if pointless, gesture. Instead he faced the grim reality that he had been overcome with fear in the face of the enemy and failed to come to the aid of his comrades. In that moment William knew that he had learned something about himself: he was a coward. He thought back to his conversation with his father about cowardice and he knew he hadn't done what was right.

He was like all those commanders in history who held back their commitment to the fight until the battle was won or lost, like all those individuals who hid until the battle was over then crept back to the safety of their lines. Despondently he walked with his now-redundant fuel for a non-existent fire back to his friends.

As he approached, he saw Cyril, a slight swelling under one eye, nursing a bleeding nose and Leonard trying to salvage what was left of their belongings. Amos was nowhere to be seen at first but then he saw him on the edge of the river, water up to his ankles, using a stick in an attempt to retrieve his socks and shoes, a little further out in the river. Leonard's head swung round, an expression of fear crossing his features as he anticipated the return of the marauders. He relaxed when he saw it was William. "Oh, there you are!" he called out.

William didn't reply as he thought Leonard's tone might be sardonic, but as he drew near, Leonard's smile dispelled his fears. "What happened?" he asked, dropping the wood on the dead fire as nonchalantly as he could.

"A bunch of yobs set on us. They took exception to us having a fire on common land or something. It was just an excuse for a bit of trouble."

"I'm sorry I wasn't here to help."

"It wouldn't have made any difference. They caught us off guard; they were older than us and there were more of them. We were outgunned in all areas," Leonard commented dispassionately.

Having satisfied himself that the bleeding had stopped, Cyril looked over at them. "It's not important. We shan't let it spoil our great day."

William said nothing. Their upbeat responses might have eased his guilt a little but paradoxically made him feel worse and almost moved him to tears. He certainly wasn't ready to forgive himself yet. His quiet contrition was interrupted by the appearance of Amos, carrying two soaking wet socks covered in some sort of blanket weed and two very wet shoes.

Amos looked at the defunct fire and shook his head. "I'll never get my shoes dry. They'll be ruined and they're the only decent pair of shoes I've got. My mum will kill me when I get home." He threw the shoes down in despair.

"They'll be all right," said Cyril. He picked up an old newspaper that he hadn't needed to light the fire and put wads of paper inside each shoe. "This will keep their shape until we get back to the boat hirers. Then you'll have to wear them home and repeat the process. Don't put them anywhere hot to dry them out or the leather will crack."

"My granddad's got some leather oil," William said. "I'll get it when we get back and you can use it after the shoes are dry to make the leather softer again."

Amos nodded his appreciation and everyone began to feel more positive. A few minutes later, they tidied up their campsite and went back to the boat, relieved that the hooligans had not done anything to it. Leonard and William rowed back down the river in silence while Cyril had a rest and nursed his various injuries and Amos cared for his wet apparel. So the day came to a desultory end and they were all glad to get home. Once or twice soon afterwards they talked about that day on the river and they gradually began to see the incident with the boys as part of the adventure of that excellent day and something they could laugh about rather than want to forget. The consensus was that the yobs may have temporarily bruised their egos and left a stain on what was otherwise a great day but that they were neither unsettled by the experience nor deterred from embarking on future adventures whenever or wherever they wished. William had no idea what the others thought inside but he did dwell on the matter after that, more often than he cared to, sometimes waking in the night and having to go through it all over again in his mind. He bitterly regretted his cowardice and was frustrated that those idiotic people would get away with their mindless behaviour and never give it another thought, whereas it would continue to gnaw away at him for who knew how long into the future. Thankfully, over time, the memory of that day gradually faded, and with it his shame.

That was the last major event of the holidays and William soon went back to school for what would be his last year. He would reach the school-leaving age of twelve in September. The headmaster called him into his study and encouraged him to see out the school year, and he was pleased to do so since he was in no hurry to lose his school friends. The Mason boys, Cecil and Stanley, had left years before and he only saw them if he or they made an effort to do so, especially after they moved to a house in Templar Road. Their sister, Lucy, had progressed through the school with him, though they had gradually gone their separate ways, perhaps inevitably drawn to friends of their own gender for companionship. In the current academic year the distance between them had grown, as the boys and girls were in different classes. There was an occasion he noticed her, almost as if it were for the first time.

After school one day in November he came out of the 'Boys' Gate as she came out of the 'Girls' and they looked at each other and smiled in recognition. But then he looked again at her and found he didn't really recognise her. With her dark blonde hair down with a bow and wearing a gymslip and dark stockings under her coat, she was dressed just as she always had been. There was something different about her, yet he couldn't put a finger on what that difference was.

"Hello," said Lucy. "Off home?"

"Er yes, Lucy. It's not a good day for doing much, is it?"

"At least it's not foggy today." She made as if to move then stopped and turned back to him. "Haven't seen you for ages. Still live in Daubeney?" She pulled on a dainty pair of brown leather gloves.

They stood still for a little while, exchanging odd bits of information about themselves and their families, then Lucy said, "Well, I'd better get going. I have a book waiting for me at the library."

Acutely aware he didn't want their conversation to come to an end, he blurted out, "I'll walk along with you if you like."

"But it's out of your way, Billy." She smiled as they began to stroll together towards the library.

"What's the book?" he asked.

"Oh, just a book of short stories, nothing exciting. I like going to the pictures more than reading; do you go to the kinema much?"

He shook his head, noticing she'd used the more fashionable term for what he thought of as the cinema. "Only been a couple of times. I went with my mum once to the Castle to see *Little Lord Fauntleroy* and my dad took me to see a cowboy film at the Pavilion. My parents aren't that interested in the kinema and I can't afford to go on my own." He felt rather pathetic having to admit to such an impecunious excuse for his lack of connection with modern entertainment. He had very much enjoyed the films he'd seen, particularly the western, but the truth was that the cinema was not at the top of the list for his limited resources.

Lucy wrinkled her nose a little, a gesture he liked. "That's a shame. Now that Cecil and Stanley are both working they go a lot, especially as the Castle's just round the corner from us, and they often take me too." She added, as an afterthought, "Where did you sit when you went to the Castle?"

"In the front stalls, why?"

She laughed. "I just wondered. I was in the circle once, you know, upstairs, and it's so small with just a few rows of seats and there was hardly anyone else there that I felt it was a special place for me, like having my own box at the theatre. It's also good that you can look down on the people below and see what they are up to. You ought to go in the circle sometime."

William nodded and wanted to ask her if she would go with him to the pictures, but he couldn't say the words. This was Lucy whom he'd known all his life and had danced and played and held hands with countless times. Yet here he was, unable even to ask her to go with him to the pictures nor contemplate touching her hand, let alone holding it.

They were at the library now and they stopped outside. "Thanks for walking along with me, Billy; it's been nice. I'll see you at school." She waited for a second or two then disappeared through the library doors he knew so well.

William wanted to follow her but froze, staring at the doors, until he was jolted back to the moment by someone pushing past him. He walked slowly back to Daubeney, full of regrets and daydreams of what might have been. He resolved to be more confident the next time he spoke to Lucy but, although their paths often crossed in the next few months, the moment when he asked Lucy to go out with him didn't come.

As the school year proceeded, his teacher, Mr Jameson, spent less time in formal lessons and concentrated on preparing the class for their future as citizens and workers. He gave them a brief introduction to the British constitution, the legal system and the main political parties. William found it quite interesting, even though practically none of the boys would have the necessary property qualifications to vote when they grew up, any more than the girls in Miss Kent's class. One boy asked if there was any point in their learning about the constitution when they had no say in what went on in Parliament.

Mr Jameson nodded. He had been asked that question many times. "It is as important in life to know the things we are not permitted to do as the things we have the right to do."

More time in class was spent in giving the boys some idea of the different occupations likely to be available to them. Jameson put a coated linen map of Great Britain up on the wall which showed the main industries and commercial activities in the country and the sort of skills they might need to learn to enter particular sectors of the economy. With most of the heavy industries located in the Midlands and North of England, Wales and Scotland, it seemed to William the main options open to him would be light industry, like his father, commerce or retailing. How he would get into any of these was a mystery to him, but his teacher told them to look in the *Gazette* and other newspapers for job advertisements and also to make enquiries if they saw items of interest on the noticeboards of local factories and other companies. William was deterred from engineering or light industry, both by a fear of unfavourable comparisons with his father and grandfather, and by a natural apprehension about the sort of work where ability and achievement would be easily measured by the worker's performance. As to the other choices, he was open to whatever came up since a weekly wage of nearly a pound would be far greater than the pocket money he currently received, even if he gave three-quarters of his pay to his mother.

A few weeks before Easter, Jack sat down with William and asked if he had decided what to do about work yet. Neither he nor Alice had objected to William staying on at school until the end of the summer term and they had encouraged him to take his time in deciding on his future.

"How would you feel about an apprenticeship?" asked Jack, sitting back in his chair while he reached into his tobacco pouch and rolled a cigarette.

"I'm not sure whether I want to do anything that involves making things, as I don't think I'd be any good at it," William replied.

"Well, not all apprenticeships involve making things; there's printing and transport and other things too."

Mr Jameson had spoken effusively of the advantages of apprenticeships, but William had his doubts. "I'm worried about spending a lot of time learning to do something without much income and at the end of it finding it's not what I want to do."

If he was disappointed, or even annoyed, by this response, Jack made no comment, merely raising an eyebrow. "Well, have you any idea of the sort of work you might like to do?"

"I thought something in retailing or perhaps a commercial area like shipping or commodities," William said, remembering exactly the words spoken by Mr Jameson in one of their class talks about employment.

Jack nodded. "I suppose that employment in those areas might be easier to get during the war than afterwards, so now's your chance to get your feet under the table. Even if you're not an apprentice you will still have to start at the bottom, though. You are only twelve, after all. I'll keep a lookout for jobs in the *Gazette* and at work or anything else I hear of and you keep looking too; it's good to try to make your own way in the world."

"Thanks, Dad. Can I ask you about something else?"

Jack sat back in his chair and puffed on his cigarette, leaving it in the corner of his mouth. "Yes, what did you have in mind?"

"Well, Mr Jameson gave us a talk in class about the constitution."

His father sat up and took the cigarette out of his mouth. "What about it?"

"It's just that as you study things like politics when we go to the library, I wondered what you thought about our constitution."

Jack raised his eyebrows and smiled. "That's a big question. Did you have any particular part of it in mind?"

"I didn't understand all of what he said, but the main point seems to be that Parliament makes the laws and the Members of Parliament are elected by the people to represent their views, so Parliament should make laws that are supported by the people."

Jack exhaled some smoke in a narrow jet into the air and

reflected for a moment. "Well, that's a very good summary, Billy. It's a bit more complicated than that, but I am impressed by your grasp of the essentials."

"But my question is, Mr Jameson said that most people, all the ladies and lots of the men, don't have a vote, so how do they affect what goes on?"

William thought his father appeared a little taken aback by this question as he said nothing for some time. He just stared at the wall and took a few more drags on his shrinking cigarette. Eventually, he looked back at his son. "That is a very important question, Billy, and it's at the centre of all discussions about the constitution. Should all the people have a right to a say in how they are governed?"

"Do you think they should then, Dad?"

"Yes, of course."

"Have you got a vote, Dad?"

"No."

"So the constitution isn't any good?"

"Let's just say that it's like the curate's egg: good in parts."

"I don't understand that."

"Well, would you eat a bad egg, even if some tiny bit of it might taste all right?"

"No." William shook his head, remembering the stomach-turning experience of opening the shell of an egg that was off.

"Well, our constitution is like that. There may be some small bits that are good, but overall it stinks."

William laughed and promised himself that he would tell the boys about the curate's egg at school the next day, although he wasn't quite sure what a curate was. "But why are you so interested in all these things to do with politics and the constitution if it's bad?"

"Because I would like to understand how it might be made better than it is. Do you remember when you asked me about

William Lovett? Well, he was trying to make the constitution better. If you are really interested, we'll talk about it when we have more time."

A week or so later, as they were walking to the library, Jack said, "I have heard of a possible opening for you to try out a job before you commit yourself."

William was relieved to hear this, as his own haphazard and uninformed research had convinced him that he was too young, too inexperienced or too unqualified or all of these things to apply for any of the positions he'd been interested in. "Oh, what's that?" he replied.

"Well, one of the blokes at work, Harry Plover, has a brother who runs an off licence and he is looking for a junior assistant. He would like to try somebody out before offering them the job. Harry has spoken to his brother and he's willing to let you have a trial the week after Easter to see how you get on. What do you think?"

William was quite excited by the idea and happily agreed to take up Mr Plover's offer. So a couple of weeks later, he turned up at eight thirty in his long trousers and Norfolk jacket, purchased by his mother on a shopping expedition to Mare Street, at Mr Plover's off licence in Well Street. Soon after he rang the doorbell, Mr Plover appeared at the door, shook hands warmly and invited him in. A jovial-looking balding man in his mid-fifties, he was dressed in a leather apron over his shirt and waistcoat, and wore silver bands round his sleeves to pull his cuffs off his wrists. After a brief conversation about background and schooling, he showed William round the shop while telling him what the job consisted of: helping to unload stock as it arrived and placing it in the right place in the cellar, keeping stocks in the shop maintained, taking small deliveries to customers, some clerical work and generally helping out. In due course he would be able to take over serving in the shop from Mrs Plover. Then he asked William some questions involving simple sums and asked him to write out a sentence with some quite difficult words. At the end of it all he offered William a trial period of two weeks. William happily accepted as he couldn't wait to get started at work and make his parents proud of him.

On arriving promptly for his first day on the Tuesday after Easter, he was greeted at the door by a kindly looking lady with blonde hair, dressed in the then-business style of a professional woman: a suit of jacket and skirt with a collar and tie.

"Welcome, William. I'm Mrs Plover," she said, shaking hands and using the title he had given himself for his new professional life. "Mr Plover is in the cellar at the moment and I think he would like you to give him a hand. I'm just making a pot of tea, would you like a cup?"

"Oh, yes please, Mrs Plover."

"Sugar?"

"One spoon, please."

She led him from the shop into a small kitchen and took a brown dustcoat off a peg on the back of the door. "Here," she said, "take your jacket off and put this on."

He did as he was instructed and put on the dustcoat held open for him by Mrs Plover. The coat was rather large for him and the sleeves went about four inches beyond his outstretched fingertips. Looking down, he could see it was too long but not quite as bad as the sleeves, as it was probably not intended to be much longer than a man's jacket and it went just past his knees.

Mrs Plover smiled and rolled up the sleeves several times. "There we are. It's a bit big for you, but we can't wait for you to grow into it; we'll get a new one for you as and when. It'll do for now."

He smiled with a mixture of embarrassment and resignation. Then he put his hands in the pockets of the coat and followed Mrs Plover out of the kitchen to the lobby, where he saw an open trapdoor.

"William's here," called Mrs Plover down to the well-lit cellar.

"Morning, William. Come down and I'll show you the layout."

He descended the narrow staircase on one side of the trapdoor and joined Mr Plover in what seemed to be a treasure trove of bottles in crates and wine racks.

"Right, William. You see this platform and pulley? I will lower some crates of beer down to you, one at a time, and you will stack them over here, exactly as those ones there are stacked." He gestured to the crates already against one wall. Then he turned to the pulley directly under the trapdoor. "The pulley's very easy to use; this rope for up and that one for down. All understood?"

"Yes, Mr Plover."

"I'll demonstrate," called Mrs Plover from above. "Cuppa tea coming down." The platform descended from above with a cup of tea and saucer standing in the centre.

William picked up the cup and saucer carefully. It was bone china with a rose pattern and was probably the prettiest cup he'd ever been served tea in. Two Rich Tea biscuits lay in the saucer, together with an apostle spoon. He stirred the tea, took a sip and a bite from a biscuit and placed the cup and saucer on top of a wooden box a few feet away from the platform.

"Right, let's get started," said Mr Plover, and climbed the stairs.

A few moments later the platform came down again with a large crate of quart bottles of beer. The platform stopped and

William took the crate with both hands, intending to swing the crate round to its designated location. Unfortunately, the weight, for which he was not prepared, caused the arc created by the swinging case to go beyond his intended stop point and the crate hit the cup and saucer left in its path. Both pieces of china took flight and smashed on the concrete cellar floor.

"What happened?" called Mrs Plover.

"I'm sorry, I've knocked your cup and saucer over," he called back, looking up and seeing Mrs Plover looking down at him.

"Oh, that's all right," she said, her expression not quite matching the generosity of her statement.

He finished the remainder of the task without incident, but he found himself wondering if he were supposed to offer to pay for the cup, thus ensuring that he would begin his first day's work with a minus remuneration for his efforts. He decided to wait for his employers to raise the matter.

The rest of the first morning went without further incident and his confidence slowly began to rise. He was given a cheese sandwich and a cup of tea (in an old mug) at lunchtime and spent the afternoon sweeping out the cellar and re-arranging the spirits cabinet in the shop, as directed by Mr Plover.

On the next day, he was sweeping the shop when a customer came in while Mr Plover was making up an order of wine for one of his restaurant customers. He called out to Mr Plover, but there was no response so, after a pause, he asked the customer if he could be of assistance.

The customer, a well-dressed man of about forty-five, looked at him in his rather ludicrous costume and hesitated before asking for a bottle of something which William completely failed to understand. So he asked the man to repeat the name and again failed to understand him. He seemed to be asking for a bottle of 'Oat, Coat D'Bone', and William wondered if it was some kind of medicinal drink. They looked at each other for a second or two while William wondered what to do.

"Would that be a tonic wine, sir?" he asked eventually.

"*Tonic* wine?"

Fortunately, at that moment Mr Plover came in from the back room. "I'll deal with this, William," he said. "Get on with your sweeping. Good morning, Mr Bradshaw. Your usual bottle of the 1912?"

William finished sweeping behind the counter and took his broom and dustpan into the kitchen. As he closed the door behind him he heard Mr Plover speaking and Mr Bradshaw laughed. Afterwards Mr Plover came into the kitchen.

"Don't serve the customers, William. It's not your job, at least not yet."

"Sorry, Mr Plover. I called out to you, but when you didn't come I was just trying to be helpful."

Mr Plover nodded and returned to the shop.

The rest of that day and Thursday were fairly uneventful, and William went about his tasks dutifully and carefully in the hope of redeeming himself in Mr Plover's eyes. On Thursday afternoon he copied some invoices and receipts into the accounts ledger. Mrs Plover checked what he had done and said his writing was very clear and that he hadn't made any mistakes. By Friday he was feeling quite confident that things were going well. On Friday afternoon Mrs Plover was out and Mr Plover called him into the kitchen for a cup of tea at about three o'clock.

"I'm just going down to the cellar to get a couple of bottles, William. The tea is poured, but help yourself to a biscuit." He smiled as he went off.

William had a sip of the tea and gave the room a closer examination. It was not really a kitchen, as he'd first thought, more a back room for the shop with a gas hob for a kettle, some crockery and a few other items to allow Mr Plover to relax during a quiet spell in the shop. Apart from the table, there were a couple of chairs with padded seats and he wondered if it would be all right to sit in one. Casually, he reached over the table to the packet of biscuits Mr Plover had left for him. As he took a biscuit and stepped back, he heard a strange trundling sound and looked down just a fraction of a second too late. The spout of the metal teapot had caught in the pocket of his dustcoat and the pot had followed him as he moved backwards. He watched in horror as the pretty teapot tipped over the edge of the table and crashed to the floor, spilling its contents, tealeaves and enough liquid for two more cups, on the carpet. In a panic he picked up the pot by the spout and put it, dent facing away from view, on the table, burning his hand in the process. Ignoring the stinging sensation, he grabbed a mop and bucket and tried to clean up the mess but could hear the ominous footsteps of Mr Plover as he climbed up from the cellar.

"Whatever happened?" he cried as he came in the room, almost dropping one of the bottles.

"I'm sorry, the pot fell. It wasn't my fault," pleaded William.

"Leave it," Mr Plover said. "I'll clear it up. I don't know what Mrs Plover will say," he muttered. "Go into the shop and fill any half-empty cigarette shelves from the packets under the counter."

Crestfallen, William did as he was told and filled the cigarette shelves with a feeling of hopelessness. Having finished, he looked for other jobs of a similar nature to fill the last hour of the day. At half-past four he went to collect his wages of ten shillings for the four days. Mr Plover gave him four half-crowns; thankfully, there had been no deductions for the damage he'd caused.

"Thank you, Mr Plover."

They looked at each in silence for a few moments until William said, "I don't suppose you want me to come in next week?"

"No, I don't think so," Mr Plover replied, shaking his head. He went off to serve a customer who was browsing the wine shelves.

Thus ended William's first foray into paid employment. During the post-mortem that evening, neither of his parents raised the question of why he had not been retained for the second half of his trial period with Mr Plover. Alice merely commented that he would have to start looking for something soon as the end of his school days was in sight. Jack observed that not everyone was cut out for the same work and asked him if there was anything that went well and that presumably he had enjoyed doing.

"Well, I spent one afternoon making entries in the ledger and Mrs Plover commented that my writing was very neat and that I hadn't made any mistakes."

"Do you think you would enjoy that sort of work?"

"I don't mind. I suppose it wouldn't be exactly the same thing all the time."

Jack smiled. "We'll draw a line under the job in the off licence and remember, any work experience is useful experience when you are starting out. Tell Mr Jameson all that you've told me and he might come up with a few ideas."

When school started again after the Easter holiday, the class size was reduced by three or four of his classmates having found work, including Cyril. Mr Jameson called each one of them up to his desk to tell him how things were going on their quest to find work. William gave him a very précised version of the work, concentrating on his successes, such as they were. Mr Jameson made a few notes and suggested that William might consider office work. He told him to seek out opportunities because they would not come of their own accord.

A few weeks later, Jack said he had seen in the newspaper at the library that there was a job going for a junior office boy in the factory of Edward C Barlow & Sons in Urswick Road and he'd copied the details out for him. The next morning William gave the details to Mr Jameson, who arranged for him to go for an interview a couple of days after that.

Alice decided to accompany William to the interview and for this he was grateful. By the time they reached the top of the High Street, where the road narrowed considerably, he was feeling quite nervous and welcomed the distraction of watching two buses endeavour to pass each other. A couple of minutes later they arrived at the factory gate and were directed to the manager's office. As they walked, Alice told him that he should go into the interview on his own, unless they asked to see her too.

"We want them to see that you are grown up enough to speak for yourself," she said as they arrived at the office block.

They entered a small reception area with doors off to left and right. Behind a mahogany counter sat an attractive young woman dressed in a navy-blue suit reminiscent of the one he'd seen worn by Mrs Plover. She looked up and smiled. "Good morning, can I help you?"

"Go on, Billy," Alice said, "and take your cap off."

He stepped forward, removing his cap. "My name is William Lovett Lyus and I am here to see about the vacancy for an office boy, please, miss."

The young woman smiled again and invited them both to take a seat while she told the office manager he'd arrived. She disappeared through the door to their left and they sat on two bentwood chairs.

"Her skirt is rather short," whispered Alice, "well above

her ankle. I don't think that's very appropriate for business premises."

William hadn't really noticed the young woman's skirt length before but was intent now on looking out for it when she returned. A couple of minutes later his eyes were focussed downwards as soon as he heard the clacking of her shoes on the lino. Her skirt was indeed a few inches above nicely shaped ankles, but he was used to seeing the girls' ankles at school and felt he took it in his stride. When he raised his eyes, she asked him to accompany her to see Mr Wilson.

"Do you want me to come as well?" asked Alice.

"Oh, yes. Mr Wilson would like to meet you, I'm sure."

They followed her through the door into a corridor, where she knocked on the second door on the right. In response to the command to enter, she opened the door and announced, "Master William Lyus and Mrs Lyus."

A thin, middle-aged man of medium height stood up and smiled warmly. "Come in, young man," he said jovially. "Thank you for coming too, Mrs Lyus. Do take a seat." He pointed them towards two chairs and resumed his own seat. "So you're interested in taking up the post of junior office boy," he said, putting on his glasses and looking at Mr Jameson's letter of recommendation. "Your first job from school?"

William nodded, having agreed with his father that he would not refer to his less-than-successful career with Mr Plover.

"Well, you have a veritably sparkling reference from Mr Jameson, your schoolteacher; all very good." He fiddled with his wing collar a little and adjusted his tie. "So tell me, what would you say the job of a junior office boy is?"

William looked over at his mother, who raised her eyebrows with an air of mild frustration while at the same time nodding encouragingly. "I think it would be doing anything somebody else wanted done and they haven't got the time to do," he replied, replicating the answer given him by Jack when he had asked the same question the previous evening.

"Such as?"

William thought he had started well but was now stumped for examples. After mentally scrabbling around for an answer for a few moments he hit on the idea of listing the jobs he had been doing for Mr and Mrs Plover, leaving out any reference to the specifics of their business. "Keeping the place tidy, sweeping up, making tea, collecting and delivering things for people, running errands, copying out receipts and invoices in ledgers, answering the telephone, going to the post box; that kind of thing."

"That's very good, William. You are right; the job of the office boy is to help other people by taking on jobs that need to be done, and done well, but not necessarily by those people. An office boy is there to assist anyone who has more urgent or important need of their time. It is a varied job and an important one, as the office boy probably knows more about the workings of the office side of the business than almost anyone else. It can't be learned in a day, so one usually begins as a junior office boy to work with the office boy who knows the ropes. That's what this job will be. Eventually you can expect to rise first to office boy and then perhaps to higher positions if you work hard and do the work given to you well. I take it you know what we produce at this factory?"

"Yes, sir, tin boxes and cans."

Mr Wilson took off his glasses, held them in his hand and waved them slightly. "Precisely, a business which will satisfy the future needs of the people for light and airtight metal containers from the housewife to soldiers at the front and explorers in the Antarctic. As it grows, so will the need for bright young men working in the offices which provide support for the manufacturing activities of the company, and you will have opportunities to grow with the company, I'm sure, William."

He put down his glasses and sat back in his chair, his thumbs in his waistcoat, and asked William a few more questions about what subjects he liked best at school, what his interests and hobbies were, and what his ambitions were for the future. This last one was the most difficult as William had no thought as to ambitions at some unspecified time to come. At the moment his only ambition was to get a job before the summer. So he made up something about one day being an office manager and learning to play a musical instrument.

Mr Wilson listened good-humouredly to this slightly diffident statement of how William saw the future then looked over at Alice. "Your son is twelve and a half so is a good age to begin the job. May I ask if you are happy for him to work here or do you have other irons in the fire, as it were, and this is just until you find something you'd rather he did?"

Alice shook her head. "Oh no, my husband and I would be very happy with this position as it gives him a rung on the ladder of working life. Billy, er, William, will be able to walk to work every day and he knows the area well, so I am sure he'll fit in easily here and will be an asset to the firm."

"I'd like to see something of his writing and arithmetic skills with a couple of simple tests."

"Of course," replied Alice confidently, and William was pleased that he had the opportunity to show his strengths.

As he expected, the tests were fairly straightforward and he had no trouble with them. Mr Wilson gave him a sheet of printed paper and asked him to copy out the first paragraph in his own handwriting. When he had completed that, he was given another sheet with various sums written on it and he had to use the appropriate arithmetic tools to find the answers. As he liked arithmetic none of this presented him with a problem. Afterwards, Mr Wilson checked his work and said that he hadn't made any mistakes.

"Excellent, William. That was all splendid. I have had other candidates for the position and I would like to see them all before I make up my mind. I will write to you within ten days to let you know if you have the position." He shook hands with them both and ushered them out of his office.

Exactly one week later, Alice looked at the post and passed a letter to William. It was the first letter he had ever received through the post, and it was from Mr Wilson, informing him that he had the job and that he was to start on Monday 8th June. Having read it three times, he passed it to his mother, who read it slowly and smiled.

"Well done, Billy. Now it's up to you to justify the faith Mr Wilson has placed in you."

By the time his father returned home that evening, William was bursting to tell him the good news. Jack read the letter and smiled broadly as he put it down. "This is very good, Billy. I am proud of you. This calls for a celebration, Alice. It's a warm evening, why don't we walk up to the Adam and Eve for a drink and buy Billy a glass of sarsaparilla or something?"

"I'm too tired to go out, maybe another day," said Alice.

Jack shrugged and that was that.

VI

IN WHITSUN WEEK THE HEADMASTER, AWARE that the leavers' class would inevitably disperse before the official end of term, arranged a service for them all at St Barnabas Church. Since he had finished his time at Sunday school William had gone less and less often to church but still remembered the prayers and rituals and was pleased to mark the end of his school days with some form of blessing from God. The vicar took as his lesson Matthew 20, the parable of the workers being called into the vineyard. In his sermon he stressed the importance of giving a fair day's work for the wage received and of loyalty to employers and fellow workers. "We must do unto others as we would expect them to do unto us. A good principle to take forward with you into your working life," he concluded.

After the service William walked back to school with Leonard, Cyril and Amos, and they were all very certain of maintaining their friendships in the future. Cyril had already signed up for an engineering apprenticeship and Leonard was to train as a jobbing builder with his father. Only Amos had yet to get a firm offer, but he was hopeful of a position as a motor mechanic. They didn't make any firm arrangements as they were sure they'd meet up soon. He saw Lucy too, and she smiled and waved at him. He thought she looked prettier every time he saw her and wanted to go and talk to her as he might not see her for a while. But he felt awkward about leaving his friends and she was talking to her friends so he stayed where he was.

His first day at the factory could not have been more different from the one at Mr Plover's off licence. Instead of working under the close direction of one person in a small establishment, he was theoretically at the beck and call of a dozen people working in several offices who might need him to carry out duties anywhere in the several blocks of the, to him, vast estate of the company. Fortunately, he was shielded from a bewildering dive into the deep end by the office junior himself, Charlie Flickill, who was waiting for him with a slight smirk on his face when William arrived at reception.

"Hello. Lyus, isn't it? I'm Charles Flickill. Do you prefer to be called William or Billy?"

"William, if you please."

"Welcome to Edward C Barlow & Sons, William," he said, shaking hands, though without much warmth. "Come with me and I'll show you where you will be based. After that, we'll take a tour round the whole site so that you get a feel for what's what."

"Thanks very much," William replied. He now realised that the smirk was Charlie's default expression, but in these foreign surroundings the guidance of even a smirking shepherd was preferable to being left as a lost sheep.

"The first thing you have to remember," Charlie said, as they walked briskly along, "is that you are the newest and least important person in the factory. You know nothing and you are unable to do anything unless you are taught by someone, and that someone is me. How old are you, exactly?"

"Twelve and three-quarters."

"Well, I'm sixteen and a half, so I am nearly a third older than you but have infinitely more experience in the factory than you, since you have none." He paused, satisfied with his exposition of the numerical properties of infinity and zero, and swept his fine straight hair off his forehead. He was a couple of inches taller than William and stood with his shoulders back to accentuate his height. He was dressed in a pair of grey flannels with a black waistcoat over a white shirt and stiff collar with a blue tie. One waistcoat pocket was decorated with several pencils and a De La Rue fountain pen clipped in position at the end. He held a notebook in one hand. "Any questions?" he barked.

"About what?"

Charlie grunted and opened the door to the general office. Six people looked up from their work as they walked in.

"Excuse me, ladies and gentlemen; this is the new junior office boy, William Lyus." He then rattled off the names and roles of the six people, beginning with the most important, Mr Frobisher, the chief clerk. He was seated at a large roll top desk and nodded to William over his spectacles before resuming his work. The names and details of the other people, William immediately forgot.

"This is your desk here," said Charlie, taking William over to a small table, not much larger than the school desk he had recently vacated. It was bare except for a blotting pad, an inkwell, two pens and three pencils, and a large pencil sharpener fixed to the edge of the desk.

"Right, now the layout of this desk gives you an indication of what one of your duties will be. Can you guess what it is?"

William was aware that some of the people in the room were watching this initiation test and could see a couple of smiling faces out of the corner of his eye. "Is it to keep everybody's pencils sharp?" he replied, opting for a humble response rather than giving a more forthright answer, which might be construed as cocky.

"Yes, good. Anything else related to that?"

He looked round the office and could see that at least some of the people had inkwells in their desks. "Keep the inkwells filled?"

"Correct," said Charlie, pleased with his successful coaching exercise. "I'll take you round the site now. I can go through your various duties while we walk, rather than disturbing the concentration of the people in our office."

He walked to the door and waited until William had opened it for him. Then they began their leisurely walk round the site: the warehouse, the factory, the workshops for design, painting and decoration, the dispatch and post rooms, the canteen, and all the other ancillary areas. Charlie was known everywhere and was on the receiving end of good-humoured banter and teasing by the foremen and workmen whose areas they intruded on. One or two chatted to William and told him jocularly to watch out for Charlie as a taskmaster and a difficult person to work for.

As they went from one area to another, Charlie outlined the main features of William's job. "Basically you will assist me in everything I do: maintaining the offices with stationery and materials, dealing with the post, incoming and outgoing, taking messages and files and things like that to other sections, clerical duties given to us by the managers and clerks such as filing or copying things out, running errands for people in the office and keeping the office areas tidy. For the first week I'll give you simple things to do and later on I'll show you more responsible jobs. You can run most of the messages and so on around the works because that'll give you an opportunity to get to know the place and all its nooks and crannies. Make sure you are in early every day as there can be jobs to do first thing. Sometimes we can get away early after all the post is done, but I can't promise. Now, do you have any questions?" He looked at William quizzically and the younger boy felt under pressure to find something to ask.

"Will I ever have to travel away from the factory to do any jobs?" he asked, showing willing.

Charlie shook his head. "You should be so lucky. It's happened to me only a few times in the four years I've been here."

Gradually, William got to know his way round the company and became familiar with what was required of him and also much of the work done by Charlie and the other office staff. Though the routine soon became largely tiresome, the money allowed him to have a little more independence and to feel more grown-up in his conversations with his father and his friends. In any case, there was much going on outside work to spice up his life.

William had been quite excited by the news of the revolution in Russia in March 1917 and the overthrow of the Tsar, whom his father considered a tyrant. Jack was impressed by the perception and maturity of William's detailed questions about the new government in Russia and what it would mean for the Russian people. This convinced him that his son was ready to understand something of his own political philosophy. They were sitting in the reading room of the library when William asked him if he thought the new Russian Prime Minister, Kerensky, would be a good leader.

"Let's see how he uses his power, Billy. New prime ministers always promise to make things better for the people but usually they mean *some* of the people. Only the people as a whole can answer whether a prime minister makes things better. You remember when I told you that I named you after William Lovett?"

"Yes, the man who gave up being a carpenter and fought to change society so that the poorer people would be better off."

Jack smiled at his son's retention of his lesson on the subject. "Well, he and the people in his group knew that only if the ordinary people of the country had some say over who governed them would the government actually make life better for most of the people. Of course, there were always rich and powerful people who tried to make things better for the poor, but there were too few of them; most people are more interested in their own needs than the needs of others. So Lovett and his friends thought the answer was to draw up a charter which would enable the whole people to decide the sort of government they wanted, rather than only the better off having a say. Do you know anything about the Magna Carta?"

"Yes, we did it at school. It was when the barons made King John respect the rights of the barons to have some say in government and it also gave people legal rights."

"That's right and 'Magna Carta' is the Latin for 'Great Charter'. The Chartists, Lovett and the others, tried to do the same for all the people as Magna Carta had done for the barons. The most important thing was that every man would have a vote and the people could elect a parliament which represented the whole people. That has not come yet, but it will soon. The suffragettes have shown that the people can bring about change if they are organised and have an objective which is just. Parliament is slowly coming round to giving women the vote and hopefully accepting that the vote should not be based on property rights so that all men will get the vote too. The charter had other aims and some of them, like the secret ballot, have come about, but most of them have not yet. As regards Russia, I'll wait and see what the new Russian government does for the ordinary people before I decide whether it's a good government or not."

It was after this conversation and other discussions about democracy and political power that William's interest in his father's ideas and beliefs changed from being a matter of filial loyalty to a genuine desire to want to follow in his footsteps, perhaps not now, but at some time in the future. William thought his father, with his noble attitude, his willingness to explain everything, his patience with questions and a refusal to rush to judgement, could be a leader of the type he praised so much. When a few months later the Bolshevik Revolution overthrew Kerensky and the provisional government, William thought Jack would be pleased as the people seemed to support it. But no, once again he said he would wait to see what the new government did to serve the whole people before coming to a view.

William's growing interest in politics had to fight to make its voice heard above the noise of the teenage years, which William had recently entered. The 'rights of man' or 'popular democracy' were concepts which could hardly compete with the reality of adolescence and all its distractions, especially when coupled with the changes in his pattern of life. He was still a boy in appearance, feelings and actions, yet he had left school and lost that relative lack of individual responsibility and camaraderie which being a schoolboy brings: the regular games and horseplay in break time, the after-school expeditions or playing in each other's homes, and the group identity of schoolmates, whether working together in class or colluding to outwit the teacher. After work and at weekends he still saw his school friends, but for much of the day he was surrounded by people much older than himself, most of whom he could hardly relate to, or they to him. Even Charlie, who was at least in touching distance in age, aspired to be accepted as an adult and was consequently averse to too much fraternising with his junior assistant.

After a few weeks he had settled into the routine of office work. Needless to say, Charlie delegated to him the simplest of jobs at first and later passed on those duties that were least to his own liking, such as filing, taking messages and simple ledger copying. William didn't mind the last of these as it gave him some insight into the way the business operated and the rest, while not exciting, were hardly onerous. Having impressed on William his hauteur, Charlie mellowed somewhat and was not a bad colleague with whom to go to the canteen and talk over the matters of the day. Relations with his other colleagues in the administration block were cordial, but he was largely ignored by the managers and clerks other than the occasional instruction. The women in the office were nearer to his own age but the gap in years was still too significant a chasm for them to see him as any more than a boy. He, on the other hand, could appreciate their attractiveness without any likelihood of ever being able to do something about it. His main interest centred on the younger of the two, the typist Geraldine, who was, he knew from Charlie, nineteen years old. She had blonde hair and blue eyes and wore what he assumed to be the latest fashion in office wear, with a long jacket and skirt showing a little of her leg above the ankle, a feature in which he had taken a considerable interest since first being apprised of it by his mother. She took a great deal of time with her appearance and used some kind of toilet water that added to her attractiveness. William thought she was beautiful and fantasised as to the possibility of using a time machine, along the lines of H G Wells, to enable them to meet at a time when they would have been nearer in age. Such were the daydreams that enveloped his thoughts while staring surreptitiously at Geraldine while he was supposed to be concentrating on his filing or getting the letters and cards ready to take to the post room.

Finally, the war neared its end. It had started when William was nine years old and by early 1918 had been going on for a third of his life without showing, as far as he could tell, any sign of ending. Over breakfast one morning in March 1918 he asked his father why it had lasted so long when neither side seemed able to win.

Jack sat back in his chair, his hands clasped behind his head. "That's a very good question, Billy, and I think it's because it's gone on for so long and with such terrible losses that every country feels it has put too much in it to give up now. The two sides are like a couple of boxers who are punched to a finish with their eyes closed and their mouths bleeding. They are just hoping their opponent will fall over so that they can say they have won and it was all worthwhile. It will only end when one side effectively runs out of men and weapons or the people decide they have had enough."

Jack's assessment frequently came to William's mind as the year wore on. Already Soviet Russia had decided enough was enough and had dropped out of the war and signed a treaty with Germany. But the balance of power did not swing to Germany because an exhausted Russia was replaced on the Allied side by a fresh United States. The Central Powers faced being overwhelmed by the arrival of these new American resources which would surely tip the balance heavily against them. The Germans now launched an all-out assault on British merchant ships in the Atlantic to starve Britain into submission, but although some rationing was eventually introduced by the UK government, it was the Germans who were running out of food. They mounted one last push for victory on the Western Front, but their allies were collapsing, and very quickly the Austrians, the Bulgarians, the Turks and finally the Germans ground to a halt and the Allies 'won'.

Though people were united in relief that the war had finally ended, there were many different views on how Armistice Day should be marked. William's parents and grandparents were among those who thought any kind of celebration was inappropriate and perhaps failed to show due respect to those who had died in the war. But there were those who wanted to celebrate the concept of 'Victory' and many more, especially among the young, who wanted to express their joy at the coming of peace. Mrs Poulter, who lived upstairs, was certainly of that view as peace meant that her husband would survive the war and be returned to her. As a gesture to her, William's parents invited her to join them for a quiet drink that evening, as she had no one to accompany her to the celebrations in the High Street. William and his friends were certainly excited by the prospect of participating in a collective letting off of steam by the nation and his parents didn't object to him joining his pals at the revelry, as long as he was not too late getting home.

In Homerton the celebrations began, low-key at first, after the armistice began at eleven o'clock and proceeded to grow all day into a crescendo in the evening. There was bunting put up in many places and several bonfires, some rebuilt from the remains of Guy Fawkes' night, blazed through the evening with an effigy of the now-dethroned Kaiser on top. On Armistice Day, restrictions on the sale of alcohol which had been in force for much of the war were lifted and a local non-alcoholic brewery switched production to real beer for the evening celebrations. Leonard, Amos, Cyril and William joined with other old friends like the Mason boys in sampling the beer, everyone turning a blind eye to under-age drinking for the night. William had a great time but envied Charlie from work, who had gone up to the West End to join the big party with Geraldine and other younger members of staff. The next morning at work Charlie told him about the high-spirited celebrations in Trafalgar Square where Nelson's Column was used as a maypole and people danced round it and all sorts of other boisterous things went on, and he wished he'd been there. Despite his sympathies for his father's pacifist stance, he did feel very patriotic that night, not so much rejoicing in the victory but proud of the bravery of the soldiers who had never given up.

A couple of days later Geraldine was not very well when she came into work and by lunchtime she was so poorly with a fever and had some difficulty breathing that Mr Wilson arranged for a taxi to take her home. She promised to see them all later in the week, but she died the following night. William's dream that he might be able to catch up with her in terms of age would materialise in a few years, without the assistance of a time machine because she would always be twenty. She was a victim of the Spanish flu epidemic which had been unreported in the newspapers because of government censorship, to forestall a panic at the end of the war. The virus had been given a boost in Britain by returning soldiers who had picked it up in France and it spread from the railway stations through the cities to the civilian population. Geraldine was one of hundreds who probably caught the virus and died after celebrating the armistice. A quarter of the population were infected and William would often see children chanting in the street a modern variation on 'Ring a Ring o' Roses':

"I had a little bird,
its name was Enza.
I opened the window,
And in-flu-enza."

Many people he knew suffered with it and, unusually, this particular strain of flu affected young people more severely than it did the old. Both he and his mother caught it, but while she was only mildly unwell, William was ill for several days. For a time he was worried about his old friend Leonard who eventually recovered after a very bad bout of it. The only other people he knew who died were a boy of fifteen who lived a few doors away from him and a girl who had been in his class at school. As with the war so it was with the epidemic: the overall loss of life was so colossal that he could only relate to its effect on those around him.

VII

AGAINST THE BACKGROUND OF THE POST-WAR turmoil of the Spanish flu and the return of thousands of soldiers from the front, the government called a general election. The government had extended the franchise so that all men over twenty-one and all women over thirty now had the vote. So William's father, who had been dreaming of the right to vote all his adult life, and his mother, who had never expected to vote at all, went to the polling station for the first time on the same day.

The last general election had been in 1910 and this was the first time that William had been old enough to appreciate its significance. He was excited by the prospect of the election campaign and the result, which was bound to be unpredictable. There was a greatly expanded electorate, the Liberal Party had split and there was the growing strength of the Labour Party. William read the newspapers avidly for their accounts of the campaign and reports of the speeches and utterances of the party leaders. He hoped that he might be able to attend an electioneering event or two.

William's grandfather was laid quite low in early December with an attack of his chronic bronchitis and William and his parents called round to see how he was and to discuss plans for Christmas. Unlike her husband, who had never been greatly interested in politics, William's grandmother was quite excited about voting for the first time and took the opportunity to ask Jack about his views on the election.

Jack supported the Labour Party, of which he had affiliate membership through his trade union and was disappointed that there was no Labour candidate in their constituency. He had been so looking forward to the election and canvassing for Labour that, when his mother asked him how he would choose from the options available to him, he seemed quite deflated. "You know, Mum, the number of people eligible to vote is four times what it was at the last general election and most of the new voters are working-class men and women, and yet there are so many seats without a Labour candidate. The choice we have is a Coalition Liberal and an Independent who used to sit as a Liberal."

"Well, you still have a choice," said Jack's father. His beloved pipe temporarily confined to its rack, he was sitting in his armchair facing the fire, a blanket round his shoulders and a hot water bottle clasped to his chest. From past experience of his attacks everyone knew he was on the mend. "I remember the days when lots of the seats were uncontested and the local toff would more or less own the seat. You'll have to choose the one who's nearest to your own inclination."

"I know who I'm going to vote for," said Alice, putting away her handkerchief and snapping shut the clasp on her handbag, signifying her determination.

"Who?" asked her mother-in-law.

"Well, I can't tell you; it's a secret ballot."

Jack laughed. "It's secret in the sense that nobody is allowed to see you cast your vote. You can tell people the truth or a lie as to who you voted for; they will never know for sure."

Alice pursed her lips. "Well, I'm minded to vote for Mr Bottomley."

Her father-in-law coughed and sat up in his chair. "Bottomley is a swindler and a charlatan, everybody knows it. He had to give up his seat before the war because he went bankrupt."

"Now, now, Bob," said his wife, "he's never been found guilty of fraud or suchlike, and he's very generous and charming from what I know of him."

Jack looked at his son and shook his head, and William smiled, pleased to be taken into his father's confidence, though not really sure who Mr Bottomley was. "Well, Mum," said Jack, "I'll not allow my personal prejudice to get in the way. I will attend the hustings and listen to their policies before I make a choice."

"Can I come with you, Dad?" William asked.

"I think we should all go, Billy."

One evening a week later, William went with his father, mother and grandmother to the church hall to hear the two candidates speak. They arrived early and it was just as well they did because a large crowd waited outside the hall; such was the attraction of Horatio Bottomley as a speaker. They were able to get seats halfway down the hall and, after about ten minutes, the two candidates arrived on the stage accompanied by the chairman of the meeting. William recognised Bottomley immediately as the man in the top hat who had distributed sweets and toasted the King's health at the coronation street party seven years before. He was a large man wearing a frock coat with his top hat held before him and he waved to the audience as he mounted the stage, a gesture greeted with one or two cheers. The other candidate, Mr Arthur Henry, was introduced by the chairman as the Coalition Liberal candidate, a Liberal endorsed by the coalition government led by Lloyd George.

"This Liberal is effectively a Tory; the Conservatives will dominate the coalition if it wins," whispered Jack when Alice asked him how this man differed from the Liberals led by Asquith.

The chairman asked Bottomley to speak first. As he rose from his seat, his hands briefly clutched at his satin lapels as he acknowledged the applause. Then he stood in a more relaxed pose, his hands in his trouser pockets. He smiled at the audience. "I must apologise if you had some difficulty getting in this evening. It's not my fault, but that of all these crowds of people round here causing a rumpus and a hoo-ha about I know not what." There was laughter in the rows of listeners and William noticed even his father smiling. Bottomley spoke of his past service to the people of the constituency as a Liberal and his work during the war to raise recruitment for the army, to some cheers. He said he was standing as an independent candidate because he did not wish to be tied to either Liberal faction, nor to any party which favoured one part of the community against another. He promised to serve the whole constituency and to work especially for the poor and the working man. Raising his hand to his heart, he said that he personally would seek to improve life for the children of the constituency through the provision of social and educational activities. As he gave his speech, a mixture of inspiring patriotism, vision for a better future and humour laced with self-deprecation, William looked around at the audience. All were listening attentively and many were moved to cheer and applaud, their faces often covered with broad smiles, as he realised his was too. Bottomley finished to a lengthy round of applause and, bowing slightly, he resumed his seat.

William barely heard anything that Mr Henry had to say. He seemed a decent man, and reaffirmed the government's vowed intention to create a country fit for heroes with a large-scale house-building programme and other social reforms. But as he went into detail, William's eyes looked over at Bottomley, sitting back in his chair with a look of courteous indifference. He knew that he had won the hall and Henry knew it too. The latter was heard in silence and was greeted with polite applause when he finished. Both speakers took questions from the floor and Henry responded efficiently and pleasantly while Bottomley drew both laughter and cheers, sometimes simultaneously, from his admiring listeners.

Afterwards, William and his family walked back to his grandmother's flat in a slight drizzle, but the weather was so mild that they could have gone without topcoats and not felt particularly cold. Instead of hurrying to get home, they walked slowly while the three voters discussed the relative merits of the two candidates. Only Jack was not won over by Bottomley, although he was impressed by his rhetorical skills. He said he would have to weigh things up carefully before he cast his vote.

The election was held on Saturday, 14th December. The count was held over until the following week to enable the votes of soldiers serving overseas to be brought home. Jack spent a great deal of time thinking about and discussing with others how he should vote. Unwilling to vote for a government dominated by Conservatives, a party which had blocked or resisted every constitutional reform he could think of, he was unable to vote for a Coalition Liberal. On the other hand, he agreed with his father about Bottomley's lack of personal integrity and didn't see how he could vote for a charlatan. He considered abstaining but, having for so long waited for the opportunity to vote, it would go against everything he believed in not to cast his vote. Eventually, he told William he could not vote for 'that scoundrel Bottomley' and reluctantly would vote for Arthur Henry, thinking of him as a Liberal, whatever his affiliations. In the event, it didn't matter how he voted: Bottomley secured 79.7% of the vote, the largest of all his majorities in the four times he had won the seat. "So much for a bad reputation counting against you," Jack muttered when he saw the result.

As an Independent MP, Bottomley was a maverick in the House of Commons, but in his constituency he did deliver on at least some of his policies, paying for day trips for schoolchildren for both leisure and educational activities and organising holidays for some of the poorer ones. Whatever his unconventional methods, Bottomley seemed to be living up to his promises and, with his newspaper and other business ventures, as well as his support of patriotic causes, William thought he was just the sort of MP he would have chosen: larger than life and outward-going, a real 'John Bull', like the title of his magazine.

VII

THROUGH THE END OF 1918 AND INTO 1919 THE process of demobilisation and repatriation of the conscript army went on. The men were released in batches to try to control at any one time the numbers seeking to resume their old careers or find new employment. The firm William worked for had promised to hold jobs open for those who had joined the armed forces and this had unexpected repercussions for both Charlie and him. Charlie had assumed that, since he was now eighteen, he could expect promotion to clerk in a matter of months, a year at the most. William would then become office boy. But this was not how things worked out.

In January, two young men were welcomed back to the office by Mr Wilson following their release from the army. The first, Richard Clapham, was about thirty and had volunteered in 1914 and joined the London Scottish, fighting in France, Salonika and Palestine. He was a quiet man, retained a military bearing and moustache, and resumed his post of assistant sales manager which had been taken by one of the clerks in his absence. The other, Arthur Taylor, was in his early twenties, and had been conscripted into the army in 1916. He had been a bookkeeper before he had served in one of the Fusilier battalions and had come back to this job. Taylor had seen service in France up until the armistice and looked old for his years. Unlike Clapham, he never referred to his war service and he was rather subdued most of the time. William noticed that sometimes his hand shook while he was writing in the ledger and once or twice he threw his pen down and walked out of the office. Nobody said anything on either occasion, but afterwards William often saw Clapham talking to him over a cigarette in the canteen and patting him on the back. Gradually Taylor became less withdrawn and taciturn.

Unfortunately, Taylor's return meant that William lost that part of his job which he had enjoyed the most, entering items in the ledger. But if he was disappointed at the turn of events it was nothing compared to the bitterness felt by Charlie. Always preoccupied with his own status, he had forsaken his shirtsleeve and waistcoat garb for a full suit when he reached his eighteenth birthday, in readiness for his expected promotion. With the return of Clapham and Taylor, he would have to put back his ambitions for some time and, without any sign of progress on the horizon, his job turned from being a stepping-stone to better things to a stone round his neck. Trapped by thwarted ambition and the prospect of endless subordination, signified by the suit that he no longer wanted to wear but could not without embarrassment abandon, his temperament festered and his hauteur increased.

One morning William came into work earlier than usual; he was the first person in the office. It was musty and he opened a window before hanging up his jacket and walking over to his desk. There was a note in Charlie's hand, "Make sure you fill up all the inkwells." He was perplexed by this note as he always kept the inkwells full and pencils sharpened as his first job of the day before the other staff arrived.

He opened the stationery cupboard and took down the large bottle of ink with its spout fixed in a cork stopper and went over to the first desk, that of Arthur Taylor. He expected the inkwell to be nearly full but as he poured the ink, it seemed to take ages to fill up. So it was with all the other inkwells; they were all nearly empty. He finished the job, returned to his desk, screwed up Charlie's note and threw it in the bin.

A few minutes later Charlie walked in. "Morning, did you see my note?"

"Yes, Charlie. I've refilled the inkwells."

"Good, mustn't get slack, you know. They were all nearly empty when I left last night."

"I don't understand it. I fill them every day."

Charlie looked unconvinced but said nothing further about it. "Today, I have to help with a stock-take over in the warehouse, so you'll have to look after things here. I'll go down there after Mr Frobisher's set out what else is to be done."

William nodded. He was used to being the only junior in the office from time to time and quite liked being in charge of the office duties. He went about his business, sharpening all the pencils, checking stationery levels and noting any shortages for reordering, getting ready the tray for collecting drinks when required by the senior staff in the offices and so on. Later he would be required to perform whatever tasks the business of the day threw up that could be delegated to him and such tasks were growing in number and complexity.

Before Charlie left to help with the stock-taking he told William that there was a pile of filing to do on his desk. William walked over and saw there were two piles of paper.

"Which pile is for filing?" he asked.

Charlie was half out the door but looked back in. "The one on the right," he said, and disappeared.

The two piles of papers were similar in size and indistinguishable in any other way, so William hesitated, not sure which pile he had referred to. He guessed that Charlie meant those on the right as he looked at them. He immediately began the tedious task of sorting the papers, held together with paper clips, occasionally treasury tags, into alphabetical order before putting them in the appropriate filing cabinet. The papers were sales orders, invoices, diagrams, queries and general correspondence, and he glanced uninterestedly over them as he filed them into the appropriate space in each of the already packed drawers. He had no idea what the other pile of papers was for but left them as they were until Charlie's return.

He had just finished the filing operation and sat back at his desk when Mr Frobisher, returning from a meeting, came into the office and picked up a document on his desk. Wandering over to Charlie's desk, he glanced through the pile of papers while looking at his document. "Do you know where the papers are that I asked Flickill to get from the filing system for me, Lyus?" He looked at William with a slight smile, his eyebrows raised.

"Er, are they the ones on the desk, sir?"

"No, I've no idea what *they* are. I have a list of the ones I want here."

With a growing sense of foreboding, William rose slowly from his desk and walked over to where Mr Frobisher was standing, his eyes drawn to the list he dangled from his hand. He recognised immediately the name 'Scrimgeour' as one of those he had filed papers under just a few minutes earlier.

"I'm sorry, sir. I think I must have filed the wrong set of papers."

Frobisher frowned. "How so?"

"I misunderstood what Charlie told me to do."

Frobisher scratched his ear. "I wouldn't have thought it required the Rosetta Stone to work it out. Well—"

"I'll get them back for you immediately, sir," William interrupted.

"I need them in five minutes," Frobisher said, and went back to his seat.

With the list, it was pretty straightforward to find the papers he'd just filed and he did get them back to Mr Frobisher in just over the time he'd been given. Then he set about filing the correct papers.

At lunchtime he went to the canteen as usual and sat with a couple of the apprentices he knew quite well. Charlie joined them after a few minutes. "What happened with the filing?" he said, his familiar smirk decorating his face.

"When you said, 'on the right' I assumed you meant *your* right."

Charlie laughed. "I was trying to help you out; I meant 'on *your* right.'"

"You should have said so then," said one of the apprentices. "It's one of the first things we learn in engineering about giving instructions: be clear and avoid possible misunderstanding."

"Who's asking for your fourpence worth?" asked Charlie.

William joined in the apprentices' laughter, but he could tell Charlie was not amused as he barely spoke through the rest of the lunch break.

After that day things seemed to go wrong at work all the time. William would be given only half the story when told to do something and consequently do it incorrectly. People in the office complained about the ink being too thick, though he always mixed it up exactly the same way. He would fail to carry out an instruction given by a note on his desk which had mysteriously disappeared before he saw it but would appear later in the wastepaper basket. Misunderstandings and misinterpretations seemed to dog his day.

At first, he put it all down to coincidence and accident,

but there were so many such incidents that he soon came to suspect that at least some of these mishaps were not chance but malicious intent on the part of someone, and that someone was probably Charlie. When he tentatively raised the matter with him he, not surprisingly, laughed it off and accused William of looking for excuses for shoddy work. There was nobody else in the office that he could raise the matter with because he didn't think they would see it from his point of view. He thought of asking his friends; they would be sure to take his side. But he suspected they would either propose retaliation of the most lurid kind or say that at their age it was something to be expected as part of growing up. He didn't want to speak to his parents. He felt he was past the stage of asking his parents to solve his problems; he should be old enough to deal with them himself. So he tried to convince himself that he was imagining Charlie's hostility towards him and just soldiered on. Then, one day there were some problems with the post going out and he was delayed in the post room until after his usual working hours. When he got back to the office, everyone was gone and he was reaching for his jacket when he thought he might as well sharpen the pencils and top up the inkwells now, making one less job for the morning. As he left the office he saw Charlie's jacket hanging up but thought nothing of it.

The next morning, he was in a good mood after a night out with the boys, playing billiards at the local hall. He knew he didn't have to worry about ink or pencils, so he looked at the messages on his desk and went off to do the various errands set out for him. When he returned an hour or so later, Arthur Taylor asked him if he would be refilling the inkwells today as his own was running low.

"I did it last night," William said, open-mouthed.

"Perhaps I've used rather more than usual today," Arthur replied almost apologetically.

William went over to the stationery cupboard to get the ink bottle. It had been half-full the previous night, but now it was empty. He took the bottle and the ink powder to the small scullery and mixed up a fresh batch of ink then took it back to the office. He filled up Arthur's inkwell and then went round to each of the others, none of which was empty, though not one was even a quarter full.

"I think you forgot to do the pencils as well, William," whispered Belinda, the typist who had replaced poor Geraldine. "But it's all right, Charlie did them for you."

Unfortunately, she gave William this message while he was carefully topping up her inkwell from the nearly full bottle. The involuntary jerk which this statement precipitated caused him to spill some of the ink on her desk. Only her quick-witted reaction with a piece of blotting paper prevented the ink flowing off the edge of her desk onto her clothes.

"Sorry," he mumbled.

"You are a silly boy; you must be more careful." Belinda smiled and patted him on the hand. He returned the smile but was mortified by her words.

He struggled to apply himself to the task at hand as he continued his journey round the inkwells, acutely aware that he was now being watched by everyone in the room, except for Charlie, who was crouched studiously over his desk, apparently deep in concentration. All the while, his thoughts were filled with the rage of certainty. *It has been Charlie all the time*, he thought, and he repeated it in his mind over and over again; *it has been Charlie all the time*. He finished filling the inkwells and walked slowly back to the stationery cupboard, retelling in his mind the story of his downfall. Most, if not all, the odd happenings that raced through his mind and had blighted his work over the past month or two had been arranged by Charlie and the latest episode encapsulated the whole. Charlie had been in the office after he had left and emptied the inkwells and the ink bottle. William couldn't believe Charlie had spent hours wearing down the pencils so that he could make them good; he must have got in early and pretended to be sharpening them as people came in to work.

William placed the ink bottle back in the cupboard and raised his clenched fists in a silent cry for vengeance. Then he opened his hands and saw they were shaking, shaking with the sad reality of powerlessness. Who would believe such a preposterous story, that their cheeky but charming hard-working office boy was capable of such a malevolent attitude towards a colleague? He sat down at his desk, staring at Charlie and harbouring murderous thoughts that he knew he would not attempt to enact. Charlie looked up and smiled at him, and it was as much as he could do to restrain himself from lunging furiously at his tormentor.

After the trouble with the inkwells, he decided that the best plan of action would be to watch Charlie like a hawk, get in before him in the morning and leave after him at night so that he could counter any more of his acts of sabotage before they took effect. This strategy was based on the hope that Charlie would eventually tire of this business and things would revert to normal. He had a key to the office so he would be able to appear to leave at night and then come back after Charlie had left to deal with any trap he had laid. It was not revenge but it at least allowed the possibility of thwarting Charlie's designs; a small victory.

Unfortunately, his plan came to nothing. A few days later he was asked to go to see Mr Wilson, the office manager.

"Ah, Lyus, do come in and take a seat."

He sat down while Wilson looked through some papers and then raised his eyes, taking off his glasses and looking at William in silence for some moments.

"You have been here, what is it now?"

"About nineteen months, sir."

"Well, we have a problem, my boy. You see, when you came here I had high hopes of you and you were very good at some of the difficult tasks that were put your way. But the return of Messrs Taylor and Clapham has meant that you have been left with only the basic duties of an assistant office boy and it seems to have affected your work. There have been complaints that you have lapses in the standard expected of you and that's not good."

"I can explain, sir."

Wilson raised his hand. "Please don't interrupt. I think the post you are in is not suitable for your ability and inclination, and it would best be filled by someone more in tune with the demands of the post. Unfortunately, with the likelihood that more of our staff who served in the war will seek to return, there is unlikely to be anything else that I could offer you for the foreseeable future. Furthermore, with extra staff returning and rumours of consolidation in our industry, I am not entirely convinced that we will any longer need an assistant office boy. So this is the parting of the ways, I'm afraid."

"But, Mr Wilson—"

"I'm sorry, but there it is. I will give you a good reference and allow you to serve a month's notice to give you time to find something else. Take time off for any interviews you obtain and I shall have the reference waiting for you whenever you need it."

He said some other soothing words, but William didn't hear them. His mind was swimming with thoughts of rejection, humiliation, injustice and hatred, and dread of having to face his parents. He trudged back to the office and, unusually, nobody looked up when he entered the room. Passing his own desk he stopped at Charlie's and looked down at him, but still Charlie didn't acknowledge his presence.

"I hope you're satisfied now," he said, leaning on the desk, his knuckles a few inches from Charlie's chin.

Charlie looked up and there was fear in his eyes. He didn't reply and seemed almost to cower, but William said nothing else and returned to his desk, ignoring the chorus of turning heads as they looked back at their work.

Sacked for a second time, William found the period afterwards worse than the actual dismissal. Instead of being able to disappear immediately, he had to endure the daily humiliation of a silent entrance to the office, the routine orders of the day from Charlie as if nothing had happened, the meaningless planning of events he would not be there to carry out, the execution of tasks he did to the best of his ability even though it would count for nothing. Worse were the sympathetic smiles of the typists and the gentle commands of the clerks when he had to engage with them. Worse still, the crocodile tears of those commiserating workers on the shop floor and the warehouse who had shown little empathy or interest in him before but seized this opportunity to criticise the management in the severest of terms. Now their vitriol towards their bosses could be sheltered under the noble banner of generosity of spirit and righteous indignation for the maltreatment of their fallen comrade.

While the passing days brought the welcome departure from his job nearer, they also hastened the moment when he must reveal the truth to his parents, see the disappointment in their faces and hear their stern or, even worse, gentle reproach. He had rehearsed what he would say to them several times but always it ended in a shambles of recrimination and despair. How could he tell them that the loss of his job was due to a campaign of malevolence from Charlie? In his mind's eye he could see his father shaking his head in disbelief and his mother dismissing his story with a look of contempt. He resolved not to tell them anything until after he had secured another job, or perhaps not at all. The next two weeks were devoted to hectic lunchtime trips to the library to search the local ads in the newspapers and after work he would scan the cards in the shop windows for 'posts vacant' for which he might be suitable. Each day the story was much the same; though he would take almost any job, he was an office junior of limited experience in competition against men and women coming back to work after demobilisation, for whom there was inevitably much sympathy. The only good news was that there would be no one leaving school to compete with him as the school-leaving age had been raised to fourteen at the end of the war. On the Monday of the third week he was turning the 'Situations Vacant' pages of the *Hackney Gazette* without much expectation when the phrase 'Office Junior Clerk' caught his eye. The brief advertisement mentioned only that an office junior with basic clerical skills and some experience of keeping ledgers was required by a small financial company in Hackney. There was a telephone number but no address.

He left the library and walked to the nearest shop which had a telephone for public use. It was the first time he had made a telephone call and the shop assistant helped him. The telephone was answered after a couple of rings by a man who sounded as if he had a cold or sinusitis. He asked William a couple of questions about his experience and current employment and then asked him to attend for an interview on Wednesday afternoon.

Just after lunch on Wednesday, William collected his reference from Mr Wilson's secretary and, with her good luck wishes ringing in his ears, he set off for the offices of Hoinville & Bates, Accountants, which were located in the upstairs rooms of a large shop on Lower Clapton Road. He went through the side door of the building and up to the first floor, where he was presented with a door glazed with frosted glass in the upper half on which was written the name of the firm. He knocked and opened the door to reveal a suite of rooms. In this first room were three desks. At one sat a middle-aged, small woman, dressed in a plain black dress with a white collar, typing a letter. At the second was a man in his early thirties, dressed in a suit, running a pencil down a line of figures and entering the total in a ledger, following a second check. The third desk was empty. The room was clean and tidy, and the furniture plain but relatively new. Behind the desk at which the woman sat were two doors, one with the name T.W. Hoinville inscribed on the frosted glass and the other F.B. Bates. The overall impression was one of a slightly old-fashioned but professional organisation.

The woman looked up when William entered, taking off his cap. The man ignored him but stuck to his next line of figures.

"Yes?" said the woman.

"Good afternoon. I have an interview with Mr Hoinville concerning the vacant position. My name is William Lyus."

The woman smiled slightly and removed her glasses. "Take a seat and I'll tell Mr Hoinville you are here." She motioned towards a row of three wooden seats with slatted backs which were against the wall.

William sat down and checked in his inside pocket that the reference was still there, in its sealed envelope. He looked up at the round clock with its wooden frame and roman numerals; he was five minutes early for his appointment.

The woman came out of Mr Hoinville's office. "Mr Hoinville won't be long," she said, sitting back at her desk to resume her work.

At two o'clock, the appointed time of the interview, Mr Hoinville's door opened and a sandy-haired man of about forty-five looked at William and beckoned him to come over.

As he entered the room, Hoinville gestured for him to take a seat while he sat behind a large desk. William was facing the window and could hear the traffic, a mixture of motorised vehicles and horse-drawn carts, in the street below.

"Well, Mr Lyus, tell me about yourself." Hoinville smiled at him quizzically and stroked his rather straggly moustache.

William recognised the nasal voice of the man he had spoken to when he rang up about the vacancy. He had spent much of that morning neglecting his duties at Barlow's while he tried to map out all the questions he was likely to be asked and to prepare answers for each of them. This first question was a variation on one of his top three likely questions and he had little difficulty outlining his school career and subsequent employment at Barlow's, stressing his clerical work and maintenance of ledgers.

"You have been at Barlow's for getting on for two years. It's a large company with opportunities, so why should you wish to leave it now?" He smiled, this time with an expression of self-satisfaction at his own shrewdness.

"The company has a policy of taking back anyone who served in the war and the possible promotion ladder has been made more difficult for me."

Hoinville nodded. "You have been pushed to the end of the queue, eh? How dispiriting. Well, we are a small firm, but we have great ambitions. Above us is another floor which is currently used for storage, but when we expand, as we surely will, that floor will enable us to take on another half dozen staff, perhaps more professional staff, even more partners. At present there is only one clerk above the position on offer so the opportunities for the right person are superlative." He sat back in his chair, his long neck rising out of his wing collar, as he stared silently over William's head, reflecting on the grand future awaiting his business.

William neither responded nor was impressed by this statement. He had heard something similar, if less grandiose, from Mr Plover and Mr Wilson, yet all he had to show for it so far was two dismissals. He was just interested in the here and now. Did he have the job?

Hoinville gave him a ledger and asked him to explain what he was looking at when he read the entries. Next he gave a few columns of figures to add up in his head and finally he asked him for some examples of his writing and spelling. After this he looked at Mr Wilson's reference.

This was the moment William had feared, the only part of the interview where he had no ability to affect the outcome. He sat waiting and watching as Hoinville seemed to take an hour to read the two-page reference.

"A splendid reference. Mr Wilson seems to believe you are destined for better things than he could offer you. Well, when would you be able to start if you were offered the position?"

William did a rapid mental calculation. He could not say immediately as that would set alarm bells ringing in Hoinville's head. He had seven days left of his notice so he replied, "I shall have to give a week's notice."

"Well, I assume you work Saturday? So if you give your notice on Saturday you will be able to start here the Monday after your notice ends."

"Are you offering me the position?"

"Yes, of course, Mr Lyus, if you want it, that is."

William eagerly replied that he did, even before he was informed that he would receive 4/- more per week than he was currently earning. Now he would not have to explain what had happened to his parents. To his relief, he would not have to tell them the whole story.

That evening he told his parents that he had become disillusioned with working at Barlow's as his prospects were diminishing rather than improving. He had therefore applied for and obtained a new job. He thought his parents would be troubled by the news, especially as he had not discussed the matter with them beforehand, but he was pleasantly surprised when his mother's face was wreathed with a big smile.

"That's wonderful news, Billy," she said. "I knew you had it in you to show some initiative. Congratulations."

Jack smiled too but wanted to hear more. "What sort of company is this, Billy?"

"Well, it's a firm of accountants. They do bookkeeping for small companies and handle clients' investments, that kind of thing. It's growing fast and hopes to take on lots of new staff. As I am starting there before the expansion happens I'll be well-placed to move up the ladder."

Jack nodded. "I'm surprised that you didn't discuss it with me first, but I suppose you are old enough to make these decisions for yourself now. I am very pleased for you. Well done, son."

William gave notice at work that he would be leaving the following week and that last week went quickly. Charlie tried to foist a lot of jobs on him that he didn't want to do himself, but William slowed down on his work rather than dance to Charlie's tune. He derived some pleasure in seeing Charlie's expressions of frustration and impotent rage. His other colleagues in the office seemed genuinely pleased that he had found something else and they signed a card wishing him good luck in the future and bought him a farewell gift of a tiepin and cuff links. Charlie had signed the card, and William smiled when he thought how much that would have made him squirm. On his last day, William thanked them all for his gift and said a few polite words of farewell then he shook hands with everyone in the office and they wished him well. Belinda even gave him a kiss on the cheek, a moment he cherished for several days. When he turned to Charlie, he smiled and gave the little speech he had prepared.

"Thanks, Charlie. It's due to all you've done that I find myself in the position of becoming a junior clerk and I hope you get there one day yourself."

Charlie's face bore a sickly grin, made worse by the smiles he could see on the faces of the typists and the chuckles he heard from Clapham and Taylor.

Lastly, William went to see Mr Wilson, who gave him his final payslip and wages and wished him well. William thought Wilson looked relieved to know that he had managed to find something else, but he didn't think that made it all right. After all, he could just as easily not have found a new job or been forced to take a worse one than he had here. It was no thanks to any of the people here that he'd been fortunate to come out of this business well. He felt he'd been treated badly, but he would try to put it behind him.

IX

Two days after leaving Barlow's for the last time, William Lyus, Junior Clerk, threaded his way through the back doubles connecting Daubeney Road to Lower Clapton Road and swiftly mounted the steps to his new offices. Not sure whether he needed to, he knocked on the door before walking in.

The same middle-aged woman and young man were seated in exactly the same positions, doing exactly the same tasks they had been occupied with on his first visit. They looked up when he came in and both smiled. William hadn't really looked at them when he came for the interview, but now he examined them more closely. The woman, whom he took to be in her late forties, was certainly older than his mother. She was a little plump and had a well-rounded figure under a purple dress that was of the current style but more conservative than some younger women were wearing. Her hair was dark brown and she wore little make-up. He thought she had a pleasant face and she gave him a kind smile when she introduced herself.

"Good morning, Mr Lyus, I'm Miss Bocking and I act as secretary to the two partners and general dogsbody for everything else. I hope you enjoy working here." She shook hands and looked over at the young man.

Her colleague had a pale, long face lightened by a cheery smile and slight dimple in his chin. He was dressed in a navy-blue suit with a dark green tie, a white stiff collar topping off a pale grey shirt. His dark hair was parted just off-centre and he was clean-shaven. He stood, putting down his pen, and strode round to shake William's hand. "I'm Biggs, Terence Biggs, chief clerk. In fact until today, the only clerk." He chortled and then guided William over to the empty desk and chair which awaited him. "You will sit here, in the 'Siege Perilous.'" He chortled again.

"Mr Hoinville would like you to take on some of my jobs and also some of Miss Bocking's, so we shall be a team with each of us knowing something of the others' work, should the need arise." He smiled.

William smiled but was slightly disappointed. He knew from his experience with Charlie at Barlow's that this probably meant that he would take over the tasks that Mr Biggs and Miss Bocking couldn't wait to get rid of. What he had not foreseen was that some of the work they did not like doing, or at least they did not mind losing, was just the sort of thing he enjoyed. He acquired responsibility for the post and paying in and making withdrawals at the bank from Miss Bocking, duties that would get him out of the office, however briefly. From Mr Biggs he took on the role of ledger clerk: the making of entries in clients' ledgers for payments made and received. He would also chase up payments outstanding and undertake some simple account reconciliation. There would be other tasks too, that had been done previously on an ad hoc basis by whoever was available, such as taking messages to clients, arranging checks on credit worthiness and so on. There were finally the mundane tasks of making tea and coffee and collecting purchases and running errands for the partners, all of which he expected. All things considered, he was happy with his pattern of work.

Settling into his new working environment would be another matter. This small firm with five staff, nobody of his own age and a lack of any staff facilities was a far cry from Barlow's. Sitting in this outer office where conversation was likely to be brief and to the point concerning work, he was unlikely to have many lighter moments. The day would be one of unmitigated work, especially with the partners in earshot behind their closed doors. This thought was on his mind as Terence was patiently going through the details of the various ledgers with him when the door of Mr Bates flew open to reveal what to William appeared a vision of rage. The man's face was a deep red, except for his toothbrush moustache, which was jet-black. His eyes were bulging behind their gold-rimmed glasses and his mouth was twisted into a snarl. For a moment William considered that the man might be having an apoplectic attack, but a high-pitched voice emanated from the mouth and almost screamed the word, "Biggs!"

Terence Biggs jumped up and so, reactively, did William. "Yes, Mr Bates," said Terence quietly.

"What the hell has happened to the Marlpool account?" Bates had a sheaf of papers in his hand which he now waved and threw on Terence's desk. "Check the circled queries and see me with some answers in fifteen minutes." He turned to go back into his office but then spun round. "What is this boy doing here?" He glared at William.

"He's our new junior clerk, Mr Bates," replied Miss Bocking.

"Hmm, hope he's better than the last one." His door closed with a slam.

Terence sat down and winked at William, who sat down slowly, grateful that he had not been the beneficiary of Bates's outburst.

"What happened to the last junior clerk?" whispered William.

"It was me," said Terence. "I'd better see to this and we'll go through the rest later."

"Come and sit with me, William," said Miss Bocking, patting the chair just behind her desk. "I shall show you round the jobs you're taking over from me."

That first day at work with Hoinville & Bates left William exhausted and worrying whether he had made the right move in his career, especially after his first encounter with Bates. However, in subsequent days it became clear that his interaction with the partners would be negligible as all his work, however it was generated, came through Terence and Miss Bocking, and he had only to meet their satisfaction as far as his work was concerned. The only time the partners were likely to ask him to do anything was when Miss Bocking was at lunch, and as Hoinville's lunch break started before Miss Bocking's and finished after it, he rarely had need of William's services. Bates, on the other hand, never deigned to speak to William and if Miss Bocking was at lunch he would wait until she returned. William was very happy with these arrangements and was pleased that his work life was concentrated in the outer office. The explosion by Bates was relatively rare, but his haughty attitude towards Terence was a permanent feature of his personality and William thought there was much to be said for being too inconsequential to be spoken to.

As time went on, the atmosphere in the office was not as severe as he had feared. The partners were often out seeing clients and then both Terence and Miss Bocking, whose name he learned was Primrose, would often exchange some light conversation over a cup of tea. When something of interest occurred in the mail or concerning a client they would share it with each other and they were quick to draw William into this social relief from the business of the day. Terence took the magazine *Punch* and would often read out a humorous or amusing titbit when they took a break.

The weeks settled into a regular pattern at work and William was soon quite comfortable in his new surroundings. His day was predictable but there was some variety and he was able to get out to the bank, the post office and occasionally to a credit agency for a reference on a client. Terence was a congenial supervisor who congratulated him on the quality of his ledger-keeping and gave him more interesting tasks to perform. William enrolled at evening classes to learn more about bookkeeping and eventually gain a qualification. Bates had occasionally been rude to Miss Bocking and Terence, but there had been no repeat of the explosion of anger in that first week. There would undoubtedly be further histrionic episodes in the future, but they would come out of the blue. The office was generally free of agitation or tension. When he reflected on matters, he was sure his career had taken a turn for the better.

As life continued its post-war return to normality the first-class cricket season began again in 1919. Born in a part of London historically situated in Middlesex, William would like to have gone to Lord's, but the Essex County ground at Leyton was both nearer at only a mile and a half away, and cheaper. So he went with his old school friends, Leonard and Cyril, to several of the matches at the ground. Though not a fashionable cricket county, Essex had three internationals in Charlie McGahey, coming to the end of his career, the captain Johnny Douglas and the stylish batsman 'Jack Russell'. Cricket always gives its aficionados time to socialise as well as watch, and the friends enjoyed talking about old times and current prospects. Leonard was still working in his father's business and, as well as acquiring the skills of his craft, was now often accompanying his father on site visits to assess the job and give a quote. Cyril was continuing his apprenticeship and was much changed, naturally physically bigger and stronger, but also no longer a shy, diffident boy but a self-confident young man with a natural air of authority. William admired how his two friends had turned out and wished he hadn't been rather left behind. Of course, he didn't know what they thought of him and would have been pleasantly surprised. His friends were interested in how William's career was developing, especially after he met them for the second cricket match and related to them the developments that had occurred in June, just a few weeks before.

It was obvious to the trio in the outer office that something was up because Hoinville was out of the office more often, and he and Bates had gone together to a couple of meetings, something they rarely did as each had his own set of clients. William had been with the firm for several months now and knew the ropes pretty well. Terence Biggs had shown him more and more of his own job to give him practical knowledge and help his studies. Though neither of them had said so, the partners appeared pleased with his progress and he had so far avoided one of Bates' temper tantrums. One afternoon, towards the end of June, he was, much to his surprise, called into Hoinville's office along with Terence. After they had taken their seats, Hoinville smiled pleasantly and turned to William.

"Lyus, how are things? I have heard encouraging news of your progress from Mr Biggs."

William glanced over at Terence, who winked at him. "Well, sir, I enjoy working here very much. I think I've settled in quite well and I am learning something new every day."

"I gather you are attending evening classes too. Very good. Well, something interesting has presented an opportunity for us that may lead to a new area of activity. Do you know what a company registrar does?"

"No, sir."

"*You* know, of course." He looked at Terence.

"Yes, it's a bank or other financial firm that maintains the register of shares of a public company and distributes dividends and information to the shareholders and perhaps bondholders as required."

"Quite, and a very lucrative activity it is indeed, with predictable costs and commitments and a guaranteed income. We are not a big practice at present and would be unlikely to attract work of this nature, but we have the chance to start on a small scale by working for Mr Horatio Bottomley."

"The MP?" asked Terence, moving a little in his chair.

"The same. He is a great champion of Victory Bonds and wants to make a stake in them open to the less wealthy members of the community by selling part shares of a bond to those interested. He has raised a significant amount of money with his backers and has sufficient to buy at least £100,000 worth of Victory Bonds. Having purchased the bonds as a whole, he will sell part ownership of a bond for as little as £1. The total interest on all bonds purchased, after costs, of course, will be distributed in the form of prizes, rather like with a gambling syndicate. Of course, not everyone will receive income, but each part bondholder will have the chance of a larger prize than an interest payment. Their capital is quite safe and can be withdrawn from the scheme whenever they want."

Terence leaned forward in his chair but said nothing.

Hoinville stopped, anticipating a comment or question, but when none came he went on. "Mr Bottomley would like our firm to help with the record-keeping and related matters. He envisages that the partners of this firm will act as trustees to ensure that all appropriate protocols are adhered to and the finances kept independent from Mr Bottomley's other business assets."

Terence leaned back in his chair and crossed and uncrossed his legs but still said nothing.

Hoinville noted the movement. "Have you any questions so far?" he asked, looking directly at Terence.

Terence hesitated. "I'm not quite clear how Mr Bottomley raised the money, sir. Was it from banks or private investors?"

"The latter. Last year Mr Bottomley launched his War Stock Combination which allowed people to subscribe to a fund to buy Victory Bonds and that has raised more than the £77,000 or so, which was his original target. Those subscribers can now convert their holdings into shares of the Victory Bonds."

Terence looked a little puzzled but continued, "Would the entire operation regarding the Victory Bonds Association—"

"Victory Bonds *Club*," corrected Hoinville.

"Would the entire operation regarding the Victory Bonds Club be based on these premises?"

"No, because this is not a conventional registrar arrangement whereby the whole administration is contracted out to the registrar. Mr Bottomley will keep the entire running of the club in his hands and will determine policy, payouts and so forth. As he is a very busy man he needs help to keep the register, collect subscriptions and deal with queries. He is suggesting that we supply a clerk for this purpose and we will be paid fees for our services."

Terence nodded. "Who did you have in mind to fill the role of ledger clerk and clerical assistant; a new member of staff?"

"Not initially, until we know how much work is involved. I thought you might set the system up and then young Lyus here could take over the day-to-day running of it, a purely straightforward clerical operation."

William had sat enthralled, up till now, listening to this exciting and noble project to help the less well-off which featured the great Horatio Bottomley. Now he was overjoyed to hear that it was in Mr Hoinville's mind to give him the opportunity to actually work with Mr Bottomley. So this was why the two partners had been out of the office so much recently, even disappearing together to go to meetings which they told Primrose Bocking nothing about. His thoughts were interrupted by Terence's next question.

"Would Lyus still work from here, where I could be of assistance at all times?"

Hoinville carefully joined his fingertips together. "Unfortunately that will not be possible as Mr Bottomley will need everything at his fingertips." He looked at his hands and separated them.

"With respect, sir, I am concerned that this venture will be under the banner of our firm as registrars, but we will not in practice have sufficient control over its conduct, notably in the matter of the distributions to shareholders."

Hoinville shook his head and then attempted to clear his nasal passages by blowing his nose through one nostril only, but to no avail. "Not at all," he said, putting his handkerchief back into his pocket. "Lyus will be seconded to assist Mr Bottomley. The position of trustees of the Victory Bond Club will be held by Mr Bates and myself in our personal capacities and there may well be other trustees drawn from appropriate people of good standing. Only when this venture has been running successfully for some time will we use our connection with it to help secure other future business. If it will put your mind at rest, I suggest you arrange for Lyus to keep you informed of his progress and raise any problems he has with you."

Terence nodded and said no more, aware that Hoinville was starting to sound a little tetchy.

"Have you any queries, Lyus?"

William was a little bothered but only because he saw that Terence was clearly worried. However, he didn't want to miss this opportunity. "When will I start, sir?"

Hoinville's expression brightened. "That's the spirit, my boy; in a couple of weeks."

After work finished for the day, Terence asked William to come with him to a local café for a cup of tea. William was surprised and flattered by this novel invitation. They ordered their drinks and sat down at a table in a corner of the simple café. It was fairly empty as few local workers heading for a drink after work would opt for a cup of tea.

"So you are looking forward to working with Mr Bottomley?" Terence took a cigarette from a packet of cigarettes and offered one to William, who politely refused.

"Yes, very much." He sipped the hot, sweet tea from a plain white mug.

"William, I do wish you well and this does seem a wonderful opportunity to mix in very different circles, but do be careful. Mr Bottomley is prominent in the worlds of politics and business, but several of his commercial activities have failed and he has frequently been accused of dishonest dealings. He sails very close to the wind and I don't like the idea of you getting caught up in anything unsavoury."

William didn't view Bottomley in quite the same way and his response betrayed a touch of irritation. "He is a good MP. He has arranged charabanc trips for the poor children to have days out and he does try to help the less well-off. I'm sure what he is doing about the bonds will be a great thing and I would like to help."

"I suppose we all believe what we want to believe," Terence said, partly to himself. "Look, I do understand how you feel, but for your own sake keep a close eye on all that happens and get in touch with me if you have concerns. Even if you just feel that something's not right but you can't put a finger on it, just telephone me."

William nodded, a little upset by Terence's disparagement of Bottomley's character and even more determined to help Mr Bottomley make his scheme a success. He was still young enough to value his own judgement above that of everybody else's.

X

A MEETING WAS ARRANGED AND TEN DAYS LATER Hoinville, Terence and William met Bottomley at his office in the City. William walked along with the two older, taller men, feeling just a touch of self-importance. His mother had bought him his first suit, a grey herringbone, which he wore with a red tie and a starched collar. He was filled with anticipation and excitement at the thought of his first business meeting and furthermore one with a famous person. They eventually arrived at the building in Finsbury Circus and found Bottomley's office on the first floor.

William was impressed as soon as he entered the outer office. A young woman sat at a desk typing a letter and immediately ceased what she was doing to welcome the three visitors with a smile.

"Good morning. The gentlemen from Hoinville & Bates? Mr Bottomley is expecting you. Please take a seat, won't you? I'll tell him you're here."

The young woman, wearing a very attractive but demure summer dress, knocked on the inner office door and advised Mr Bottomley that his guests had arrived. A moment later she reappeared and asked them to go straight in.

William walked behind the other two, adjusting his tie and patting down his hair, which appeared more golden in the rays of the sun piercing the room through venetian blinds.

The recognisable figure of Horatio Bottomley stood to greet them. As usual, he was well-dressed in a charcoal grey frock coat and double-breasted waistcoat. A flash of gold was visible on his blood-red tie and his buttonhole sported a pale pink rose.

"Gentlemen, please come in and make yourselves comfortable. I am delighted to see you again, Mr Hoinville." He walked over and shook Hoinville's hand.

"How do you do, sir, may I introduce my colleagues, Terence Biggs and William Lyus?"

Bottomley shook hands with them both, looking each in the eye with a broad smile. He gestured to the two armchairs and small sofa which provided the seating for guests in the office. "A glass of sherry or port, perhaps?" He walked over to a table with several bottles of spirits and other drinks and waited for their orders.

William, who rarely drank anything stronger than a pint of mild, wasn't sure if he should accept the offer of a drink and he waited for his colleagues to give a lead. Hoinville asked for a dry sherry and Terence for a glass of port. Remembering that his grandmother usually had a glass of port at Christmas, William thought that would be a safe bet and, after Hoinville had given him an approving nod, also asked for port. Bottomley poured himself a dry sherry and gave his guests their drinks with the merest hint of a flourish.

William sat on the sofa, his senior colleagues having taken the two plum-coloured armchairs. He looked round the office and reflected that he had never been in a room so grand. It had recently been decorated in a subdued flock wallpaper and grey paint. All the fine reproduction Sheraton furniture was new.

Though William was neither aware nor particularly interested in the detail of the furnishings and decor, he felt this must be what people referred to as 'opulence'. In response to Bottomley proposing a toast to a 'fruitful co-operation' he drank a little of the port and found to his surprise that he quite liked it.

By way of making conversation, Hoinville asked the MP if he was satisfied with the way events were going in the country. Bottomley replied that he was enjoying holding both main parties to account from his position as an Independent.

"There is much to do, so much to do, I'm afraid. But now to business, gentlemen," said Bottomley, putting down his schooner glass on the green leather of the desk in front of him. "All is ready for the launch of the 'John Bull Victory Bond Club' next week. There has already been advance notice of the club and how to purchase subscriptions by coupon in the *John Bull* and advertisements will go out at the weekend in *The People*, *Reynold's Newspaper*, etcetera. In addition, there will be bills stuck all over the place and posters on hoardings, especially in London, like this one." He produced a poster with a picture of John Bull offering a man in a cloth cap membership of the Victory Bond Club and pointing at a poster for Victory Bonds. "I expect the postal orders to come flooding in soon after that. So we need to be ready; the first week is likely to be the busiest. Is everything prepared at your end?"

"Yes, most definitely," said Hoinville. "I have asked Mr Biggs to look after the management of our activities and he will be here for the first few days to set the process rolling. Young Lyus will act as clerk and bookkeeper for you here for as much and as long as you require him."

William was concerned that Bottomley might be less than impressed that such an inexperienced person as he had been given such an important role, but the MP merely looked in his direction and smiled benignly. "I shall be honoured to work with you, Mr Lyus. I began as an office boy and moved up and so shall you."

Hoinville continued, "Mr Biggs will ensure our procedures are set up to your satisfaction and will be available to assist Mr Lyus if any difficulties occur while you are engaged elsewhere."

"Good, that all seems very satisfactory. May I refill your glasses?" He brought the bottles round and, afterwards, William was thankful that this time only a small amount was poured into his glass.

They talked at length on the detailed workings of the club and Bottomley showed them the certificates which would be issued and the ledgers that would need to be kept. Terence asked one or two questions about the auditing of the club's books, but Bottomley was charmingly vague about this and assured him that all would become clear once the operation was up and running. Finally, William and Terence were shown the two new desks which were waiting in a storeroom along the corridor. William thought it so much better than his present one with its faux leather top and lockable drawers, and could barely wait until the following Monday when he would begin his new role.

When the meeting had ended the staff from Hoinville & Bates walked out into the bright sunshine and William felt slightly woozy after his introduction to fortified wine. They took a bus back to the office and William sat in silence while his two senior colleagues discussed their opinions as to how the meeting with Bottomley had gone. Hoinville appeared to be perfectly at ease with the outcome, whereas Terence once again voiced his misgivings about the whole venture, especially as William was being 'thrown in at the deep end'.

William had listened carefully to every word in the meeting and was sure that he would be able to do the job well and that Terence was being overly protective of him. Hoinville was also sure that William would be able to cope, especially as Terence would be there for the first few days to iron out any problems. As far as he was concerned, there were sufficient safeguards to forestall any calamities and he suggested that perhaps Terence was looking for problems. Terence, based partly on his understanding of what had been agreed and partly on his knowledge of Bottomley's past activities, could see nothing but pitfalls. Three people, three perspectives: the unconscious incompetence of the junior, the blind arrogance of the partner based on past success and future expected rewards, the risk-averse caution of the managing clerk aware of Bottomley's failings. The different perspectives were patched together in an unspoken agreement to go ahead with it for the simple reason that Hoinville had already committed them to it.

If William had any qualms, they arose from the uncertain reaction of his parents to the news that he would be working for Mr Bottomley. When he arrived home, he was prepared for a grilling from his father, due to the possible uncertain outcomes of any business in which Bottomley had a hand. His preparations for the onslaught were not in vain. He countered his father's expressions of concern and disappointment with a rigorous argument for the Victory Bonds Club and his role in it. He defended the right to be given another chance in the case of Mr Bottomley, stressing his genuine desire to raise the opportunities for the working class, as he had done in other ways for the children of Homerton and the rest of South Hackney. He said the firm of Hoinville & Bates were well aware of the need to protect their own reputation and would ensure that the club operated with integrity and that all would be above board. Then he stressed his own competence and that of Terence in ensuring that the processes and procedures of the club were beyond reproach. Finally, he pointed out that the work he did was determined by his employers and he was in no position to refuse what were duties within his ability.

His father was so taken aback by his son's eloquence that he soon abandoned any attempt to persuade William from doing what he knew he was obliged to do and bowed to the reality of the situation. Alice sided with their son and said she would be pleased to take part in the Victory Bonds Club.

The following Monday morning, brimming with confidence and joie de vivre, William took the train to Broad Street Station and made the short walk to Finsbury Circus. He arrived early, but Bottomley's secretary, whom he remembered from the previous week, was already there and offered him a cup of tea. He was pleased to see the offices of Horatio Bottomley had lost none of their charm over the weekend and was pleasantly surprised that someone was making *him* a drink at work for the first time. The secretary introduced herself as Millicent Porter and said she was pleased to have a work colleague at last. She explained that Bottomley was often at the House of Commons or at the publishing offices and she sometimes spent the whole day at work without seeing anyone. They passed a few other pleasantries before Terence arrived and went through a similar exchange of courtesies with Millicent. Then Terence and William turned to look at their desks.

They were confronted by a huge pile of envelopes on one desk and a stack of deep red registers on the other. William looked over at Millicent and she smiled with her eyebrows raised. "They came in with the first post at eight o'clock. There will be another three deliveries today. I'll help you later: first, that cup of tea I promised." She knocked on Bottomley's office door. "Messrs Biggs and Lyus are here."

Bottomley came, slightly puffing, out of his office. "Welcome, gentlemen. Glad to have you both on board.

A good start, by the look of it." He gestured to the pile of envelopes then went straight back into his office.

A good start, by the look of it." He gestured to the pile of envelopes then went straight back into his office.

It was a warm day and William took off his jacket and hung it on the hat stand. Then he looked at the pile of envelopes and gingerly picked up the first one.

Millicent came into the office from the little kitchen opposite with a tray containing cups of tea and biscuits. William picked up the pretty flower-patterned cup and saucer and, remembering his first day at Mr Plover's, placed them carefully on the desk, out of reach of his elbow. Millicent lifted up her chair and went to bring it over to his desk, but William quickly came to her aid and placed the chair next to his own.

"Thank you, Mr Lyus," she said, and, with a pencil and notebook, sat between him and Terence.

William liked being called 'Mr Lyus' even if that was really his father's title, but he had no illusions about his real status. "How shall we do this?" he asked Terence.

"How do you think we should do it?" replied Terence, giving William the opportunity to show some initiative.

"Shall one of us open the envelopes and dictate the person's name and address to another who enters the details in the register? Meanwhile the third person notes the amount received in the cashbook and the form of payment: postal order or cheque or whatever?"

Terence nodded in agreement. "Yes, let's try that and see how well we get along. We can always change tack if the need arises. Miss Porter opens the envelopes, reads out the details and passes the subscription form and money to me to make a note of each payment while you enter the register."

Millicent carefully leaned over William and took a bundle of the envelopes, the smell of her eau de cologne momentarily distracting him while he got his registration books ready.

Millicent had waited patiently while the other two agreed their strategy. Now she began to read out the details of the person in her clear, almost neutral accent and William wished he spoke as she did, instead of his East End accent, with its tendency to a glottal stop and a dropped aitch which he had difficulty controlling. But for now, he had only to listen as he entered sum after address after name in his neat hand, pausing only to turn to the correct book as designated, to check a spelling or clarify a detail. Each envelope contained one, sometimes two or even three, coupons and it took less than a minute to complete the registration and accounting procedure. Some straightforward ones took less than thirty seconds, but there was some time lost in repeating the details or spelling them out, occasionally a discussion over a potential or actual irregularity in the coupon or the form of payment and a very occasional chuckle over a name or address. After an hour they had completed one hundred and ten submissions with subscriptions of £440 and the pile of envelopes had declined in size from a mountain to a hill. During the course of the hour Bottomley appeared and asked how things were going before disappearing again to a meeting elsewhere in the City, with a promise to return after lunch, which Millicent advised would mean after two-thirty, unless his anticipation got the better of him.

On they worked, stopping for a cup of tea and more biscuits mid-morning when Terence and William asked Millicent how she'd arrived in this particular post. She gave a brief résumé of her past life. During the war she had attended classes for young ladies in typewriting, shorthand and bookkeeping at Clark's College. After that she had worked in an insurance broker's office until taking up this post a few months previously.

"What's Mr Bottomley like to work for?" asked William.

She shrugged. "All right. He doesn't make me work very hard and as he knows shorthand himself, he's good at dictation.

Actually, I'm not strictly speaking Mr Bottomley's secretary," she said, biting into a Bourbon biscuit which she held daintily. "He has a secretary who deals with all his parliamentary business and another office at Odhams Press, where *John Bull* is published. I think he uses that office for his various activities to do with newspapers and the magazine. This one is just for the Victory Bonds Club and related matters."

William admired her candour. He also thought her very attractive, with her chestnut-coloured hair worn up off her slender neck, big brown eyes, pert nose and well-shaped mouth. His regard for her looks was purely aesthetic as he realised the age gap between them eliminated him as someone of any likely interest to her. He mused that if the age gap were the other way round it would not seem odd at all. By the charm and gentle flattery that Terence was employing, it was clear he found her attractive too.

Another postal delivery arrived and this prompted them into returning to their work. William was beginning to fret that if this continued they would be overwhelmed by the sheer numbers by the end of the day. They were getting slightly quicker now as they had almost worked their way through the first mountain while the second one waited on the floor. They stopped again at lunchtime and Millicent went out and bought some sandwiches of tongue and corned beef, which they ate with more fresh tea.

Bottomley returned after lunch but only in the sense that the lunch hour had long since passed. He arrived just after four with a bag which he took into his office before asking how the work was proceeding.

Terence took his pencil from behind his ear. "Well, sir, we are making progress, but we have been emptying envelopes all day and have opened and registered around nine hundred, but we have opened less than half of the late morning post and the afternoon post is unopened. If there is another post this evening we will be swamped. If it continues at this scale all week I believe more help will be needed."

"That is splendid news," said Bottomley, gently punching the air with both his closed fists. "The fact you have to work so hard means it's a success. I shall get some help over to you tomorrow. Have you kept a summary of the total money so far?"

"Yes, sir, it's about £3,600 pounds."

Bottomley smiled. "Excellent, but we must not leave all this loose money lying about. We shall work on this evening, for which you shall all receive appropriate reward, and what we do not complete we shall leave till the morning."

He went back into his office while the team picked up where they had left off. They could hear Bottomley talking quite loudly on the telephone with the occasional laugh and after about half an hour he came out to join them.

"I have arranged to have six people here tomorrow morning to help with the registration process and there is a room available for them to work in. I assume you will direct operations to match your own high standard, Mr Biggs, and allocate your resources in whichever way you wish. I am depending on you and I am sure you will not let me down. Now, how can I be of assistance right now?"

William for one felt daunted by the possibility of actually working with the Great Bottomley, but then Terence's answer made that possibility less likely. "Do you have a safe, Mr Bottomley?" he asked.

"Why, of course. There is one in my office."

"Well, may I suggest we concentrate on sorting the money out and leave the registration until later? We open every envelope, check that the postal order or cheque or money order matches the form it comes with as to the amount, and then we put the forms in a pile for completion and the money in the safe. Perhaps you might be so kind as to bundle the money into the various types: cheques, cash etc., ready for banking in the morning."

"An excellent idea," said Bottomley.

The new approach speeded matters up considerably and they had cleared the backlog by the time the evening post arrived. One more hour and they were finished. Despite warnings to the contrary in the public offer, the subscriptions included a great deal of cash and Bottomley put the money into the safe and locked it. Then he walked over to the bag by his desk and produced a bottle of Veuve Clicquot in a small pack of largely melted ice. "A celebration is called for, my friends," he announced, releasing the wire and gently removing the cork before pouring into four champagne glasses which seemed to have appeared from nowhere.

William felt heady even before he had raised his glass and taken his first ever sip of champagne. The day, already seemingly apocryphal, had now entered the realms of fantasy and he loved it.

"Well done to you all and let us hope for many times like this in the days ahead. You must all be very hungry; drink up and then we'll have some supper." He topped up their glasses and Millicent giggled as her glass threatened to overflow before the bubbles retreated. Terence gave his apologies, saying that he had a social engagement that evening, and he left soon after they had finished the champagne.

When all was locked up for the night the other three left the office and walked into the cool, still light evening. William felt, justifiably now, a little light-headed. They walked out of Finsbury Circus into Liverpool Street and round to Old Broad Street and Gow's Oyster Bar. Once there, Bottomley regaled them with amusing anecdotes of his past before and during the War while they enjoyed platters of smoked salmon and brown bread and more glasses of champagne.

"Well, time and tide, you know," said Bottomley, signalling for the bill after forty-five minutes or so.

They walked out into the air and stood for a moment on the pavement.

"Mr Lyus, I trust I can impose on your courtesy to see Miss Porter to her means of transport home. I shall see you in the morning. Goodnight." He touched the brim of his hat and marched off in the direction of the Bank of England.

He turned to Millicent and asked, "Where do you have to go to get a bus?"

Millicent smiled. "Don't worry about me, William. I've only to go to Liverpool Street and get a train to St James Street."

"Well, I have to go that way to Broad Street, so we can go together."

She took his arm and they walked along. The City was very quiet as the theatregoers and diners had yet to arrive for the evening. They reached the steps up to Liverpool Street and Millicent disengaged her arm. "Thank you, William," she said. "I'll see you tomorrow for another eventful day."

She began to walk into the station and William watched her go with a wistful, undefined longing. Then she stopped and looked round and gave a little wave, and William, feeling slightly caught out, waved back and set off for Broad Street. Millicent watched him till he disappeared from view.

If champagne is quick to make its impact, it is equally quick to relax its grip, and by the time William got off his train at Homerton he had sobered up, much to his relief. His mother was concerned that he was home after nine, but he explained that he'd had to work late without warning.

"But your evening meal!" she exclaimed.

"Mr Bottomley treated his secretary and me to a champagne supper."

Alice's face lit up. "Where, in the City?"

"Yes, at Gow's Oyster Bar."

She beamed. "Well, I never." She cheerfully took his meal from the oven and put it in the bin.

When he went to bed that night, William was very tired, but he willed himself not to go to sleep. 'Well, I never' is right, he thought as his mind played over the events of the day, again and again. He wanted to savour each moment and commit it forever to his memory: meeting Millicent, working in a team with her and Terence, the avalanche of the applications, Terence involving him in the decision-making, celebrating the sense of achievement and triumph with Bottomley, the champagne, the supper at Gow's, Millicent taking his arm, everything! He was certain this had been the best day of his life, at least at work, and it would probably never be this good again. He would certainly remember it.

The days that followed were a hectic blur. William had allowed for his registers to cope with tens of thousands of investors, but still they kept coming. Extra books were purchased for the team of clerks, who were kept fully employed. William went to the bank twice each day and paid in several thousand pounds on each occasion. They stayed late every evening to cash up and balance the books, and Terence and he had a drink after work once or twice. Bottomley made only one fleeting appearance and there was no repeat of the champagne supper.

By the middle of the second week the money paid into the Victory Bond Club account exceeded the £100,000 in Victory Bonds available to the club. After another two weeks, subscriptions paid totalled £450,000. Concerned that nothing was being done to repay these over-subscribed funds, William raised the matter with Terence, who told him just to carry on processing the applications, as Bottomley would deal with the issue of refunds. Two weeks after that, Terence and William sat down together to assess the situation over a cup of coffee.

"Well, William, things are calming down now. I have been very pleased with how you have worked to make this a successful operation."

"Thanks very much, but you organised everything; I just carried it out."

"Not at all, we did it as a team. I am very happy with how it's gone and I know I can pass control on to you now to continue the good work. I'll be available to discuss any problems and you can give me a regular update on events when you call into the office."

"So I don't need to be here the whole time?"

"No, divide your time up as you think fit."

Entrusted with both the management of the Victory Bonds Club register and his own timetable, William enjoyed a less regimented existence. He would spend two days a week at his firm's office, resuming some of his old duties, but he was always glad to get back to the Finsbury Circus office, where he was his own master.

The months went by and William's role at the Finsbury Circus office went through different phases. After the very busy early weeks, a pattern had developed in which he was now only at the office once or twice a week, and then not for the whole day. The subscriptions slowed to a trickle and there were just as many requests for refunds which he passed to Millicent for Bottomley's attention. Bottomley had, meanwhile, opened a similar club in France linked to French bonds and William was thankful not to be involved in that. After a while Millicent came to the office less often, as more of her time was taken up processing applications for refunds.

When he was at the Victory Bonds Club office all day he often had little to do, so William based himself at Hoinville & Bates' office most of the time. Bothered about the rise in demands for refunds, he suggested that perhaps the partners, as trustees of the Club, or Terence as manager of the operation, might wish to establish what had happened to the excess payments made by subscribers. Terence spoke with Hoinville and informed William that the partners did not feel it necessary to intervene at this stage, so there were to be no changes in the arrangements for Club administration. William comforted himself with the knowledge that he had drawn attention to his concerns and it was no longer his responsibility.

XI

WITH THE END OF SUMMER, THE FOOTBALL LEAGUE resumed for the first time since the war and William hoped he might start attending football matches with his grandfather. But when he raised the subject, the old man shook his head and said that he didn't feel up to it at the moment. William, knowing his grandfather's health was declining, understood this really but, like most adolescents, he was reluctant to give up all the traditions of his childhood. However, Leonard was quite keen on going to the football occasionally, so they went together to the first match of the new season. Coming out of the ground after the match they saw Stanley Mason, William's old friend and neighbour from his days living on the High Street.

They talked outside the ground for quite a long time. Stanley and William had lost touch a little and Stanley hadn't seen Leonard for a couple of years. Stanley was very interested in hearing about Horatio Bottomley and the other jobs William had had. He shook his head and smiled. "I'm very impressed, Billy. You've done well and I'm sure you deserve it."

"Thank you, but my job's nothing special. I'm just a pen-pusher who spends most of my time filling ledgers. It's just the person I work for that makes it sound exciting."

They had a lot to talk about and as they were about to part company, all three agreed to go together to the next home match and a new tradition was established.

One day, as they walked back from the ground along Chatsworth Road, Stanley suggested they go to his house in Templar Road for a cup of tea and a piece of cake. Leonard made his excuses, but William said he'd like to.

"My mum hasn't seen you for ages; she often asks how you are getting on, and Cecil and Lucy too. They were pleased to hear how well you are doing and would love to see you again."

William nodded. He hadn't seen Cecil for a couple of years and Lucy not since they had left school. It was Lucy he was most curious about.

They turned right off Brooksby's Walk into Homerton Row and along the dark walls of the Eastern Hospital before turning into the terrace of small houses that was Templar Road. Stanley pulled the string with its hanging door key out of the letterbox and let them in. "I'm home and we've got a visitor," he called out.

The first to appear in the front room was Cecil, the oldest Mason sibling. "Hello, Billy, long time, no see. How are you doing?"

William smiled and shook hands with Cecil, whom he thought must now be nearly twenty. He was every bit a man now, evidenced by a day's stubble on the chin, above which a cigarette hung from his mouth. They reminisced a little about the old days and Cecil told William about his work as a porter at Liverpool Street Station and his aspirations to work on the trains.

"I'm on at ten o'clock tonight, night shift. Anyway, how did they get on?"

"They won, 4-0," said Stanley.

"Blimey, that makes a change; first win at home, isn't it?"

"You don't ever fancy going?" asked William.

"I play in a team over the marshes when I can, but I've got a gammy leg at the moment." Cecil tapped his knee.

Before William could reply, Mrs Mason came in the room, drying her hands on her apron. "Hello, Billy; quite the young man, aren't you, now? I saw your mum in the butchers in the High Street the other day. I've been hearing about your exploits in the City, working for the MP and everything. Good for you." She walked over and leaned up to kiss him on the cheek. "Cuppa tea?"

William thought she looked much older than he remembered, but she still had a cheery smile. "Yes please, Mrs Mason. Keeping well, I hope? And Mr Mason?"

"Yes, love; we're all very well. Bert's out this afternoon, he'll be sorry to miss you." She bustled off to the kitchen and the boys turned their attention back to the match and Stanley gave Cecil a brief report on each goal.

When the door opened again it was pushed by the foot of Lucy, who came in with a large wooden tray, on which were four cups of tea and a plate with slices of fruit cake. She smiled at William. "Hello, Billy, you all right?"

William could only nod, as he took in the change that had overtaken his former classmate. It was a very cold day for late September and she was dressed for autumn rather than summer. She had on a navy-blue woollen dress with a nautical collar and, with her hair pinned up, she looked to William very grown up – so different to when he had last seen her. He was lost for words.

"You must be frozen," she went on. "They've had snow up north."

"Yeah, it's surprising South Shields didn't do better. They should be more used to this weather," said Stanley, and they all laughed.

"Stan tells me you're working in Spokes?" said William.

Lucy smiled. "Yes, in the shoe department. I'll see what I can do for you if you pop in sometime."

William grinned and said nothing, though he put the remark away for consideration later. The four of them reminisced about their school days and joked about their teachers over tea and cake for forty minutes or so before William headed for home.

The next time he was in the office of Hoinville & Bates he took a walk to Mare Street in his lunch hour and thought about going into Spokes but didn't, nor did he the next time he passed the shop. Afterwards he wanted to but somehow didn't get round to it and then it seemed too late. He thought that perhaps Lucy was just teasing anyway.

William's friendship with Stanley, however, once renewed grew to be one of his most important. Stanley, even at a young age, seemed to understand himself well enough that he avoided most of the pitfalls of youth. He did not indulge in far-fetched ambitions or hopeful fantasies that crashed in disappointment, nor was he someone who played safe, afraid to take chances and regretting missed opportunities. He treated life with total equanimity. He did not balk at risk nor did he fear making a fool of himself. In a given situation he took the first decision that came into his mind and didn't give it another thought if his plans came to nothing, never wallowing in self-pity or remorse. To the envy and admiration of his friends, this attitude seemed always to be to his benefit. Girls were attracted by his openness and lack of jealousy, his colleagues at work respected his absence of mendacity and disregard of ambition, and his friends knew he could always be relied on to be honest but loyal to them. Over the years, he was the friend William would most often regard as a confidant.

When people think back over their lives, they nearly always express a regret that they left something they wished to do until it was too late. This is especially true in the matter of human relations. Barely had William come to terms with his failure, once again, to pursue his interest in Lucy when a far greater cause for regret invaded his thoughts. Busy with his social life with his friends and building some sort of career at work, William had stopped visiting his older relatives, even with his parents. One day in November his mother asked if he wanted to visit his Granduncle Charles, the kind man who, when out on his rounds, had always treated the young William if he saw him. He hadn't seen his granduncle for a couple of years and though, perhaps because, the old man was in poor health, William declined the request, saying he was too busy at present. Ten days later, Charles succumbed to pneumonia and died. William's inner guilt was not totally remitted by attending the funeral and it was further exacerbated when the reading of the will revealed that Charles, a childless widower, had left his not-insubstantial house in a road off Morning Lane, not to his sister still living but to William's mother.

Alice began making plans to move soon after the funeral and took William round with her to decide what should stay and what should go of her uncle's possessions. They dealt with the furniture quite quickly. It was of decent quality and not old so it would be kept, except for the beds and most especially the bed on which Charles had breathed his last. Apart from a few books and some photographs, Alice decided that most of the personal possessions, letters to and from his wife, records from his business, and various keepsakes could all be disposed of. Rather than consign them to the dustbin and later to a 'foul grave', William started a bonfire at the bottom of the garden and threw the papers and other combustibles on it. He watched the great shallow wicker basket with its ribbon reading 'Gentleman

Purveyor of Cat's Meats' erupt into flames then, all trace of his granduncle gone, he joined his mother in the house.

"Why did he leave *you* the house, Mum?" he asked, as they sat down to a cup of tea.

"Why shouldn't he?"

"No reason, but your mother is still alive and she was his sister after all."

"He knew she was quite comfortably off; she married well the second time, not that we've ever seen anything of it. He wanted to give us a leg-up in life and he was fond of us." She took a handkerchief from her sleeve and wiped her nose. William stared in vain for sign of a tear. "Anyway, he left his money to my mother and my aunt Agatha, so they'll be all right."

They were both silent for a while then his mother continued. "The house couldn't have come at a better time. You may as well know that your father is hoping to have a new job soon, an office job. We are moving up in the world, nearer to where my family came from and where we should be."

"He's going to be a manager?"

"Not exactly. If he's successful at the interview he'll become a trade union official. It's what he's wanted to do for years. That's what a lot of his studying was for."

"Why didn't Dad say anything to me about it? When's the interview?"

"Next week. He didn't want to tell you in case nothing came of it. You know what he's like."

William acted afterwards as if he'd heard nothing and the following week his father gave him the good news. He had been appointed a trade union official at the Amalgamated Engineering Union and would be starting in his new position early in the New Year.

"Congratulations, Dad. You'll be able to fight for the charter now."

Jack smiled. "Nothing as poetic as that, Billy. It's important work, mind you: sorting out disputes, standing up for workers' rights and trying to get workers to see they are better off in a union. You know what people are like; when things are going well they begrudge paying their union dues, but they're glad of the union's help when employers treat them badly. The working class can only get what's due to it by using its strength in numbers and unity of purpose."

"It's like having insurance, isn't it? It seems a waste of money until you have a problem."

Jack nodded and talked about his expectations in the job, and William could see how proud his father was to be doing something that he was convinced was worthwhile.

There were occasions when William felt the same about his work for the Victory Bonds Club, especially when he heard people expressing their excitement about the forthcoming prize draw. This was due after the January interest payment was received on the club's holding of Victory Bonds.

Although it made him uncomfortable, even a little ashamed, when he had doubts about the workings of the club, especially the matter of over-subscription, these doubts continued to nag away at him. Despite the fact that there was a process in place to manage refunds, he had heard of not even one person who had had their application money returned. There seemed no point in raising the matter again with his employers since the partners had dismissed his previous concerns, while Terence was very busy with a large new client recruited by Bates. He decided instead to broach the subject with Bottomley directly and, after several attempts, managed to speak to him on the telephone.

"My dear chap, I do so appreciate your conscientious attitude to your work and the well-being of the club's members. However, there is absolutely no cause for concern. There have been some delays in sending back some of the refunds due partly to administrative difficulties at the Odhams office. In addition, my recent purchase of two more newspapers has kept me away from the office and I confess I have not been punctilious in my stewardship of the club. In retrospect I wish I'd handed the whole job into your capable hands, my boy, but there it is." The subject was closed.

William was a little mollified by Bottomley's explanation but in January 1920 his confidence was undermined again by the total silence regarding the payment of prizes which were due to take place in a few weeks. After several queries to Millicent at Bottomley's office, he finally received a notification that the draw had taken place for prizes arising from the January interest payment on Victory Bonds. Bottomley would be distributing the payments himself so William need not concern himself with the matter. Tentatively reassured, he buckled down to his work and resolved to put any lingering doubts out of his mind.

His determination to adopt a positive attitude to life was given a boost by the family's house move. With all the probate and conveyancing details completed, his family had taken possession of their new home. They now had three bedrooms and two spacious reception rooms, as well as a kitchen. Under the supervision of Alice, Jack and William began the process of redecorating each room in turn, using paint supplied by Berger's at the special price available to William's grandfather. William could not remember the last time his mother had appeared so happy. She helped with the wallpapering and pottered about giving assistance here and encouragement there, and even her criticisms were constructive. William liked to think the new home signalled a new beginning for his family and happier times ahead.

Although Alice had received none of her Uncle Charles's money, the fact that they owned the house outright represented a rise in net income, as they no longer had any rent to pay. Coupled with Jack's higher wage and William's contribution, this meant that they were better off than they'd ever been. Jack went as far as having a telephone installed so that he could be reached out of office hours, for Alice another sign of their embourgeoisement. She even began referring to them being 'lower middle class', which Jack dismissed with the rebuke, "If you *must* climb the social ladder, why not 'upper working class'? I wouldn't think you'd want to be 'lower' anything. Anyway, don't ask me to distance myself from the people I'm supposed to represent."

William thought that these nuances of class were meaningless labels. To him it was a case of whether you took the orders or gave them, and he definitely took the orders. He was not troubled by this, as he took a pride in his work and in the fact that he could handle anything that was thrown at him.

In part, William's equability in the face of rising responsibilities at work was due to a more varied social life, which had nothing to do with his employment, other than a steadily rising wage enabling him to pay for it. He was enticed into playing the odd football match for Leonard's team which played on Sunday mornings and this added numbers to his well-established group of friends. Saturday evenings he would often have a few soft or mildly alcoholic drinks at one of the local pubs with friends followed by a card game in one of their homes. There was also the occasional local dance where tentative steps could be taken both in dancing and in making conversation with the young women who attended. On Saturday afternoons there were the home matches at Clapton Orient every other week or so which he attended religiously, if not always adoringly. The fairly successful season was coming to an end and the high spot was the impending visit of the Prince of Wales, the future King Edward VIII, to their last home match of the season against Notts County. This, the first ever visit by such a senior member of the royal family to a Football League match, was to thank the club for its extraordinary commitment of players and staff to the armed services in the Great War.

Remembering his grandfather's pride on that day in 1915 when the players had marched round the ground in their uniforms, William asked him if he would like to go to the match. Much to his surprise, the old man, now into his late seventies and walking with the aid of a stick, agreed without hesitation.

"Now, Bob, it'll be too much for you," said his wife. "There's bound to be a crush to see the Prince of Wales and how will you stand for ninety minutes?"

It was true that the ground would be packed. Even without the presence of the Prince, the club was enjoying its highest average attendance of any season before or afterwards. "We'll sit in the grandstand," William said, elated by his grandfather agreeing to go to the match, "and we'll get a taxi there and back."

William spoke to his uncles Bob and Ted, and they were keen to go too. So he booked the tickets in advance and on the 30th April all four of them assembled at his grandfather's flat and took the short taxi ride to the ground. Leonard and Stanley were there too but, respecting William's alternative arrangements for the day, went on their own. The Prince of Wales inspected the two teams before the match and William's uncles helped their father stand with the rest of the grandstand as the prince walked out onto the pitch to loud cheers. In the new world of photojournalism and cinema newsreels, the diminutive figure with his still-boyish features was instantly recognisable under his trilby hat.

"He seems to be wearing a sling on his right arm," said Uncle Ted.

"He's probably giving the right arm a rest, all the shaking of hands he has to do," said a voice behind them, and Ted nodded, having heard that story before.

To cap the day, the Orient won 3-0 and the family party went back to the High Street in a taxi to celebrate a successful season with a drink in the Corner Pin. They were joined by Stanley and Leonard a quarter of an hour later in what became a rather longer celebration than they had originally envisaged. They dispersed at about half-past six and William took his grandfather's arm as they walked across the High Street and wearily climbed the stairs to his flat.

"Hello," said William's grandmother with just a hint of relief. "Did you have a good time?" she asked her husband as she took of his cap and coat.

"It was wonderful, to see the future king at our little club and then a fine win to crown it all. Very big crowd. The boys forked out for a seat for me; they wouldn't take the money. I'm very grateful." He smiled and reached out for his pipe and tobacco, evincing a frown from his wife which he pretended not to notice.

"Well, I hope you haven't overdone it." She looked reproachfully at William for a moment before busying herself to make them some tea.

Not having seen his grandparents for a while, William stayed for a meal of ham and eggs and afterwards met some friends to go the pictures to see *The Cabinet of Dr Caligari* at the Pavilion. Though the dialogue shots in the film had been replaced by English-language ones, the film retained its exotic character and William enjoyed his first horror film very much. Afterwards they had a few drinks to round off what he thought had been a near-perfect day.

XII

AFTER A LENGTHY QUIET PERIOD, WORK FOR THE
Victory Bonds Club flared up later in 1920. William received
an instruction from Bottomley stating that it had been decided
to merge the club with the Thrift Club and William, now given
'an overseeing role of the whole operation', would be required
to update the registers, which translated to 'more work'.

Throughout the rest of the year, William spent much
more of his time at the club office in Finsbury Circus. There
was a constant churn of new investors, existing club members
converting their subscriptions or adding to them and a growing
number of members applying to withdraw their investments.
He was informed the prize draws went ahead, although he was
never given details of how much was paid out or to whom, and
he was not asked to distribute such payments. Intentionally
or not, his employers took a decreasing interest in his role
with the Victory Bonds Club. They had taken on several
new clients arising out of their self-proclaimed expertise in
the management of large-scale investments and they were
preoccupied with them. Their offices had spread to the upper
floor of their premises and these were occupied by three new
members of staff. William barely recognised the place when

he made one of his infrequent visits to his employers and with each successive, rare visit he felt less and less that he belonged to the firm.

The sometimes frenetic nature of the work for the club continued to the end of the year and into 1921. In February Terence telephoned him to ask if all was well with the Victory Bonds Club work. "I don't want to appear to be fussing, but I have heard rumours." He sounded a little apologetic.

"What sort of rumours?"

"That there have been complaints about the workings of the scheme: no prize money distributed, delays in refunds and repayment of subscriptions, no reply to queries. The kind of difficulties you have raised with me in the past."

"Well, I have been keeping the registers updated. Mr Bottomley has advised me that the prize draws have been made and that there have been delays in payments but they will be going out soon. The new arrangements over the Thrift Club have bedded in and, according to Mr Bottomley, there have been fewer problems with late refunds recently."

"I admit it does seem as if things are going in the right direction, but we have had assurances before. You're quite sure that there are no issues requiring my attention?"

William was irritated that Terence, for so long showing little or no interest in the work for Bottomley, seemed to be giving him a veiled criticism. "I'm not totally sure, but no trouble to speak of, for the moment anyway."

"Good, just get in touch anytime you need anything. I must go; such a lot on my plate at the moment. Don't forget, you can call me if you have a problem."

"I will, thanks." William replaced the receiver with the vague feeling that Terence knew something he didn't.

In the weeks that followed, the daily postbag was heavier than it had been for months: more subscriptions, more demands for refunds, more complaints. Then the people came. At first, a trickle, half a dozen standing outside the door of his office, angry or upset or both, demanding instant action after their letters had been ignored. William was surprised by this as the address of this office had never been published. All notifications and advertisements had merely directed enquiries to a Post Office box number. But he remained calm, explaining that their complaints regarding refunds should go to Mr Bottomley's office at Odhams but taking all their letters and promising to forward them to the correct person.

One day he arrived very early and collected the mail before anyone had assembled outside his office. He made as little noise as possible and kept the door locked in the hope that the seeming inaccessibility of the premises would deter any potential callers. There were a few desultory knocks on the door but nothing more. Once again he went through the motions of dividing the envelopes into the different categories and entering everything in registers before slipping out to the bank and having a cup of tea and a scone at one of the local cafés. The rest of the day went on as before and the next day and the next. This was the new norm. Like the proverbial frog placed in a saucepan of cold water and boiled to death before he realised the water was too hot for him, William did not notice that the number of complaints letters and demands for refunds was growing relentlessly each week or that each day he was working longer hours to finish the job.

Early one afternoon he had a pleasant surprise when Millicent, after a lunchtime visit to a friend in Lothbury, called in to see how he was managing on his own. The first he knew of it was a rattling of the office door handle.

"Who is it?"

"It's Millie."

He unlocked the door. "Hello, Millie, what a surprise."

She smiled. "Why was the door locked?"

"Oh, it's just a habit. In the mornings I often get irate customers turning up to complain and there's not much I can do for them."

Her smile faded. "I did wonder. We've had some of it ourselves."

He took out his handkerchief and wiped the dust off her chair, before she sat down and put her parasol under her desk. "Are you managing all right, William?"

"Not too bad, thank you. I'm always busy, but I can cope." Nonetheless, he was pleased when she offered to help him with the evening post.

"A lot of these letters are very abusive," said Millie, reading a particularly acerbic one from a very disgruntled member of the Thrift Club, demanding his money back and telling Bottomley and anyone else who read the letter what he thought of them.

William smiled. "D'you think so? I suppose some of the people are a bit cross."

"Cross? I have seen more very angry letters in one hour than I see at work in a month of Sundays, well, perhaps not that long." She laughed.

William laughed too. "I suppose I'm used to it. People join these schemes hoping for more than they can reasonably expect out of them."

"Or perhaps even those who expect very little are anxious because of all the rumours."

William merely grunted.

When they had completed their work he decided to leave the book entries of the post until the morning and put the money into the safe. They finished at about a quarter to seven and walked back to Liverpool Street Station together. Since his family had moved home, it was quicker for him to take a train to Hackney Central than to Homerton and he was soon walking through the dappled shade of Hackney churchyard. It was Midsummer Day, sunny but not too hot, and the evening seemed so young that he was reluctant to go home. Reflecting on the pleasant hours he'd spent with Millie, his cares seemed of no real consequence and on balance he felt all was well in his world.

This sense of well-being persisted through the fine summer: quieter periods at work, long days spent in the country or at the cricket, outings to the seaside or on the river, an attempt with Cyril and Leonard at emulating Jerome's *Three Men in a Boat*, though only from Teddington to Henley. But for him the summer ended abruptly before the autumn equinox when he returned home from work to hear unwelcome news.

He unlocked the front door and his mother met him in the hall. "Your grandfather's been taken ill. He's very bad."

"What's happened?"

"They think it's a stroke. He was his usual self this morning but then collapsed just after climbing the stairs. He's in the Hackney; your dad's with him."

"I should go."

"There's nothing you can do. Have something to eat first."

William did as he was bid and half-heartedly ate the meal his mother had prepared for him. Then he rushed to the hospital with Alice and they stood with Jack and his brothers watching the old man, apparently asleep, breathing shallowly and one arm moving once or twice. His wife sat by the bed, holding the quiescent hand, her face slightly stained by dried tears, but calm. After a while the three brothers arranged to keep vigil in turns through the evening with their mother while William and Alice returned home. When he woke the next morning his father told him it was all over.

With such fond memories of his grandfather, William expected to mourn his passing over a lengthy period, before the grief gradually faded, as it is both inevitable and necessary that it will. But barely had the funeral taken place and he'd toasted his late grandfather in the pub afterwards when, as he well remembered later, it seemed all hell had broken loose at work.

He was strolling towards Salisbury House, distracted by the flowerbeds in Finsbury Circus with their late summer displays, when he saw a crowd of people standing outside the main entrance. He was used to a handful of people calling at the office most days now, but he had become adept at dealing with them. As none in the crowd knew who he was, they merely shifted slightly as he squeezed into the lobby and walked to the porter's desk.

"Morning, Percy, any post for me?" he asked looking at the snaking queue that in single file mounted guard on each step of the stairs.

"You gotta be joking," said Percy, picking up a full mailbag and, with difficulty, hoicking it up onto the counter. "Like the old days, isn't it? Something has to be done about all these people, though, Mr Lyus. They could cause a riot: very intimidating for other people coming into the building. I told them to sling their hook, but all I got was a mouthful for my pains."

William smiled grimly. "Sorry, Percy, I'll sort it out." He picked up the heavy bag and went over to the lift.

The sentinels on the stairs watched his every move. They had heard the conversation and now knew who he was and he knew they knew, but none spoke. He took the lift to his floor and humped the bag towards his office and the head of the queue. He paused at the door and that was the signal for the queue to break ranks and advance in a swarm.

"When will Bottomley be here?" said a gruff man with a high colour.

"I'm sorry, but I couldn't possibly say. I am not informed of his movements." The more he responded to them the greater the number of voices were raised to demand action. Speechless, he looked out on a sea of clamouring mouths and waving fists.

A woman pushed her way to the front, brandishing a pamphlet of some sort. "He should be here to explain what's going on. Have you seen this?" She pushed the pamphlet towards William and reluctantly he took it.

He read the title: 'The Downfall of Horatio Bottomley MP. His Latest and Greatest Swindle'. He gazed at the people behind the woman and many of them were holding their own copy of the document. "I haven't seen this before," he said. "I know nothing of it. You'll have to take the matter up with Mr Bottomley."

"Well, where will we find him?" said another woman.

"He has offices at Odhams Press in Long Acre."

This firm response seemed to unsettle the certainty of the crowd, who looked round at each other. William took the few seconds' grace he had bought to open the door, throw in the bag and step over it to close the door behind him. The bag prevented the people at the front from pushing the door open more than a few inches and as soon as the pressure relaxed a little he locked the door.

He realised he still had the woman's copy of the pamphlet and he tried to read it while people hammered on the door and called out, at first persistently and loudly, until the voice of Percy could be heard telling them to leave or he would call the police. After that the noise slowly subsided and then petered out. William could now concentrate on reading the pamphlet. It was by a man named Reuben Bigland who had known Bottomley for many years and by his own admission had participated in a number of his business activities. He set out in considerable detail how Bottomley had swindled money from gullible poor people to use for his own business interests. With each line he read, William's loyalty and sympathy towards Bottomley, already under strain from months of having to defend the Victory Bond Club, grew more tenuous. However, he reminded himself that Bottomley was innocent until proven guilty.

Uncertain how to proceed in the new febrile atmosphere and in need of assistance to deal with the huge quantity of post, he telephoned Millie at the *John Bull* office. During a long conversation she revealed that the situation had become highly unstable, with Bottomley having severed his financial links to *John Bull* and Odhams trying to dislodge his control of the magazine. In addition, Bottomley was considering suing for libel over the Bigland pamphlet. In response to William's news, Millie offered to come over to Finsbury Circus to help with the vast quantity of mail.

William put the phone down feeling a little more in control of the situation. He began the laborious process of emptying all the envelopes and, as he had surmised, almost every one contained a request for return of funds. Later, Millie arrived and soon they were working together, using the system of recording and registering they had perfected over many days like this.

"Is Mr Bottomley really going to sue?" asked William as they took a break.

"I think he shall have to. If he doesn't, Mr Bigland's pamphlet will lead to a run on the club's investments and it will collapse."

"It's pretty near to a run now," said William, looking at the great pile of demands for refunds. "I think it would help if I had a list of the monies that have actually been returned, so that I could tie them up with my registers of members."

Millicent agreed. "I'll get the list tomorrow from Tom Flint and bring it over."

"That would be a great help. But how will you be able to spend so much time over here?"

She smiled. "I think I've been forgotten about in the office. I'm still officially the reception and secretarial support for the club and I can spend as long on it as I have to. Nobody ever queries it."

William was puzzled. "But after such a long gap?"

Millicent looked at him sheepishly. "I'll tell you a little secret. I have very occasionally used a so-called trip over here to take the odd hour off."

William tutted theatrically. "Really, Miss Porter, I don't know what to say." Then he laughed. "I'll ask Terence if he can lend a hand as well."

The next morning, the queues outside the offices were, if anything, even longer, but William had arrived very early to be sure he could get to his office before the crowds arrived. When Millicent appeared she had to run the gauntlet of the irate crowd. A degree of forbearance was, however, shown towards her after her hat was accidentally knocked off as she tried to push her way to the door. A man returned it to her and called on the crowd to show their manners.

"Phew," she said as she entered the office, tossing her hat onto her desk. "Does this happen every day?"

"Pretty well. Are you all right?"

She laughed. "It's all rather exciting, isn't it? 'The barbarians at the gate' and that sort of thing. I managed to get the information from Tom." She produced a sheaf of papers from her bag and handed them over.

William flicked through them and realised that the member registration system was in a complete mess. All the registers were out of date with some members owed refunds for months and others having been refunded twice. He telephoned Terence and arranged a meeting at the end of the week to discuss the situation, and on the Friday he went to see him in his new office at Hoinville & Bates. This was situated on the upper floor, just off a general office seating half a dozen junior clerks and two secretaries. The lower floor had been reconfigured to have a reception area containing Miss Bocking and the significantly expanded offices of the two partners. When he arrived in reception, William was struck by how much the previous, slightly seedy, atmosphere on this floor had given way to something approaching the grandeur, if not on the same scale, of Bottomley's now seldom-used office.

Miss Bocking looked up from her work. "Good afternoon. William. How nice to see you. Mr Biggs is waiting for you. His office is on the next floor; I think you know it?"

Terence smiled broadly and shook hands warmly when he saw William. "So glad you could come over, William; we have a lot to talk about." He motioned to a smart new chair and William sat down.

William took out a notepad in which he had written the issues he wished to discuss. But before he could speak Terence said, "Matters have turned rather sour with respect to Mr Bottomley, William. I believe he has had no choice but to sue over the inflammatory pamphlet."

"I know." William opened his notebook containing his questions for discussion, but his attempt to open up the conversation was thwarted by an interruption from Terence.

"The libel case will delay matters, but if there is any truth in the accusation that Bottomley has been siphoning off funds for his own purpose, the Victory Bonds Club will collapse. We cannot afford to be associated with it any longer."

William could feel a sense of unease rising in his chest.

"But it's not the fault of this firm, surely. We have done everything correctly."

"That may be so, but mud sticks and we must not be seen to be at fault if the club collapses. What are we to do?"

Terence looked at his papers carefully and then spoke sonorously. "Under the terms of our contract, made specific by Bottomley, the contract may be severed by either party with one calendar month's notice. Mr Hoinville has already given, three days ago, due notice and we shall terminate our arrangement on 14th October."

As he listened to Terence, William thought how much he now spoke like Mr Hoinville. "Do I carry on in the meantime? Perhaps bring the registers over here? It's very bad at the moment at the club office, so many people clamouring to have their money refunded, and some of them are very angry."

Terence stroked his chin and stared ahead for a moment, in the manner of Hoinville. "I don't think that would be a good idea. We must keep our association with the club at arm's length. Batten down the hatches and work out the next four weeks as best you can. Why not deal with the post then take the registers home and work from there? That way you will avoid any potential trouble with clients."

"Perhaps I could have one of the junior clerks to help to clear the backlog?"

Terence shook his head. "I'm sorry, William, it would not be in our interests to increase our involvement with Bottomley now. Just do your best. Now, what are these concerns you wanted to bring up with me?"

For William it seemed the moment to raise concerns had passed. It was all over bar the shouting and he was certain Terence knew more than he was revealing about the parlous state of the Victory Bonds Club's finances. "It was mainly that the financial procedures in the club are not very efficient and I haven't been kept informed of refunds made by Mr Bottomley's office. There is so much money owed to shareholders and much of it may have been lost in refunds being paid twice."

Terence shook his head. "This is why we must break our links with Mr Bottomley; we were not given full control of the operation. Never mind, it will soon be over as far as we're concerned. Well, if that's all, thank you for coming over, William. See you in a few weeks." He stood and William felt he was being ushered out of the office.

William looked through the glass at the new, large general office, but there was no one there he knew and he walked uneasily down the stairs, said goodbye to Primrose Bocking and returned to his former bastion, now stockade, in Salisbury House. When he arrived he had to knock on the office door. Millicent had locked herself in while he was away to avoid difficult encounters with awkward customers. She smiled as she let him in then returned to the task she'd been doing when he'd left her: opening envelopes and putting them in the usual piles. The piles were instantly recognisable from their size, the one for new subscribers now a solitary application form.

William picked the subscription form up and looked at it. "Poor devil," he muttered. "Have we still got some stamps here?"

"Yes, in my top drawer," said Millicent.

He wrote on the form 'subscription full' and placed it and the accompanying postal order for two pounds in an envelope, which he addressed to the sender, ready to return.

"Everything all right while I was away?" he asked.

Millicent nodded. "I'm afraid I've got some bad news, though."

"Oh, what's that?"

"I think my coming over here regularly has finally aroused an interest in what I do with my working day. My manager telephoned me this afternoon, just after you left. After today I won't be available to help you anymore. I'm sorry, William."

"Well, it was good while it lasted, for me at any rate."

"And for me, I've enjoyed working with you over this time."

"I have news to tell you too. The firm I work for is cutting its links with the Victory Bonds Club in four weeks, so I shall be finishing here soon anyway."

Millicent nodded but said nothing for a few moments. Then she said brightly, "Let's have some cake, especially as it's our last day." She went over to her desk and produced a Victoria Sponge from the bottom drawer.

It was nearly four o'clock by the time they sat down to tea and cake, and they had agreed, without saying as much, that they were finished for the day. They chatted about life away from the office and reminisced about some of the more interesting, exciting or difficult episodes they'd encountered working together. At about five thirty, William collected the evening post, which usually came early on a Friday, and put it, unopened, in the safe, despite Millicent offering to help go through it.

"You have opened your last letter for the Victory Bonds Club," he said.

"Well, that's that," said Millicent, taking her personal things from her desk and looking round the office for one last time.

In the final analysis, the only pleasant part of William's work for Bottomley had been working with Millicent, and he was sad that this was coming to an end. On an impulse he asked her, "Will you let me take you for a drink?"

Millicent smiled, but not out of sympathy, or worse condescendingly, as William feared she might. "I don't know, William," she said hesitantly.

"I don't expect you to go to a pub; I was thinking of Gow's or somewhere like that. I'd like to thank you for all you've done for me here."

She smiled again. "It was a pleasure. I don't need to be thanked for it."

"It was my birthday last week and I was too busy to celebrate, so I'd really like it if we could make up for it just a little today."

"Well, we've had the cake, so I suppose we ought to have the drink to go with it." She laughed and walked over to a mirror to inspect her hair and dress.

They left the office, said goodnight to Percy at the porter's counter and strolled along to Gow's. They were escorted to a table of their choice in the quiet restaurant, the City deserted by the Friday-evening rush to the country.

They looked at the menu, William patting the pocket containing his wallet, the wallet that had once belonged to Granduncle Charles. "What would you like?" he asked.

"Oh, I don't know. I'll be having a meal later, so just something light, please, William."

William ordered some sandwiches and glasses of the house white wine.

"Well, here's to a belated 'Happy Birthday', William," said Millicent, raising her glass. "You know, it is worrying that you have been working so hard that you couldn't even take time to celebrate your birthday."

William smiled and thought how true it was that work, and this work in particular, had taken over his life. In recent months he had regularly worked until eight o'clock. His mother had become used to putting his evening meal in the oven, latterly not even bothering to cook for him. Having been given an expenses allowance by his firm, he now regularly dined in one of the cheaper restaurants near his office. It occurred to him that the cost of this meal could be accommodated in his expenses, if spread over a few evenings. "Well, it's kind of you to say so, but I suppose I could have got off for that evening if I'd wanted. I just forgot all about it."

"That's the point."

The dainty finger sandwiches and glasses of Muscadet arrived.

"Was it an important one?" asked Millicent.

"Important what?"

"Your birthday; was it a special one?"

William wondered if she was fishing for his age as he'd never told her, nor had she ever asked. "No more than any other."

"I never forget my birthday, but everybody else does."

"Why's that?

"It's the 26th December. Everyone is too busy and, when I was little, my birthday present was always combined with the Christmas one. Only my mother took the trouble." She shrugged. "Now, I'm at the age when your birthday comes round too quickly. It won't be long before I start staying at the same age year after year."

"I don't think you're anywhere near old enough to do that."

"Why, how old do you think I am?"

William realised he was about to enter a dangerous area and sought to delay matters by reaching for a sandwich. Unfortunately, despite the fact that neither of them had thought they were particularly hungry and he didn't recall eating anything, the sandwiches were all gone. He could sense her waiting for his reply and took a sip of wine instead.

"Well?" she said, smiling at him.

"Um, I'm not very good at guessing ages."

"That's no answer."

"Well, twenty-two?"

"I'm twenty-four, so I'll say that's a good guess." She laughed.

Seven years' difference: she must see me as merely a boy, thought William. He waved to a hovering waiter and asked for two more glasses of the same.

"Why, William, I'm not sure I should have another," she said, but not until after the waiter was out of earshot. "I wonder what's in your mind."

He felt himself colouring even though nothing other than being hospitable had entered his mind. "Would you rather…"

"No, of course not; I'm only teasing. Take no notice of me."

There was an awkward silence for a few moments and it was William who broke it, unable to resist asking the question that had been in his mind when they had chatted over tea and cake earlier in the day. "How is it that someone as attractive as you is not yet married?"

The fresh glasses had arrived and Millicent reached for hers, a slight expression of sadness suddenly replacing her carefree smile. "I could say that the right person never came along or that I was in love with someone and they were killed in the war, but the simple truth is that there just aren't enough men of the right age to go round for all us women. I shouldn't have been so choosy when I had the chance."

"Sorry, I didn't think."

She had resumed her smile. "It's just the way it is; all those young men cut down in their prime, or before their prime, and all us women left over. Now we have to compete for the young men coming up with the girls of their own age, not an enviable position."

William nodded sadly. He couldn't help but be pleased at finding himself on the right side of supply and demand but hesitated to investigate the possibilities.

"Well, William, I must be going. It's been lovely; thank you for inviting me. I will pay the bill."

"You can't possibly."

"It's your birthday celebration; you mustn't pay on your birthday." She picked up her handbag.

"No, really. I can claim some of this on my expenses account."

"Very well, they certainly owe it to you. I won't be a couple of minutes." She went off to the ladies' room while William settled the bill.

They walked out into a still-light evening and strolled to the station. He considered taking a Chingford line train with her but thought the farewell would be more complicated if they got off at different stations, so he left her at Liverpool Street.

"Goodbye, William, it has been so nice to work with you and I wish you every success in the future." She held his hand for a moment and kissed him on the cheek.

XII

THE LAST FOUR WEEKS AT THE VICTORY BONDS Club office passed for William in a form of solitary confinement. The impending libel trial against Reuben Bigland had led many of the club members to hang on for its result, either in hope or expectation, so he was less inundated either by mail or by disgruntled people. Despite several requests for help to wind up the registers and refunds, nobody else appeared from Hoinville & Bates, so he plodded on alone, updating his books, returning the monies of any foolish enough still to wish to hand their savings over to Bottomley and marking the calendar as each day passed.

It was early in the third week that there was a knock on the door, but not the familiar signature knock of Percy the porter. Expecting a disappointed club member, he called out, in his usual refrain, "We are closed. All queries to be taken up with Mr Bottomley personally."

"Police."

He shot up and stared at the door for a moment. There was a second knock, this time louder and more insistent. He walked swiftly to the door and opened it.

A well-built, stocky man in his mid-thirties stood in the

doorway, coat open and hat in hand. "Mr Lyus, Mr William Lyus?"

"Er, yes?"

"I am a detective from Scotland Yard. I have a few questions for you."

"What about?" asked William.

"May I come in?"

The man spoke politely in an accent William thought was probably Irish. He stood back and let him in.

"My name is Lynch. I am based at Scotland Yard."

"Not City of London Police?"

Lynch smiled. "I work for a special enquiries team, but we do observe all the correct protocols with other forces. I am currently examining some matters connected with the Victory Bonds Club. I believe you act as registrar for that organisation?"

"I'm only the clerk that maintains the register. My employers, Hoinville & Bates, are the official registrars."

"Quite so. I have been in contact with Messrs Hoinville & Bates and they inform me that the role of registrar was effectively delegated to you."

"What do you mean by that?"

"Only that you were permitted to work on your own without direct supervision. As you rarely referred questions of procedure or decision-making to your superiors, the inference to be drawn is that you felt competent to work on your own initiative and to take on your shoulders the responsibility this implied."

"But I am still just a clerk. I have had no say in the running of the club."

"You underestimate yourself, Mr Lyus. You would not be the first person to bear the title 'clerk' and possess considerable authority. The fact of the matter is you are still in charge here whatever your precise title. But let's not dwell on semantics. I'm interested in the nature of your duties and what you know about the workings of the club. Of course, others are accountable for the management of the scheme and I shall see them in due course."

William nodded. "Please sit down, Mr Lynch. Would you like some tea?"

"No thank you, sir." He took off his coat and threw it and his hat on one seat before sitting on another opposite William. Then he slowly and deliberately took a notebook from his pocket and checked the point on the small pencil that he removed from the spine of the book. "Perhaps you would like to begin by telling me how it was you took up your duties with regard to the Victory Bonds Club and what your job consisted of."

Relaxing a little, William went through the reason for the decision by Hoinville & Bates to act for Bottomley and the meetings which led to him being given the job of clerk for the register of members. Then he outlined his principal responsibilities. Lynch occasionally interjected for clarification or more information but spent most of the time writing and nodding his head.

"Did you have any concerns about the workings of the enterprise, insofar as you were involved with it?"

"Not at first. It was rather hectic but seemed to be going well. It was very popular with all sorts of people and the money kept pouring in. I was first concerned when the number of applications was so large that the club seemed to be over-subscribed, but I was not asked to organise refunds."

"What did you do about your concern?"

"I asked Mr Biggs what he thought and he told me not to worry about it. He said Mr Bottomley was handling the financial administration side of the club and would have his own way of dealing with it."

"Anything else?"

"There were always delays in the payment of prizes, but when I raised the matter I was reassured by Mr Bottomley's office that everything was in hand. Then there was the merger with the Thrift Club which Mr Bottomley had been operating separately in France. Mr Biggs thought that the merger might be illegal under French law, but then Mr Bottomley changed the arrangements. After that, club members could convert their original subscription into French bonds and receive interest on them."

"Were you aware that those club members who exchanged their subscription shares for Credit National bonds were charged £15 per unit in spite of the fact they could have purchased them on the market for £9?"

"No."

"What next?"

"There was a steady rise in complaints and demands for refunds, and I discovered the system of repaying money was out of control. Some people were refunded money twice and others seemed unable to obtain a refund at all. Gradually things seemed to fall apart."

"Did you try to do anything about your suspicions?"

"As I didn't have the full picture there was not much I could do. When I did raise issues with Mr Bottomley's office I was fobbed off with excuses. My employers didn't really take much interest in what was going on until the problems became well known and then they decided to pull out of the arrangement."

"So if I understand you correctly, you felt that all was not well with Mr Bottomley's administration of the club but, despite several attempts, you were powerless to do anything?"

"Yes."

"Did you think that there was fraud involved?"

"No, I thought it was just not run very well."

"I should like to see the registers and any other relevant papers you have, such as bank receipts. I will need to take them away to have them properly examined."

"I might need to get permission from my employers first."

"Certainly."

William rang from Bottomley's long-empty office and was informed by Terence that, as far as the partners were concerned, there was no objection to releasing the books and other documents.

"Did you know the police would come to see me?" asked William.

"Well, yes. That chap Lynch came to see Mr Hoinville last week and took your details. I meant to let you know but it slipped my mind. Still, don't worry, William. Just tell the truth and you've nothing to worry about."

The detective then telephoned a colleague and began piling up all the registers, over twenty of them, on Millicent's old desk. He went through all the other papers in William's possession, retaining receipts and other documents relating to the club before turning to the safe. While William watched, he looked through all the documents lodged there by Bottomley and removed most of those too. Finally he gave William a signed receipt for all of the papers he was taking with him.

By the time Lynch had finished this exercise, two uniformed policemen had arrived with a sack barrow and they took the registers and other papers to a waiting van.

"Thank you very much for your co-operation, Mr Lyus. One last question: who were your contacts with Mr Bottomley's administration office while you were here?" He took out his notebook and pencil again.

"There was Miss Millicent Porter, who was the secretary for the office here. She was on the staff of the *John Bull* and was usually located there but helped me here when it was

very busy. Her office was within the Odhams premises at
Long Acre. There was also a Mr Tom Flint, who dealt with
club refunds and other financial matters. He was at the same
offices as Miss Porter, though I never actually met him or even
communicated with him directly in any way."

With a determined full stop, Lynch finished writing and
put away his notebook. He held out his hand. "You have been
very helpful. Thank you for your time. I hope not to have to
trouble you again. The registers and other documents will be
returned to your firm's headquarters in due course. Good day
to you."

William locked the door behind the detective and sat back
in his chair. With the last vestiges of his belief in Bottomley
and the Victory Bonds Club lost, his tools of work removed
and none with whom to share his sense of despondency, he
felt emptied of any purpose. Yet still he had to keep going;
eight more days working in an office where anything achieved
would be devoid of meaning.

After a break from the office, he felt refreshed and organised
a new work schedule. He found an unused, spare register in
the cupboard and for the last week and a half recorded every
letter he received. The steady stream of refund applications
was forwarded to Tom Flint and he sent back to the sender
those few new subscriptions to the club, which often came with
letters praising Bottomley and regretting that he should have
been maligned by so many. These letters he deposited in the
safe. Finally, the day came when he could vacate the office. He
left the register he had compiled and the last few bank receipts
in the safe and returned the keys to Percy, walking out into
Finsbury Circus with a sense of freedom on the verge of elation.

The following Monday William made his way to the Hoinville
& Bates offices in Lower Clapton full of hope at the prospect

of a new start with his firm. There was just the slightest sense of insecurity because his old post had been swallowed up in the new scheme of things and so he was not sure where he would fit in. He climbed the stairs and walked into the reception area, expecting the reassuring gaze of Primrose Bocking. Unfortunately her gaze was not reassuring.

"Oh, good morning, William," she said without any warmth. "I was asked to tell you when you arrived to wait here to see Mr Hoinville and Mr Bates."

"Good morning, Primrose." He smiled, but Primrose averted her eyes and looked back at her typewriter. "Are they in yet?"

"Not yet," she said, without looking up.

William waited for twenty minutes. People occasionally came down the stairs to speak to Primrose or to get files from the archives or to go out on a business matter. He didn't recognise any of them and none of them gave him anything but a cursory glance.

Eventually the two partners arrived together. They acknowledged Primrose, Hoinville with a jovial greeting and Bates with a grunt. Neither acknowledged the uncomfortable young man perched on a chair against the wall. They proceeded into Hoinville's office with Primrose and, after two or three minutes, William heard footsteps on the stairs and Terence Biggs came into the reception area.

"Good morning, William," he said, with a slight smile, on his way to Hoinville's office.

A couple of minutes later, Miss Bocking appeared and asked William to go into Hoinville's office.

The three men, the two partners and the chief clerk, were seated behind Hoinville's desk, and William had no option but to sit in the chair opposite them.

"Well, Mr Lyus, we meet under unfortunate circumstances."

Hoinville interlaced his fingers and rested his hands on his waistcoat, just under his watch chain. His nasal tone sounded more threatening than William remembered.

"Er, yes, Mr Hoinville, I suppose we do," William replied.

"This Victory Bonds Club business has not been very successful and it does not reflect well on this firm that we should have been associated with it." His thumbs beat a gentle rhythm on his waistcoat.

William looked at Terence and Bates. Both were shaking their heads slightly. William noticed that Terence was wearing a gold watch chain and not the brass one he had sported when first they met. He had also taken to wearing a wing collar like that of Hoinville.

"You see," continued Hoinville, "Mr Bottomley has not been as open as he might have been about the success of this venture and there are now doubts, not only about its viability but also its probity. This unfortunate business with Mr Bigland will inevitably drag the reputation of Mr Bottomley through the mire and, if his libel suit is unsuccessful, have very severe consequences for him. You see the difficulty for this firm?"

William did see the difficulty but wasn't sure it was exactly the same difficulty to which Hoinville was referring. "I believe that we have behaved entirely properly in our dealings with Mr Bottomley and his business," he replied, attempting to speak with the same degree of gravitas as his employer.

"Indeed," said Hoinville, "but it is not enough to behave properly: we must be *seen* to have behaved properly."

"Well, Mr Lynch, the detective from Scotland Yard took the books away last week and I am sure he will confirm they have been kept in order, to the best of my ability."

Hoinville leaned forward, his interlaced fingers resting on the desk. "That may well be the case. However, a registrar has a duty of care to ensure that the number of shareholders does not exceed the number permitted by the charter of the organisation, as this could affect any payout due to shareholders. It might be that some would seek to imply that we had been somewhat negligent in this regard."

William was not inclined to respond to this comment; this was surely a matter for those who had set up the contract with Bottomley. But all three were looking at him and as the seconds ticked by he felt a compulsion to say something. "I raised the matter with Mr Biggs when I noticed the club was over-subscribed. I was told not to worry about it as Mr Bottomley would refund the over-subscriptions in his own way." He looked directly at Terence as he said this.

"But you should have followed it up as time went on, William," said Terence.

"But I did raise the matter on other occasions and suggested that you or someone else in the firm take action as trustees. Surely, as a clerk, it is not my place to ensure that the firm meets its obligations to shareholders, other than by doing my job properly."

"You were given a great deal of responsibility to work on your own initiative and as you never asked to be relieved of that responsibility we assumed you were up to it. It appears we were mistaken." It was Bates, intervening for the first time, his tone beginning as a sneer and then becoming more menacing.

Painted into a corner though he was, William was angered by the injustice of this remark and refused to be cowed. "With respect, Mr Bates, I was given to understand that you and Mr Hoinville were the main trustees of the Victory Bonds Club and if the club fell short in its duty to its shareholders surely that would be a matter for the trustees."

There, he had said it; he had poked the dragon with a stick. He thought he caught a flicker of a smile cross Terence's face before Bates crashed his fist down on the desk.

"How dare you tell us our job!" Bates thundered, his face red, his mouth wide open in rage, if not exactly foaming. "You were trusted to look after the interests of the firm and the shareholders of the club and were rewarded with a rise in salary and extremely generous expenses with liberty to determine your own way of working. You pay us back by failing in your responsibility and leaving us in ignorance of irregularities and misconduct for which the firm could in part be held accountable. You deserve nothing but contempt." He had risen a few inches off his seat during this tirade but now he sank down.

"Taking an arrogant position will not help anyone, Mr Lyus," said Hoinville. He paused while he held his forefinger on one nostril and breathed deeply through the other. "This firm must protect its reputation and cannot be expected to be brought down by the independent actions of one of its staff who was effectively contracted out to another party and didn't take sufficient steps to alert us to the dangers."

"Mr Biggs *was* kept informed, regularly." William looked over at Terence, silently appealing for help. Terence looked away.

"We are afraid we have no alternative but to dispense with your services, Mr Lyus."

In those few seconds between his last statement and the coup de grace administered by Hoinville, William had realised what was about to come, so when it came he was prepared. "I always did my best," he muttered.

"We will give you a month's salary in lieu of notice and a reference. Please clear any belongings you have here immediately after this meeting and collect your notice money and reference from Miss Bocking. That will be all."

William left the office and found himself in an empty reception area, Miss Bocking having left the room for whatever reason. He looked at her desk on which there were two envelopes addressed to him. He had nothing else here of his own but, on a whim, he walked over to the stationery cupboard and took a hardback journal with a burgundy cover and put it in the pocket of his raincoat. As he closed the cupboard, Miss Bocking came back into reception.

"I am very sorry, William," she said. She went to her desk and gave him the two envelopes. Seeing the tears in his eyes, she squeezed his arm. "Everything will be all right; you have your life ahead of you."

He smiled. She could not know that the tears that stayed suspended in his eyes were neither of sorrow nor of self-pity but of righteous anger. He shook her hand and left the offices of Hoinville & Bates for the last time.

XIV

AFTER HIS DISMISSAL, WILLIAM WAS IN NO RUSH to go home. He thought of going to Spokes to seek out a friendly face in Lucy, but he didn't want to burden her with his woes. Instead, he walked to the ABC in Mare Street and had a cup of tea and a bun while he checked his payslip and wages. His expenses, including his trip to Gow's, was in there too: all correct. Then he opened the letter of reference. Some might think it a perfect example of damning with faint praise, but William was thankful it did not mention his role in the Victory Bonds Club; his anger had subsided into resignation.

14th October 1921

TO WHOM IT MAY CONCERN
Mr William L. Lyus

The above-named has been in our employ since March 1919. During that time he has held the post of junior clerk. We have always found him to be punctual and he performed his duties satisfactorily. There is nothing known to us that would preclude our stating him to be honest and of good character.

Yours faithfully,
Hoinville & Bates

He put his wages into his wallet and returned the reference to his inside pocket. He briefly contemplated beginning his search for a new job, but his heart was not in it. He needed all his strength for what was to come: the meeting with his parents and the explanation for his dismissal from his post. Wearily he put on his coat and walked down Mare Street, ignoring the shops, his thoughts everywhere and nowhere. He thought about cutting through the churchyard but carried along the road, crossing without purpose but then, on the corner of Amherst Road, stopping to look idly in the window of Gibbon's furniture shop at a very attractive desk. Then he remembered the fine desk he'd had at Salisbury House and suddenly the acceptance of resignation gave way to the cold grip of despondency. He trudged on, under the railway bridge while a train rumbled above him as he crossed Graham Road before passing the Hackney Empire and the old town hall. He found himself standing opposite Hackney library.

The library, a place of happy memories shared with his father. With a lump in his throat, he entered the building, seeking in it, like an old friend, a source of succour. There, he spent an hour or so in the reference library, looking up things he didn't really care about and then immersing himself in subjects that took his fancy for a few minutes at a time. Eventually he removed the empty journal from his raincoat pocket and stared at it. He knew the root of his undoing was the disaster of the Victory Bonds Club and the cavalier behaviour of Bottomley. Even so, it was the behaviour of Hoinville & Bates that rankled above everything; they had treated him despicably and he was more sure of that than of any other reason for his downfall. Worse, there was nothing he could do to right the wrong of their disloyalty and lack of fairness. He stared at the burgundy-coloured book until the detail of the weave burned into his eye and he made an unspoken vow. He would never again allow injustice towards him or others he knew to pass without a fight.

Hungry and no longer seeing any point in delaying his return home, he put his journal in his coat pocket, exited the library and turned down Morning Lane.

"What are you doing home?" asked Alice. She was seated at the scrubbed kitchen table peeling some potatoes.

"I've been given the sack," he replied simply.

"What? What did you do?"

William had expected this response and was barely troubled. "Why do I have to have done something wrong?"

"Well, haven't you?"

"No. I've been working so long for Mr Bottomley they've got used to me not being there and now they don't need me."

Alice frowned. "That doesn't seem fair; you worked hard and often late."

"It's not fair, but they don't want any links between the firm and Mr Bottomley, and I am the main link."

His mother tutted. "Did they give you a reference?"

"Yes, and four weeks' pay in lieu of notice."

"Well, I don't know what your father will have to say."

I do, thought William.

"D'you want a cup of tea and a sandwich?"

"Yes please, I'm starving."

"I don't know why they have been so hard on you; there had to be a reason. You must have a knack of rubbing people up the wrong way."

"Can we not talk about it at the moment, Mum? We'll have to go through it when Dad gets home so let's wait until then."

Alice desisted from probing further about William's

misfortune but, sensing that she was straining at the leash, he thought it best to relieve the pressure on both of them by going out for a walk. After eating his sandwich, he went up to his room, took off his suit and hung it up, and then put on a blazer and grey flannels. On his way out, he looked in at the spare bedroom and at the half-painted woodwork of the only room still to be decorated since the family had moved in. With time on his hands, he would finish painting the room a week early so that the smell would be gone long before it was needed. His grandmother had finally agreed to move in with them in a couple of weeks. She was nearly eighty now and the flat in the High Street was far too big for her on her own, and Alice, and especially Jack, had convinced her that it made sense to move into her own room with them. He stroked the undercoated architrave and, satisfied with its smoothness, went down the stairs, cursorily explained what he was doing and went for a walk. For no reason in particular he walked to the High Street and then down to the marshes, across the Triangle and on to Temple Mills Lane. There was the White Hart Inn, over four hundred years old and a supposed stopping place for Dick Turpin when active in the area. The bar was open and he had a pint of mild and bitter while he sat outside and watched an old horse with its even older cart haul some timber up the lane, its driver, reins in hand, walking by his horse's side, coaxing and encouraging.

When, eventually, he got home he went straight upstairs, changed into his overalls and painted for an hour or so, lost in daydreams.

Jack, who had spent the day visiting a company in Bromley-by-Bow, was home earlier than usual. He listened in silence, smoking a cigarette and taking the occasional drink of tea from a large mug, while William told his sad tale. When William had finished, Jack showed no emotion. He merely nodded and commiserated with his son. "I'm sorry for you. You have not been treated right, whatever way you look at it."

"Thanks, Dad."

"Well, Billy, if nothing else I hope you've learned a few lessons from all of this. First, a leopard never, or at least very rarely, changes his spots. I understand: you saw an opportunity for yourself and that dominated your thinking. Despite all you knew of him and my warning, you were willing to give Bottomley a chance and you clung to your hopes even as you learned more about his shenanigans. The fact of the matter is Bottomley is by nature a crook. He may have good intentions when he sets out on some of his schemes, but when he sees a way of carving a little bit more for himself, he can't resist the temptation. If something goes wrong he will put himself first, however much damage he does to the interests of others. Your mother and grandma and many others can afford to lose a couple of quid, but stealing a little from a lot of people rather a lot from a few doesn't make it all right. You made an error of judgement there, son, but not as great as your employers and there's a second lesson. There have been many good individual employers who have genuinely cared for their workers, but most of them will only pay what they have to and regard their workforce as expendable. Hoinville & Bates paid you what you were worth because they wanted the job done but, as soon as their investment in Bottomley was proved faulty, they had no hesitation in cutting you loose to drown. They just saved their own skins, what they referred to as their 'reputation'. The last lesson is that individual workers cannot stand up to unscrupulous bosses alone and that's why they need a union. The tragedy for office workers is that they believe their professional standing or class will give them individual power. The truth is that this is a myth propagated by those who possess the real power."

William hadn't expected anything less than a lecture from his father and he didn't see any reason to challenge his father's assessment of the situation. After all, Jack had expressed his reservations about Bottomley, so it wasn't as if he was being wise after the event. He smiled and nodded. "I know," he replied.

"Still, they gave you a reference and you have had some exciting times no doubt working with Mr Bottomley. Put it all down to experience."

"But he's got to find another job, Jack," said Alice, plaintively, though not quite wringing her hands.

"He's got plenty of time; he'll find something, won't you, Billy?"

William nodded, and his mother gave a resigned grunt and went out to the kitchen.

Silently, William and Jack had colluded to mislead Alice. Getting another job at the same pay he'd received at Hoinville & Bates would not be easy. The post-war recession with falling wages and high unemployment was only now coming to an end and Jack had spent much of his working time negotiating to maintain wage rates for his members. Though the economy was now improving, many businesses had still to recover their pre-war levels of profitability.

They knew that for William, the situation was little better. He had been elevated beyond his role of junior clerk because it suited his previous employers, but he would find it difficult to move into a new job with the same status. At a lower level, he had to contend with competition from juniors willing to take a lower wage, especially school leavers now coming into the job market. Starting near the bottom again would involve a large pay cut. It was a choice between employment and self-worth: work for less or wait for something which suited him to come along.

There was another lesson he had learned in addition to those spelled out by his father. Whatever the apparent glamour attached to working for a particular person or an area of commerce, the actualities of a role were always the same: you would still be a clerk or a bookkeeper or a driver or a cleaner. In future, he would seek to achieve satisfaction in his life in activities outside his work. When, a few days later, he began looking for a new job he paid no attention whatever to the industry, trade or profession with which a prospective employer was connected.

In his search for work William applied for several posts. He avoided, for obvious reasons, any mention of his association with Bottomley but did emphasise that he had worked often on his own and without direction. After a few weeks this did eventually result in him securing the post of office assistant and bookkeeper with a large garage in Swiss Cottage. The job involved looking after the car hire business, paying bills and wages, maintaining the accounts, and looking after the office when the owner was away. Although he had taken the position without concerning himself with the nature of the company, the owner turned out to be an interesting character nonetheless. With business and other activities outside the garage, he was frequently away from the premises and depended on the surefooted management of the workshops and motor factoring by his foreman. An able and responsible office assistant would enable him to spend even less time on the premises when he wished. He might have looked for a more mature man, but William, though only seventeen, could pass for someone older: he had now developed a deep voice, lost much of his accent and spoke with an acquired timbre of seriousness and responsibility. In addition, his dark hair was well-groomed, his natural curl repressed into a just off-centre parted haircut and he wore a well-cut suit. As his employer was only in his mid-twenties the gap between them in age probably seemed smaller to both of them.

William soon settled into never-ending days of taking and entering bookings for one of the garage's services, dealing with invoices and payments, typing the odd letter and bill, and attending to the occasional customer services query. He also greeted and attended to female customers who could not be expected to enter the male purdah of the accessories shop and service area. His spent most of the day alone and he was perfectly happy with that; he felt he had the balance about right. Sometimes, he would see an interesting motor car pull into the garage forecourt: a stylish Sunbeam coupé, a Star two-seater, or a grand car like a Daimler or Lagonda, and he would take a casual walk round it while it was filled with petrol. Otherwise, he had enough interaction with customers and staff and was pleased to be left alone to his work, his library books and his thoughts.

After his mild flirtation with the reckless, Icarian wing of the free enterprise culture personified by Horatio Bottomley, he was glad to settle into a working environment with neither great excitement nor ambition. Instead, he now embraced more warmly his father's political and economic values. He accompanied him to lectures at the Fabian Society, the Co-operative Party and other political organisations, and he devoured books on political economy from Harrington and Locke through Bentham and Stuart Mill to Marx and Lenin. Such fiction as he picked was suggested by his father too, such as *The Ragged-Trousered Philanthropists* and novels by George Gissing, Thomas Martin Wheeler and others who showed the 'real world', as his father put it. In practical terms his commitment to his father's view of the world augmented his already-heightened sense of justice and fairness.

Relations with his new boss were pleasant enough but not what one could describe as warm. Bertram Drogo, amateur racing driver and occasional batsman for Hertfordshire County Cricket Club, enthusiast for the gaming tables and dilettante in a variety of business activities, could only see William as a clerk and bookkeeper. He doubted he had much in common with William and it did not occur to him to find out. He respected him as he would an efficient NCO, much like the very capable corporals and sergeants he had served with in the war. Their only social interaction was at the work drinks party just before Christmas when crates of beer were bought in for the entire garage and workshop workers. At the end of the party, William was asked to join Bertram for a brandy and soda in his office.

"Well, here's to a Merry Christmas and a successful New Year," he said, raising his glass. "I hope you are happy here, Lyus, old boy, I think you have slotted in very well."

"Thank you, Mr Drogo. I am very happy here and I am glad you find my work satisfactory," responded William in reciprocal terms, without giving the question much thought.

In truth he was quite content with his new position, even though the work was rarely stimulating and mainly repetitive. The set up suited him, his boss was never too demanding and he experienced little difficulty in his relationships with his fellow workers. He always kept in mind his father's warning that he earned his wages and that his employer would always put his own interests first. Nowadays, he was never tempted to confuse pleasantness with loyalty. He had made that mistake with Hoinville & Bates, and he was reminded of that when Horatio Bottomley came to trial at the Old Bailey in the following February.

Bottomley's criminal libel case against his former associate, Bigland, began in January 1922. By now, Bottomley's methods had come fully to light and, to avoid further damaging disclosures in court, no evidence was offered by his counsel and Bigland was discharged. Bottomley had also, rather foolishly, brought another charge against Bigland of attempted extortion and this charge was heard in Shrewsbury in February, where again Bigland was acquitted. His own position having been under investigation by the police for several months, it was not surprising that Bottomley was in turn charged with fraudulent conversion. He was sent for trial, also at the Old Bailey, in May 1922.

William wondered if he might be called as a witness himself, but he was not. Inspector Lynch had clearly been aware that William was not involved in the distribution of funds, only in their acceptance and payment into Bottomley's account. Hoinville & Bates also evaded scrutiny by lodging a statement in which they claimed to have been misled by Bottomley as to his conduct in managing the Victory Bond Club funds.

On one occasion, William attended the trial. As on every other day of the trial, the proceedings began with an adjournment of fifteen minutes while Bottomley prepared himself by drinking a bottle of champagne. Afterwards, he defended himself as best he could, but the weight of evidence against him was damning and William could not but feel sorry for the forlorn wretch, a shadow of his formerly ebullient self. Despite the trouble Bottomley had brought on him and his career, William took no pleasure in hearing he had been sentenced to seven years' penal servitude, after being found guilty. He was surprised that he felt no animosity towards Bottomley, despite suffering personally from the man's criminality, and put it down to the fact that he took no pleasure in kicking a man while he was down.

XV

AFTER THE DEMANDING WORK FOR THE VICTORY BONDS
Club, the relaxed atmosphere of Bertram Drogo Motors gave
William more time to do what he should have been doing:
enjoying being a young man where play was as important as
work. No longer working late most evenings, he spent more
time with friends. The variety of pleasure pursuits on offer was
growing in the 1920s so, apart from playing football and other
athletic sports, they could enjoy time together while playing
cards or listening to music on the new record players, go out
for a drink, play billiards, visit the cinema or go to dances.

As he neared his eighteenth birthday, William's thoughts
also turned towards girls. Not in a sexual sense, as he assumed
that this would be a matter which would arise at the same
time as marriage. At present, he was thinking purely in terms
of recapturing the fleeting pleasurable moments which he had
enjoyed when in the company of an attractive young woman,
as when he had worked with Millicent and especially when
he had taken her to Gow's. The likelihood of meeting girls
at work was negligible and he lacked the courage to seize the
initiative in a chance meeting, so the likeliest opportunities
were at social events, such as dances.

Typically, at these dances, many of the invitations to dance were gently rebuffed. Of those that were accepted most would lead nowhere as either William or his partner would decide to take the matter no further. Other filters would result from meeting each other in the cold light of day or the struggle to find anything in common, but a few times a date did lead to William having a brief social relationship with a young woman of about his age. In particular, there was Violet, a vivacious brunette who worked in a button factory; Eileen, a shy shop assistant who liked going to museums and art galleries; and Lavinia, a primary schoolteacher who shared William's interest in politics. None of the relationships became serious or lasted for a long time, and in part this was due to William's mother.

Whenever he acceded to Alice's request to invite a girl round to meet her, she never seemed to warm to them. An initially polite welcome would seem always to chill as the meeting proceeded. Afterwards, Alice would give her son a brief comment of approval followed by a list of failings which made the particular girl unsuitable: Violet was too noisy and out-spoken and lacked polite table manners, Eileen was too mousy and didn't have anything to say for herself, Lavinia was argumentative and headstrong. While William did his best to rebut or at least ignore such comments, he was unable to dispel them completely from his mind and, in any case, the young women were not keen on repeating the experience. Perhaps because he had not formed a particularly strong attachment to any of them, or they to him, the eventual end of each relationship mattered little to him. But then there was Esther.

One evening, William accompanied his friends, Cyril and Amos, to a dance held at the Hackney Hospital. There, a dinner-suited quintet played a mixture of music, some from the latest sheets and others of a pre-war vintage. Young men in lounge suits or the occasional dinner suit struggled gamely with waltzes and slow foxtrots in their efforts to win the approval of pretty young women in sleek dresses and headbands. The women, despite higher heels and long skirts, in most cases moved more confidently than their partners. Most of the young men, huddled in their small groups, spent much more time assessing the relative attractiveness and approachability of the young women than actually doing anything about it. Those who could not summon up the courage to approach the women usually disguised their timidity in a negative assessment of those available.

Having the courage to ask and the mettle to accept refusal, William approached a very pretty young woman who had sat out a couple of dances and who presented too intimidating a challenge to his friends. Much to his surprise, his offer was accepted. After a reasonable attempt at a waltz, the music turned to a rag and he relaxed to dance a one-step with the smiling girl. He was relieved when she thanked him after the second dance and delighted when she did not dismiss him when he walked her back to her chair but accepted the offer of a glass of fruit punch. When, after a lengthy conversation, he returned to his two smiling friends, he dismissed their hints that he seemed to have made a conquest and skirted round their question of whether he would see her again. In fact, riding the wave, he had asked her out and she had agreed to see him the following Saturday.

The young woman, Esther, lived near Stamford Hill and that Saturday afternoon, after finishing early at the garage to give himself time to change, he took a 53 tram and met her at her local cinema. His memories of her prettiness, grace and charm were not in any way diminished by the bright light of day as he looked at her standing outside the cinema, before she spotted him.

They saw a couple of fairly forgettable films, a melodrama and a light comedy, enlivened only by some vigorous piano playing from the musical accompanist. Afterwards, they went to a small café which served what Esther described as 'continental cakes'. He hadn't presumed to ask her age but guessed she was a little older than him. She was certainly assured and seemed at ease in any situation. After a slightly stilted conversation at first, they soon relaxed, and the talk flowed more freely as they moved on to their second cup of tea. He had a very enjoyable time, exchanging edited facts of his life with the engaging, pretty brunette in her attractive turquoise dress. Esther Portnoy worked in the City as a clerk in a shipping office not very far from the unlamented Victory Bonds Club. She was aware of the workings of both the Baltic Exchange and Lloyds but had never been in either of them, having learned most of what she knew from the paperwork which went through her hands. She lived in a road near Clapton Common with her parents and two younger brothers.

"My father works as an insurance broker. I suppose that's how I ended up in the City. What does your father do?" she asked, holding a chocolate éclair carefully and ensuring her napkin was in position to catch any debris.

William was proud of his father's work, but it always seemed so definitive, so encapsulating of his personality, compared to being a greengrocer or a railway signalman. "He works for the Amalgamated Engineering Union," he replied, without going into detail.

Esther nodded. "So you have no brothers or sisters?"

"No, my sister died when she was three: diphtheria."

"Oh, William. How sad."

"Yes," he replied. He hadn't thought of Kitty for a while, but the memories that came flooding back were the good ones and for that he was grateful, even if they made him unable to speak. He raised his teacup to his mouth and pretended to drink.

Esther thought she should change the subject but did not wish to appear callous, so she too reached for her cup of tea.

Composed once again, William resumed the conversation. "I suppose I count as an only child, really. I envy you your brothers."

Esther laughed. "Well, perhaps not *my* brothers, but I know what you mean."

After tea, they walked across Clapton Common and into Springfield Park, chatting constantly, not yet knowing each other well enough to be comfortable in silence. Esther left him at his tram stop, refusing with thanks his offer to walk her home. They exchanged work telephone numbers before they parted.

William thought it right not to appear pushy and rationed his attention to Esther to a weekly date and a visit to the cinema or music hall. It suited him to have all the personal satisfaction that went with enjoying the company of an attractive young woman without the need to curtail any of his other social arrangements, especially as Saturdays often involved his sporting activities. After three dates he realised he enjoyed her company very much and looked forward to the next time that little bit more.

When that day arrived, he was in the kitchen, one foot on a chair while polishing his shoes in readiness for the evening out, when his mother came in.

"Going out with your young lady this evening?"

"Yes, Mum."

"It would be nice to meet her some time. Perhaps you ought to invite her round for Sunday tea."

Following previous occasions when he had brought a girl home, he now thought it was the last thing he wished to do. "I haven't met her family yet either."

"I wonder why; hope there's nothing wrong with them."

"Wrong with them? Don't be silly, Mum. Her father's an insurance broker and they have a house in one of those nice roads near the Common. Anyway, we're just friends."

His mother made one of her non-committal sounds. These always left the irritating impression that she was displeased about something without knowing exactly what it was. She was fussing around behind him in the kitchen while he was finishing his shoes and adjusting his tie, and he could tell she was itching to say something. So he waited and watched while she kept herself busy doing nothing.

At last she spoke. "This girl Esther, might she be Jewish?"

"What? Jewish? I've no idea."

"What's her surname?"

"Portnoy."

"Then she is Jewish. There was a man with a stall in Ridley Road market who had the name Portnoy and he was Jewish."

"That doesn't necessarily follow. But what does it matter if she is Jewish?"

"They don't like their children to marry outside their faith."

"Who said anything about getting married? We're just friends."

She took off her apron and folded it up with that precision which usually signified a conclusion to the conversation, but not this time. "Perhaps she's from a strict family who wouldn't approve of her going out with somebody who isn't Jewish and that's why she won't take you to see them. They probably don't even know she's going out with you."

"Would *you* mind if she was Jewish?" He put the shoe brush away and took his coat from its hook, wishing his father was in the room to hear this nonsense.

"Well, I've got nothing against the girl, but there are differences in the way they see things. That can lead to misunderstandings and difficulties. It's usually for the best that people stick to their own kind."

William's sense of well-being was totally deflated. Nothing had changed in his life but somehow his mother had introduced a complication, an invisible impediment to things going on exactly as before. At some point he might feel impelled to have a conversation or ask questions that he had never considered, nor wanted in his head. He was used to his mother being less than complimentary to any young woman he showed interest in, but this time she had managed to raise her doubts without even meeting her. He made sure he had his wallet, put on his coat and left, calling out a half-hearted farewell to his mother.

Half an hour later he met a smiling Esther outside the cinema and they went to see a film he had been looking forward to and that she had only agreed to see to please him: *Nosferatu*.

Sitting in his seat and watching the film with Max Schreck in the monstrous image of Count Orlok, William was swept up in the story and horrors of the film, and forgot about his mother's strictures, especially when Esther grabbed his hand during the more disturbing scenes.

Afterwards they went to their regular café and had a cup of coffee and a salt beef sandwich. They laughed and joked about the film, mainly as a relief to the revulsion and horror they had experienced watching the repulsive unfolding of events on the screen. William commented that he had seen more than one person in the audience cover their eyes during a particularly lurid scene.

"I must admit I closed my eyes once or twice," said Esther. "Why do they make films like that?"

William smiled. "Presumably they make money because people like them. They allow us to indulge those parts of our nature that we usually keep hidden."

"Such as?"

"Fear, cruelty, violence, hatred. When you think of children's fairy tales they are nearly always about horrible things befalling an innocent person and usually end with something worse happening to the bad person or monster. As civilised human beings we are supposed to abhor violence and cruelty and revenge, but we are allowed to experience these feelings within a fictitious environment in which the evil one is so terrible we feel no guilt about wanting them to be destroyed."

Esther laughed. "That's a good answer. You must have thought about it quite a lot."

William nodded. "I suppose I have. People can be cruel and nasty, and if these films act as an outlet for negative thoughts and desires perhaps they are a good thing."

"I find them frightening, and I suppose that has a strange attraction, but I don't think I like watching violence or people being cruel."

"That's because you are naturally a kind person." He looked down the menu. "I like the food here," he said. "Is this possibly a Jewish restaurant?" After he asked the question he was aware that one or two heads were turned in his direction.

Esther coloured a little. "Yes."

"Are you…?" he began, seemingly unable to halt the sequence of interrogation but then trying to stop short at the last. Other heads were turned now.

"Why do you ask?"

"No particular reason."

"Can we get the bill now? I should like to go."

Esther stood up and pulled on her coat while William hurriedly settled the bill with the proprietor.

They came out of the café, William still putting on his coat. "Have I done something wrong?" he asked, inwardly cursing himself.

"I suppose not, but I felt uncomfortable; people were looking at us. Why not ask me questions like that when we are alone or somewhere private?"

They had turned away from the café and were heading towards the Common, though it was dark and cool, and a walk there was not an attractive proposition. "I'm sorry, I didn't think it mattered," said William.

"Well, it obviously matters to you otherwise you would have waited for me to tell you in my own time."

He took her hand and she didn't resist. "It doesn't matter to me. The thought just entered my mind."

They walked in silence. "I was going to tell you," she said eventually. "I know it does matter to some people and I didn't want to know if you were one of them."

"But I'm not," he said, squeezing her hand.

It was too early to go home and they both wanted to continue this positive exchange, but he could not consider taking her into a pub. They were approaching the Common. "What would you like to do?"

She shook her head. "I don't know."

"If I walked you home we could have a cup of coffee or something," he suggested.

She smiled. "That's the other reason I hadn't told you. I'm not quite ready to take you home to meet my parents."

"Why not?"

"My family is very conservative about mixing with gentiles, especially relationships between the sexes, and I haven't had the courage to tell them about you yet."

"Is your father one of those men who dresses in black and—"

She shook her head. "You mean Hasidic? No. But it would be difficult for him if I took you home out of the blue; my mother too, I think. You see, my grandparents are very traditional and that would probably influence the way my parents feel too."

"How do you know, unless you try?"

"You're right. I suppose I'm a coward."

"So where do your parents think you are tonight?"

"At the cinema with a friend, Miriam, the one I was with at the dance when we met."

"But this deception can't go on forever."

"I know. I will tell them soon."

"Perhaps you shouldn't have come out with me if it was going to become awkward."

"That's what Miriam said. I'm sorry."

They had walked to the Common now and were circling back. They had somehow talked themselves into a dead end and neither could think of anything constructive to say, so they carried on in silence, holding hands, until they were back where they started. After agreeing to see each other soon, they kissed, and Esther, at her insistence, made her own way home.

"You're back early," said Alice when he arrived home.

"Yes. Where's Dad?"

"He went out for a drink with his brothers. So, have you met her parents yet?"

"No."

"Did you find out?"

"Find out what?"

"If she is Jewish?"

"Yes, but so what?"

She gave her non-committal grunt and put the kettle on.

Lying in bed that night William found his conversations with his mother and Esther going round and round in his head. Alice had been right about Esther's unwillingness to take him to meet her family and she had made a good guess about why that was so. Perhaps she was right about everything; was it too hard to keep a relationship going if the families were not supportive? Was it worth trying to? He envisaged difficulties if the relationship were to become more serious but consoled himself with the thought that it was never going to get to that stage. He was right; it never did.

William and Esther went out again a couple of times more, but somehow there was a slight unspoken awkwardness between them. She did not invite him to her home and he thought it probable her parents still did not know about him. William felt things slipping away and couldn't see the relationship going anywhere if it couldn't be out in the open. When they hadn't seen each other for two weeks he realised he was unable to find the enthusiasm to ring Esther. Another week passed and eventually Esther rang him at the garage.

"Oh, hello, Esther. How are you?"

"I'm fine, thank you. What about you?"

"Yes, thanks."

"I wondered why I hadn't heard from you."

"Well, I've been so busy, you know how it is."

"Are you busy this weekend?"

"I'm not sure. Can we leave it for a while?"

"Yes, of course. I hope to see you soon."

"Goodbye," he replied, but she had already gone.

He felt a twinge of regret and intended to ring her again, if only to tell her that he couldn't see any future for them. But he put it off for a week and then another week. With each successive week the invisible impediment grew larger and he thought she had probably come to the same conclusion.

They never spoke again and a few weeks later his mother picked over the bones.

"You haven't seen your young lady lately," she said one evening, when he told her he was going out with a couple of the boys.

"No, it didn't work out."

"Never mind, if things don't work out it's for a reason. It's probably for the best."

William did not reply, nor did he agree. He guessed she would have felt the same if Esther had been a Catholic or a Hindu or from another country. The war had shown how easy it was for people to see in those of another country only their national identity, rather than their humanity. How sad it was that such labels should have to intrude even into personal relationships. Of course, the barriers often existed on both sides. Not that he blamed Esther; she was a victim of these barriers. But it pained him that she hadn't thought enough of him for her at least to ask the question of her parents.

XVI

THE FIRST ANNIVERSARY OF HIS EMPLOYMENT AT Bertram Drogo Motors was approaching and William was quite excited at the prospect of the opening of the new showroom for the sale of second-hand sports cars. Drogo chose not to sell new cars as this would probably tie him into a contract with one company and he wanted to offer the cars in which he took a particular interest. This was for him as much about enjoyment as profit, but he thought this new venture would provide both. He knew there was a growing number among both sexes who were, like him, exhilarated by the growth of organised motor sports and who wanted to be associated with this world of speed and flair. Those who were willing were also becoming more financially able as the post-war recession had finally come to an end. He was confident the time was right to branch out into car sales.

The office in which William had been located was knocked down together with the spares shop. The area made available plus an empty space adjacent to it provided the site for the showroom and William's new office. Most of the cars for sale would be stored at the back of the workshops while Drogo displayed his current four most eye-catching vehicles in the showroom. He took on the role of sales manager himself but appointed a part-time sales assistant from among his team of motor mechanics to handle sales while he was away. William was reluctant to get involved in sales, knowing nothing about selling or about motor cars. However, he agreed to take customer details and set up appointments when Drogo was out. He would also arrange for the sales assistant/mechanic to show a seriously interested client under the bonnet and organise a test drive.

The new showroom opened at the end of November and William was recruited to dispense drinks and bonhomie at the open day, which was held soon afterwards. Aside from potential clients, most of the guests were involved in the motoring industry in one way or another, including a number of racing drivers, some of whom he was introduced to. Drogo took the guests on a tour of the showroom in small groups so they could admire, perhaps even buy, his prize exhibits: four tourers with varying degrees of sporting prowess, two Sunbeams, a Lanchester and a Crossley.

The next morning, Drogo was, unusually, in the office before William and was clearly in high spirits when he greeted his office manager. "Good morning, Lyus. Thanks for all your help last evening. It went very well; I think I've sold the 1914 Sunbeam. We're on the threshold of a new era, old boy." He took a cigar from a box on his desk and lit it, puffing between phrases as he continued. "Cars have definitely come a long way from the old horseless carriages, but in the next few years designs will become sleeker and sports cars will diverge much more from saloons. I've seen some of the prototypes – wonderful, and we'll be in on the ground floor."

"Perhaps we should be selling the latest models in that case," replied William.

"Good point," puffed Drogo, "but we'll be a specialist with a range of makes and at a price more people can afford, and soon we'll be selling cars a year old, after the original owner becomes tired of them. With our team of mechanics we'll be able to fix almost anything that needs doing to make them like new."

The change in the emphasis of the business did have its teething troubles since Drogo was not on the premises as much as he thought he would be. Customer service fell through the two stools of the well-dressed young man who knew nothing whatever about cars and the articulate and helpful mechanic who did not quite look the part in an operation aiming to have a degree of swank about it. Furthermore, William's time was now spread more thinly and he often could not complete his regular work on time. Eventually, Drogo was persuaded to take his sales assistant/mechanic out of the workshop, creating for him a new role centred on sales and customer relations.

With the arrival of spring and the resumption of motor racing, Drogo was missing from the office more than he was there. 1923 was a watershed year in the history of the sport with major developments in Grand Prix racing and the first Le Mans 24 hour race, and Drogo wanted to be in the thick of it. Much of his time was spent, at Brooklands or other venues, in the pits, watching, advising or actively racing. When he was back at the garage he worked hard, seeking out special items for his stock of cars, preparing them for sale and fine-tuning them ready for the road, finally using his considerable charm in the showroom. William got used to meeting Drogo's friends in motoring, mostly young men from a public-school background with the financial independence to permit them to devote their time to racing. There were others, less well-off, who used their connections in the motor trade to help fund their pursuit of speed. All of them would call in to discuss upcoming events or to collect Drogo for lunch and while there inspect his latest offerings.

A particular friend was Jack Barclay, a partner in the Rolls-Royce sales outlet of Barclay and Wyse. Young and dashing in appearance, with very dark hair and a determined expression, he had an unassuming nature which added to his charm. He called in one day to wait for Drogo, who was out seeing a client, and took up William's offer of a cup of coffee while he waited. He was chatting away to William about the latest developments in motor cars when his ears pricked up. "That doesn't sound too good," he said, walking over to the window. A Vauxhall 25 D-type had limped onto the forecourt and the driver was waiting for someone to attend to him. To William's amazement, Barclay, who was wearing a pale summer suit, strolled out to the car and, after a brief discussion, took his jacket off, rolled up his sleeves and soon had his head under the bonnet. He had diagnosed the trouble and got the engine running by the time a mechanic had arrived from the workshop. Barclay gave the driver his card and, wiping his hands on a rag, came back into the office.

"That was kind of you, Mr Barclay," said William.

Barclay smiled. "Thanks, but nothing to it, really. I know those Vauxhalls inside out. May I use your washroom?"

Over the next few years, William was never anywhere except on the periphery of Drogo's motor racing activities, but that was enough for his knowledge of and interest in motor sport to increase over time. From overheard conversations, the reading of relevant paperwork and discussions with other employees, William, almost unaware of it, became steadily more familiar with the cars for sale in the garage and also more confident in dealing with customers, even on technical matters when necessary. From Drogo he would hear the latest news on motor racing, especially the results relating to the people he knew, had met or at least had heard of, and he derived a degree of team spirit out of it.

Drogo was away in May for the inaugural Le Mans 24 hours, where the only British team came equal fourth in a three-litre Bentley. Then in July he was off to France again to see Henry Segrave win the French Grand Prix in Tours. He returned a couple of days later and produced a bottle of champagne to celebrate the victory 'one last time', as he put it, while he poured drinks for William and the salesroom assistant Alf Travis.

"Here's to Segrave," he said, "incredible effort by him, and the mechanic too. A real nail-biter: Segrave driving with a slipping clutch at first but steadily moving through the field. It looked all over when with five laps to go Salamano had a lead of over four minutes on Divo and Segrave and then," he punched his palm with his fist, "everything changed. First Divo came into the pits and his filler cap jammed so he had to run on the reserve tank and refill after every lap. Next, instead of Salamano coming past the pits it was Segrave who flashed past. We realised that Salamano had run out of fuel when we saw his mechanic running towards the pits. He filled a can, but the judges wouldn't let him use a bike, so the poor chap had to run back to the car with the fuel. It was too late. The Sunbeams of Segrave and Divo came home first and second. What a day for British motor racing."

Although Drogo's primary cause of celebration was the victory of a friend, he was fully aware the success of the Sunbeams certainly did no harm to his business. The cachet attached to a Grand Prix win was sure to raise the profile of the marque and he usually had a few Sunbeams in stock as it was one of his favoured makes. While the sales business was certainly growing, the expertise of the garage in the repair and servicing of high-performance cars further added to its rising reputation. As a sideline, the garage occasionally allowed customers to hire one of the sporting tourers to enjoy a weekend away on the open road and Drogo, with his growing reputation at Brooklands, was becoming something of a celebrity among followers of motor sports.

William enjoyed the reflected glory of his association with this glamorous sport and soon all of his friends had made the journey over to Swiss Cottage to look round, gawp at some of the illustrious vehicles in the showroom and hope to meet, as several did, *the* Bertram Drogo. Over the following two years William went to a few races at Brooklands with Stanley who, as well as being a lover of speed, was a keen motorcyclist and was able to take him on the back. They stood behind the picket fence and watched Alvis 12/50s, Austin Sevens, Frazer Nashes and Lee Francis cars battle over non-championship distances with the teams of two battling against each other and the various difficulties thrown up by the track and the reliability of their vehicles. Stanley was in thrall to the excitement of it all and was always keen to attend a race when the opportunity arose. He sometimes placed a bet on the race, though he knew the outcome was always extremely unpredictable, and referred to it as 'just a bit of fun'.

In 1925 Drogo drove at Brooklands on a few occasions and for the first time invited William to attend as his guest in the paddock. "Bring along a chum. It'll be in the record as William Lyus and guest so you can bring who you like on the day. Alfie will drive you down in one of the cars."

William asked Stanley if he would like to come and Stanley was absolutely delighted to be asked, calling it a great thrill to watch a race from the paddock. They would both take the Saturday morning off and Stanley would pick William up on the way to Swiss Cottage. That morning, William dressed in his best suit and most flamboyant tie and was ready a good twenty minutes before Stanley was due to call. He opened the front door wide as soon as he heard the knock. It was not Stanley standing there but Lucy.

He hadn't seen Lucy for at least a couple of years as whenever he called for Stanley she seemed to be out or doing some chore or other. The pretty girl of a few years before was now a very attractive young woman. She was wearing a blue cloche hat and a beige and blue drop-waist dress which stopped just below the knee. As always seemed to be the case when he saw Lucy, he was unprepared and could only stare.

She smiled. "I suppose this is a bit of a surprise?"

"Where's Stan?"

"He's had an accident."

"What? Is he all right?"

"Yes, nothing to worry about. He came off his motorbike last night, slipped on some oil or something, he said. He twisted his ankle and can't walk very well this morning so he asked me to come instead, if you don't mind."

"I don't mind at all, but do you really want to go?"

"Oh yes, I want to see some of these cars that Stanley is always on about and, of course, the racing drivers." Her smile faded a little. "You are happy for me to go?"

William nodded vigorously. "Poor old Stan. I'm sure there will be other chances later."

They walked to the bus stop, telling each other what they had been doing since they last met. Lucy was now a section head at Spokes and reiterated her past offer to give him a generous discount should he ever come to the store. They went to Liverpool Street and took the Metropolitan line to Swiss Cottage Station and then to Drogo's garage.

Alfie was waiting for them, leaning against a gleaming, burgundy Alvis 11/40, its roof up but the sides open. Alfie looked surprised at first but said nothing. He touched his hat as Lucy approached.

"Hello, Alfie. This is Miss Lucy Mason; she will be taking her brother's place as he is indisposed."

Alfie nodded. "Sorry to hear that. How do you do, miss?" He smiled. "Alfie Travis. Well, shall we start?"

"Everything all right in the showroom?" asked William.

"Yes, young Tommy Shelts is looking after it today. He'll take names and telephone numbers, etc. Here are your paddock badges." He handed each of them a small pass card attached to a treasury tag. William secured his in the buttonhole on his lapel and Lucy affixed hers to her brooch.

They climbed in the car, William not sure whether to join Alfie in the front or Lucy in the back but deciding on the former as it would be less of a squeeze. Lucy did not comment but arrayed herself elegantly on the rear seat. Alfie started the car and they set off for Weybridge and Brooklands.

When they arrived, Alfie swept into the paddock and jumped out to open the small door for Lucy. William got out the other side and took in the atmosphere of the paddock: the roar of engines being revved up, the shouting of instructions above the noise, the small mechanical sounds of tapping and clanging and wrenching and filing, the curses of mechanics and drivers as yet another solution failed like all the rest they'd tried, the chatter and laughter of the spectators, the smell of oil and grease and petrol, the clouds of exhaust and cigarettes and pipes and the occasional waft of perfume.

"There's the boss," said Alfie, pointing over at the Frazer Nash of Bertram Drogo who stood by the side of his car, talking to a smiling Archie Frazer Nash and laughing about something. Alfie pointed out some of the other drivers here for the 150-mile race including Malcolm Campbell, the world land speed record holder, with his Bugatti and Woolf Barnato leaning against his Bentley. As they walked around, William recognised Jack Barclay, who would be driving a Vauxhall TT, and waved at him and another friend of Drogo's, Mytton Thornycroft. At six foot three, Thornycroft was a tall man to be a racing driver but managed to squeeze into a Hispana-Suiza. While the drivers were too busy to stop and talk, most of them managed to be distracted enough to notice and smile at Lucy. William was pleased about that.

Alfie had been given an allowance for refreshments and he bought them both a drink before the start. The race itself took over two hours and was like a real-life version of snakes and ladders. Drivers experienced a series of unfortunate mishaps such as mechanical failure, irregularities on the track surface and shortage of fuel. There were regular pit stops at which mechanics worked as fast as they were able to send the car out again, often with a cigarette in their mouths even when refuelling. The leader changed lap by lap and there was no certainty about who would win the race until the chequered flag was waved. William, Lucy and Alfie had an excellent position from which to view the excitement, and they waved and cheered as Drogo went past. The winner was Jack Barclay, but Bertram Drogo came a very respectable fourth and Thornycroft finished, which was more than some of the illustrious names in the sport managed to do. Everyone ended up in one piece to enjoy after-race drinks.

After a brief conversation with Drogo and one or two others and a congratulatory wave to Jack Barclay, they went back to their places to watch a second race, a shorter one this time, with a nasty spill for one of the drivers, who fortunately was able to walk back to the pits. Afterwards they had a walk round the paddock, spoke to all the drivers William knew and then went back to their car and set off for the garage. Lucy was given a tour of the site and allowed to sit in some of the cars by Alfie while William went through the business of the day with Tommy Shelts, making a phone call to one potential buyer. Then he and Lucy set off for Homerton and the walk to Templar Road.

As they approached her home Lucy told him how much she'd enjoyed the day. "I had a lovely time, Billy. Thank you very much for taking me. It's an experience I shall never forget."

"I'm glad you were able to go with me. I had a great time."

They arrived at her house and Lucy put the key in the lock. "You'll come in, won't you? Stan will want to hear all about it."

He nodded and took off his hat as they went in the front door.

"Hello, Billy," said Stan. He hobbled into the front room as they entered it. "How did it go?"

"Jack Barclay won and Bertram came fourth. It was a great race: lots of ups and downs and pretty close at the end. How's the ankle?"

"Getting better; it was only a bad strain. I'm sorry I had to pull out. I was really looking forward to it. Did you enjoy it, sis?"

"Yes, and I was lucky to be able to go. I dare say Cecil would have been first choice for the spare ticket." She winked at her brother.

Stanley smiled. "You'll never know. Anyway, he couldn't change his shift at such short notice. What car did you go in, Billy?"

"An Alvis 11/40."

Stanley whistled. "Great car; lucky old you, Lucy. Did you meet the drivers?"

"Yes," Lucy said, "I got them to autograph the race sheet for you." She rummaged in her handbag and produced a neatly folded sheet with the signatures of Barclay, Drogo, Thornycroft and one or two others.

Stanley smiled and looked at the paper wistfully.

Lucy went off to make some tea and the two young men chatted about the racing and the atmosphere in the paddock.

"How was Lucy; did she *really* enjoy it?" asked Stanley.

"Yes, why?"

"Well, she's never shown any interest in cars and when I offered her the place I thought she might not be keen, but she jumped at the chance. I'm glad she wasn't disappointed." He sighed and looked at the sheet again, reading every word on it. "There'll be another time, I'm sure."

It was briefly like old times, the two Mason children and their friend from their old home, drinking tea and laughing together. Mr and Mrs Mason also looked in and asked after William's family.

"How's your grandmother?" said Mrs Mason. "She must be…"

"She was seventy-eight last week. She's not too bad, thank you, but she's having some trouble with her memory and does get some strange ideas into her head. A couple of weeks ago she got herself ready and set off to visit her mother in Stratford. I had to run after her and bring her back. Obviously, her mother's been dead many years."

Mr Mason shook his head. "Just old age. They call it senility these days to make it sound posher. Shame, though, nice old lady; she and her husband, your grandfather, were in the house when we moved in, so I've known *her* a few years."

Mrs Mason was getting ready to serve the evening meal and William knew it was time to go. "Thanks for the tea and cake. I'll see you all soon, I hope."

Lucy took him to the front door. "Thanks again for taking me to Brooklands. I think I understand what all the fuss is about now," she said. "Perhaps I'll see you soon?"

"I hope so." An idea went through his head. "How about that trip to the Castle we never get round to doing?"

"Yes, that would be lovely. When?"

"How about next Sunday?"

"Yes, second performance?"

"I'll meet you outside." He smiled and turned to go home, Lucy watching him until he turned the corner at the end of the road.

His mother greeted him as he came through the front door. "Hello, have a nice time?"

"Yes, it was really good."

"Stanley enjoy it as well?"

"He couldn't go; he's got a sprained ankle."

"Oh, that's a shame."

"Lucy came with me."

"Lucy? Really? Is that the right sort of thing for a young lady to go to?"

William laughed. "Lots of ladies go to motor racing; it's like going to the horse racing, perfectly respectable."

"Go and spend a bit of time with Grandma while I finish getting tea."

He walked into the living room. "Hello, Grandma."

The old woman looked up from her doze and smiled. "Been out with Granddad?"

"No, Grandma, just some friends. You remember the Masons?"

A flash of recognition crossed her face. "Yes, Flossie and Bert."

"No, their children, you know, Stanley and Lucy."

She nodded and closed her eyes, humming the old Mexican song 'Cielito Lindo'. William sat down in an armchair and closed his own eyes. It had been a long day, full of excitement and enjoyment, and he went through it all, hoping to impress the memory in his mind. His reverie was interrupted by his mother looking round the door.

"Bring Grandma into the kitchen," she called.

His father was already seated at the kitchen table, his collarless shirt undone at the neck and his sleeves rolled up.

He had just finished an afternoon in the garden and was now reading the *Star*. "Hello, Billy. Have a good day?" he asked, without looking up.

"Yes. It was really good. You should come with me sometime."

"I'm not that keen on sport, as you know, especially one which is only open to members of the moneyed classes. This massacre in China makes grim reading," he added, referring to an article in the newspaper.

William did not reply. Of course he agreed with everything his father said in the matter of politics, but did it have to be politics all the time? He thought back over the day, its edge not taken off by his father's comment, and refused to despise all those drivers just because they were not on the right side of the class struggle. He turned to his grandmother and helped her cut up her sausages.

"Did you see many famous people today?" asked Alice, ignoring her husband's distaste for the world of motor racing.

"Well, we saw Malcolm Campbell and Woolf Barnato and Ernest Eldridge and—"

"I meant apart from racing drivers."

As he had when a child, William tended to equate fame of any value with noble achievements like those of the Antarctic explorers, war heroes and sportsmen, especially those who put their lives at risk. So his reply should not have been too unexpected.

"I'm not sure if I would recognise many famous people apart from racing drivers. I dare say some of the people in the paddock were famous for being something, but whether they are famous for anything worthwhile is another matter."

Jack laughed. "Well said, Billy."

On the following Sunday, William met Lucy at the Castle and they sat in the fairly full circle, halfway back on the end of the fourth row. They listened to the pianist warming up before the first feature while they talked about work and their hopes for the future. As the lights went down and they settled to watch the first film, William wanted to hold her hand but wasn't sure if he should. They had known each other virtually since they were born, almost like a brother and sister. How could they be anything other than just friends? His hand, having slowly moved towards hers, retreated to its former position.

After the cinema they walked to Templar Road and William went in for a brief chat with Stanley and the rest of the family. When he left, Lucy saw him to the door.

"Thanks for today. I really enjoyed it."

"Me too. Hope to see you soon."

But he didn't see her soon. He was caught in the web of a dilemma and he could not find a way out of it. He was very fond of Lucy and wanted to have a romantic relationship with her but wasn't sure it could or even should develop, against the background of their childhood friendship. Furthermore, he couldn't broach the subject with Lucy in case she regarded him purely as a family friend and could never imagine a romantic attachment. Any such conversation then would be an embarrassing, possibly even a toe-curling, situation. So he let matters slide.

William's growing enthusiasm for motor racing found further outlets when he and Stanley decided to take their summer holidays in short bursts, touring round the country to see racing on the sands of Southport, Pendine, Weston-super-Mare among others, staying in bed and breakfast accommodation, or occasionally a small hotel. He also began to make plans for 1926 as the proposed dates for motoring events were revealed, including the first ever British Grand Prix at Brooklands, which he was determined to attend. He toyed with the possibility of one day taking up driving himself, especially after his friend Amos achieved his ambition of moving at up at his firm from mechanic to lorry driver. For the first time he could envisage a future career in a job which was related to his own sporting interests and where he would grow as the company grew.

XVII

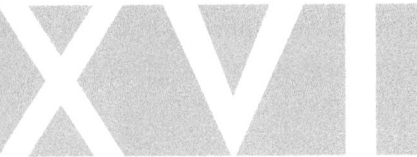

THE NEW YEAR COULDN'T HAVE BEEN BETTER FOR William's career. The dramatic growth of cars on Britain's roads, which tripled between 1910 and 1923 and would triple again by 1930, opened great opportunities for someone with the business acumen of Bertram Drogo and he opened a new branch of his garage in early 1926. He appointed a new manager for this site in Kilburn and, while acting as manager for the Swiss Cottage garage himself, promoted William to financial controller with responsibilities over both sites.

It was this change in his work, now involving travel between the two garages, which convinced William that it was time to take up driving. He felt he ought to be able to drive between sites to reduce journey times and give him greater flexibility, a view which Drogo shared. William obtained a driving licence and Alfie Travis took him out for lessons every evening after work until he was reasonably proficient. There was no driving test required, so he could take to the road alone as soon as he felt comfortable enough to do so. Not able to afford a car, he was permitted to use whatever car was available from those on sale at the garage and he soon became familiar with a wide range of makes and models. He had soon driven cars with gearboxes, handbrake positions and other controls so varied that he began to doubt there was any car he couldn't almost immediately adapt to.

As spring arrived William began making plans for the motor-racing season. He hoped he might attend some events under his own steam in a car borrowed from the garage. However, his planning was interrupted by a national event which, as far as he was concerned, came completely out of the blue.

One evening in the middle of April, he had just finished his evening meal. Alice was upstairs feeding William's grandmother, who was no longer well enough to take her meals downstairs. He looked through the newspaper, which was full of commentary about the difficulties in the coal industry and another breakdown in negotiations between management and trade unions.

"This mining dispute seems to be getting worse, Dad," he remarked to his father, who was reading a book.

Jack took off his glasses and looked up. "Yes, I think it almost certain we'll have a strike now."

"I don't understand it; I thought miners were well-paid."

"They used to be, but the war messed things up. We exhausted a lot of our best mines during the war and these days we are no longer as competitive as we were. Overseas rivals like Germany and Poland can undercut our prices. So profits keep falling and the bosses keep cutting wages; miners were on £6 a week in 1918 and now it's less than £4. They won't stand for another cut in wages, especially as the owners are expecting them to work longer hours as well."

"But if the industry is in decline, sooner or later wages will have to go down or jobs will be lost. It's simple economics."

Jack shook his head. "Simple economics are too brutal to be let loose. Over the long run, industries must come and go, but for the here and now it's different. These people live in mining villages with no other jobs to turn to and working lives not long enough to start again. They have no choice but to fight change."

"I can't see how they can win a strike if their position is so weak."

"They have the support of the TUC and other big unions, so we'll see."

Jack's prediction of a strike was proved correct. Two more weeks of fruitless negotiations finally broke down on the 1st of May and the Trades Union Congress announced a general strike 'in defence of miners' wages and hours', to begin at a minute to midnight on the 3rd May.

William was faced with a conundrum. Sceptical about the likely success of the strike, he nonetheless did not wish to hinder it in any way, mainly out of loyalty to his father. He was determined not to cross a picket line nor offer any support to those seeking to break the strike, but how would this sit with his responsibility to Drogo? On the 3rd of May he went into work as usual and saw that Drogo was in the middle of a conversation with the mechanics. They were all standing outside the workshop, despite the temperature, which was well below average for the time of year. William watched the group for a while; the conversation appeared to be calm and good-natured rather than heated, so he went into his office.

He was joined after another ten minutes by Drogo and Alfie Travis.

"Morning, Lyus," said Drogo breezily. "I think we need to have a discussion about the strike starting tomorrow." He planted himself in the chair opposite William's desk and Alfie leaned against the windowsill.

"What did you have in mind?"

Drogo took out a cigarette and lit it. "I've spoken to the

chaps in the workshop. None of them are members of a union and they are happy to go on working, though a couple would feel uncomfortable if they were subject to intimidation. My own view is that we have a duty to stay open and keep private motorists on the road as public transport is going to be pretty non-existent. What do you think?"

"So you are anticipating that we carry on as usual?" asked Alfie.

"That's what I wanted to ask you. As I understand it, the strike is only by certain unions so our mechanics would not be affected anyway. However, as private cars could be used by people unable to get a train or bus we could encounter some hostility. Is it worth keeping everything open when we don't know what the strike will be like in practice? Are people likely to want to buy a car in the middle of all this? Or want any unnecessary work done on their car?"

"I doubt it," said William.

"Nor do we want to give cause for any disgruntled striker to be provoked into doing something silly. I am inclined to close the showrooms here and in Kilburn, keep the petrol forecourt open in both places and have a couple of mechanics here and there to carry out emergency-only repairs, just for a week until we see how events develop. It may be difficult to get into work, so I suggest that each of us comes in for one day during the remainder of the week to keep an eye on things. I'll pay full wages to all the staff while this is going on, at least for the first couple of weeks. How does that idea appeal to you?"

"Sounds fine to me," said Alfie.

"Perhaps we should put all the cars round the back while this is going on, otherwise I agree," added William.

"Good idea; see to that, will you, Travis? I'll come in tomorrow, then Lyus on Thursday and Travis Friday. When you're on duty give me a call in the evening to let me know how it goes and we'll all come in next Monday to review the situation."

On the evening of the 1ˢᵗ of May Jack had been full of energy and anticipation. The first day of May was a symbolic day, the date chosen by the Marxist International Socialist Congress of 1869 to commemorate working-class demands for an eight-hour working day and celebrated in so many countries as Labour Day or Eight Hours Day. It was not recognised as such in Britain but it being the eve of a general strike made the date's significance for Jack palpable. It was as if his life had been leading up to this moment. It was his destiny to be a torchbearer, albeit a minor one, in a long line of English champions from Wat Tyler through the Diggers and Levellers, the Luddites, the Tolpuddle Martyrs and the Chartists, for the noble cause of obtaining universal human rights and decent living standards for ordinary working people. He would rather it had been a battle for political power, but the TUC had deliberately limited strike action to certain key industries, to play down any suggestions that this strike was intended to support revolutionary political change. However, he knew that, as Marx had made clear, it is economic power that determines who has political power. Victory for the trade union movement in this strike would shift the balance of power between the classes. He chose not to contemplate the thought of defeat.

The following day he was at his union's London office, meeting with colleagues and planning co-ordination with other unions, particularly in transport, which would play a significant part in disrupting the ability of non-union and non-striking labour to get to work. There was a degree of frustration because his own union had been slow in committing to the strike, but now he was able to execute his own plan of action.

He would stay near his home area, attending and supporting picket lines, and liaising with strikers keeping the bus and railway stations closed.

On the next morning at seven o'clock he was raring to go. First, he visited the iron and steel works in the area to ensure his own shop stewards were maintaining picket lines on unionised sites. At each site he congratulated the steadfast, encouraged the wavering members of his own union and exchanged fraternal messages of goodwill with members of other unions. In his suit and tie he was instantly recognised as an official from head office. He was accorded both respect and fellowship from most of his members, but the odd disgruntled remark from those who would rather be at work. There were some engineering workshops that were not unionised and not on strike, and he had no alternative but to accept these were outside his influence, as was most of the working population. Satisfied he had done all that he could with his own comrades, he went through the churchyard to Mare Street and Hackney bus station.

Having successfully stopped the trams running in London, the Transport and General Workers' Union was intent on preventing buses leaving their depots. Non-union volunteers, often from the middle classes, were acting as drivers and conductors, and Jack watched as a volunteer-manned bus left the station with a policeman walking in front. There were boos and shouts from the watching strikers and a couple of bricks were thrown at the side windows, though most of the behaviour appeared to be fairly good-natured. After a quarter of a mile or so the policeman waved the bus on and the driver continued down the road. Jack could see more strikers in the distance and wondered how far the bus would go before it was mounted and the driver ejected from his seat. The transport union officials on duty at the depot were confident the makeshift volunteer drivers would soon lose the enthusiasm for their strike-breaking.

"They're mostly young toffs and university types," said one of them. "They see it as a bit of fun and a kick up the pants for the working class; put us in our place. They'll soon get fed up with being dragged out of the buses and sent packing. Mind you, this rag doesn't help." He handed a newspaper to Jack. It was the *British Gazette*. "This so-called newspaper is full of lies, look!"

With the print workers on strike, there were no national newspapers, but both the unions and the government decided to produce their own. The TUC would the next day bring out the *British Worker*, largely in response to what it saw as scurrilous propaganda by the government newspaper, the *British Gazette*. The latter was edited by Winston Churchill, the Chancellor of the Exchequer.

Jack looked at the editorial of the *British Gazette*, which ridiculed the strikers and claimed that the aim of the strike was to bring down the government and overthrow the constitution. "The people will never believe this rubbish," he said, handing the newspaper back.

"Some people will believe anything if it's in the paper. That's why we need to get our own one out. Hold tight, there's another bus on its way." He pointed to an AEC S-type bus with its open staircase at the back, protected by a policeman while a young man with a fledgling moustache and bright red cravat sat crouched over the steering wheel and moved funereally out of the depot. The union official walked over to join the pickets in their peaceful attempt to obstruct the progress of the bus.

Jack spent the rest of the day inspecting the picket lines and groups of dedicated union activists, thinking this would be as near as he was likely to get to the revolutionary barricades of Paris or Petrograd. He worked energetically all day and returned home that evening satisfied with his efforts.

Up early the following day, Jack repeated his tour and inspections as before and was pleased to see all the arrangements and picket lines were still in place and his union members were holding firm. When he went to the bus station there had been a strengthening of the police protection being given to the volunteer drivers, most of the buses having broken windows and wire netting installed where the windows had been. The transport union officials were disappointed that the Underground was managing to run some trains that morning. As the day wore on Jack became convinced the strikers had to prevent workers getting into the City if they were to be successful in bringing the economy to a halt. It was an ambition being frustrated by privateer transport operations joining the strike-breaking. There was, apparently, a local road haulage company in Lauriston Road which had, the day before, begun ferrying workers into the City. He discussed the options with his colleagues and readily agreed to help organise a group of strikers who would try to prevent this haulage company carry on its strike-breaking activities.

That evening he discussed the situation with William. Aware that William had no choice, as a member of staff in a non-unionised company, other than to fulfil his contractual duties, he did not expect him to play any part in the strike. It was not a question of loyalty; whatever the government might pretend, this was not a constitutional struggle but an industrial action in which William had no part. On the contrary, he was rather pleased that Bertram Drogo had taken a neutral stance in the matter, not attempting directly to undermine the activities of strikers.

William had had an uneventful, quiet day at the garage with regulars calling in for petrol but nothing going on in the workshop, except one tyre repair and a job fixing a radiator leak. He listened quietly while Jack outlined how the strike was going locally and his own part in it. "What are your plans tomorrow, Dad?" he asked.

"There's a local haulage firm running a sort of cattle truck bus service to the City. I'm hoping to make it as difficult as possible for them to keep going so the City workers will give up. We have to stop people getting to work otherwise the strike will not hold up."

"Can I help? I don't have to go to work tomorrow."

"Well, if you want to." Jack was visibly pleased.

The next morning at seven o'clock a posse of bus workers was rounded up at the bus station and they set out with Jack and William to cover the likely routes a lorry might take from its garage near Victoria Park. Jack split the strikers into three groups, each one positioned at a possible exit point onto Mare Street once the lorry had picked up its passengers. He and William led the group at the end of Victoria Park Road and there they waited. At about a quarter to eight they heard the slightly high-pitched whine of a lorry, in chocolate and cream livery, as it came along the road towards them. It had taken a circuitous route to pick up as many passengers at a shilling a time as it could before heading for the City. As the lorry approached the junction, the striking busmen linked arms and spread across the road while Jack and one of the strikers approached the vehicle. The driver, alert to the danger, immediately attempted to turn right, hoping to cut through to another route. But, realising it was a dead end he reversed out again to turn back up Victoria Park Road. Jack could see the bowler-hatted passengers standing in the back of the lorry, holding on to ropes used as hand straps. He ran round the lorry towards the front as the driver, panicking and unable to find a gear, finally found one and lurched forward, foot hard down on the accelerator. As he looked up, the driver saw with horror a man with his arms waving just before he ran over him. He jumped from his cab and ran to the front. "Jack, oh, Jack," he cried as he realised he knew the man lying before him with the marks of the wheel across his stomach.

William and the busmen were there in a few seconds and William knelt over his father and held his hand. "It's Billy, Dad. We'll get some help."

Jack's eyes were closed, but he opened them and William thought, and he wanted it to be so, that Jack smiled slightly.

"Let me through, please, I'm a doctor."

A man in a black jacket and grey pinstripes had appeared, presumably from the lorry, and was kneeling down on the other side of Jack. He held Jack's wrist and said, "Can you hear me?"

Jack's head moved slightly.

"We're calling an ambulance; it won't be long," said the doctor as he looked up at the crowd. Someone nodded and ran towards a telephone box at the end of the road.

The doctor opened his Gladstone bag and began to prepare a syringe. "Are you in much pain?"

"No pain. Tell driver not his fault," Jack said faintly, blood running from the corner of his mouth.

The doctor was feeling gently over Jack's body for signs of injury but after a few seconds he stopped and put his head to the injured man's chest and William gripped his father's hand harder. The doctor tried for a pulse again while the world stood still then he placed Jack's hand on his chest and stood up, removing his hat. The busmen removed their caps and the driver turned away and sobbed quietly into his hands.

"Are you a friend?" the doctor asked William.

"He's my father," said William, barely able to speak.

"I'm so dreadfully sorry I couldn't help him. He had severe internal injuries."

The sorrowful tableau dispersed: the passengers alighted from the lorry and walked a respectful distance before discussing their options; the strikers stood to attention, unexpectedly pallbearers for their fallen leader; the doctor placed his handkerchief over Jack's face and waited for the police and the ambulance to arrive. William walked over to the driver.

"It wasn't your fault, Amos." He put his arm round his friend's shoulder.

"I am so, so sorry. I wasn't looking; I just wanted to turn the lorry round. I am sorry, Billy." He broke away from William, rejecting any attempt at solace.

A policeman arrived and spoke to the doctor.

"How did it happen, sir?" he asked, taking out a pencil and notebook.

"I can't say. I was in the back of that lorry which was being used as a makeshift bus. The driver is over by the lorry. He's clearly shocked at what occurred."

"You'll kindly stay until the ambulance arrives, sir?"

"Of course."

The policeman walked over to the lorry where Amos stood, calmer now, though still obviously distraught.

"I need to take a statement from you, driver. Are you up to it, son?"

Amos nodded.

He took down Amos's full name and address and his employer's details. Next he examined Amos's driving licence. "Now, tell me in your own words what happened."

"I was driving along this road, Victoria Park Road, and saw a group of strikers spreading out across the street. I think they wanted to stop me turning into Mare Street."

"Why would they wish to do that?"

"Because I was carrying passengers and they wanted to stop buses getting through their picket lines."

"What did you do next?"

"To avoid any trouble I tried to change direction by turning right but then I realised that road is a dead end."

The policeman pointed. "That road?"

"Yes. So I reversed out of it again to go back the way I'd come. I suppose I panicked a bit, but I couldn't get into gear, and I looked down at the gear stick while I tried. I had the other foot on the accelerator so when I did finally get into gear and engage the clutch the lorry shot forward. I looked up and saw Mr Lyus, but it was too late and I hit him. I think the wheel went over him."

"There was no intention on your part to drive forward, knowing that Mr Lyus was there?"

"No, I wouldn't do that, especially not to him. I knew him and I liked him, he was the father of one of my best friends." Amos's voice broke a little and tears ran down his face.

William patted Amos on the shoulder. "I'm Mr Lyus's son and I know what he said is true. My father's last words were 'Tell driver not his fault.'"

The policeman nodded. "Thank you for that information, Mr Lyus." He entered William's statement in his notebook and turned to Amos again. "I don't think I need to detain you any longer. Just make sure you call in at the station in the next day or so to make a full statement otherwise you'll receive another visit from us. Leave the lorry here for now and collect it later when you are less shaken up."

Amos nodded to the policeman, expressed his sorrow to William once again and trudged slowly back to the garage, accompanied by a concerned passenger.

William watched as his father's body was taken to the ambulance and accepted the commiserations of the strikers before setting off home. He managed to go through the ordeal of telling his mother and watch her break down, console his bewildered grandmother, and, later, visit the mortuary and the undertaker, though the funeral would be delayed by both the strike action and the inevitable inquest.

Unsurprisingly, in the aftermath Jack was paid generous tributes by the unions, which held him up as a hero. Some went so far as to accord him something approaching the status of a martyr, a noble upholder of the rights of the working people mowed down by a pawn of capitalism. Later, the inquest would be conducted with sober rectitude, though the coroner, in finding for accidental death, pointed out quite firmly that Jack had not considered blame, let alone a malicious motive, should be attributed to Amos. He said that a man's last words, especially in matters of judgement, had always been treated with great solemnity and trust, and those who sought to use this case for political or propaganda purposes should respect his wishes. After the inquest William tried to speak to Amos, but his friend made a quick exit, speaking to no one.

The funeral was very well attended, not only by family and friends but also by union officials and members, notably the busmen who had marched with Jack and acted as pallbearers. Drogo was very understanding and told William not to come into work for the following week as he and Alfie could manage. William was grateful for this, as there seemed to be so much to do. Once all the tasks connected with his father's death had been dealt with and the funeral was over, his firm composure defrosted and the thaw of grief set in. Whatever the eulogies and tributes heaped on his father at this time, they would fade from memory, even in the minds of those who made them, when the strike was over and new preoccupations took centre stage. For his son, Jack would always be a hero and the inspiration for the values he held and aspired to. His sense of loss was immense and at the same time he knew his father's death had been meaningless, given what happened afterwards.

The general strike which had begun with such optimism barely lasted to the end of the following week. Stark statistics explain why the confidence was misplaced. Trade union membership in Britain had peaked at 8.3 million in 1920 and had been in decline since then, so there was barely more than half that number of union members in 1926. Having deliberately chosen to restrict the strike to industries in transport, printing, docks, iron and steel to avoid charges of a politically motivated strike, the TUC had the active support of only 1.7 million union members on strike. With nearly nine per cent of the working population unemployed and over eighteen million people still working in a workforce of over twenty million when the strike started, the TUC did not have the strength in numbers necessary to bring the economy to a standstill. The key area was public transport, and as each day of the strike passed, more and more buses and trains were running in London and throughout the country. By the beginning of the second week the strikers began returning to work in growing numbers and the TUC accepted defeat that Friday.

William didn't know the details, but as he watched the collapse of the strike he could not but believe his father's death had been in vain and he wanted someone to blame for it. Not Amos, who had panicked in a situation he couldn't control. Nor the striking trade unions, who had supported a noble cause but had been undermined by the circumstances. For him, the blame lay at the hands of the government, and particularly Winston Churchill. It was the government led by Stanley Baldwin which had insisted on making the strike a political issue with its claims that the strikers' aim was to overturn the constitution. It was Churchill with his inflammatory language in the *British Gazette* who was the key propagandist in the government. William was certain that it was because of Churchill that many middle- and upper-class people saw the strike as a threat to the government of the country and were motivated to volunteer on public transport to break the strike and save the constitution. This need to apportion blame gnawed away at William and gradually evolved into a vague desire for retribution, though he doubted he would ever see it materialise into action. For now, he noted the events of the strike and his conclusions about it in his journal.

On his return to work, William found Drogo as sympathetic and supportive as he had been at the time of his father's tragic death. "I am glad to have you back, William," he said, unusually referring to him by first name. "I know this has been a terrible time for you and the nature of your father's death while he was doing his duty must have made it doubly appalling for you. I hope you know that, whatever my view of the strike, I have nothing but the sincerest sympathy for what happened."

William nodded. "Thank you, Mr Drogo. I do appreciate your support during this time. It never crossed my mind that you would think other than you do about all this. I know it was just very bad luck and has not altered my attitude about anything." William didn't really believe that, but he genuinely liked Drogo and wanted to carry on working for him. In any case, he had little choice for now.

In the week after his father died, William had seriously considered a career move to something more in keeping with his father's values, working for a charity or the Co-operative movement or perhaps even for a trade union. But when he mentioned it to his mother she was not enthusiastic.

"William, we can't afford for you to try something else with less money after we've lost your father. You are the man of the house now. I can't go out to work; I've got your grandmother to care for. Neither of your father's brothers has offered to take her off my hands, so I just have to get on with it and so must you." As usual, she folded the cloth in her hands as a figurative sign of closing the matter.

In a way he knew she was right. He was the family breadwinner now and he must take his share of responsibility and he was willing to do that. But his mother did not make it an easy burden to carry. When he came home from work she expected him to share the care of his grandmother. "I have had it all day, clearing up after her and trying to make conversation," as she described it.

He began to feel awkward when he went out in the evening. Alice might say, "Out again? I wish I could go out, but someone has to sit in with your grandmother," or, "I have no company in the evenings; stuck in with no one to talk to. Still, you have a good time, but don't be too late in, I miss the company." It reached the stage that he was apologetic when he went out and sometimes turned down invitations, especially if he had already been out once that week. He fought against this feeling as he wanted to maintain his dwindling circle of friends. He hadn't seen Amos since the day of the accident and he saw Cyril less often too. When he asked why, Cyril apologised. "Sorry, Billy, but Amos can't face meeting with you at the moment, he feels so guilty. I think for the time being I ought to be trying to cheer him up."

XVII

INCREASINGLY, WILLIAM'S TIME WAS DEVOTED TO the world of motor racing, both at work and at leisure. He spent more time at the racing tracks, even during working hours, as one of the 'faces' of Bertram Drogo Motors, and there was an almost seamless link between his professional and pleasure activities. Once at the track he could always find a good reason to stay on after the racing had finished, talking to Drogo's friends and clients and members of the racing teams. It was at Brooklands on the 7th of August, the day of the first ever British Grand Prix, that he met Sylvia. He had planned as usual to go to the track with Stanley. However, his friend had a date early on in the evening so he had brought his motorbike for a quick getaway. William drove down and met him at the track.

There was a sense of excitement everywhere as a large crowd turned out to watch this historic event. All the entrants were in the colours of either France or Great Britain and the British drivers had a range of vehicles: Talbot, Bugatti, Aston Martin and Alvis as well as the private entries of J G Parry-Thomas and Frank Halford. William and Stanley looked out for Malcolm Campbell and Henry Segrave and were hoping to see Parry-Thomas race in his Thomas Special. The French

Talbots were painted in British racing green, to promote
Sunbeam, the British arm of their parent company.

The unpredictability of motor racing in that era was in
full force as there were several withdrawals before the race,
including both Thomas Specials, so only nine vehicles started.
It was a hot day and a number of the cars over-heated and
equally over-heated drivers were often replaced by a substitute
when they stopped in the pits. Due to various mechanical
failures, the numbers were whittled down and, after a race
lasting over four hours, only three cars finished: Delages in
first and third places, and the Bugatti of Malcolm Campbell
in second. The third-placed car was brought home by André
Dubonnet, dressed in a lounge suit. He had taken over after
the original driver, Benoist, was overcome by the heat in the
car. Malcolm Campbell was cheered at the chequered flag as
much as the winning team of Sénéchal and Wagner.

After the race and presentation, Stan went off on his
date and William, reluctant to go home and enjoying the
atmosphere and the late summer evening, had a drink and
observed the fanatics crowding round the cars. In the paddock
he watched the drivers and technicians as they held their post-
mortems on the racing and tinkered here and there to improve
this or moderate that for the next time.

"They're all so keen, aren't they?" A woman's voice
penetrated his reveries and he looked round to meet the eyes
of someone he'd seen before at the racing but never spoken to.
"I take it you are not quite so keen?"

William smiled. "No, I don't particularly like receiving a
cloud of exhaust fumes in my face or getting my hands dirty
unless I have to. I like driving and watching others drive, not
the mechanical side."

"How refreshing," she said, playing with long beads and
waggling a loaded cigarette holder in his general direction.

William produced his father's lighter and lit her cigarette.

"Thanks." She held out her hand. "I'm Sylvia Napier, how do you do?"

"How do you do? William Lyus."

"You don't smoke?" she said, a slight smile curling the corners of her mouth.

"No," he replied.

"Perhaps you're not old enough yet?"

He laughed and looked at his empty glass. "Would you like a drink?"

"Thank goodness you have some vices. Have you a car?"

"Yes."

"Let's get away from here for a while and have a drink somewhere more civilised."

"What about your..."

"My husband? Oh, he'll be fiddling about with his toys for ages and then... well, let's just say he can look after himself."

They walked out from the bar towards the car park. "Did you enjoy the race?" he asked.

"Yes, it was wonderful, and the drivers are so brave and resourceful. It's the unpredictability of it all that makes it so exciting; one minute a car seems certain to win then a problem occurs and they retire or spend ages in the pits. Then another looks the favourite and misfortune befalls them and on we go again. It's not much good being a skilled driver if the car conks out."

"Perhaps being able to nurse a car home is what counts, and that's a skill too."

"Good point," she said as William stopped by his car. "Very nice," she said. "I have been in one of these, different colour."

William was pleased he had brought the almost-new Sunbeam 14/40, a blue open-top two-seater with plenty of leg room and the appropriate cachet for a day at Brooklands.

She waited while he opened the door and then sat on the black leather bench seat, carefully arranging her short summer dress and making sure her hat was on tight.

"Had you anywhere in mind?" asked William.

"Well, there's that pretty little inn a couple of miles that way." She pointed to the right with her deep red nail-varnished index finger.

William knew the place; he'd been in there once or twice before with Stanley. Starting the car, he went off at a fair pace and they arrived at the inn in a few minutes. Sylvia slid against him as he turned in sharply and they both laughed.

They went into the saloon bar, ordered two gin and tonics, and sat in the window, stared at by an old collie. "Well, that's better," said Sylvia. She took off her hat, revealing her dark, waved hair, cut in a Charleston bob.

William looked at her. He had seen her with her husband, a balding, heavily set man of around forty, and guessed she was probably in her mid-thirties. She looked young enough to pass for under thirty, especially as she was dressed very much in the latest fashions. Beautiful and extremely elegant, she was, in just about every way he could think of, out of his league.

"Are you any relation to Montague Napier?" he asked, changing the subject on his mind.

"No, although my husband likes to think he is a distant cousin. He certainly doesn't disabuse people of the idea if they think he's something to do with cars and aeroplanes. I'm afraid my husband's family made its money in nothing nearly so exciting – walking sticks."

William laughed. "Just as important in their way."

Sylvia nodded and took out a cigarette, offering one to William, which he took, lit and left to smoke itself after one companionable puff.

"I've noticed you about on racing days. Are you connected with the racing business?" she asked.

"Only in the most tenuous way; I work for Bertram Drogo."

"Ah, I see. Doing what?"

"I'm the accountant of his garage business and I'm another available contact for clients on racing days." William wished he had something more interesting to offer but knew it was always best to be honest about one's status to avoid embarrassment later on. "That isn't my car outside, it belongs to the garage."

She nodded and smiled. "I don't own the car I drive either. It must be fun to drive different cars all the time, especially as Mr Drogo probably deals in rather sporty ones."

"Yes, it is, though sometimes they're quite a lot to handle. Same again?"

"Yes, let me get this one," she said, reaching for her handbag.

"No, thank you, it's fine," he said. When he had started work his mother had always taken the bulk of his wage packet and returned him some spending money for clothes and leisure activities. As his pay had risen faster than the cost of living, he had thought it not unreasonable to fail to inform her of some of his pay rises. This ensured that he could afford to entertain a girl when he wished to do so, rare occurrence though it was.

The conversation flowed, never drying up, and they had a third drink which Sylvia insisted on buying, passing the money to William surreptitiously before he ordered. They talked about their families. Sylvia was an only child, as William had been for most of his life, though unlike him she did not regret it. She described her father as a 'not particularly well-off' retired member of the colonial service who had been posted to several colonies including Grenada, Jamaica and Mauritius. She said her husband wouldn't dream of her going to work so, as she had no children, her day was often quite hard to fill. When she asked about his family and learned that he lived at home with his mother, she didn't have to ask if he was married. In any case, the conversation about his family swiftly turned to his father's death, for which she expressed great sorrow, taking his hand in hers, a gesture he admitted to himself he found thrilling. Afterwards, however, he wondered whether she saw him merely as a boy and was mothering him. Not that he cared; he was enjoying being with her.

Sylvia looked at her watch. "I'm sorry, William, but would you mind taking me back to Brooklands? My husband will be ready to leave now, I'm sure."

"Yes, of course. I'm sorry if I've made you late."

"Don't be silly." She touched his arm. "It's my fault, if anyone's."

Bidding goodnight to the landlord, William opened the bar door and followed Sylvia into the sunny evening and the smell of her perfume carried on the breeze. He drove more slowly on the return journey.

As they pulled into the nearly empty Brooklands car park she turned to him. "Thank you very much, William, for the drinks and your company."

"Thank you. I hope we can do it again some time."

"Me too." She smiled and walked nonchalantly towards the paddock while he sat in the car, unable to take his eyes off her.

On arriving at work the following week, William went straight to the calendar to look for the next Brooklands racing day, the last of the season, and inserted the date in his Letts diary. When the date came round, a few weeks later, he asked Alfie if he might take the lavender Lagonda 12-24 LC which had just been serviced prior to going on sale.

Alfie raised his eyebrows. "That's the boss's pride and joy at the moment. Are you sure?"

"Do it good to have a run out, I think."

Alfie shrugged. "I'll make sure it's ready for you tomorrow."

Absorbed by vague plans for the day, William had to consider what to do about Stanley. Unwilling to let down his friend, he arranged to go over to Swiss Cottage with Stan, resigned to the fact that he wouldn't be able to stay after the racing for very long. He consoled himself with the thought that Sylvia might not attend the races anyway. Nonetheless, as soon as they were at the track he found himself looking towards the area where Sylvia usually sat. Unable to see her, he concentrated his attention on a fine five hundred-mile race in which Drogo drove well, though was not highly placed due to a fault in the carburettor of his Alvis.

After the race, William and Stanley walked through the paddock and he saw Napier in a conversation with one of the drivers.

"Fancy a drink?" asked Stanley.

"What?" said William, who was thinking, *If he's here, she might be too.*

"Fancy a drink?"

"Oh, yes." He glanced around while they walked towards the bar, hearing Stanley talking but not listening to a word.

The bar was pretty full and they had to wait for some time to be served. They took their drinks outside and William saw Sylvia talking to a couple over by the paddock. It was cooler today and she was wearing a long-sleeved dress but still the large-brimmed hat she had worn before.

"Great race today," said Stanley. "One or two new drivers breathing down the necks of the veterans. Pity Drogo's car played up."

"Yes." William was staring at Sylvia, but she did not turn round.

"Glad I didn't put a couple of bob on him."

"Yes."

"I suppose we ought to make a move soon, I've got a date with Lily tonight."

"Yes."

Just then Sylvia turned, looked towards the bar and waved when she saw William, who waved back. She finished her conversation with the couple and walked towards him.

"Do you know her? She's very attractive," said Stanley.

"Yes, she's married to one of the people who put up the money."

"Good evening," she said, smiling at them.

William touched his hat. "Good evening, Mrs Napier. This is my good friend Stanley Mason."

"How do you do, Mr Mason?"

"How do you do?" replied Stanley.

"Did you enjoy the racing?" she asked.

"Yes, it was excellent," answered William. "I hope Mr Napier's favourite did well."

"Yes, I think so."

"Are you on the way to the bar? If so, I'd be pleased to escort you," said William. He was conscious that Stanley's head shot round with a look of amused surprise.

"Actually, I was going to ask you if you would mind awfully doing me a very big favour."

"Oh, if I can I'll be glad to."

"Well, my husband is going to be tied up for ages and I thought if you are going into town you might be kind enough to drop me off at my flat. You see, I have an appointment to keep early evening."

"Well, I'd be glad to. We were just leaving anyway, weren't we, Stan?"

"Er, yes."

They walked over to the Lagonda. "Another very nice car," said Sylvia as William opened the rear door for her.

"Where do you want to go?"

"Portman Square, if you would be so kind."

"Will you be all right for time if I go via Hackney?"

"Yes, there'll be plenty of time."

"I'll drop you off first, Stan," he said, as they set off.

"Won't that be out of your way?" asked Stan.

"Saves you having to wait while we go to Portman Square and then on to Swiss Cottage, before we go home."

"Well, if you're sure." Stanley sat back in his seat as the car sped through the Surrey suburbs.

Traffic was light and they took the A3 through south London until they branched off for Tower Bridge and on through Whitechapel to Hackney and Homerton. When they arrived at Templar Road, William stopped only long enough for him and Stanley to say their goodbyes before he set off for Marylebone. They'd gone barely two hundred yards before Sylvia tapped him on the shoulder. "Stop," she said, leaning forward.

William stopped the car and got out. "Is anything the matter?"

"No," she said. As he opened the door she jumped out and joined him in the front, their bodies touching on the bench seat as she climbed in. "That's better, you're not my chauffeur."

They set off again, William trying to ignore the closeness of her body but finding it difficult to concentrate on anything else.

"I'm glad I spotted you," she said.

"Yes, I thought you weren't there."

"You looked for me?"

"Yes." He coloured a little. "What would you have done for a lift if you hadn't seen me?"

"Oh, I'd have managed."

William was left silent, slightly disappointed that he was not regarded as irreplaceable. In just over twenty minutes they pulled up in Portman Square.

"Would you like to come in for a drink?" she asked as he opened her door.

"I thought you had an appointment in the early evening."

"I have: with you."

They went up to her flat on the third floor. Sylvia turned the key in the lock and the door swung open to reveal a square hall or lobby in which was a console table and off which were several doors. William barely had time to look around before she opened the double doors facing them and he was astonished by the image which confronted him. This living room was so much larger than he had expected, and the furnishings and decoration were like nothing he'd ever seen before in the flesh. The decor reminded him of some of the sets he'd seen in American films at the pictures. He gazed around at the gold and black of the frieze round the top of the walls with its theme reminiscent of ancient Egypt, the vivid patterns of the fabric covering the square furniture, the glass objets d'art and nude statues in ebony, the rich carpets on a beautiful wooden floor, and the iron and copper grill which served as an ornate screen for separating one part of the room from another. There were two different sets of sofas, one round the large marble fireplace and the other over by the window, a baby grand piano, a desk, a bar and several occasional chairs.

"What a lovely room," he said.

"I'm glad you like it." She took off her hat and threw it onto a chair.

"Is the whole flat decorated like this?"

"Yes," she said. "What would you like to drink?"

"I'll have whatever you're having, please."

She walked over to the bar in the corner of the room and mixed them two cocktails. "Chin-chin, William," she said, and raised her glass a little.

"Cheers," he replied, and raised the brownish orange drink to his lips. "I like this very much, what is it?"

"It's a whizz-bang." She laughed. "Silly name, isn't it?"

"I can taste the Scotch and some sort of vermouth, but there's something else."

"Perhaps it's the absinthe."

"Absinthe!"

She laughed again. "Just a couple of dashes."

William was afraid of appearing gauche in this intimidating setting and was pleased that his knowledge of alcoholic drinks, which had matured under the tutelage of Drogo and Thornycroft, could now hold its own in the world of cocktails.

She walked over to an elegant red and gold-covered sofa. "Come and sit next to me." She patted the seat as she sat down.

He took his seat next to her, almost overwhelmed by the scent of the Guerlain perfume, although he had no idea what it was, and the sense of her presence, despite the gap between them.

She took a cigarette from the box before her and he lit it with the table lighter which nestled in what looked like a glass discus. To have rubbed shoulders with people like her had itself been an experience worth retelling, but to be in this flat as the guest of this woman was something he had only dreamed of, in fact had not dared to dream of. He looked around the room, without actually seeing anything, to avoid staring at her.

"You're very quiet. Are you all right?"

"Yes, I'm just admiring your taste." Seizing on something to illustrate his statement, he pointed to a picture which appeared to be of Greek architecture with an unreal perspective. "Is that an original?"

"The de Chirico? Yes, I like him very much; I've another one in the dining room."

"I like it, but I don't quite understand it; real objects but not in a real world."

"It's surrealism. I'm glad you like it, you have good taste."

William smiled. He thought she was being kind as he knew nothing about art whatsoever. He finished his cocktail and put the glass on the table.

"Shall we have another?" she asked, reaching over to pick up his glass.

"I don't want to impinge on your evening."

"Not at all. Roger won't be home for ages and I have nothing planned."

"All right then, thank you." He didn't really want a drink, but he was in no hurry to go.

She poured two more whizz bangs and brought them over, this time with maraschino cherries on cocktail sticks. They toasted each other again and sat down on the sofa, this time a little closer. William asked about the decor in the room and Sylvia told him of a trip to Paris the previous year. She had gone to the International Exhibition of Modern Decorative and Industrial Arts and become very interested in art deco. On returning to London she had persuaded Roger to allow her to transform their apartment in this style.

"So all this is new?"

"Not all of it; the piano and the pictures I already had and a few pieces of furniture. But all the decoration and most of the furniture I acquired since the exhibition. I do so like the look: modern but with classical touches. It's very in vogue."

"In vogue?"

"The finding of Tutankhamun's tomb and the whole

business of Egyptology has had a big impact on fashion in recent years, and it seems to complement modern design, don't you think?"

"Yes, I suppose so; I never really thought about it before. I do like the modern designs and streamlined looks coming through in cars and trains and aeroplanes."

"Well, there you are. I have seen Segrave's new car, the Sunbeam, the one he's hoping to set a new land speed record with. It's streamlined and modern, perhaps even futuristic, and its style fits in so well with art deco." She smiled as she thought of it and William thought that perhaps she was more interested in motor racing than she pretended to be.

"I think I should be going," he said.

"Oh. Must you? What a pity." She stood up and he did the same, disappointed that she did not try to delay his departure. "Where did we put your hat?" she said, looking round the room.

"I left it in the car."

"Ah, yes. Well, that's pretty much the end of the motor-racing season; I shall miss our little chats."

"So will I." He walked towards the door.

"You must come over for dinner one day, or perhaps lunch."

"Yes."

"May I have your card?"

He took out his wallet and handed her his business card. She looked at it for a moment. "Well, goodbye." She shook his hand.

"Goodbye, Mrs Napier."

"Sylvia," she corrected. "Goodbye," and she closed the door behind him.

William walked down the thickly carpeted steps, acknowledged the porter's call of "Goodnight, sir" and wandered over to the Lagonda for the drive back to the garage.

It was after eight o'clock by the time he'd parked the car in one of the lockups, placed the keys in his own desk drawer and set off for home.

"Where have you been?" said his mother, as he walked through the front door.

"At the motor racing, as I told you I would be." He hung his hat up in the hall. "What's the matter?" he added, noticing his mother's drawn expression.

"Grandma's had a bad fall down the stairs; the doctor is sure it's a broken hip. She's in the Hackney. It doesn't look good."

"I'll go to see her tomorrow. We could go together."

"Not that she'll know you. Doesn't see you often enough."

They visited his grandmother the following day. When they arrived for the long Sunday-afternoon visiting session they found her asleep. She was in one of the new airy pavilions, in a Nightingale ward, with a very high ceiling and opposing windows to allow for a through draft of fresh air. Each metal-framed bed had a locker on one side and a chair on the other.

As soon as he saw her, William thought she looked suddenly very tiny, only her white-haired head above the sheet, folded over the counterpane, her face shrunken even more by the absence of her false teeth. Alice sat down in the chair near the bed and William took his grandmother's hand, which felt cold and virtually lifeless. He spoke to her, but she didn't open her eyes, and he wondered if he would ever hear her speak again. He sought out the ward sister, who, in response to his questions, said his grandmother was quite weak and the surgeon was not sure she would come through an operation at present. She was being kept under observation for now.

He returned to her bedside and held her hand again. Somebody had told him that hearing is the last faculty to be lost. "Hello, Grandma. Are you all right? Can you hear me?"

She opened her eyes and smiled. "Hello, Jack," she said. "I'm all right, son." Then she closed her eyes.

She went gently downhill a little more each day and visiting time was spent in silence as she slept right through it. She died three days later and the funeral followed the next week. William reflected that his church attendances seemed always to be for funerals. He couldn't remember the last time he'd gone for any other reason. It was almost the only time now that he met his uncles Bob and Ted and their wives or his other relatives.

At home afterwards, when everyone else had left, his mother changed from her black dress into something less severe and William thought it a symbolic gesture, liberation from responsibility and looking forward to the future.

"You'll have a lot more free time now, Mum. A chance to do more of the things you've not been able to do lately."

She shook her head. "I shall miss your grandmother very much."

"Yes, I understand that, so will I. I just meant your time will be more your own."

"I'm forty-seven, a bit over the hill to start a new life. All I'm good for is looking after the house and you. That's my job now."

William felt she was inviting a response, but he refrained from giving one. He thought of going out, but he didn't do that either.

That weekend he was supposed to be going to a dance with Leonard and Leonard's friend Gordon, but he felt uncomfortable about it; was he supposed to be in mourning? After mulling it over for a time, he found himself unable to resist broaching the subject with Alice the morning of the dance.

"Well, it's entirely up to you, Billy. If you can still enjoy going to a dance just a few days after poor Grandma was laid to rest I don't suppose she would mind."

"But you don't mind?"

"Nothing to do with me. I shan't be enjoying myself, but don't let that stop you."

William did go to the dance but didn't actually do any dancing, thinking that an appropriate gesture out of respect for Grandma. While Leonard and Gordon were on the floor with various young women, he chatted with Charlie Bond, a former neighbour of his from Daubeney Road. Charlie said he had 'an inbuilt aversion to anything to do with moving in time to music' and was only there to escort his sister and take her home afterwards. Charlie enjoyed a few pints and William, in keeping up with him, had rather more than usual and was glad that his mother had gone to bed by the time he arrived home. The next morning she asked him how he had enjoyed the dance.

"I didn't actually do any dancing. I felt I ought to go as I'd told Leonard I would, but I didn't feel much like dancing, what with Grandma and everything."

"I should think so too. I had a miserable evening myself, thinking about Grandma, and your father as well. It's been a terrible year. The days will only get lonelier now."

"You have your friends."

"But in the evening, with you out and about."

"I don't go out very much; I've sometimes not accepted an invitation to go out to keep you company. Anyway, we could go out together, to the pictures or the music hall or a pub with a lounge bar."

"It's not becoming for a lady to go to a pub."

"Well, don't say I didn't ask you." He picked up the newspaper and turned to the cricket scores.

XIX

Trade was very busy at Bertram Drogo Motors, and at the Swiss Cottage headquarters it became increasingly obvious that William could not undertake alone all his office duties because of his other commitments. So he was given the assistance of a receptionist-cum-secretary, a young woman of about twenty, Mary Baker. She sat in a reconfigured front office and answered the telephone, greeted visitors and did all of the secretarial duties for both Drogo and William.

One morning the telephone rang and William leant over to answer it, stopping himself when he remembered that Mary took all the calls now. She buzzed through a few seconds later. "Mrs Napier for you, Mr Lyus."

After a few opening pleasantries, Sylvia said, "I meant to get in touch before. Would you like to come to a dinner party at the flat?"

William's first thought was one of excitement, but there was also a tinge of apprehension. "Well, that's kind of you, but I don't know any of your friends."

"That doesn't matter. Would you like to bring a lady companion?"

"I don't think so."

"That's fine, just asking to make the numbers right. Is your diary handy?"

"Yes."

"We're looking at Thursday, 14th October, say seven for drinks?"

William hesitated; the evening was clear, but sometimes he was kept late at the garage. After a pause he replied. "Yes, I think that will be fine, I just need to check something. I'll ring you by tomorrow if I can't make it. Is that all right?"

"Yes, of course. Hope to see you on the 14th. Bye."

The opportunity of seeing Sylvia again triumphed over a slight apprehension and he looked forward with rising anticipation to the date of the dinner party. When at last the day arrived, he left work early to give himself time to change. Once home, he put on his new, as yet unworn, bespoke dark grey pinstripe suit from Collison and Coleman, a tailor he couldn't really afford. With a burgundy tie and gold pin he felt he looked rather good and even his mother complimented him on his appearance as he left the house.

"I hope you have a good time, William," she said. "It's good to mix with a better class of people. After all, our family was once of a higher class; my grandfather's second cousin was a Queen's Counsel."

William took the train into the City and then the Underground to Marylebone. He was a little late due to a holdup on the line but finally arrived just after ten past seven. He rang the doorbell and was surprised to see the door opened by a maid.

"Good evening, sir," she said, taking the flowers he'd brought and his hat. "What name is it?"

"Lyus, William Lyus."

She opened the double doors and announced, "Mr William Lyus."

William nodded to the maid and marched into the room. Three men and four women looked in his direction. Sylvia smiled and came over to him.

"Hello, William, so glad you could come."

William's expression was frozen in a half-smile by the sight of the three men; they were all wearing dinner suits. At once, the mask of savoir-faire that he had carefully built up in preparation for this evening cracked.

"I'm sorry, I didn't think about the suit," he muttered as he took her hand in his now limp, damp paw.

"Oh, that's all right, my fault. I should have mentioned 'black tie'. Come and meet everyone."

He traipsed behind her as they walked over to the bar area.

"May I introduce William Lyus, a colleague of Bertram Drogo, whom I met by chance at Brooklands. He kindly gave me a lift home when Roger was held up after the racing and I had to get back to town. First, the couple: Monty and Fiona Benstock." She gestured to a tall, sombre-looking man of about fifty with dark hair and a matching military moustache and a slightly old-fashioned, if well-dressed, woman with mousy hair who smiled broadly.

Next, Sylvia introduced a friendly-looking man in his early thirties with his fair hair in a slightly rakish style, whom William recognised as Roland Punter, one of the drivers from Brooklands. He was standing next to a rather ostentatiously dressed woman in her early thirties, with a plunging neckline dress, strong make-up and jet-black hair topped off with a headband sporting a feather. She was introduced as Mrs Janet Blenkinsop, a friend of Sylvia's. Then there was a younger woman of about William's age named Tillie Clark, who was also dressed very fashionably but less dramatically than Mrs Blenkinsop. Finally, there was Roger Napier, who smiled and said he thought he'd seen William at Brooklands and was grateful William had got Sylvia home on time.

"Thanks very much, old boy. I'm afraid the time runs away with me when I'm chatting to Roland here or one of the other drivers."

As the drinks and the conversation flowed, William could not help but feel self-conscious about his being under-dressed. His accent, though modified over the years, still grated slightly, to himself if no one else, when he responded to the cut-glass accents of the other guests. Just as his equanimity was returning, he was approached by Monty Benstock.

"Haven't seen you around much," he said, finishing off his 'Old Fashioned' and holding out the glass, assuming somebody would replenish it. "Are you a friend of Roger's or Sylvia's?"

"I don't know either of them very well."

"Why no black tie, old boy? No time to change?"

"Er, no," he lied, and could feel himself blush.

Benstock smiled in a knowing, slightly supercilious way but did not pursue the matter. "So what do you do exactly?"

"I am the accountant and office manager of Bertram Drogo Motors."

"Ah, trade. At least you don't have to get your hands dirty, I presume."

William wanted to grin and treat it as banter, but not even a flicker of a smile could push through his expression of discomfort. "What about you?"

"What about me what?"

"What do you do for a living?"

Benstock laughed. "A good question; I dabble in this and that. Where's my refill?" He looked around for the waitress. "What's happened to the girl?" he added, seemingly oblivious to the fact that Napier had been serving the drinks himself.

The host brought over a refill for Benstock and William and joined them both.

"So how did you get to know young Lyus here?" asked Benstock.

"Through Sylvia. You met at Brooklands, didn't you?" he said to William.

"Yes."

"Amazing the different types one meets at Brooklands," observed Benstock. "Not a bad suit, though." He touched the hand-stitching on William's lapel.

"Yes, a nice suit," agreed Napier, and they smirked at each other.

William could tell that they were engaged in some kind of private joke, though he was sure he would never be party to it or even quite understand it. They made a couple of other what seemed to William odd remarks and then Benstock asked Napier about a rumour he'd heard in the City and William took the opportunity to seek out someone else to talk to.

He turned round to face the slightly startling appearance of Janet Blenkinsop, who was holding a long drink with the dark pink hue of a Singapore Sling.

"Hello again." She smiled, her long eyelashes fluttering slightly. "So you are in the Brooklands set?"

William smiled wanly. "I do go to Brooklands quite often."

"Are you an aspiring racing driver?"

"Not exactly. I watch rather than do."

"Ah well, we can't all be good at everything. Personally, I prefer only to engage in activities where I can do it myself."

"Such as?"

"That would be telling," she said, and leaned over to take a cigarette from the box on the bar counter, William having difficulty averting his gaze from the plunging neckline.

William lit her cigarette and, contemplating her last

enigmatic statement, thought this conversation might prove to be just as tricky as the one with Benstock. As she puffed on her cigarette in the long holder and sipped her drink, he tried to take the measure of her. He thought she must be about the same age as Sylvia, maybe a little older, and had opted for the vamp look, presumably to attract men. While he thought her certainly attractive, in a scary way, he doubted he could meet her expectations and anyway, where was her husband?

"Have you known Sylvia long?" he asked, aware that she was sizing him up too.

She raised her eyebrows. "Absolutely ages; we came out together in 1920, the first proper season after the war. We've been friends ever since."

William was struggling to find anything else to say and, hearing the orchestra of Paul Whiteman in the background from a fine gramophone, said, "I like Paul Whiteman's band very much."

She listened for a moment, but he could tell she wasn't particularly interested. "Yes, there's lots of good dance music today."

They were both victims of small talk and were relieved when the maid's voice was heard calling them to come in for dinner. Everybody trooped into a much smaller room, also decorated in the art deco fashion with black skirting boards, architraves and picture rails, and furniture with a chrome and mirrored theme. The table, laid for eight, had space for ten or perhaps twelve, so they were not limited for room as they took their seats. William found himself at the lower end of the table, between Sylvia at the end to his right and Tillie on his left. He held the seat for Tillie and she smiled at him as she sat down. The positioning of the guests confirmed his suspicion that Tillie had been chosen as someone he could relate to, at least in terms of age. He was not exactly pleased to see Benstock opposite him and hoped that either the charm of Sylvia or the zest of Janet would keep him busy.

Eight is an interesting number at a table, on the edge of being able to maintain a conversation inclusive of all, though more likely to break into smaller groups. Yet it permits everyone to hear the conversation of anyone else at the table, should they have a mind to. William stole a look at Sylvia, who was being charming to Benstock, and then turned to Tillie. Like the other women, she was wearing an evening dress, hers a similar style to daywear but longer in the skirt and with a beaded adornment on the fine material. She was pretty and seemed very friendly. She began the first course and looked at him.

"We didn't get much of a chance to speak over drinks. Tell me about yourself."

William hated talking about himself. He always felt he was being interviewed and consequently searched his mind for something very interesting or at least unusual that he had done or had happened to him. But the unusual events in his life, the loss of his sister, the Bottomley business, the nature of his father's death, were not the sort of events he would relate to a stranger.

"Well, I am twenty-two and I work for Bertram Drogo, the racing driver, as the accountant at his garage. I live in Hackney, more precisely Homerton, with my widowed mother. I like motor racing, football and cricket, and am interested in political philosophy." He looked at her face. She was slightly frowning as her eyes flickered while she appeared to struggle to find something to say in response.

"Hackney, isn't that a dangerous place? Don't you have to be careful when you go out at night?"

William laughed. "I've never found it dangerous. Perhaps I'm one of those that people are scared of."

Tillie stared at him for a second then realised he was joking. "Sorry, one hears such silly things about the East End and so on."

"I'd be reluctant to let my daughter go there alone," intervened Benstock. "If you are born into it you probably wouldn't notice."

Tillie half smiled, but Benstock did not return the smile and she tried to lighten the mood. "I presume you count as a cockney then?"

William was not enjoying this conversation but went through his standard response to a question he'd been asked many times. "I suppose so, though strictly speaking you should be born within the sound of Bow bells and I was not. Homerton is too far north, unless you have extremely good hearing." Out of the corner of his eye he could see Benstock watching and smiling humourlessly at their rather odd conversation.

Tillie turned back to her pâté and looked at Fiona Benstock to her left, but she was deep in conversation with Roger Napier.

"How do you know Sylvia and Roger?" asked William.

Tillie looked back to him. "My father is a friend and colleague of Roger; they are both directors of 'Napier and Blackwood'."

"Do you work for the family firm?"

She screwed up her features in mock horror. "No, thank you; I work for Cintra."

"What do they do?"

"It's a fashion house."

"That must be very interesting. Are you involved in making the dresses?"

"No, I'm on the publicity and representation side of the business. They wouldn't let me near a pair of scissors."

William smiled. He found it more comfortable talking about her. "What is Tillie short for?"

"Matilda, but I don't ever use my proper name; it makes me feel so old."

William thought Tillie amusing and entertaining and would have been quite happy to talk to her all evening were it not for Sylvia, who was the only reason he was here at all and was the only person he was really interested in. He looked over at her and their eyes met. She smiled and asked both the young people if everything was to their liking and then seized the moment to talk to William while Tillie turned her attention to Fiona Benstock.

"Thanks for coming this evening. I'm sure you could have found something more interesting to do."

"No, I wouldn't rather be anywhere else. Thank you for inviting me; lots of interesting people and a very good dinner." He was aware that Benstock was listening to them and smiled at him until Benstock looked away. Their conversation could not be private, so William asked about the wine they were drinking and made some complimentary comments about the food. They soon tired of careful chatter and Sylvia brought Benstock into the conversation by asking him about the state of the economy and the stock market.

After dinner, the women went off to the drawing room and William was left with the three other men, a bottle of port and a box of cigars. Napier and Benstock hogged the conversation with a discussion about the Gilts market and the investment outlook. William was silent, feeling out of his depth and that his very presence here was no more than a charade. Their conversation turned to the economy and they berated the trade unions and made disparaging remarks about the worth and expectations of the working classes, especially the miners.

William bit his tongue for some time but eventually could contain himself no longer. "The miners have had their pay cut several times since the war; how many times have you had your pay cut in the last few years?"

Benstock smiled. "Ah, an apologist for the working class. Hardly helps their cause if their solution is to bring the economy to a halt."

"They felt they had no choice," said William.

"I think it shows what the general strike was really about: an attempt by the radical socialist leaders of the working class to seize power and overthrow the constitution," said Napier, pouring himself another glass of port.

"Neither the Labour Party nor the TUC supported constitutional change," said William.

"There was a lot of propaganda going on," said Punter, reaching over for the port.

"It was still a class struggle and the working class lost." Benstock smiled.

"It was not about class; it was about justice," William said, feeling his anger rising.

"What a load of tommyrot," said Napier.

"Well, the King didn't think so," said Punter, silencing the other three. "I was reliably told he remarked to somebody, 'Try living on their wages before you judge them.'"

That brought the debate to an abrupt end, and Benstock and Napier resumed their discussion about the stock market.

Roland Punter winked at William and started chatting about the latest trends in motor racing. He was particularly excited by the developing rivalry between Malcolm Campbell and Henry Segrave to break the world land speed record of Parry-Thomas and his car 'Babs'. Eventually, this conversation attracted the attention of the other two and Roland was asked about his recent racing record. He downplayed his own success and entertained all three of them with amusing stories about motor racing and the people in it. For the first time that evening William relaxed, drank a few glasses of port and let the conversation flow around him until they decided to join the women. William turned down the offer of making up a fourth for bridge as he hadn't a clue how to play the game and instead listened to Janet play the piano and give very decent renditions of 'Always', 'Do Do Do' and 'Baby Face', insisting on making him the focus of her attention while singing the last, much to his embarrassment. When she then played some Chopin, he was able to talk a little to Sylvia while Roland was engrossed in a copy of Philips' *Atlas of World History*, and the Benstocks, Napier and Tillie played a few rubbers.

At about ten thirty the party began to break up and William was one of the first to leave as he wanted to make sure he could get his travel connections. Roland Punter left at the same time, telling William he didn't want to be the only young man around while Janet was on the prowl.

William laughed. "I know what you mean. Do you know her well?"

"Not really, not as well as I know Sylvia, obviously."

"You have known her a long time?"

"For some time; she's quite a girl, great parties, very obliging."

"Yes," said William.

He was still mulling over Roland's last remark when they stopped at a parked Bentley and Roland offered him a lift into town.

They talked about Brooklands and other racetracks on their journey to the station and when he dropped William at Broad Street Roland asked, "Have you ever been round Brooklands? On the track, I mean?"

William shook his head. "No."

"Give me your card and we'll have a go one day next week, now that racing's finished. I'll call you when it's all arranged." He waved to William as he shot off, back to his flat in Bloomsbury.

When he arrived home William's mother was waiting up for him and asked him all about the evening. He gave her the edited highlights and she thought the whole evening had been a great success and recommended he cultivate this entrée into the 'world of the wealthy with its evening soirées and grand dinners', as she put it.

"Fancy you mixing with people who have servants and the ladies retire after dinner and all that."

"Fancy," said William.

WILLIAM WROTE TO SYLVIA THANKING HER FOR A most enjoyable evening at her dinner party. By return of post he received an invitation to lunch with her alone at her apartment the following week, which he promptly accepted. Not wishing to be tight for time, he arranged to take the afternoon off and arrived at Sylvia's apartment a few minutes early. The door was opened by Sylvia herself.

"No maid today?"

"It's her afternoon off. Just a light lunch today; I hope you don't mind."

"Not in the least," he said. He found the situation so much more relaxed than at the dinner party. They knew each other well enough now for the conversation to flow easily and they had many areas of common interest. They talked about the dinner party the previous week and Sylvia was very amusing with her comments about Janet and the Benstocks, especially Monty.

"He is a bore and at times a boor as well. What about Tillie? She's a nice girl."

"Yes, I liked her and we got on well, but I think she was surprised that someone as common as me could hold a knife and fork properly."

Sylvia laughed, exposing her perfect teeth, and William thought how much he loved seeing her laugh.

"She was meant to be your potential flirt for the evening, but I'm glad she wasn't too big a hit. What about Roland?"

"We got on very well and I liked talking to him about motor racing. He's invited me to Brooklands for a run round the circuit on Friday."

"What fun; I envy you."

"Why don't you come too?"

"I'd love to, but it might look a bit odd."

"Why? Roland said lots of nice things about you after the party so he would be glad to see you, I'm sure."

"He might wonder what the two of us are doing together."

"He said you were very obliging, what did he mean by that?"

For the first time since he'd known her, Sylvia seemed less than totally composed. She coloured a little and took a cigarette, which William lit for her. She inhaled deeply. "How should I know what he meant? I believe the dictionary definition would be 'helpful' or something like that. Why so many questions? I assume you found the party rather irritating."

Still with questions in his head, William chose not to go on. "Not really but, to be honest with you, I didn't feel I fitted in."

"Oh, really, I thought you did rather well. Surely, no one was unpleasant to you, apart from Monty, perhaps, and he's unpleasant to everyone when he feels like it."

"It's not that. I live in a different world to your friends: debutantes, the stock market, country houses and servants. It's not like anything I've ever experienced."

"It's my world too, William."

"I know, but when we are on our own I forget that."

"You poor boy, I meant for you have a nice time."

"I did have a nice time but, you know."

The brief moment of agitation forgotten by both of them, she sat down next to him. "Well, we're on our own today and I'll make it up to you." She put his glass down and kissed him gently on the lips. "Let's have some lunch!"

They went into the dining room, where a table was laid with a buffet of cold salmon and chicken. A bottle of Chablis was waiting in an ice bucket. The lunch was what William knew it would be: amusing conversation which never seemed to run out, excellent food and wonderful wine. Afterwards they returned to the drawing room for coffee and more drinks, and as they sat on the sofa together he wished every day could be like this and he told her so.

She smiled. "You are sweet, William. We'll have lots of days like this: a friendship of just us two." She patted him on the hand and kissed him again, this time not so chastely and he wanted more, but dismissed the temptation.

"When shall I see you next?" he asked, moving away from her a little.

She smiled. "Do you like art?"

"Well, yes, though I don't know much about it." He thought about the picture in Homerton library of an old woman walking along a pretty lane with trees and chocolate box cottages, the only oil painting he'd ever looked at closely. He thought the name was 'Sunnyside Terrace' or something like that.

"Why don't we go to the National Gallery one afternoon and have tea afterwards?"

"Yes, I'd like that."

William took Friday off with the blessing of Drogo, who hoped he enjoyed the experience and asked to be remembered to Roland. He met Roland at the course at around ten o'clock and found him in the pits with a mechanic, fine-tuning his Bentley.

"Hello, William, glad you could make it. Do you know Harry?" He nodded towards the mechanic.

"Only by sight. Hello, Harry."

The mechanic nodded and resumed his work.

"Soon be ready. We're just souping her up so she can go through her paces," said Roland.

Ten minutes later, Roland eased the Bentley to the starting line of the circuit and then they were off, the engine picking up from a deep purr to a throaty roar as Roland took the car through the gears. The speed was over eighty miles an hour by the time they were on the banked part of the circuit. William had never travelled at such a speed, but as the wind in his face took his breath away his feelings were of exhilaration untroubled by fear, even when some of the bends came up so fast it seemed impossible to take them. Round the circuit they went for eight laps, each lap faster than the last, shouting their comments to each other over the background noise, until finally they slowed down and cruised towards the pits.

"That was fantastic," said William as they came to a halt.

"Would you like a go?"

"Really? Well, I'd love to."

They swapped seats and off they went again, Roland occasionally giving advice on taking corners and choice of gears but otherwise leaving matters to William. The racing-track novice made no effort to imitate the driving of Roland, content instead to experience the thrill of speed and the excitement of the course at a more sedate pace for half a dozen laps.

"Thank you so much, that was a wonderful experience," said William as he jumped from the car and shook Roland's hand. "Can I buy you lunch?"

"Thank you, yes. I'll just have a word with Harry." He walked over to where Harry was tidying up in the pits and put some money in his hand.

They went to the inn where William and Sylvia had first shared a drink and had a relaxing hour reminiscing about the highlights of the motor-racing season and Roland's ambitions for the following year. Roland outlined his plans, including weeks on the French Riviera in Cannes, Nice and Monte Carlo, and trips to Biarritz, Rome, Milan, Paris and elsewhere, all strategically aligned with his various racing commitments. He told William all this in a matter-of-fact way without the slightest hint of bragging. As he listened, William thought that, much as he got on well with Roland and knew him to be a decent man, the reality of their lives was so far apart that true friendship was hardly practicable. Roland offered to share the bill but did not insist when William would have none of it.

William very much enjoyed his trip to the National Gallery with Sylvia, especially the Pre-Raphaelite paintings, which rekindled in him his affection for the bowdlerised tales of King Arthur, and the Knights of the Round Table, which he had read as a boy. His renewed enthusiasm was such that afterwards he read Mallory's *Le Morte d'Arthur* for the first time and realised what flawed heroes Arthur, Lancelot and the others actually were. He hoped his relationship with Sylvia would be the chivalrous, unsullied love that those knights had aspired to.

As the weeks and months passed, they saw something of each other more or less every week, sometimes in Sylvia's flat but usually on an outing, cocooned from the different worlds they inhabited and avoiding any discussion of their relationship. In February, William considered sending Sylvia a Valentine's card but wasn't sure she would welcome it. She invited him for lunch that day and he took her some flowers as an alternative gesture to a card. Only ten days before, Malcolm Campbell had broken the world land speed record in his Napier-

Campbell 'Bluebird' and she said that Roger was basking in the reflected glory associated with the name. William could see Roger's point of view as he was himself enjoying a similar feeling, having actually *met* Malcolm Campbell and knowing someone in the motor-racing fraternity who bore the name Napier.

They had a long, languid lunch and sat together on the sofa, their arms round each other as they kissed.

"You know you can have me if you want to," she said, her head on his chest, her hand on his leg.

"I do want to, but I can't." He let go of her and she moved away a little.

"Don't feel bad about Roger; he has a colourful life of his own."

"It's not about him; it's how I want to feel about myself and about you."

She shook her head and smiled. "A man of principle; just my luck."

"If you left Roger it would be different."

"You want me to leave him and what, go to live with you?"

He nodded. "We could marry."

"William, you are a sweet boy, but you are such an ingénue. How can that possibly happen? Even if I were prepared to give up everything I have now, it would have to be *me* divorcing Roger; the alternative would be too awful. Either way it would be messy, particularly if our names appeared in the *News of the World*. Then what would we be? You struggling to keep me in the manner to which I am accustomed and probably resenting it, and me dreading the day when you realise that you are still a young man and the woman that you loved in her prime has become a middle-aged frump. The end will come when someone mistakes me for your mother."

"You don't love me at all?"

"Of course I love you, but love is not enough to make a go of anything." She walked over to the bar and poured another drink.

"What do we do now?" asked William, his mythical world in ruins.

"Carry on as before if you want to. Nothing's changed and the offer still stands."

But something *had* changed. The surface tension which somehow enabled his political and social ideals to co-exist with his admiration and tangential engagement to the lifestyle of Sylvia and her circle had been disturbed and he was unable to reset it. The conundrum of how to reconcile values with personal interests and aspirations, while presenting few difficulties for most champagne socialists, had become for him a source of inner conflict, highlighted by the truncated debate about the general strike at Sylvia's party. The concord between him and his upper-middle-class friends he finally recognised as a sham. It was a relationship of convenience for him and a passing fad for them in which the social differences between them were politely ignored and could never be discussed. However charming, friendly and well-mannered they were towards him, he would never be fully accepted and his beliefs would be an anathema to them.

This gulf between him and them was no smaller even with Sylvia, who had evaded the issue by indulging his childish game of make-believe. She would no more leave her own class than he would ever gain access to hers. In the class war she was just as much the enemy as supercilious snobs like Monty Benstock. The mere acceptance of this fact by William began their drift apart. There was no argument, split or recrimination. They saw each other still, but first the ardour cooled and they met with growing infrequency until they metamorphosed from near-lovers to old friends who bumped into each other, exchanged pleasantries and went their separate ways. As Swinburne put it:

> *And the best and the worst of this is*
> *That neither is most to blame,*
> *If you have forgotten my kisses*
> *And I have forgotten your name*

Except that William never forgot Sylvia's name.

XXI

In William's professional life little changed as the years passed. He worked as hard as ever for Drogo, whom he liked as a person and for whom he continued to have much respect. However, after the ending of his relationship with Sylvia, he found himself reassessing his personal life. This led him to think once again of the work and beliefs of his father and his own commitment to those ideals, which he had neglected over recent years. All the visits to the library, the books he'd read on philosophy and politics, the lectures attended with his father or on his own; all had been pushed into the background by his flirtation with the high life and aspirations to be something that he wasn't. It was time to turn over a new leaf, literally, and return to the path he had sought to follow in his father's footsteps. He took out his journal, opened it at a fresh page and wrote, "My true vocation henceforth will be to further the beliefs and aims of my father, and I will work to this end in whatever way possible." He read it over and nodded, thinking it a bit pompous but heartfelt.

He sat back in the chair, glancing through the various entries he had made in his journal, and found a note he had once scribbled about Lenin. It was Lenin's view that those who want to bring about a revolution should not alert their likely opponents to their intentions nor intimidate the uncommitted by giving the appearance of revolutionaries. They should dress conventionally and respectably like members of the lower middle class and speak and behave in ways that did not make obvious their radical perspective, so that those who feared revolution might be lulled into a false sense of security. William smiled as he read what he had written underneath. "I will dress, speak and behave as someone whom people would regard as a reasonable man with appropriately limited middle-class ambitions. My views and aims for society will be very different to those assumed of me but others will not become aware of this until I judge the time is right to reveal them when the revolution comes."

Much as William admired the acumen and achievements of Lenin, he had long ago abandoned teenage fantasies and self-deceit in which he pictured himself as an English version of some heroic revolutionary like Bolivar, Garibaldi or even Lenin himself. He no longer believed that Britain, and especially England, was the sort of country that was fertile ground for a revolution and all the upheaval that entailed. In the general strike there had been no attempt to seize power by the working class. The unions had repeatedly spoken in support of the current system of government and the strike itself had been conducted generally in a climate of restraint and tolerance by both sides. He remembered on the fateful morning he had accompanied his father to the bus station that the majority of strikers had had expressions of humour rather than vitriol on their faces. There had been no verbal, let alone physical, attacks on Amos when his bus ran over Jack, just a sense of sadness at misfortune and tragedy. Instead of waiting for a revolution which would probably never happen, he would, like his father, support peaceful change to bring about a fairer society, supporting whatever political group and course of action seemed most likely to be successful. In the meantime he would continue in his present job, tacitly accepting the current political and economic status quo.

Gradually William found his interest in motor racing waning. Despite the excitement and thrill of it, he thought it too closely identified with wealth, both in the way the teams were financed and the pool from which the drivers were recruited. He could not envisage how it might ever be a sport for the unprivileged and this made him uncomfortable with the whole set-up. However, when the 1927 season came round he felt obliged to go to some of the races out of loyalty to his good friend Stanley's continued enthusiasm for motor racing, as well as for his own business contacts. At the first meeting they attended, he found himself looking out for Sylvia, but when they passed in the paddock there was no awkwardness; they just waved and smiled.

After the last race, he and Stanley had a drink as usual and Stanley said, "I've got something for you," handing him an envelope.

It was addressed to William and he could feel it contained a card. Inside was an invitation to him and his mother from Mr and Mrs A Mason to the marriage of their daughter Lucy to Mr R J Stone. A pang of dismay and regret came over him as he read the card and reread it.

"What do you think of that, then?" asked Stanley.

"Well, I am surprised. You didn't mention that she was engaged."

"I didn't know. They kept it quiet and then sprang it on us a few weeks ago. Dick is in the merchant navy and they have to fit the wedding round his time at sea."

"She doesn't mind that he'll be away a lot?"

"I guess not. Won't get fed up with each other, will they? Absence makes the heart grow fonder."

William smiled. "What's he like?"

"Dick? Haven't seen much of him. She's brought him round perhaps three times. Seems like a nice bloke, though. You'll come to the wedding, won't you?"

"Yes, tell Lucy I'm very happy for her. Let's have another drink to celebrate." He ordered a couple of double brandies and gulped his down so fast that Stanley stared in disbelief.

William and Alice did attend the wedding in June at the Lower Homerton parish church along with fifty or so others. Lucy wore an ivory dress below the knee with a handkerchief hem while her groom was dressed in his uniform as a Third Officer in the merchant marine, as was his best man. Lucy had two bridesmaids; one of them William recognised from school.

"Don't they look well together?" whispered Alice as the bride and groom went to the vestry to sign the register. "She's done well for herself, when you think where she came from."

"The same house as us."

She looked up at him, her eyes half-closed. "We have different roots when you go further back. *You* know what I mean."

A wedding reception was held in the church hall afterwards and William felt at home with the Mason family and their friends, whom he was delighted to see again. Naturally, Lucy was in great demand, but he managed to speak briefly with her and her husband.

"I'm very pleased to meet you, Billy," said Dick. "Lucy's told me a lot about you and the times you shared when you were children."

William smiled. "It was a long time ago but doesn't seem like it."

"Yes, it's as if it were yesterday." Lucy patted his arm.

"How long have you got before you go back to sea, Dick?"

"About ten days, so we have time for a short honeymoon." He smiled at his wife, who blushed a little.

William thought what a strange life they would have together. "I wish you both the very best for the future." He kissed Lucy on the cheek and shook Dick's hand.

"We'll keep in touch, though, Billy," she said, and she turned to smile at him as her husband whisked her away to the next group of guests.

He continued his tour of the room, renewing acquaintances with old friends, but when his mother said it was time for her to go he was glad to walk home with her.

In the next few weeks and in pursuit of his aim to follow his father's political beliefs, William began by joining the local Labour Party. He dutifully attended branch meetings and gave the occasional help in distributing leaflets and canvassing. He found the party meetings less enjoyable than he had hoped. There were often pointless arguments about what the party should have done in the general strike or debates dominated by idealists or armchair revolutionaries, who were convinced that capitalism was about to disintegrate but were less interested in the here and now. When, however, discussions were on practical issues such as the alleviation of poverty or unemployment he learned much that made him feel ashamed of his ignorance. He had been to Wales and to parts of the country north of the Home Counties but only on holiday and never to one of the big cities or industrial areas, let alone setting foot in the North-East or Scotland. Not only had these places suffered most in the post-war recession, neither production nor employment had recovered to the levels of 1914. Unemployment in many areas was always over ten per

cent and often families survived on the dole. These were the
issues that he wanted to see addressed by politics, rather than
the search for the perfect form of government.

The 1929 general election was an exciting event for
William. Aged twenty-one just before the 1924 election, his
name had not made it on to the electoral register so, at nearly
twenty-five, this was the first time he had voted in a general
election. He embraced enthusiastically the whole process from
canvassing and attending political meetings to cheering the
return of the Labour candidate in his constituency, Herbert
Morrison, to the House of Commons after an absence of five
years. Labour won the general election and formed a minority
government; William had high hopes for change.

Within a few months the government was confronted by
the economic turmoil which followed the Wall Street crash
in October. Feeling bound by the established principle of a
balanced budget, the Labour government, confronted by
falling tax revenues and rising unemployment payments, was
immediately under pressure to cut government expenditure.
Like many others, William despaired at the government's
failure to explore more radical measures to help the economy
but saw hope in the proposals of one relatively junior
government minister, Sir Oswald Mosley. In a memorandum
to the cabinet published at the end of 1930, he called for high
tariffs to protect British industries, state nationalisation of
the strategic industries and a programme of public works to
tackle the problem of rapidly rising unemployment. He also
appeared to support corporatism with its aim of giving a
formal status to both trade unions and business interests in
the formation of economic policy.

Despite the support of many prominent Labour figures,
Mosley's memorandum was not adopted by the cabinet and
he resigned from the government to establish his own political

movement, the New Party. William was disappointed both by Labour's unwillingness to consider a new approach and Mosley's petulance and disloyalty, but he still hoped the Labour government would find a way through the crisis. What actually happened he found inexplicable.

In May 1931 the Labour cabinet split over the decision to make huge cuts to public expenditure to try to balance the budget. Unable to win a vote of confidence in Parliament, the Prime Minister, Ramsay MacDonald, reluctantly agreed to form a national government at the request of the King. The bulk of the Labour Party refused to support the new government and expelled all those MPs who remained loyal to MacDonald. The government continued in office, supported by the Conservatives and a few Labour and Liberal MPs. A general election was called for October.

When William attended the next meeting of his constituency party, the vast majority of speakers supported the decision to expel MacDonald and his supporters and for the party to go into opposition. William listened patiently to the discussion but grew increasingly frustrated by the trend of the debate. Finally, he asked a question.

"If I understand the situation correctly, we had a Labour government which was attempting to protect the working people from the worst effects of an economic crisis not of its making. The party refused to support the government's budget for understandable reasons which led to the fall of the Labour government and a new national government dominated by Conservatives. The few Labour MPs who chose to support the Prime Minister, presumably with good intentions, are vilified and have been expelled from the party. The new government will introduce a budget similar to the one the party rejected, but now Labour will be in opposition and powerless to protect the very people it pledged to do. In what way is this outcome good for the ordinary people of this country?"

There was silence in the room for a few seconds. Ten minutes later, arguments of matters of principle and mockery of his lack of understanding assailing him from all sides, he left the meeting and walked home. That night he read through the Mosley Memorandum again and tried to envisage his new strategy to bring about the radical economic and political change that was needed in the current crisis. He wondered if an upper-class figure like Mosley, with backing from different parts of the political spectrum, could get policies accepted that would be unpalatable when put forward by the Labour Party. The New Party had been launched with considerable goodwill and a clutch of MPs had defected to it from each of the main parties. In the euphoria which followed, it attracted more and more interest, received support from several newspapers and proceeded to inflate on high hopes and impossible ambitions.

Having considerable sympathy with Mosley's policies, William decided to attend one of his meetings and he was initially very impressed by it. Mosley spoke at length in his strong, rather high-pitched voice, using flamboyant gestures to make his points. It was not a style to William's taste, but it gripped the audience and at the end they were raised to a level of fervour that William had never seen before at a political rally. He found Mosley's stare rather disconcerting, with one eye not looking exactly in the right direction, but thought perhaps it assisted his ability to mesmerise and electrify the audience. There was nothing he found to quibble about in the policies advocated in the speech, though he did find the rabid atmosphere a little disconcerting. He was reassured by the attendance of moderate mainstream political figures such as John Strachey, the Labour MP, and Harold Nicolson, the former diplomat and *Evening Standard* journalist, who was editing the party's newspaper.

However, he was troubled by the presence of a party militia called the 'Biff Boys' whose role was apparently to keep order at the meetings. As the party had received a positive response from much of the press and drew support from across the political spectrum, William didn't see why it should need these people to keep order. Rather their probable effect would be to intimidate any potential antagonists who attended.

Already softened by the existence of the Biff Boys, William's early enthusiasm for the New Party soon began to drain away. The weeks passed and the party quickly attracted many members from the British Fascists, another political grouping, and soon there was a mass defection of Fascists to the New Party. As the party moved to adopt more authoritarian policies, William realised he had made a mistake, as did many of the moderate politicians who had joined the party, and he gave up any thought of supporting it. He didn't actively campaign in the general election but voted for his sitting MP, Herbert Morrison.

The general election was a disaster for the New Party, which lost all its MPs and did very badly in most of the seats it contested. It was also a disaster for Labour, which lost four out of every five seats it held and two million votes. Morrison lost his seat to the Conservatives.

William reflected on the election for some time and then wrote in his journal: "The result of the general election confirms my view about the latent tendencies of the British electorate. Too conservative and too moderate to support a revolution from the Far Left, the same qualities make it unwilling to support a party of the Far Right. During a crisis the voters turned not towards upheaval and change by the radical right or the radical left but to stability. They voted for the status quo of the national government, as they had every democratic right to do."

After the election, Oswald Mosley went on a tour of Europe and, on his return, pronounced that he was convinced that Fascism was the true path for the renewal of the political and economic system, and the British Union of Fascists was formed, absorbing the New Party. This further shift in Mosley's ideology led William to assume that Mosley probably had few guiding principles in his politics, a view reinforced by Mosley's later adoption of anti-Semitism and the replacement of erudition with rabble-rousing and intimidation at his meetings. Despite its brief attraction for some members of the upper classes and occasional revivals in support among the disgruntled working class, the British Union of Fascists failed in its many attempts to win even one seat in Parliament.

XXII

WILLIAM'S DISENCHANTMENT WITH PARTY politics came at a time when work was occupying most of his attention. The Great Depression which afflicted Britain in 1930 had a huge impact on the car industry; three-quarters of the two hundred British car makers collapsed in the early 1930s and others went through a considerable period of regression, including the marques in which Drogo Motors specialised. By 1931 Bertram Drogo's business was in serious trouble and William was using all his accounting skills to keep it afloat. To cut back on expenditure, Drogo gave up motor racing and sold his beloved Frazer Nash, but it was not enough. The cloud of economic depression hung like a pall over the business and the Kilburn branch was closed in 1931. William could see from the books that Drogo was still leaking money and his debts, partly due to his earlier motor-racing ventures, were unsustainable. He made savings where he could, striking a harder bargain with suppliers, improving systems and work rotas, but there was only so much that could be done. In 1932, an apprentice mechanic was the first to go at Swiss Cottage, followed by Alfie Travis in car sales, and the writing was on the wall. It was almost a relief in early April when Drogo came into William's office after a long meeting with two bank officials.

He was carrying a bottle of Scotch and two glasses, which he put on William's desk. "Well, William, it's all up, I'm afraid." He poured two drinks. "Chin up," he said, looking at William's crestfallen expression as he raised his glass and took the contents down in one gulp.

"Perhaps I could find some more cost savings. I would willingly take a cut in pay if it would help."

"Kind of you to offer, old boy, but we both know it's gone too far for that. The bank won't give me any more time – they're calling in their loans. My father has offered to help out, but it would just be throwing good money after bad; pouring water in a bucket with a bloody great hole in the bottom." He refilled his glass and topped up William's barely touched drink.

"So what will happen now? Administration?"

"I can't see anybody taking this on as a going concern; too many debts. So it's liquidation, I'm afraid. They sell everything off dirt cheap and give the debtors a few bob in the pound and we'll hand the keys back to the landlord."

"I'm sorry it's ended like this."

Drogo shrugged. "Yes, it's a bastard thing."

"What will you do?"

"Oh, I'll be all right. There's a bit of money in the family and I've got a few contacts. I'll start again somehow. It'll be harder on the boys I'm turning out and you, of course; you've been here a long time."

"Over ten years." William drank some of the Scotch; he wasn't a connoisseur, but it certainly tasted like a very good one.

"Only two fewer than me," said Drogo. He shook his head. "You're still a young man, William. Things will come out the other side; they always do. The bank has given me a couple of months to see if I can get a buyer, but I don't have much hope and they don't have any. I'll pay your salary for the two months so perhaps you will be able to sort something out. I'm sorry about this, but it's an impossible position." He finished his drink. "Help yourself to another," he said. "I'll go and talk to the men in the garage. Would you mind telling Mary; it might come better from you?"

William nodded and sat down at his desk, watching his boss walk over to the garage workshops and shrink into the distance, mirroring the shrinking away of his business. He decided to postpone the refill to his glass until after he'd spoken to Mary.

She stopped typing and looked up with a look of trepidation as he walked into the reception area. "It's bad news, isn't it?"

"Yes, the worst, I'm afraid."

"Oh God, how long?"

"I'll make sure you get more than the usual notice."

"It's such a shame." She took a pretty handkerchief from her sleeve and dabbed under one of her eyes. "I love working here. What will my mother do with Dad out of work as well?"

William remembered her mentioning a month before that her father had lost his job. "Your dad hasn't found anything yet?"

She shook her head.

"I'll help you find something," he said, ignoring the challenge this posed.

She smiled disbelievingly.

William went back to his office and looked out the window, mentally calculating what could be raised in sales of the equipment, fixtures and fittings, and stock before the shutters came down. After a few minutes, he saw Drogo reappear from the workshops and walk slowly to his office, his head bowed.

On the way home that evening William pondered how best to break the news to his mother. Personally, he did see a silver lining to this particular cloud. Inertia, loyalty and a liking for the job had kept him with Drogo for eleven years, and this enforced change in circumstances gave him the chance to try for something more in keeping with his political beliefs, although he wasn't sure what. He knew his mother would not take it well and it was only a matter of which particular harrowing path of self-pity she would choose to pursue. It was impossible for him to predict what for him would be the least wearing tack to adopt.

"Hello, Mum," he called as he came in and threw his hat on the coat stand in the hall.

Alice called out, "I'm upstairs."

He picked up the morning newspaper and skimmed through it while he waited for the descent of his mother. None of the stories registered with him.

Alice went out to the kitchen and put the kettle on, and about ten minutes later she came into the sitting room with tea and biscuits. "Busy day?" she asked, setting down the tray.

"You could say that; the business is closing down."

"Closing down? You mean moving to new premises?"

"No, closing down for good; it's finished. I've got two months' notice."

Alice put her hand to her mouth. "I can't believe it."

"I did tell you about the closing of the Kilburn branch. It was only a matter of time the way business has being falling off, month after month."

Alice shook her head slowly and extravagantly. "Can't anything be done?"

"No, Drogo is broke. He would have kept going, I think, but the debts are being called in."

"So you will have to find another job."

"Yes."

"What will become of us? I can't do so much sewing now with my eyesight what it is; what if you can't find work?"

"I'll find something."

"You say that."

"What else can I say? I'll do my best to find another job."

"I don't suppose it'll pay as well as this one."

"That had crossed my mind."

"Sometimes I do believe we must be cursed; you working so hard but losing jobs through no fault of your own and your poor father." Her voice wavered a little and she wrung her hands, looking up to Heaven. "God give us strength," she added plaintively.

William didn't reply. He leaned over and took a malted milk biscuit from the plate in front of him, stared at the embossed image of the cow on it for a second, then put it in his mouth.

"Don't take the whole biscuit in one go, you'll choke."

"I can think of worse things," he replied, taking another biscuit.

The next morning William saw the 'For Rent' sign outside the garage when he arrived for work. Drogo was in the yard, over by the cars for sale, talking to a tall, well-built young man whom William recognised as a racing driver from Brooklands. This was W B Scott, known to everyone as 'Bummer' Scott, though William had no idea how the nickname had come about. Scott was skilful both at driving and dealing in high-performance motor cars, and William guessed he might be in the market for one or two of Drogo's best models.

William went into the office and continued his inventory of the company's declining assets. He made a few phone calls before calling Mary in to take some letters to potential buyers of items for sale. While phoning, he also enquired about possible vacancies for Mary but without success.

That's how it was for the next few weeks: cars disappearing, staff, machinery, stock, fittings, all disappearing. Few of the items sold for anything near their true value but at least they realised more than at an auction or fire sale. Two mechanics remained to service a few old customers' vehicles and man the petrol pumps. In the third week Mary's notice ran out. William went out to complete a sale of their office furniture on Thursday afternoon but on Friday he was back in the office. He was tying up the loose ends on Mary's work and trying once again, despite her protestations, to find her a position when Drogo came in, unusually for him without knocking.

"Ah, Mary, there you are. I'm afraid I've found a discrepancy in the cash box; ten pounds is missing since I counted up the money yesterday lunchtime." He paused as if not certain to go on but then continued. "Mr Lyus was out of the office yesterday afternoon and you are the only other person with a key, so I assume you borrowed the money without permission. If you'd care to pay it back now nothing more will be said about the matter." He didn't sound angry, just weary and almost apologetic.

Mary went very pale and looked terrified. "I can't," she said.

William intervened. "She can't because she has already given it to me. Sorry, Mr Drogo, I've been so busy this morning I quite forgot to return the money to the cash box." He took out his wallet and produced two five-pound notes, which he laid on the desk. "I have reprimanded Mary for this transgression, but I hope you understand; difficult times."

"Of course, all forgotten." He smiled, picked up the money and went to leave, then stopped. "Oh, I'll take your key to the cash box now, Mary. Don't want to forget it, do we?"

Mary, her hands shaking, took the key from her key ring and handed it over to Drogo. He thanked her and left. As the door closed behind him, Mary, who had retained a ghastly, sick colour throughout the conversation between her superiors, collapsed into a chair. She put her hands to her face. "Oh, my

God, thank you, Mr Lyus, I am very sorry. I will pay it back; it's just that I can't at the moment."

William poured a glass of water and gave it to her. "Tell me what happened."

"We're behind on the rent and my mother had to clear the arrears, or most of it, by last night. There was nowhere to go to get the money, so I took it from the cash box."

"Presumably, you were hoping to make your escape today before it was noticed."

She nodded.

"Then what? I suppose you hoped Mr Drogo would not pursue the matter?"

She nodded again and looked down.

"You are probably right about him, but you know that makes it worse, somehow. You could have asked for help."

"I know, it was stupid of me, I'm sorry. How did you happen to have so much money on you? If you don't mind my asking."

William smiled; her curiosity was intact even if her nerves were frayed. "It was pure luck. Yesterday afternoon I visited the firm buying our office furniture and they paid ten pounds on account as a holding deposit. I was going to make the entry in the ledger and pay the money into the bank this afternoon. Now, I shall have to draw from my own bank and do it that way."

"I really am sorry. If you give me your address, I'll pay you back the money as soon as I can, I promise."

William took the view that a loan once made is instantly forgotten and he doubted he would get his money back, despite her good intentions. Nonetheless he went through the ritual of writing his address on the back of his business card and gave it to her. Then he went off to the bank and transferred the sum of ten pounds to the garage's account. Mary left that afternoon with more promises of repayment and by the end of the following week the workshop was closed, and only William and a petrol attendant/spares person were left.

With most of the business sold off, he turned his attention to his own future. Drogo had given him an exceptional reference and he now had experience in industry, professional accounting and the retail business. On a piece of paper he wrote the heading 'Curriculum Vitae' and listed his work experience in order since he had left school, describing briefly the various duties and experience gained in each role. Next he recorded his few certificates of attainment in accounting and cost management. Finally, he added his interests: sports, particularly cricket, football and motor racing, reading, music, and politics, which he changed to political philosophy to make it more anodyne. He read down the attainments of his life so far and thought, *What a paltry record for fifteen years at work and no prospects.*

In the next few days he sent off a score of letters with enclosed CVs to all the organisations he could think of which worked for the causes his father and he espoused, seeking any position for which his experience and qualifications might be suitable. He received a polite, sympathetic and negative response from each one. Meanwhile, he responded to adverts he saw for other jobs that he was definitely qualified to do, but each reply said either that the vacancy was already filled or that he was over-qualified for the post which would suit a younger or less-qualified person. Each day that passed was filled with disappointment, exacerbated by his mother's reaction, consisting of a forlorn expression coupled with questions and advice which could never quite be described as reproach.

With only a couple of weeks to go before Drogo's generous notice expired, he was contemplating attendance at the Labour Exchange. He had seen pictures in the newspapers of long queues of the unemployed stretching away from an exchange, so he was not very hopeful but could see no alternative to at least giving it a try. But then he had an idea. He opened his address book at the Amalgamated Engineering Union and the name he had forgotten: Arnold Fleming, Regional Manager, London Region. It had been six years since they had met at Jack's funeral, but it was worth a go. He took out some writing paper and commenced writing a letter. The third draft he thought good enough.

Dear Mr Fleming,

You will recall my father, Jack Lyus, who served as an official for several years with the union. I met you at his funeral after he died during the general strike. I hope you won't think me presumptuous in writing to you at this time, but my current employment is terminating in a few weeks and I have been considering my future options. I should like to find employment in an area which works for the causes my father held dear, in particular the rights of the working people and the development of a fairer society under a progressive government. The trade union movement is an obvious example and one with which I have personal affinity and some personal knowledge. I am not an engineer but believe there will be areas within the union's sphere of responsibility where my particular skills and experience would be of some help. I enclose a copy of my curriculum vitae for your information.

As someone whom my father always found helpful and generous with his time I would greatly appreciate any advice and suggestions to possible opportunities which you think I might explore.

With best wishes,
Yours sincerely,
William Lyus

He read the letter over several times, thought it probably a bit smarmy, but it was a long shot anyway. What did he have to lose? He attached a special copy of his CV which alluded to his active membership of the Labour Party and sent it off in the post.

William did not receive a reply for over a week and, unable to gauge whether that was encouraging news or not, he decided to assume he probably wouldn't receive any reply at all. Then, in the morning post a letter arrived with the name 'Amalgamated Engineering Union' printed in the top corner of the envelope. He held the unopened envelope between his thumb and forefinger and savoured that moment when all possibilities exist before the envelope is opened. Then he cut through the envelope with his paper knife, preparing for the worst.

Dear William,

What a pleasant surprise to hear from you again and I hope you are well. I do remember meeting you at your father's funeral and afterwards when I discussed the pension arrangements and so forth with your mother. Jack was always a popular and well-respected member of our establishment here and is still much missed, especially on account of his tragic death. That sad incident is marked by a plaque next to the war memorial in our foyer.

As to the reason for your writing, unfortunately we have no vacancies on our staff at the moment for anyone with your qualifications and work experience. However, out of the friendship and admiration I had for your father I should like to assist you in your career aspirations in any way I can, especially as you may soon be without employment. I note that you have had considerable experience in registration work and we shall have a

vacancy in our registration department at the end of July.
The manager of that section would be pleased to interview
you for the post if you are able to wait that long. I have
to point out that the salary is considerably less than your
current emolument, but if you would be interested please
let me know by return of post.
    Yours sincerely,
    A D Fleming

William breathed a sigh of relief and hastily responded to
Fleming to confirm his interest in the job. The next afternoon
he received a phone call from the union office inviting him
in for an interview the following Thursday, if convenient. He
had no difficulty with the date as he would be out of work
by then. The petrol pumps had run dry and been closed, and
with it the last employee of Drogo Motors had left. William
had, some time before, finished off the last sales of assets and
settled the gas and electricity accounts. The following day, he
would prepare a final profit and loss account for Drogo, make
sure the telephone was cut off, close the premises and hand
over the keys.

    The next morning he arrived at the garage at ten o'clock;
there was no point in being any earlier. He packed his
few personal items in his briefcase: a thermometer, some
pens, pencils and a ruler, leftover postage stamps, a framed
photograph of him and Bertram Drogo at Brooklands, and the
badge taken from a Sunbeam car, mounted on a base by one
of the mechanics as a Christmas gift one year. He went round
the offices and workshops one last time, checking there was
nothing that couldn't be left to whoever occupied the premises
next. There was nothing. Even the old pieces of scrap metal
and wood, kept by the mechanics 'in case it comes in handy',
were gone. The whole site was a near-pristine void. Only the

concrete floors and drive with their marks of ingrained oil and grease remained as a reminder of what this place had once been. Drogo had not been near the garage for two weeks and, as he looked around for one last time, William could understand why. What was this now other than a reminder of lost dreams and ultimate failure? Drogo had moved on and so must he.

Satisfied that he had done all he could to save and then wind up this ailing business, he locked the premises, dropped the keys in at the estate agents and walked to Drogo's apartment in St John's Wood. He had been to the apartment a couple of times before, once to deliver some papers and the other time for a meeting. He noticed that there were tea chests in the hall and the pictures had been removed from the walls, only the telltale shadow of each remaining.

"Come in, William. Take a seat. Would you like a drink? Bit early, I know, but it's probably our farewell to each other."

"Yes, thanks. I'll have whatever you're having."

Drogo poured them both a large whisky and soda and added ice. "Well, cheers."

"Cheers."

"Thanks very much for all you've done, especially the closing-down part. Everything go to plan?"

"Yes, there are a couple of cheques for you to sign; they're ready to post. I've brought you the final accounts for your records." He laid the chequebook and the accounts on the table.

Drogo signed the cheques and put them in the appropriate envelopes. He didn't bother to look at the accounts. "Have you something fixed up for yourself?"

"Well, I have an interview next week and I'm fairly hopeful I'll get it; I know someone on the inside."

"Excellent, always gives you the best chance. Same sort of position?"

"Not exactly, it'll be quite a drop in salary, but you know, beggars can't be choosers."

Drogo nodded. "You're a good man; you'll work your way up in no time."

"I see you are moving."

Drogo smiled. "Yes. I've been offered a job in the oil industry; every car needs oil and petrol, so I should be all right. I'm going to Persia in a couple of weeks. Looking forward to it; only trouble is they don't play cricket out there."

"Congratulations; I hope it works out for you." William raised his glass and took a drink.

"I've been lucky, connections and all that. When will you start in the new job?"

"Beginning of August."

"That's a long way off. You'll be able to manage?"

"I've got savings. I can wait."

"As long as you're sure?"

They had another drink and chatted about the past and the future for a half hour or so, mostly the past, and they knew it was time. Drogo produced a business card from his wallet. "If you fancy a go in the oil business, give me a chance to get my feet under the desk and give me a call. I'll see what I can do. Well, good luck for the future."

XXII

WITHOUT A JOB, WILLIAM TOOK STOCK OF HIS financial position. Though he had savings, he wouldn't be paid for at least two months even if he got the position at the Amalgamated Engineering Union so, unless he could get some casual work to tide him over, he would have to tighten his belt. A few days after he left Drogo's, he strolled along to the Labour Exchange where he found a long queue so decided to leave it to a quieter time. A member of staff was giving out leaflets explaining how to claim unemployment benefit and William took one to read.

His mother was out when he arrived home. After her mother-in-law had died, she had gradually started to build up a social life. For this, William was grateful as he felt less likely to be silently reproached when he pursued his own activities outside the home. Today was her weekly trip to the cinema, an interest which she had embraced more enthusiastically with the arrival of talkies. He went to the kitchen, made himself a cup of tea and a cheese sandwich, and read through the leaflet, stopping at the regulations governing 'the dole'.

He concluded he was eligible, in that he was eligible to be assessed. He would be means-tested and that meant his mother's pension, his savings, her savings, if she had any, valuable possessions that were not necessities such as jewellery and so on would all be taken into account to determine if he received anything. He totted up what he knew about his and his mother's items of value and income, and thought he would probably be entitled to very little, especially as the dole had gone down by ten per cent the previous year. He threw the leaflet on the table and went for a walk in the garden. His family had inherited a well-maintained garden with flower borders and a small vegetable plot, and his father had enjoyed looking after it as a relaxing hobby. William had no interest in gardening, but he cut the grass and left his mother to look after the plants. The vegetable patch had received little attention for the last few years and William stared at it wistfully.

His mother arrived home at half-past four.

"Good film?" asked William as he brought her in a cup of tea and some biscuits.

"It was all right. Mrs Warren enjoyed it more than I did." She sipped her tea. "So you're officially unemployed now?"

"Yes."

"Let's hope and pray you get that job next week, otherwise what will we do?"

"I'll have to look elsewhere; that's all I can do. I got a leaflet from the Labour Exchange today. I can sign on, but I doubt I'll get very much as they take into account family income and savings."

"I suppose I could try to get some work, but I shan't be able to do cleaning, not with my wonky knee."

"What wonky knee?"

"You know, the left one. Too much bending or kneeling and it blows up like a balloon."

"I don't suppose it will come to that. Anyway, you are a good seamstress. You could take that up again."

"Eyes permitting, of course." She shook her head. "I don't know. When your father was alive and you had that promising career with Mr Drogo, I thought our family was going to get back to where it belongs. My grandfather's second cousin was a Queen's Counsel."

William settled back to hear the sad story of her family's decline once again.

"It was two early deaths that did it. My great-grandfather had that cheesemonger's business in Marylebone and he passed it on to my grandfather, who moved it to the City. But then my grandfather died young and my grandmother couldn't run it so she sold up. My father got a decent job in a drapers and then he died when he was only forty and my mother was left with nothing. She thought I married below my status when I married your father as his family didn't have two ha'pennies to rub together. But I wasn't likely to do any better after she was reduced to working in a laundry."

"At least you married him for love."

"Yes, I did and he worked hard, your father, to get where we did. We were doing all right, especially after Uncle Charles left me this house. I was always his favourite niece. Everything was looking brighter as we climbed back up the ladder. Now it's one bad thing after another and down the snake we go."

As William had anticipated, her voice wavered a little at this point and she took her handkerchief from her sleeve and blew her nose.

William felt impelled to comfort her in some way and patted her hand. "Don't worry, Mum, it will be all right."

"The only blessing is that you are not married with a family to worry about."

"No."

The following week he attended the interview for the job. After thinking it over, he decided not to wear his best suit but an off-the-peg work suit. The headquarters of the Amalgamated Engineering Union headquarters was on Peckham Road in London. It was a magnificent building with a carving which depicted two workers holding a huge cogwheel over the main entrance. Inside the foyer was a memorial to the employees who had lost their lives in the Great War and, by the side, a plaque commemorating those officials who had died while serving the Union. William felt a lump in his throat as the most recent name was that of his father. He gave his name to the receptionist and, while waiting, read the details on the plaque and fondly reminisced about his father. After a few minutes a man of about sixty, named Bunkall, came for him and took him into a small meeting room, where they went through the formality of an interview. There was a brief discussion about William's career history and a cursory examination of his experience and qualifications. After a short run-through of the duties attached to the post, Bunkall offered it to him. The salary was less than two thirds of what he was paid by Drogo and with none of the perks, such as the use of a car. Bunkall apologised that the pay was less than William was used to but said that he was retiring in the next few years and William could expect to be promoted to his job if all went well in the meantime. William had no hesitation in accepting the post, to commence on the 3rd of August.

With six weeks to go before he started his new job, William searched around for something to earn some money. It would not be easy with national unemployment at over twenty per cent and, without a union ticket, he could not consider unionised industries, especially as he was only looking for temporary work. He was willing to have a crack at labouring but, after years in a sedentary occupation, he doubted he would be able to perform to the standard expected. The large number of temporary workers in agriculture would not be needed for a few weeks yet. He tried for casual work as a van driver, a chauffeur, a shop worker and a commercial traveller, all without success.

At the weekend, despite the admonition of his mother, who thought savings should be preserved, he went out for a drink with Leonard and Stanley. They had continued to go to the football over the years, but not as frequently as in their youth, and all of them had other demands on their time. Leonard was married with a young son now and Stanley was engaged so neither of them was usually free on a Saturday evening, so this was something of an occasion, the celebration of Stanley's birthday, which had taken place the previous day. Not having seen each other for several weeks they had much to talk about, especially the economic situation.

Stanley admitted he was a little worried about his job as a charge hand in a local pencil factory. "Exports are down, but obviously people don't give up using pencils even during a depression. I'll probably be all right as I've been there for a long time, but it's put me off marrying Joan until things pick up. What about you, Billy? I bet it was a wrench, you having to leave Drogo's after all that time."

William smiled. "Yes, I did enjoy working there. Still, I'm lucky to have something else, even if it isn't for a month or so."

"What are you doing in the meantime?" asked Leonard.

"Nothing at the moment. I've been trying to find a temporary job, but there's not much out there as far as I can see."

"What about working for me for a few weeks?"

"Really? You could give me some work?"

"Yes. Things are definitely picking up in the building trade now, even housing."

Leonard explained that his father was nearing retirement and had handed over much of the management of his building business to him. They undertook some small building contracts of their own, but much of the work involved sub-contracting for larger firms.

"Well, it's kind of you to offer, Len, but I'm not sure I would have the skills to do much to your satisfaction."

Leonard laughed. "Don't worry. I'm not going to let you loose on bricklaying or plastering or plumbing. When we get onto second fix on a building there's rubbing down and painting, levelling off the garden, cleaning up after everyone; that kind of thing."

"Well, that would be great. When can I start?"

"I'll pick you up on Monday morning, quarter-past seven sharp."

They agreed that William would leave the last week in July free for a holiday and for the next month Leonard kept William busy on the various sites where Leonard's firm was involved. In the first week William spent his time in a large new warehouse using various colours of paint to stencil the numbers and signs of the different sections and areas of work. In later weeks he cleaned areas and did the preparation for painting, priming and undercoating but leaving the topcoat, dug trenches (slowly) and cleared rubble, levelled a garden, helped put up a shed, and cleaned out drains and gutters. All of these experiences he enjoyed to a greater or lesser extent as Leonard was not a hard taskmaster and more than once had difficulty finding something for William to do. Apart from the odd backache, blistered finger and cut or bruise here and there, he was none the worse for wear each day and the five weeks went quickly. Leonard gave him the going rate for the job in cash with a payslip each week and, at the end of it all, said how much he'd enjoyed having William working with him.

"Thanks for everything, Len," said William. "I *do* know how much you put yourself out for me. I shan't forget it."

Leonard dismissed the compliment with a self-effacing grunt and a pat on the back. "Any time," he said.

William told his mother he would be taking a few days away and, in her relief that he'd managed to bridge the gap between his two jobs with some income, she was quite encouraging. "You deserve a break," she said. "Where will you go? The coast? Broadstairs is supposed to be nice."

"I thought I might go somewhere further north, perhaps the Midlands."

Alice looked sceptically at him. "Well, it's up to you."

After a little research into Britain's early industrial revolution, William spent a week in Shropshire, in Ironbridge and around Coalbrookdale. He also hired a car to travel round Birmingham and the Black Country. His aim was to get to know one of the heartlands of British industry so that he might understand more about the sort of places in which the majority of his union's members lived and worked. He witnessed more poverty than he had in London, certainly since the war, and saw at firsthand how much worse the Depression was when one travelled away from London and the South-East. When he explained his professional interest in engineering works, he was fortunate enough to be shown round a couple of factories and met some of the workers, all of which he found very enlightening. So also were the evenings he spent in the small commercial hotels where he stayed, talking to those who knew the industries of the area in depth. He returned to London aware that he had gained no more than a flavour of industrial Britain but at least he no longer felt totally ignorant of it.

On Monday the 3rd of August he reported to Mr Bunkall and spent the first day learning the ropes. Much of the work he was familiar with, albeit in a different context, and it was merely a case of learning new styles and ways of procedures, protocols and practices. Apart from Bunkall, the only other members of the team were a young, ebullient junior clerk and a secretarial assistant, a youngish woman who at first seemed very shy but was quite outgoing once she got to know him. He found his colleagues and working conditions very agreeable and he settled in almost immediately. Taking a note of the membership details of his old school friend Cyril, he made a resolution to renew their acquaintanceship, especially as he still lived in Homerton.

The new job was pretty straightforward and he was rarely stretched. After work he was hardly ever tired when he arrived home and he could devote his evenings to whatever he wanted to do. The first weekend after he started at the Union HQ, he called on Cyril, whom he hadn't seen for a long time. The door was opened by a young woman of about twenty.

"Good evening," he said. "Is Cyril in?"

She smiled. "You're Billy Lyus, aren't you?"

"Yes." He didn't recognise her but guessed she was Cyril's younger sister, Barbara. "Hello, Barbara. How are you?"

She smiled again. "No, I'm the next one down, Anne."

"Sorry, Anne. I seem to have lost track of the years."

"I'm very well, thanks. I haven't seen you for ages. Come in, Cyril's only upstairs."

He followed her in and she led him to the front room.

A few minutes later the tall, now-bespectacled figure of his old friend appeared. "Billy, what a great surprise! How are you?" He gripped William's hand in his and shook it vigorously. "I've kept meaning to get in touch, but I never seemed to get round to it."

"Me too. How are you?"

"Great, thanks. Where are you working now, still at the garage?"

They exchanged the details of their lives over the previous

five years. Cyril had not long finished his apprenticeship when they last met but now was working as a design engineer at a company based in Whitechapel. "I'm sorry we lost contact a bit," he said. "Amos was so cut up about what happened to your father that I felt I had to stand by him and I didn't want him to think I was reporting back to you how he was getting through it. So that's it, really. It was probably wrong to worry about that, but it seemed right at the time."

"I understand. How is Amos now?"

"He doesn't talk about it anymore, but I know he still feels guilty. His firm were very good and kept him on. But he doesn't drive the big lorries anymore, pantechnicons and so on; just the small ones."

"I wondered if you'd like to have a drink sometime."

"Yes, but we'll have to make it soon. I'm moving up to Derby in a few weeks; got a new job."

So a friend that was lost was found but then lost again and William's social circle continued to dwindle. He still saw Stanley and Leonard from time to time, but more often he spent his evenings at home with his mother or alone at the cinema or a concert. He began to go to lectures on socio-political or economic matters organised by London University colleges, the Fabian Society and others, most of which he found very enjoyable, especially as he met many new and interesting people during the coffee intervals.

After one lecture in early November on Stalinism in the Soviet Union, he found himself talking to a man of about thirty whom he had seen once or twice before but not taken much notice of.

"Very good speaker, I thought," said the man, as they turned away from the drinks and biscuits.

"Yes, it was excellent. It raised a lot of questions, so it's a pity there was only a brief question and answer session afterwards. I would have enjoyed a longer discussion of the various points the speaker made."

"I agree with you, but there's rarely enough time to explore the subject fully. I take it you enjoy political discussions, especially about the current situation in the world?"

"Yes, I suppose I do. I often find myself with ideas and questions about politics that I can't really talk about with anyone else."

"Well, I belong to a political discussion group. It's quite small, only a dozen or so members. Perhaps you'd like to come along some time? We usually meet above a pub in Islington once a fortnight. We've got a meeting next Monday, if you're interested?"

William was slightly hesitant, wondering if he was being recruited for some odd organisation or other, but he was also intrigued, so he agreed to go.

"That's great. My name is David Harris."

"William Lyus."

"Very pleased to meet you, William. I'll see you on Monday. If it's not your cup of tea you need never come again." He handed William a card with the name of the group and the address of the pub, finished his tea and wandered over to another part of the room.

XXIV

WILLIAM LOOKED FORWARD TO ATTENDING DAVID Harris's political discussion group and duly arrived at the pub at the appointed time of 7.30. It was a large Victorian pub with several bars and, having bought himself a pint of beer in the Public Bar, he went straight to the upstairs room where the meeting would be held. The stairs were uncarpeted and his noisy footsteps gave advance warning of his arrival so that ten pairs of eyes were fixed on him as he opened the door. The room was congenial, with a patterned rug covering all but the edges of the wooden floor and a large table, round which were perhaps a dozen bentwood chairs. Other seats were scattered around two smaller tables and there were window seats too. He looked for and was pleased to see David Harris.

"William," David said, jumping up. "You are most welcome." This greeting prompted some of the other faces to light up with a few smiles and one or two nods. "Let me introduce you to the rest of the group." He gestured to each in turn, eight men and two women, and gave their names, and William did his best to remember them. There was one man in his sixties and a woman of about fifty-five, but the others seemed to be between twenty and forty. "There are three not yet here," said David, "so we may have a full house yet."

"I think we should start, anyway," said the older man, stroking his grey beard. He reminded William of a picture he'd seen of Charles Darwin. Another man, in his thirties, and presumably the secretary, read the minutes of the previous week's meeting. The title for discussion this evening was 'Social Democrats: Friends or Enemies of Socialism?'.

The Darwinesque chairman invited a man with a black goatee beard and moustache to take the floor. It was a short paper which took perhaps seven or eight minutes to read. The speaker had a slightly husky voice which sounded as if he had a perpetual need to clear his throat. There then followed a lively debate from which William abstained, finding himself swayed this way and that by the views of successive speakers. Despite the different views expressed, the speakers did not split into two sides. Nobody actually said that social democrats were friends of socialism, but some would not go so far as to say they were indisputably the enemy in all situations. These were jocularly teased for their tendency to lean against the fence, if not actually to sit on it. There was no vote on the matter and everybody seemed satisfied with the general tenor of the debate.

A whip-round ensured that everyone contributed to another round of drinks and then people split into groups of three or four for relaxed discussions on whatever appealed to them. David Harris invited William to join his group which, in addition to him, consisted of Felicity Pelham and Ronald Pierce. Felicity was in her early thirties and dressed in what William thought a rather unconventional way: her dark auburn hair was mostly hidden under a turban of some kind, her dress longer than the prevailing custom and of a severe cut. She wore no jewellery or make-up, though this did not prevent her being reasonably attractive. She was smoking a cheroot and drinking what looked like a pint of stout. While she had refrained from making any comment during the discussion earlier, Ronald Pierce had spoken in the debate. He had observed that social democrats may well have the same suspicion towards socialists that socialists had towards them, and there was a danger that in fighting each other they were doing the work of the fascists and reactionaries for them. His remark received one or two nods, but the general response was that he was an apologist for collaborators, which evinced a smile from him. Pierce was a balding man of perhaps forty. In his appearance he was entirely unnoteworthy to the point of blandness: grey suit, greyish tie and grey shirt. He spoke with a refined accent and had a pleasant voice, and the good-natured way he took criticism seemed to endear him to the rest of the group.

David Harris re-introduced William to the other two then asked, "So, William, what did you think of the discussion?"

"I thought it very interesting, plenty of food for thought."

Felicity dragged on her cheroot and sent a stream of smoke to join the dark cream patina on the ceiling. "But what conclusion did you come to?" she asked.

"I did not come to a conclusion; just more questions."

"Like what?" interjected Harris, smiling.

"Well, the balance of the debate seemed to be that social democrats weaken the strength of true socialists by accepting the status quo of the economic system. Is that a fair assessment?"

The others nodded.

"If we take the example of the Labour Party, which contains both social democrats and others you might accept as true socialists. The split over Ramsay MacDonald's decision to form a national government resulted in a weakening of all those factions who opposed the leader because they lost office and, in the general election that followed, lost most of their seats. As a result, they are now confronted by a national government with a huge majority, dominated by Conservatives."

"So what is your point?" asked Felicity, turning the matchbox in her hand over and over on the table.

"That if the party had kept together and supported MacDonald's original budget there might still be a Labour government which, while taking some unpleasant decisions, would have been better placed to represent the interests of the working people. They could have mitigated the worst results of the crisis as far as the poor are concerned."

"Good point," Roland observed. "You can't achieve your policies if you are never in government."

"A clever and beguiling argument which I've heard many times before," said Felicity. "But if we prop up the wishy-washy moderates posing as socialists they will drag us down with them."

"In what way drag us down?" asked William.

"When they fail to deliver socialism and end up in a mire of compromises with nothing achieved, the people will lose faith and blame socialism, whereas in fact socialism would not even have been tried."

"I think this is where we came in this evening," said David. "Interesting to hear your views, William. Where would you say you stood in the political spectrum?"

"I am a member of the Labour Party and I work for a trade union, so I suppose I am in the mainstream of the Left, though not quite sure exactly where."

"Which union do you work for?" asked Ronald.

"The AEU."

"As an organiser?" asked Felicity, sitting up and putting her matchbox aside.

"No, I work in the registration department. My father was an organiser; he was killed in the general strike."

"How dreadful! What happened?" she asked.

"He was trying to block the way of a transport lorry acting as a temporary bus when he was run over."

They all appeared shocked and reacted sympathetically, changing the tenor of the conversation. It soon became clear to William that this personal tragedy gave him a position of honour of some sort through the noble death of his father; he was a hero once removed, as it were. While Ronald went to buy him another drink, William talked of the values and beliefs he had inherited from his father. Even Felicity appeared to lose her slightly frosty attitude towards him and thrilled to hear of his humble origins as part of a family living in two rooms in an apartment which was not even their own. As the conversation meandered through the labyrinth of political philosophy, William was enthused and energised. All the discussions with his father, all the reading he had done, all the time reflecting on these matters: at last he had found a forum where he felt comfortable expressing his ideas and submitting them to examination.

At the end of the evening he was asked by David if he would like to become a member of the group, which bore the title 'JM Group'. David explained it was named in honour of Julius Martov, a leader of the Menshevik revolutionaries, the more moderate of the groups which engaged in the 1917 revolutions. William was pleased to join and asked why they thought so highly of Martov.

David explained, "He was a man of peace and a democrat. Not everyone in the group agrees with Martov, but we all believe that when socialism loses its belief in democracy and peaceful opposition it loses its heart."

Every fortnight, William attended the group, listening

to, and later participating in, the debates that took place. The topics varied from esoteric philosophical nuances to policies for dealing with the current economic problems or world affairs. They were usually very serious debates and often quite heated, but rarely was anyone rude and it was a rule of the group that everyone had the right to be heard. Given the general leanings of the group members and the topics chosen for discussion, it was probably inevitable that those of a very different political persuasion were not inclined to attend their meetings and certainly not likely to become members.

The third time William attended the meeting was on a Thursday to celebrate the fifty-ninth anniversary of the birth of Julius Martov. Everyone was asked to make a small donation to pay for the group's administrative expenses, chief of which seemed to be financing the so-called 'Winter Festival' party arranged for the following month, just before Christmas. The chairman, Arthur Crane, delivered a paper on 'The failure of the Mensheviks' and was quite critical of Lenin, though not all the group agreed with him. There was a toast to Julius Martov and 'The Internationale' was recited, not sung, as the landlord was known to be concerned lest his other customers thought he supported revolutionary politics. William did not know the words and merely stood to attention.

At each meeting William got to know more members of the group. They could not be described in any way as homogenous, either by their backgrounds or their political beliefs. Arthur Crane was not the leader, either of the group or a faction within it. He had been one of its founder members and was chosen as chairman on the basis of his experience as a prominent member of the Social Democratic Federation before its decline following the formation of the Labour Party. He derived further kudos among the group through having known personally both Friedrich Engels and Eleanor Marx. He acted as a generally silent and gently moderating chairman of the group's discussions. The lady of fifty-five or so was Hilda Craddock, a former suffragette and a longstanding history teacher at a girls' high school. Her views were naturally conciliatory and she often brought debate to a convivial conclusion by her engaging summations. David Harris, John Billings and Fred Sweetman were three easy-going members of the group who rarely got over-excited by the debates. A South African of Indian descent, Krishna Narain was perhaps the quietest of the members. He had known Gandhi before the Great War and campaigned with him for Civil Rights but had come to England, where he felt he was more likely to be able to pursue a legal career. He was reflective during debates and seemed content to listen. Among the others was a young art student whose views seemed to vary from one week to another, a politics lecturer from the London School of Economics who spent more time making notes than speaking, even in the break-up groups, and a rather gaunt-looking aesthete in his late twenties who often quoted the Greek philosophers in his comments, seeking to draw allusions to modern democracy from the greats of ancient Greece. There was also a quiet man in his mid-thirties who worked in Derry & Toms, the department store, and who was often preoccupied with the fear that his employer might learn that his politics did not reflect those of his company.

Ronald Pierce, the man whose discussion group William had sat with on his first evening, was the nephew of a viscount. This fact he had never sought to divulge, but it had come to light when members of the group were asked, as part of a discussion on backgrounds, to describe their class origins. He then admitted that his mother was aristocratic. Since then this revelation, coupled with his tendency to moderate views, had occasionally been cited as the probable reason for his inability to take a more radical line politically.

Tired of such insinuation, Pierce, when next he was asked to bring a paper forward, chose the topic 'People of aristocratic backgrounds are incapable of being Socialists'. William, unaware of Pierce's origins, was startled to hear the chairman announce the title and assumed that he would hear an attack on the upper classes. Instead, Pierce asked how constitutional change in Britain had come about, in the absence of a revolution since at least 1688. He argued that much of it was the consequence of some members of the upper class acting counter to their own political and class interests. They had supported the expansion of the suffrage, the end of rotten boroughs, the secret ballot and other democratic measures in the nineteenth century. So, if an aristocrat is capable of acting against his own class, why should he not be capable of believing in democratic socialism? Though some of the group suggested the support of reforms could have been out of self-interest to deter revolutionary settlements, Pierce won the argument intellectually, at least as far as William was concerned. Looking round the group he wondered how many of the others there were of a working-class background. If they were not, they would have to accept that class could not be the only factor determining a person's political beliefs.

XXV

IT WAS THE LAST MEETING OF THE JM GROUP for the year. It was an extra meeting for the group members to hold their Winter Festival party and the chairman delivered a tongue-in-cheek paper on 'Father Christmas: paternalist or capitalist stooge?'. The debate which followed was short, light-hearted and humorous, and the rest of the evening turned into a very pleasant event. A few of the members of the group were abstemious, but most threw themselves into the party spirit. Towards the end of the evening, William found himself talking to Felicity, who was drinking her third or fourth pint of Guinness, she couldn't remember. William had also had several beers, certainly more than he was used to, and he found her less intimidating than usual. They soon drifted away from political topics to talk about themselves.

"I loved hearing about your childhood at that other meeting, and how you left school at twelve and had to make your own way in the world," she said, lighting one of her cheroots. "You are virtually the only one of the group who has really struggled over adversity to get where you are. The rest of us mean well, but we will not suffer terrible hardship if the world never changes. Most of us are just as far from knowing the real working class as dear old Ronald."

"So why are they here?"

"Ideals, principles, debating, company, who knows? We won't change the world talking about it, though."

"Why did *you* join the group?"

"All of the above, probably. But I would like to *do* something that made a difference. I hope that at some point we'll stop being merely a talking shop and come up with a plan of action for change that we all agree on. I think the Labour Party is too demoralised at the moment to seize the initiative."

"There's always the Communist Party if you think Labour is not socialist enough."

She nodded. "I don't think I'm ruthless enough to be a communist, but you may be right. We mustn't let the fascists win the argument, must we? So what made you decide to join us?"

"I met David at a lecture and he invited me along to a meeting. I was interested to hear other viewpoints than my own; I accept the likelihood that sometimes my views are misinformed or of dubious validity. Anyway, I like political discussions and most people aren't interested, whereas there's always plenty of debate in this group."

She smiled, looking round the slowly emptying room. "Getting near to closing time. Time for one more?"

"I'll get them." He took their glasses and went down to the bar. When he returned he saw Felicity talking to Henry Brisk, the young art student, who then leaned over to give her a kiss. William came to a halt, holding the drinks, uncertain what to do. But the young man was actually leaving and wished William the compliments of the season as he passed him on the way out.

"Thank you, William, cheers." Felicity raised the pint to her lips and took a sip.

"Cheers," replied William, wondering if this idea of another pint was a very good one. "You included yourself in those not part of the working class, but I don't know much about you."

She lit another cheroot. "Not a lot to tell. I'm thirty-two and I teach art at a local girls' school. It's a case of 'those who can't, teach', I suppose."

"You wanted to be an artist?"

"Still do; sculpture is my preference."

"You look like an artist."

She was dressed in her usual, slightly exotic style, given a seasonal enhancement of sprigs of holly and ivy made into a kind of brooch worn on her right breast. "That's the easy part. The world is full of people who dress up to look like the person they wish they could be."

"Perhaps I could see your art sometime?"

Their conversation was suspended as they bid goodnight to other members of the group who were on their way home. Suddenly, there were only Arthur Crane and David Harris still there, tidying up the remains of the snacks that had been served at the party and making sure the furniture was left as they'd found it. "I think I ought to give them a hand," Felicity said, and William joined her. It only took a few minutes.

"Well, thanks very much," said Arthur, putting on his overcoat and pulling his jacket down underneath to prevent the collar rucking up. "Happy Christmas and I'll see you both in the New Year."

"Glad you decided to join our little group, William," said David, shaking his hand. "Have a great time. Bye, Felicity." He kissed her cheek and walked off with Arthur.

"Well," she said, "party over and we've been abandoned. Would you like to come back to my flat for a little nightcap? It's not far."

"I don't want to put you to any trouble," he said.

"No trouble. You can give a critique of my latest piece of work." She put on her deep red overcoat and scarf and waited for him.

They walked downstairs and waved to the bar staff and the last customers, and William grasped the brass handle of the door to propel them into the cold night air. Except it didn't seem that cold.

Felicity loosened her scarf. "Phew, it's almost warm," she said. "Suits me; I hate white Christmases and all that sentimental tripe." She saw William's surprised reaction and laughed. "That's why the Christmas truce in the war didn't last; the soldiers were just being sentimental. If they'd really believed it was madness to fight they would have refused to return to the trenches. They exchanged one myth for another, for just one day."

William shrugged. "One day is better than nothing, perhaps."

"I suppose so, but it makes it seem even sadder that it changed nothing."

They walked the last few yards to her flat, the ground floor of an early Victorian house on one of the side roads off Upper Street. She let them in and gestured to the rooms – "Living room, bedroom, studio" – as she led him along the hall to the kitchen. This room was very warm and they both took off their coats. Felicity removed her concoction of a headdress, half-scarf, half-toque, and William saw her hair properly for the first time. It was curly and the deep shade of auburn looked almost mahogany. He wondered why she covered it up so much. She saw him staring at her and he looked away.

There were the remains of a fire in the grate and a pot was on the range. She took the lid off with a cloth. "I'm starving, would you like some soup?"

"Yes, please."

"I thought it might warm me up if it was a cold night when I got in. It's only vegetable."

"Just the ticket."

Felicity produced a couple of soup bowls and spoons from a cupboard and took a loaf from the white, blue-edged enamel breadbin. She ladled some soup from the pot and gave a full bowl to William. He held his spoon over the bowl and looked at the soup. The colour was normal, but the components were nothing like any vegetable soup he'd ever seen. Instinctively, he gave the surface a generous scattering of salt then plunged his spoon into the exotic under-surface, dredged up a spoonful and, with a quick blow over it, he tasted the soup gingerly. He looked over at Felicity, who was smiling.

"Is it all right?" she asked, before taking a spoonful herself.

"Yes, thank you." It was certainly not unpleasant and he took another spoonful. It was good, quite peppery and with a slight taste of lemon. "I don't recognise the vegetables."

"There are no potatoes or other root vegetables in it."

"Why is that?"

"I don't eat them."

William looked perplexed. "Really? Are they not to your taste, or perhaps there are health reasons?"

She smiled. "No, nothing like that. It's a long story, you'd find it boring."

"No, I'm interested," said William truthfully.

"Don't say I didn't warn you. I suppose you know what a vegetarian is?"

"Yes, of course."

"Well, I'm a kind of vegetarian, except that I take it a bit further. You see, I don't think it right to kill any living being for food when we can have enough to eat by coexisting in harmony with all life and harvesting from nature, without destroying the source of what we eat."

"That sounds much the same as vegetarianism to me," said William, now quite enjoying the soup.

Her usual expression of amused disinterest had given way to an earnest smile. "Except that I believe that plants, in their own way, are every bit as evolved as animals and entitled to a similar respect."

"But surely plants don't think or feel pain or care what's happening to them?"

"One might argue that some lower forms of animals can hardly be said to think in our meaning of the word. In any case, plants respond to stimuli and can exhibit stress, which is related to pain. I know I cannot avoid some injury to plants, but I choose not to destroy a living plant to feed myself. So I don't eat root vegetables and I don't eat plants which have been planted as annuals purely to exist for one year to feed me."

William nodded and replaced his spoon in the bowl.

"Would you like some more?"

"No, thank you, but I did enjoy it. So what *do* you eat?"

"Fruit, nuts, seeds, the leaves and flowers taken from perennial vegetables. I also eat food from animals which I believe causes them no pain or stress, such as eggs from chickens, honey from bees, dairy products and so on from animals who are well cared for and have a certain amount of freedom."

"This soup..."

"Has loads of different plants: sorrel, Good King Henry, wild leeks, a kind of Egyptian onion where the bulbs grow above the ground, beans, artichokes."

"How can you be sure that the vegetables you buy are from perennials and not annuals?"

"I grow a lot of my vegetables and as they are perennials I can keep them over the winter in a cold frame if they are tender. Of course, when I buy vegetables, I have to be careful, but sometimes you just have to do the best you can. It's a principle not a religious duty."

William nodded. "Do many people follow this kind of vegetarianism?"

"I've no idea. It's just something I believe is right for me to do. I don't tell anybody else how to live, so I'm not interested in seeking converts."

"Is there a name for it?"

Felicity laughed. "Not a universally accepted one that I know of. In one of my more pompous moments I did come up with a name. It's 'Demetarianism', after Demeter, the Greek goddess of the harvest." She picked up the bowls and spoons and put them in the Butler sink. "What would you like to drink? I've got sherry, port, whisky and gin."

William looked at his watch; it showed nearly half-past eleven. He thought he ought to be going. If he missed the last bus it would be a long walk. But he answered, "Could I have a whisky with soda or water, please?"

"Of course." She poured them both large drinks and brought one over to him. "We can sit in the living room if you like, though this room is probably warmer."

"Aren't you going to show me your latest sculpture?"

Her eyes lit up a little. "Would you like to see it?"

"Very much."

She took him into what had been designed to be a morning room but was now her studio. The room was full of art materials and tools. The walls had daubs of paint and sketches drawn on them, and in the centre, on a base, was a three-foot-high sculpture of a woman seemingly coming out of the stone, reminiscent of Michelangelo's 'Prisoners'. It was a nude of a woman with the legs not yet begun and the arms not fully formed. The face had a slight smile, half quizzical, half encouraging.

"You did this?"

"Yes, what do you think?"

"It's really good."

"I wouldn't say that, but it's not bad."

"It must weigh a ton."

"Quite a lot. I had to have the floor reinforced when I moved in. After I finish a piece I put it in the garden until I find a buyer, if I ever do."

"I'd like to look at the ones in the garden, if I may."

"It's rather dark, but if I put the outside light on you will get an idea." They walked back into the kitchen and she switched on the outside light then switched off the kitchen light.

The moon was in the last quarter and didn't help, but he could make out a couple of small figures, one a young girl, and a fish of some sort. "Very impressive," he said.

She put the kitchen light back on and refilled their drinks. Then they went to her living room where another fire was almost beyond help. She opened the damper and worked the hand bellows hard for a few minutes until the embers glowed brighter and she carefully arranged a few pieces of coal on the fire to give it the best chance. Then she sat in an armchair opposite William.

He had been looking round the room. The furniture was good quality, walnut or mahogany, but not new, and he thought the room rather old-fashioned, save for the walls. One was painted a plain green and decorated with stencils and painted objects to give the impression of a jungle scene. The others were hung with abstract artworks. "Have you lived here long?" he asked.

"About seven years, since I have lived on my own."

"I've never lived on my own."

She smiled. "You are probably thinking 'Poor Felicity', but actually I am quite happy. When I lived with my parents I couldn't expect them to put up with me making everywhere a mess for the sake of my art." She paused and posed with the back of her hand on her forehead while she looked upwards with a look of intensity then laughed. "I realised that living with anyone else I would always have to make compromises with how I lived and it wouldn't be worth it. Alternatively the other person would have to live their life fitting in with me and that wouldn't be fair either, not that I'm overloaded with offers anyway."

He looked at her and made a private critique of her physical appearance. She was attractive, but not conventionally beautiful. Her features were a little heavy and inclined to make her appear severe in her attitude. Her figure and legs were wrapped in a long loose garment that gave nothing away. Her hair was most certainly her crowning glory yet she kept it mostly hidden. Perhaps she was not interested in her appearance or reluctant to put it to the test. What did it matter? It was her choice.

"You never get lonely?" he asked.

"I've got friends and a busy life." She looked over at the door as it opened slightly. "And I've got Scopas."

At that moment, the cause of the door opening became apparent as a large ginger cat walked silently into the room, glanced at William and jumped up on Felicity's lap.

She tickled him behind the ear and stroked him under the chin, his feet taking turns to gently stamp up and down. He settled into a comfortable position admiring the fire and closing his eyes in a friendly gesture to William.

"Unusual name," said William.

"He was a Greek sculptor, famous for a copper statue of Aphrodite. It seemed appropriate at the time and he's happy with it. Aren't you, Scopas?" She stroked his head and received a lick on her hand. "I make all the compromises in our relationship and neither of us minds in the least."

William smiled and finished his drink. It was well after

twelve and there was a very good chance that his mother would have bolted the door, as she always did if he was away for the night and often did if he came home after twelve. After an hour-long walk it would not be the best end to the evening, but needs must. "Well, I think I ought to be going. I don't want to overstay my welcome and I have work tomorrow."

She looked at the clock on the mantelpiece. "Gosh, is that the time? You'll not get a bus and taxis are impossible round here after eleven."

"I can walk. It's only an hour at the most."

She stood up, Scopas reluctantly jumping to the floor but soon settling on the rug in front of the fire. "But if you have work tomorrow you mustn't get to bed after half-past one. You can stay here."

William looked at the furniture in the room. There were two sofas, but both were two-seaters. A night of discomfort followed by a morning of stiff joints beckoned. "I don't want to be an inconvenience."

"Nonsense, we'll sort something out."

William was tired; it had been a long day. He abdicated the decisions to her and sat down in the armchair while Felicity went off to do what had to be done. He stroked the cat, which had moved enough for one night and was settling down into a sleeping position.

A few minutes later, Felicity returned. "I've considered the options and I don't think you'd be very comfortable on a sofa or in the chair. We'll share the bed."

William looked alarmed. "I couldn't possibly. It wouldn't be right."

"Don't be silly. We are not going to bed *together*. We are going to share a bed. I have a six-foot bolster; we'll put that down the middle of the bed and we won't cross into each other's half. I've put clean sheets on."

"Aren't you worried about the neighbours?"

"No, *honi soit qui mal y pense*. Would you like anything else before you go to bed?"

"Are you sure about this?"

"Yes, I trust you. Shouldn't I?"

William made a gesture of futility and accepted her offer of one last drink while she went to the kitchen to wash.

"I'm going to the bedroom to change. You can wash in the kitchen if you like. The lavatory is just outside and round to the left. There's a little oil lamp and a box of matches just inside on the right."

William nodded and, leaving the Scotch for now, went to the kitchen and washed and took a trip out to the lavatory, managing the lighting of the lamp without difficulty. When ready, he went back to the living room, finished off his drink and entered Felicity's bedroom. It was smaller than the living room and was dominated by the double brass bed, over which hung a watercolour of a pastoral scene. A nude in the style of Toulouse-Lautrec stared at him from another wall. The room was warm and the bed looked inviting. Felicity was in the bed, only her nightdress-covered shoulders and head visible. William was pleased she was not wearing curlers.

He went to the other side of the bed and took off his clothes, all but his underwear, and slipped into the bed, his thigh touching up against the bolster and recoiling a little, like a boat bouncing gently off a harbour wall.

"Goodnight, William. Thanks for a lovely evening," she said, and rolled over to go to sleep.

"Goodnight and thank you for the hospitality; it was great." He lay on his back, positive he wouldn't get a wink of sleep, and woke up with an alarm ringing in his ears and with Felicity's hand on his arm. He lay still until she woke, apologising when she removed her hand and getting up immediately.

"I'll put the kettle on," she said, putting her slippers on and gathering up her clothes.

He watched her walk to the door, thinking how attractive she was and also how generous. Then he lay back, that initial moment of tranquillity and warm feelings towards Felicity pushed aside by the awareness of discomfort. His head was aching, his mouth dry, his stomach tender; he had a hangover. After a few minutes he got up and slowly put his clothes on. He consoled himself with the thought that the office was winding down towards Christmas; he could pace himself when he got to work. He came out of the bedroom and was attracted to the kitchen by the noise, painful though it was. Felicity was dressed and had breakfast almost ready: boiled eggs, tea and toast.

"Sleep well?" she asked, stirring the pot before pouring two large cups of tea.

"Like a log; I hope I didn't disturb you?"

"Not at all, I went out like a light. You behaved impeccably too. You see, I am a good judge of character. I don't let just anyone share my bed."

"I'm glad to hear it." He tried to sound jocular even though he was just the tiniest bit disappointed that he was regarded as so safe, even if he knew it to be true. He hoped she hadn't guessed he had never before spent the night with a woman.

"Thanks for breakfast, very kind," he said, changing the subject. "Where are you spending Christmas?" he asked, tapping the egg before slicing the top off with his spoon. The egg was just how he liked it: firm white and not too runny a yolk.

"With my parents in Hemel Hempstead, as usual. My brother and sister and their families will be there so it will be very lively. What about you?"

"Just me and my mother. I have no brothers or sisters and my grandparents are dead."

"Poor you."

He smiled. "It's only one day."

After breakfast he looked in a mirror in the hall. He had popped into a barbers for a shave just before the party and his beard was not too heavy this morning and would do for work. The breakfast had ameliorated the hangover somewhat and so, after a quick wash and the use of Felicity's hairbrush to comb his unruly hair, he was ready for the office. "Thanks for last night and this morning. It's been great. Have a Merry Christmas and I'll see you at the next meeting."

"Happy Christmas." She kissed him on the cheek and he went to work, feeling that sense of elation associated with an adventure, even when nothing had really happened at all.

When he arrived home that evening his mother greeted him with a look that somehow managed to combine annoyance, concern and suffering. It was one of her several visages she had worked on and perfected over the years.

"What happened?" she asked. "I've been worried out of my wits."

William maintained his composure. "I am sorry, Mum. I went to a party, as you know. It went on longer than I'd expected and I missed the last bus. A friend put me up for the night and I went straight to work this morning. I thought you would guess something of the sort as I could hardly telephone; I didn't want to wake you."

"Well, it was thoughtless to let me worry."

"If you were that worried, why didn't you phone me at work today?"

"I didn't like to. What if you'd not been there? They might have thought you were skiving off work and I would have been even more worried. Who was the friend who put you up?"

"Oh, no one you know. Just a friend."

XXVI

As 1933 began, William viewed the world from two distinct, though overlapping, perspectives. At work, he was preoccupied with the economic situation manifested in the loss of businesses and markets and the consequences this had for his union. For the members it meant prolonged unemployment, fewer opportunities, falling living standards and poverty while the union was suffering falling membership and reduced reserves to support the members who remained. His immediate concern and that of his work colleagues was to care for the welfare of the union membership. In his role as deputy to the head of registration he was involved in the union's schemes to help members and their families who had fallen on hard times. He also helped in giving advice on retraining and other opportunities open to those union members who had lost their jobs during the depression. He found the work rewarding, if at times frustrating, as the union could not do all it wanted to.

Yet away from work, in his political activities, he was increasingly troubled by the world situation, especially the rise of authoritarianism, notably in Europe and particularly in Germany. He was perfectly aware that, in regard to historical events, hindsight is a marvellous thing. If world leaders or generals had known the consequences of their actions before they embarked on them they would often have chosen differently. Surely the great powers in 1914 would have pulled back from the brink if they had known what awaited them in the Great War. However, he believed that foresight was possible too and sometimes there is an opportunity to detect signs of the direction history is taking. Without claiming powers of prophecy himself, he was convinced there were such signs for all to see in Germany.

Early in 1932 he had begun keeping in his journal a log of those political events in Germany which seemed to be pushing the country towards authoritarianism and perhaps foreign expansionism. His first note was in April when the German chancellor Heinrich Bruning banned the SS and the SA as the chief cause of political violence in the country. "A brave decision but illustrated how far the Nazi Party and its adherents had already changed the landscape of politics in Germany," he wrote. Subsequent entries in his journal reinforced this view. At the end of May: "Bruning is dismissed as Chancellor and the new government of Von Papen openly questions the value and continued existence of the Weimar Republic." In June: "The ban on the SS and SA is lifted." In July: "The democratically elected government in Prussia is deposed by the army on the orders of the government." Two weeks later the Nazi Party won thirty-seven per cent of the votes in a general election and became the largest party in the Reichstag. With the World Disarmament Conference in December approving Germany's right to re-arm, William concluded that neither the world powers nor the German people recognised the dangers posed by Hitler and the Nazis.

Now, in 1933 he wrote the last four entries in the journal concerning the deteriorating democratic situation in Germany.

January: "Hitler becomes Chancellor." February: "The Reichstag fire, followed by the curtailment of some German civil liberties." Early March: "Federal election in which the Nazi Party wins 43.9% of the vote and all but two areas of the country." Late March: "Hitler given dictatorial powers and the virtual end of democracy in Germany."

In April it was William's turn to deliver the discussion group paper and he chose as his title: 'If it can happen in Germany, it can happen anywhere'. Using examples from the past, he presented his hypothesis that Europe was periodically subject to a wave of political and philosophical change in which a philosophy or powerful argument was propounded by a dedicated and determined minority. In time this could cross boundaries and sweep across most of Europe like a contagion. He concluded, "At the present time there is, in much of Europe, a desire for strong government to solve economic and other problems, and this has led to an acceptance of dictatorships, even in countries like Italy and Germany, with a long record of philosophical and cultural maturity. If democracy can be lost in Germany, in how many other countries can it be expected to survive?"

The group listened to him quietly and sombrely, and none of them challenged the basic premise of his argument. In the discussion afterwards there was a consensus that a Europe of dictatorships would be more likely to lead to another war, especially if they were not all of the same political ideology.

"What a good paper that was," said Felicity as she and William left the pub after the meeting.

Since Christmas they had always shared a drink or two after the meeting, and this time she had invited him to a light supper at her flat. They had one of those hard-to-define relationships where they always spent time together after the regular group meetings, sometimes on their own and sometimes with other members of the group, but didn't meet apart from that. They were more than acquaintances but not fully-fledged friends. So to William this invitation to supper seemed to be an upgrading of their relationship, although still nowhere the level of chaste intimacy of that night after the Christmas party.

"It's kind of you to say so," he replied. "I've been mulling over this potential nightmare for months and it's good to get it off my chest."

"Everyone found it thought-provoking and it is frightening that so many countries have become dictatorships. You didn't seem too worried about Britain, though."

William shrugged. "I'm just basing it on how few votes Mosley got in the 1931 election. I just can't see half the country voting for Fascism here. Our biggest problem is complacency. Hitler is a posturing, self-important braggart, but at some point he will feel impelled to prove something so we must be prepared."

Felicity smiled. "What did you do over the Easter break?"

"Football matches on the Friday and Saturday and nothing much else. What about you?"

"At the last minute I went to Rome, for the art mostly, and obviously I saw the sights."

"Rome, that's exciting. I've never been to Italy," he replied. In fact, he had never been abroad.

"I'd been to Rome before, when I was about twenty, and it was as I'd remembered it but oddly different."

"Because of the Fascists?"

"Yes. Everywhere there are signs that the Fascists are in power: the pictures on billboards, the symbol of the Fasces, the propaganda. There is a system of state-sponsored art which puts over the message and the artists I met felt, not controlled exactly, but subject to strong censorship. Then at six o'clock every evening everyone has to stand to attention if they are out in the streets or piazzas and listen to a broadcast of some nonsense from Mussolini and give the Fascist salute. If you don't, the police are likely to take a dim view. But, it's still Rome and I did have a good time."

They had arrived at her house and as she opened the front door, Scopas was waiting and purred loudly as Felicity picked him up and stroked him under the chin. "Come on; let's see if your bowl is empty." She took him to the kitchen and fed the cat before cooking a meal of spaghetti al burro followed by omelette fines herbes.

"I brought back some wine from Italy and I thought we might have a bottle tonight," she said, raking around in the cutlery draw for a corkscrew.

The meal was excellent and the Chianti too. "That was great," said William, lighting Felicity's cheroot. "You are a good cook."

"Not hard, cooking, unless you make it difficult by trying to do things that are either for show or stretch the ingredients beyond their limits. But glad you liked it." She poured them both another glass of wine and the bottle was empty.

William had become used to Felicity's dismissal of compliments and guessed it was a sign of embarrassment or modesty rather than tetchiness. He liked her little quirks of behaviour, so just smiled. He watched her blow the smoke from her cheroot into the air and thought her better-looking than she used to be, quite pretty in fact. Perhaps there was something she was doing different with her looks, though he couldn't think what. Whatever the reason he found her very attractive this evening. He insisted on washing up, one over-enthusiastic splash of water sending Scopas scurrying out of the room. While he was drying up she offered him another drink in the sitting room.

She had already poured the drinks and was sitting on the sofa with the cat half on, half off her lap.

"It's warm, isn't it?" said William. A fire had been lit earlier in the day and though it had all but died out, the heat still permeated the room.

"It is, now you come to mention it." She shooed the cat onto the floor and with a swish of the tail it settled down on the fireside carpet. She stood up and removed her burgundy cardigan to reveal her short-sleeved blouse and sat down again.

William asked her about the art she'd seen in Rome, at the Vatican and the National Gallery of Modern Art. She launched into an enthusiastic summary of those pieces that had most enthralled her, usually by painters he'd never heard of. He looked at his watch a few times, but there was never a good moment to interrupt her, and suddenly he had missed the last bus again.

"I really had better go, it's rather late."

"Oh, I'm so sorry," Felicity said. "I just keep jabbering on."

"It's not your fault. I very much enjoyed the evening. We've always got so much to talk about and never enough time."

"You can stay again."

"It doesn't seem right to impose."

"I'd like you to. I bought a razor just after Christmas, in case you ever needed one."

William raised his eyebrows in a mock admonishment and she laughed. "How about a cup of tea before we retire?" and she went off to the kitchen.

William took off his jacket and undid his collar while he waited for her return. He was thinking about being in bed with Felicity and what might happen, his hopes a mixture of longing anticipation and noble restraint. But a vision of his mother intervened, saying how worried she was when he was away all night, and the spell was broken. He took the whisky bottle from the table and poured himself another small drink. After what seemed an age, the door swung open and in marched Scopas followed by Felicity with a tray and the tea.

"Sorry I was so long; I thought the kettle would never boil. I used the time to get ready for bed so you won't have to wait too long." She was wearing a different nightdress to the one she had worn at Christmas, this one in a finer material, and William averted his gaze in order not to stare.

They drank their tea almost in silence, apart from the odd unimportant comment or observation and a brief discussion about their plans for the day ahead.

"Right," she said, finishing her tea and re-assembling the cups on the tray, "I won't be a minute and then the kitchen is yours. I've left you a new toothbrush there if you want to use it."

He watched her go out, admiring the shape of her figure under the nightdress, and waited until he heard her go into the bedroom before he went to the kitchen. While he cleaned his teeth he looked at the big iron bath on the wall and wished he'd been able to have a bath before going to bed. He had been nervous when presenting his paper that evening and hoped now that he hadn't sweated much. *Oh God*, he thought and, now a little anxious, he crept along to the bedroom.

Felicity was already in bed, sitting up and glancing through a magazine.

He stripped down to his underwear and, almost apologetically, climbed into the bed.

She put down her magazine and turned to him. "I so enjoyed our evening." She moved a little nearer him. She smelled of soap, or was it a scent of some kind? He liked it.

He realised they were very close and there was no barrier between them. "No bolster tonight?"

She smiled. "Would you feel better if it were there?"

He shook his head.

"I trust you not to do anything I wouldn't want you to," she said.

Although this statement was open to various interpretations, he took it as an invitation at least to kiss her, which he did. They kissed and cuddled for a while, but William was not demanding; after all, she had invited him to her bed to sleep. As she didn't encourage him to go further, this passage of physical entwining was enjoyable but relatively brief, and they turned round and went their separate ways to sleep.

The next morning, they woke early and lay together for a while, comfortable with each other's presence, before the alarm urged them to get up. William, until now unsure of their relationship, asked her over breakfast if they might meet again later that week and found himself unexpectedly overjoyed when she agreed.

Over the next few weeks their relationship developed with trips to the cinema, an evening at the Playhouse Theatre to see a young Laurence Olivier in *The Rats of Norway* and several visits to art galleries and museums. At his insistence, Felicity educated him in the painters and paintings she liked best. With their time spent together in the discussion group, they saw each other twice, sometimes three times, a week and William reflected that he was as happy in his personal life as he had ever been.

Though they did not think of themselves in that way, they had become a couple. They looked for each other first when they arrived at the JM Group meetings and sought each other out at the end of the formal proceedings. They adapted the rest of their social life around the times they spent together and they shared with each other the experiences and thoughts which filled their time apart. However, they had not met each other's families nor did they announce their relationship to anyone else. Others, like the members of the group, observed and assumed they were now a couple, and as far as any newly joined members of the group were concerned, they might always have been together.

One Saturday in early summer, they went to the seaside and after their return they sat talking about the day. William said, "It's still early, would you like to go out for a drink?"

"Is that what you would most like to do?"

"Not particularly."

"What *would* you most like to do?"

"Whatever *you* would most like to do."

She smiled. "They might be the same thing, but I don't think you should have to go along with what I want to do."

"Why not? There are ample opportunities for us to pursue other interests when we're not together. We don't live in each other's pockets."

Her expression became serious, though not sad or apologetic. "There is something I must tell you. Do you remember I said that I didn't want to live with anyone because I would find the compromise too much?"

"Yes," William replied half-heartedly. He tried to prepare himself for what might be the termination of their relationship.

"Well, I feel we are at that stage in our relationship when sooner or later the question of sex will arise and I think it only fair to tell you that I don't believe it right that we have sexual relations."

"I see," said William.

She smiled. "I don't think you do. It's not a matter of morals or ethics; personally I believe in the idea of free love, with people able to do whatever they please with whoever they want. The problem is that as soon as most people have sex with each other they want commitment: women generally expect the man to marry them and men demand fidelity from the woman, even if they don't expect it from themselves. That's why an open marriage, though a good idea in principle, rarely works. It requires both partners to maintain the same degree of detachment between what their partner gets up to and their commitment to each other, and that often proves impossible. So we are left with monogamy as the only solution. That involves the biggest commitment of all, which puts us back where we started."

William thought she had probably used this little statement of her values before; it was so well-worded. He shrugged. "If you don't want to have a sexual relationship I am happy to continue as we are."

She sighed. "It's not that I've got an aversion to sex. I'm not a virgin; I'm nearly thirty-three, for God's sake! Will you promise me that you will never ask me to marry you?"

"Yes, I promise. But you can still ask me to marry you."

"Let's go to bed," she said simply.

They went up to the bedroom and William could feel his pulse racing. He undressed with his back to her, as usual. He went to climb into the bed in his underwear, but she stopped him. "Everything off," she commanded.

He did as he was told and lay facing her, a few inches apart. As they kissed she came into his arms and he felt the exhilarating shock of her naked skin and the pleasing touch of her hands on his back. It briefly went through his mind that he was glad it wasn't her first time; that seemed too great a responsibility.

Afterwards, they lay in each other's arms, the covers back. He glanced down at her body for the first time and thought how beautiful she was. "What made you change your mind?" he asked.

"I didn't change my mind. You made me a promise and I will hold you to it and everything that goes with it."

This new development in their relationship did not change anything else. They maintained their independence and demanded nothing of each other. A few weeks later, Stanley informed him that he was getting married to Joan, his fiancée of a couple of years, and asked William to be his best man. William felt honoured to accept and asked Felicity if she would like to accompany him. She gently refused and explained that her going to a wedding would be the height of hypocrisy as she would have nothing but pity and dread for the couple. In any case, she would know nobody else and, with him busily engaged with the wedding, she would be a pure supernumerary. William fully understood and instead was accompanied to the wedding by his mother, who was delighted to attend.

The wedding day arrived, the Saturday of that traditionally very hot third week in July. William arrived at the bridegroom's house with his mother and, as he walked into the front room, the first person he saw was Lucy. He hadn't seen her since her own wedding day, six years before, but she hadn't changed at all, perhaps a little more beautiful. She looked over at him and smiled then gave a little wave to his mother.

"Hello, Billy," she said, walking over and kissing him lightly on the cheek. "You remember Dick?" She pointed to the man leaning on the mantelpiece.

"Yes, of course." William shook hands with the tall, tanned man whom he had last seen in uniform, looking just as fit and handsome in a well-cut suit and tie.

"Nice to see you again," Dick said.

"Bit of a swelterer, isn't it?" said William, pulling his starched collar away from his neck.

"Yes, luckily I'm used to it. I've just got back from the Med."

"This is my mother, Alice Lyus."

"Yes, I remember you well from our wedding, Mrs Lyus. Dick Stone." He shook her hand.

As they were going through the introductions and small talk, Stanley came into the room. "Hello, Billy. Let's go in the other room and we'll run through everything once more."

The wedding was not a complicated affair. They would make their own way to the church on foot and the wedding breakfast with fifty guests would be held in the church hall. The vicar knew his job, there were no ushers to instruct, so all William had to do was make sure that he had the ring in his pocket, ensure there was a car to take the happy couple away and give a short speech at the breakfast.

Ten minutes later the two men were walking cheerily to the wedding, William checking every so often that he had the ring while Stanley waxed lyrical about his plans for his new home in Cambridge Heath. Feeling it was his duty as best man to offer one last word of caution but not wishing to raise doubts with his friend, he said, "I can tell you are absolutely certain about today and that you have no doubts about marrying Joan whatsoever."

Stanley smiled. "You're right there, Billy. I've been going out with her for over three years and we've had plenty of time to learn each other's good and bad points. Of course, we haven't lived with each other yet and I dare say I'll get on her nerves and she on mine from time to time, but as long as we've got a room each to get away from the other till the dust settles I reckon we'll manage."

William smiled and patted his friend on the back.

The wedding went smoothly. The bride, in a long wedding dress, looked lovely, the bridesmaids just as pretty and even a little page boy, Joan's nephew, handled his role well and was composed throughout. The minister was efficient and delivered a suitably platitudinous homily. At the wedding breakfast all the speeches were short and mildly amusing, the food and drink were up to standard and neither ran out.

Nobody stood on the bride's dress, nobody made a fool of themselves, nobody was taken ill, nobody overstayed their welcome, the bride looked very pretty in her going-away outfit and everybody who needed one got a lift home. In short, the wedding passed without incident and the best man thought the day had been splendid. The only irritation for him was the frequent comment, "Your turn next!" from other guests at the wedding.

What added to the day for him personally was that he had the opportunity to talk to Lucy and Dick. They appeared to be very happy, although William detected a hint of frustration that as yet there had been no sign of a child on the way. Dick was now a Second Officer in the Merchant Navy and had his First Mate ticket. They still lived in London but also had a holiday bungalow on Point Clear, near Clacton.

"Are you able to use it very much?" asked William.

"Yes, it's very convenient for a holiday break when Dick's home," said Lucy. "Dick's keen on sports and he can pop over on the ferry to do a bit of sailing on Mersea Island."

"There's also a golf course on the island where I play sometimes. Lovely position: opposite Brightlingsea with the Colne and the Blackwater around you as they enter the sea. You must come and stay with us some time. We could play a round together," added Dick.

"Yes. We'd love to see you, Billy," said Lucy. "And your young lady if you're courting?"

William smiled and said he hoped to see them soon. But that's what people always do at weddings and funerals: promise to keep in touch but never do. Everyone means it at the time but keeps to the rules otherwise the population would be inundated with unexpected visits from distant relations and long-lost friends. For a few weeks William was tempted to get in touch. He was a little concerned that

Lucy might be lonely at times with Dick, even when home, spending time sailing or playing golf or enjoying his other interests, but he thought it not his place to keep her amused and let the idea drop.

XXVII

AFTER THE SUMMER, THE JM GROUP RETURNED revitalised and with many new members, thanks to the recruiting efforts of old hands like David Harris and one or two others. There were now over thirty of them and the atmosphere had subtly changed: less informal and intimate, more organised and pro-active. With each member having fewer opportunities to present papers, a new item appeared on the agenda: 'Members Reports and Activities'. At each meeting it was open to members, on a rota basis, to report on news in their own spheres of interest and everyone could draw members' attention to important events coming up, in which they might wish to participate. Often, the group would send a delegate to a conference or a representative detachment of members to a rally in support of some campaign they wished to support.

For most of the JM Group the biggest domestic issue was the increasingly forthright anti-Semitism of the British Union of Fascists. They now often held rallies in Jewish areas to provoke unrest and lead to violence between protesters and the so-called security forces of the BUF. It was too close to home for William not to be aware of it with large Jewish communities distributed throughout North and East London. These events brought back a sense of shame for William for having briefly leaned towards the New Party, even though it was before the party revealed its true colours and policies. It also brought to mind his brief relationship with Esther and how they had been driven apart through a belief that differences of background and culture were too insurmountable for their relationship to develop. He regretted that he had not tried harder to resist this obsession with difference because now he was seeing where this could lead: the exploitation of 'difference' as a means of seeking to raise one race or creed or culture above another and stamping on it.

Inspired by the crusading spirit in the group, he readily joined a number of members who attended a BUF meeting in Birmingham, including Fred Sweetman, David Harris, John Billings and Ronald Pierce.

How different it was to the last time William had heard Mosley speak. This time he entered the darkened auditorium in a blaze of light and surrounded by a parade of flags to the music of a German military march. The name 'Mosley' was chanted by the loyal faithful. Then he gave one of his stirring, fluent speeches, delivered without notes and in a strong voice. As the speech moved from one crescendo to another most of the audience grew increasingly enthusiastic and even sceptics like William couldn't help but be impressed by this powerful oratory. There were repeated standing ovations and loud cheers, broken only by occasional booing from a small minority, including some of the JM Group. Suddenly a man in front of William was grabbed by two Blackshirts and dragged from his seat. Those next to William booed and protested and then their row was attacked. William tried to fend off someone grabbing Fred Sweetman from behind but was punched in the face and pulled out of his seat as well. In a whirl, William was carried, struggling to no effect, out of the hall by two men. Within seconds, he and three of his friends were outside in a side alley. Fred's wallet came out of his pocket as he was thrown to the ground and a Blackshirt picked it up and looked inside.

"Jewboy, eh?" he said, examining the driving licence inside. "Causing trouble while you've still got the chance, eh?" He kicked Fred in the face and stamped on his glasses as they fell to the floor.

"I bet you're a yid as well, you'd better get back to the ghetto," said another to William, and cracked him on the head with a truncheon.

William felt a terrible pain on the side of his head, but he didn't pass out. Dazed, he waited for the next blow, but it never came. The Blackshirts had gone into the hall to deal with more 'troublemakers'. He looked over at Fred and another man he didn't know who was lying on the ground without moving. Fred was trying to staunch the flow of blood from his nose. "Are you all right, William?" he asked.

"My head hurts and my ears are ringing, but it didn't knock me out. What about you?"

"Nose might be broken, glasses definitely are. I won't be able to drive back." He looked behind him to where William's eyes were fixed.

The prostrate man had still not moved, and William scrambled to his feet and gingerly walked over to him. As he bent over, nearly falling on the man in the process, he heard footsteps and looked up with relief to see it was David Harris with John Billings.

David stopped by Fred. "We couldn't get through the mêlée," he said, bending down and helping him up.

John had run over to William, who was trying to turn the man over. John helped him and knelt by the side of the man. "Can you hear me?" he asked.

The man, not young, probably well over fifty, mumbled something. Blood was seeping from his receding grey hairline. "We need an ambulance," said John. "Are you all right, William?" he added as he saw William sway a little.

"Sorry, didn't hear that."

"Are you all right?"

"Just took a bash on the head. I'll get an ambulance."

At that moment the man opened his eyes. "What happened? Was I run over?"

John was holding a handkerchief to the man's head. "No, someone hit you on the head. You were in there." He pointed to the hall.

The man sat up. "I remember now, I was dragged out here and I felt something hit me."

"We'll get an ambulance."

"No, thank you. I'll go home and my brother, he's a doctor, he will see to me."

"Do you live in Birmingham?"

"Yes, not far from the Bullring. Where is my friend, Benny? He was here with me. He will help me."

At that moment, a portly man in a black Homburg came running over. "My God, Sam, what has happened to you?"

"I'm all right, don't worry. Harold will see to it. Just get me home."

"It needs to be checked out," said William. "He was unconscious for a while."

"I will be sure to have him looked at," said Benny. "Thank you very much for your help, you have been very kind. Come on, old friend."

As Sam was helped up, he turned and thanked John, apologising as he returned the blooded handkerchief.

The JM Group members found Fred's car and William drove back to London, saying he felt much better except for a raging headache and a ringing in his left ear. When people spoke to him from the back of the car he couldn't hear what they were saying and Fred Sweetman insisted on his staying at his house that night. After dropping the others off, they finally arrived at his house in Cricklewood in the early hours of the morning and Fred's wife gave them tea and toast and cared for their ailments as best she could, both promising to see the doctor the next day.

In the morning William awoke, lying on his right ear. Without moving he could see the clock on his bedside cabinet; it was nine o'clock. He closed his eyes again and thought how quiet and peaceful it was here, even at this time. But it was not quiet; it was silent. He turned over and the noise of traffic and drone of a machine somewhere were picked up by his right ear. He pressed his right ear with his finger and there was silence again. He felt the bump on the head above and behind his ear; it was sore, but he didn't care about his head.

After breakfast he and Fred went to the doctors, where both were examined by an amiable, middle-aged GP who repeated to William the advice he'd given to Fred about the folly of attending 'rumbustious political meetings'.

He put down his otoscope. "Well, you are deaf in one ear and that you know already. I can't see anything untoward, so we have to put it down to the blow to the head. Do you have any sounds in that ear, nothing to do with what's going on outside?"

William shook his head.

The doctor nodded. "That's one blessing. Some people are stone deaf and still hear ringing or other noises in their ear all the time: tinnitus."

"Will I get my hearing back?"

"Difficult to say; could be a loose wire, as it were, and it might go one way or the other. Sometimes the injury does permanent damage and that's it, I'm afraid. I could try to get you an appointment with a specialist, but there's no guarantee."

"I'll think about it," said William. "How much do I owe you?"

"Forget it, I couldn't help. Let me know if you want a referral."

"Thank you, Doctor."

Fred was waiting with a large plaster on his nose. It had been broken, but the doctor had reset it. "Glasses next," he said. "I'm sorry about your ear, William. Perhaps the hearing will come back."

"I've still got one good one," said William breezily.

Feeling better, if not quite himself, he went to work after thanking Fred and his wife for their hospitality. That evening he went to see Felicity first. He needed time to prepare to face his mother.

"You poor thing," Felicity said, examining the lump on his head. "I wish I'd gone with you last night. I might have been able to help."

"You had to be in early this morning. Anyway, it was no place for a woman who wasn't ready to cheer the great leader and his cronies."

"Won't you stay so I can make a little fuss of you? I do think you should see a specialist about the ear."

It was the first time Felicity had come anywhere near to mollycoddling him and he was tempted but shook his head. "I have to go home; I've got so much to do."

He had warned his mother that he might stay in Birmingham, so she was not in the least worried about him until she spoke to him in the kitchen and he didn't hear her. Then she noticed the bump.

"What happened to your head?"

"Nothing, just a bash from one of the thugs surrounding Mosley. It's affected my hearing, but I'll be all right."

"You should never have gone to that Mosley meeting. What was the point of you going, when there was bound to be trouble, if all you get for your pains is a bump on the head and problem with your hearing? It doesn't stop him doing what he wants."

"Mum, it really isn't my fault if someone hits me with a truncheon for no reason whatsoever."

His mother merely huffed but then did apply a cold cloth to try to get the swelling down and cooked him a nice meal.

At the next meeting of the JM Group there was a discussion about the Birmingham rally and those members who had not been ejected from the hall reported that any booing or attempt to challenge what was said on the platform led to those people being thrown out and some obviously experienced violent attacks. There was a great deal of anger within the JM Group and some called for a common front with other anti-Fascist groups to meet violence with violence. Arthur Crane called the meeting to order so that Krishna Narain could be heard.

"As you know, I worked and campaigned with Gandhi in South Africa and he convinced me that non-violent protest will eventually triumph over evil, whereas when violence is used to settle a dispute there is no guarantee that the right side will triumph. If we engage in battles with the Blackshirts we will be seen as just a left-wing version of the BUF and the moderate, law-abiding majority will not distinguish between us. But if we protest peacefully this will stand out in stark contrast to the violence and intolerance of the Fascists and they will lose support. Every victim of violence will lose the BUF ten supporters. This will cause them to become frustrated and more extreme, and for each act of extremism they will lose a hundred supporters."

The debate went on for a while and at times was very heated, but Krishna's position won the day and this was the policy followed when the JM Group attended BUF rallies during 1934 and later years. Although some of the group was disappointed by its relentlessly peaceful stance at such meetings, Krishna Narain's forecast was proved to be correct. However much the BUF tried to protest that trouble at its meetings was stirred up by extreme left-wing groups, it had become tainted by violence and, despite the occasional upsurge in support, it was in long-term decline.

Nothing that happened in Europe over the next couple of years did much to reduce William's pessimism about where the world was heading. Dictatorships, in absolute control of their own countries, were now seeking to expand their influence on weaker neighbours and were meeting little opposition from either the League of Nations or the Western powers. The one bright spot was Spain, where democracy seemed stronger than it had ever been. But in 1936 a coup was launched by part of the army under General Franco and civil war broke out in the country.

In early October, the JM Group met and gave their support to the International Brigades of foreign volunteers who were going to Spain to fight for the Republic. David Harris and John Billings said they were going out to Spain themselves and would organise the travel arrangements of anyone else who wished to go. Several others said they were minded to go and a few did take up the offer. William knew it was time to make a stand against Fascism and perhaps this was his moment of destiny. He looked at Felicity; she was silent and seemed reflective, almost ignoring the noise and excitement going on around her.

After the meeting ended she told him she didn't want to stay for a drink; she needed peace and quiet to think. They walked to her house in silence. It was quite cold and they both wished they'd brought a coat. She put her arm through his and held him close. When they got in, she went straight to the kitchen and put the kettle on. He did not go to the living room as usual but sat in the kitchen, watching and waiting for her to reveal her thoughts. While the kettle was boiling she turned to face him, her arms folded.

"I've decided to go to Spain," she said quietly.

"Are you sure?"

"It's nothing to do with tonight; I've been thinking about it since August, when Metaxas staged his coup in Greece. I can hardly believe that Italy and Greece, the so-called cradles of philosophy and democracy in Europe, are now dictatorships, and look at the rest of the Mediterranean: Portugal and Albania dictatorships, and Yugoslavia on the edge. If Spain goes too, can even France survive? We have to make a stand."

William was simultaneously proud of her and full of anxiety. They had been friends and lovers for a couple of years, and she was such a part of his life that he found it hard to imagine their being apart for any length of time. The last time she had left the country, for a week in Normandy, he had gone with her. He had not broken his promise about never mentioning marriage, but as far as he was concerned his feelings and loyalty to her were no different to that of a married man. He repressed his doubts and concerns and tried to be supportive.

"Will you join the International Brigade?"

"I don't think so. I'm not really a communist, certainly not a Stalinist, and I'm not sure I could shoot to kill. I thought I would offer my services as a stretcher bearer or an ambulance driver or something like that."

"I'll come with you," said William.

She smiled. "No, you won't! You know me, I don't want anyone worrying about me and I don't want to have to worry about anyone else. You've already lost one ear in the cause; it's enough."

"It's not right that a woman should go when I don't."

"Don't be silly. If you went, you would be bound to fight; they would expect it. A woman isn't expected to fight. They'll be glad to have me helping out as a non-combatant."

"It will still be dangerous."

"I'll be careful."

"What about your job; will it be kept open for you?"

"The headmistress was very good, she's an old suffragette. She's given me a nine-month sabbatical from the beginning of next month which means I shall not be required until next September. After that we'll see."

William remained both concerned for Felicity's safety and unconvinced by her arguments against his going. The next day he broached the subject with his mother, though he was in no doubt what her view would be.

"Why would you want to go to Spain and get involved in their civil war?" she asked, looking at him with a look of stupefaction.

"It's a matter of principle. The Spanish people elected a socialist, republican government, and Franco and his troops want to replace that by force. All over Europe, democracy is being replaced by dictatorship and we all have to try to stop it."

"You take after your father with your political principles and fine gestures. Where will this leave me? I'm not getting any younger and I have no other close family. If anything happens to you I shall be left on my own."

"You have sisters."

"They have their own families to think of. It's time you thought of your family. Everything I have will be yours when I'm gone; surely you can spare me the worry of you marching off like this."

"But everybody who goes leaves a family behind, like they did in the war."

"They were going off to fight for their country, for us, not the Spanish."

"I haven't made up my mind yet," he said, feeling himself wilt under his mother's barrage of objections.

He didn't go to Spain. His mother thought it was out of concern for her, and Felicity believed he had acceded to her request. He didn't know whether both or neither of them was right, but he was surprised by his willingness to stand back from the struggle for the Spanish republic, when he had believed so fervently that it was time to resist Fascism. Yet one of the things his mother had said troubled him. She had talked of fighting for the Spanish, but there were Spanish on both sides and he found the prospect of helping one Spaniard to kill another Spaniard disturbing. Or was that just another excuse for not standing up for his principles? He didn't know.

Six weeks later the JM Group was out in force to see seven of their members depart for Spain from Victoria Station. Apart from David Harris, John Billings and Felicity, there was the artist Henry Brisk and three newer members of the group, all in their early twenties. Their plan was to go first to Barcelona by train, provided there was no interruption to the route. Once there, some would enlist with the International Brigades and others, in the case of Felicity at least, with the Spanish Medical Aid Committee which had been set up by the Popular Front.

Felicity had not informed her parents that she was going in the hope of saving them from anxiety, so only William saw her off.

He had brought her some artists' materials and a portable stand. "In case you get the chance to paint a bit; I thought a piece of stone might be too heavy," he said as he gave it to her.

They walked down the platform together, William holding most of her luggage. He waited as Henry Brisk helped Felicity get her luggage to their compartment then the window opened and she leaned out and put her hand on his shoulder.

"You'll write, won't you?" he asked.

"Yes, but don't be surprised if letters take a long time to get to you."

"Be careful," he said, squeezing her hand.

"Now, now, no sentiment, we agreed. Look after Scopas for me."

"Of course."

The couple in the upstairs flat of Felicity's house had agreed to look after Scopas, but William promised to look in on him from time to time even though, as Felicity admitted, "He's even less sentimental than I am."

They kissed as the whistle blew and she leaned back and stood, waving from the window to him until he was a speck on the platform.

XXVII

To William's surprise, Felicity did write regularly, though the missives were usually short, almost terse and quite properly avoided mention of the Republican units she was attached to or where exactly she was, other than on the Madrid front. After arriving in Barcelona, the volunteers had gone their own ways and she had registered with the Popular Front. After a time spent kicking her heels while they decided what to do with her, she was finally assigned to a convoy of equipment and medical supplies to Madrid. The convoy had to skirt round Nationalist-held areas and the route was often disrupted by bomb damage or shelling.

Once in Madrid, she was appointed a nursing auxiliary at the central military hospital and willingly accepted the most menial tasks to support the professional medical teams. She had spoken no Spanish when she arrived, but soon she picked up enough words to be able to help the nurses more, eventually being assigned to duties like dressing wounds and washing patients. Dealing with the terrible injuries suffered by the casualties was very difficult at first, but she learned to concentrate on the job at hand and separate that from the sorrow she felt for the wounded. The fighting was ferocious and she was shocked by the number of casualties among the Madrid defenders. The Durutti Column, a force of anarchist troops, had arrived in Madrid in early November and by the time it had withdrawn from the fighting two weeks later, it had lost 2,600 of its original count of 3,000, either killed or wounded. Felicity arrived in the city as the worst casualties were still being nursed before being discharged, sometimes to return to the front.

It came as such a relief when, by the end of November, the two sides were deadlocked and a front line was established, easing the pressure in the hospital a little. Felicity shared some quarters with other nursing volunteers, British, Americans and a couple of Canadians, her bed vacated by a nurse on the night shift when she came home at the end of her day. She didn't make any particular friends; she didn't see enough of anybody for that to happen. However, in the few precious moments of rest and relaxation, whoever was around would get together, smoke cigarettes, drink cheap wine and share stories of their lives before they had come to Spain and what they would do after the war. They rarely spoke about their work; they all knew more than enough about what went on already.

At the beginning of December, Felicity had her first day's leave for ten days. With the number of men in the hospital and among the city defenders far outnumbering women, there was no shortage of invitations to dates and fervent hopes of physical comfort of some kind, though to many of the younger men she must have appeared more of a mother figure. She went out in a group once or twice but was not interested in individual entanglements of either a social or sexual nature, even with young men keen to fulfil their 'older woman' fantasy. In the weeks that followed, the lull in ground fighting gave her more time to herself and she did a little painting of areas less damaged by the incessant bombing. Although unimpressed by the quality of her work, she found it a release of tension and an escape from the horrors she encountered every day. In the relative respite at the end of the year, Felicity's letters to William became more reflective about the war and the importance of human life and less about her daily events. She confessed herself unable to become hardened to the scale of the daily bloodshed and the stories of terrible retribution and mass executions by Nationalist forces. The Republican government dismissed counter-claims against Republican forces as propaganda, but she didn't believe all of it was false. For her, the only truth was that war debases humanity and modern warfare in its destructive capability debases humanity entirely. The individual cases of honour and valour, whatever their singular virtue, did nothing to change the reality.

A cynic of the usual Christmas festivities in Britain, she was nonetheless surprised that the public celebration of Christmas was considered such an anathema by the Republican authorities in Madrid that it was effectively banned. A mild atheist herself, she hadn't considered the possibility that atheists could be as fanatical as Christians and thought it an unnecessarily harsh move if only because of the negative effect on civilian morale; after all, not all the Republican supporters were Communist. A couple of the nurses she shared her lodgings with decided to make Christmas cards for the children in hospital wounded in the bombing and she was pleased to illustrate them in her spare time.

For her personally, the deprivations and lack of festivities made little difference. Food shortages and the need to support the troops with what meat was available resulted in a diet most days of rice, lentils and a few vegetables, which she did not regard as an inconvenience. Finding time to make a Christmas card for William, she attached her address in case he wanted to write and enclosed an unusually long letter which finished:

I have found a purpose here but also a clearer understanding of how precious all life is and that we must resist being overwhelmed by brutality, whatever the cause. I know now how much those I love mean to me, and you especially. I am not foolish enough to plan for the future while there is so much uncertainty in life, but I have had my own little epiphany here and I long to share the new me with you.

With my fondest love,
Yours ever, Felicity.

William read the letter several times that day and the next before sending her a Christmas card with a long letter, relating the main details of the relatively bland and uneventful weeks he'd spent since he'd seen her, purely to give her some link with a sense of normality. Finishing with a few lines of his affection for her and the pride he felt in what she was doing, he knew her well enough not to overdo the praise.

At the beginning of February, the Nationalists launched another offensive against Madrid in an attempt to cross the Jarama River and sever Madrid's connection to the Republican capital, which had now been relocated to Valencia. Although little progress was made, the fighting was intense and the casualties being brought back to the hospital rose once again to almost unmanageable heights.

The civil war had become a world war: Soviet and Italian fighters engaging in dogfights over the city, German and Italian bombers pounding the city almost every day, Italian and Moroccan troops supporting the Nationalist forces, and the pro-Republican International Brigade volunteers she tended came from every country in Europe, the Americas and further afield. In the morning she might hold the hand of a dying New Zealander and in the afternoon that of a Bulgarian. Often a dying man asked her to say a prayer for him and she did, even though she did not believe in it.

With the Republican side now having more control of the skies, the bombing of the city was concentrated during the hours of darkness. One evening she was working later than usual because of the terrible losses in the battle for the so-called 'Suicide Hill' and it was after eight o'clock when she left the hospital. It was bitterly cold and she hurried to get home for a hot drink. She had not long left the hospital when the air raid siren started, but she didn't want to go back; she needed to be away from the place and its horrors for a while. So she began to walk briskly to her home and the nearby shelter. Around her the street was filled with frightened civilians turning this way and that for the nearest shelter. As she turned the corner, a little girl ran straight into her. She was perhaps three, certainly no more than four, and she was crying. As they collided, Felicity held on to her.

"Where is your mother?" she asked in her halting Spanish.

At first the girl just cried, but then she calmed down a little and spoke, pointing back the way she had come. Felicity couldn't quite understand the girl's reply, but she picked up the word 'perdida'. She looked around for someone to help, but everyone was moving so fast, without casting an eye towards them. She held the little girl's chin and said they would find her mother. Then she took her hand and they turned the corner. She could hear the planes overhead and gripped the girl's hand tightly as they walked at the girl's pace towards the shelter. Hearing a bomb fall not far away and sensing the urgency of the situation, Felicity bent down and picked her up as the bomb landed on the building behind them.

The rescuers found them under the rubble, the little girl still alive in the dead arms of Felicity. Church services had not been allowed in Madrid for six months, under government regulations, so Felicity did not have a Christian burial, which would have caused her no regret. She had left details of her parents as next of kin and they were advised. Her parents knew nothing of William as Felicity had never mentioned him to them so neither they, nor anyone else, informed him of her death. Meanwhile he, inspired by the warmth of her last few letters to him, had begun to write regularly to her at her quarters. When the letters from her stopped in February, he assumed there had been disruption in deliveries to and from the Spanish postal service and continued writing, in happy anticipation of a bundle of letters from her in due course. Sure enough, when he arrived home from work one day his mother said there was a small package for him and his heart quickened a little as he saw the Spanish stamps on the front of it, above his name and address, written in a different hand to that of Felicity.

He took the package up to his room and opened it with eager anticipation. But he was stunned to find a small, neatly wrapped bundle of letters, not to him but from him. They came with a letter from a Dorothy Slater, dated the 19th March.

Dear Mr Lyus,

I do hope you won't mind my opening your letters to Felicity, but I felt I must, so that I might write directly to you.

I am most dreadfully sorry to be the bearer of bad tidings, but you have obviously not yet been informed that Felicity died on 12th February. She was killed in an air raid after she came off duty and died protecting a little girl, who mercifully survived. Felicity was buried in the city after a civil ceremony which was attended by several of her co-workers and friends, including myself.

I did not read your letters but realise that she was important to you so I hope that knowing she died saving another will be of comfort to you at this time. I did not know her very well but, like others here, I was touched by her kindness and selflessness and was pleased to count her as one of my colleagues and comrades.

Please accept my deepest condolences and heartfelt sympathy.

Yours sincerely,
Dorothy Slater

William sat on his bed, holding the five letters he had sent to Felicity but which she had never read and only one of which had ever been opened. He did not read the covering letter again, every word already engrained in his mind. He felt nothing but emptiness: unable to feel, unable to articulate his loss. After a while he walked downstairs.

"Wasn't that from Spain? Was it important?" asked his mother.

"A letter telling me that someone I knew has been killed in the war." He had never mentioned Felicity to his mother, not even as a nameless person, never mind as an individual. As he had spent a night at her flat even before they had been in a relationship, it had been easier to describe Felicity as a 'friend' and let his mother make the appropriate assumptions. Once this pattern was established, it avoided all the awkward discussions about a relationship with all the opportunities it provided for questions, analyses and critiques which would almost certainly have undertones of judgement, criticism and disparagement. So now he had said all there needed to be said rather than have to talk about a grief he couldn't discuss.

"Did you know him well?"

"Quite well," he replied, and that was the end of the conversation.

At each meeting of the JM Group, there were reports from the war in Spain, whether from group members themselves or other information which they gleaned from the press. Ten group members had travelled to Spain in a variety of roles, and one had already been killed in the fighting. One evening William reported the death of Felicity and two minutes' silence was observed. Afterwards, Fred Sweetman, Arthur Crane and others, who knew he had been close to Felicity, commiserated and said she would always be remembered. After three weeks, Felicity was no longer mentioned at group meetings.

William carried on going to the meetings for the rest of that year, but his heart was no longer in it. He could never attend without thinking of Felicity and it became too painful. In any case, he'd heard all the philosophical theories and arguments about politics and political action, and he wasn't interested in hearing them over and over again. He was settled in his conviction that democratic socialism of some sort was the best chance of a fair society; the only questions for debate were the means by which this would be achieved and the details as to the desired ends.

He was now only concerned with action. He still had faith in his father's words that one day he would be destined to do something of worthwhile importance and he would know when that moment came. In the meantime, he followed events in Europe as the war in Spain became a proxy for a future European war. He thought of going to Spain, not to fight, as he had promised Felicity he wouldn't, but to visit her grave. He was held back by the fact that Madrid was constantly under siege and he feared he may not even be able to find where she was buried. So he put that out of his mind until peace had returned, if it ever did. He was certain that once the war in Spain was over there would follow a real European war which might well be resolved in a victory of either fascism or democratic socialism.

XXIX

NOT LONG BEFORE HIS EXECUTION DURING THE French Revolution, Camille Desmoulins described his age of thirty-three as 'the age of the good Sans-culotte Jesus: an age fatal to revolutionists'. The age of thirty-three can presage the end for a revolutionary in ways other than death, however: the decline of revolutionary fervour, a tempering of enthusiasm as middle age beckons or the desire to pursue other paths in life which are less self-sacrificing. William was thirty-three in 1937, but it was not fatal to his revolutionary zeal; rather he became a sleeper, waiting for the time when his hour would come, as he was certain it would, as certain as he was that there would be another Great War in Europe.

While he waited for the call, he worked hard in his trade union role as the British economy and jobs in engineering continued to recover. He was a dutiful son to his mother as she moved towards late middle age. Despite hardly ever attending meetings of the JM Group, he remained a good friend to several of its members, writing to those who were still in Spain, especially David Harris, and joining protests against the BUF. His best friend from the group was Fred Sweetman and he was often invited for a meal with Fred and his wife, Joyce. He also maintained as much as possible his old friendships with his former schoolmates, though they were all married now and had other demands on their time. But the great interest, almost obsession, of his life lay in his role as an amateur grand strategist, trying to anticipate and outguess the steps which were pointing to the next war.

He purchased and hung on the wall of his room a large, coloured, linen-backed map of Europe similar to those used in schools, except that, as well as country boundaries it also illustrated the main language divisions. After examining the map in great detail, he placed flags on all those areas where, contrary to the principle of self-determination laid down in the Treaty of Versailles, minorities had been cut off from their own ethnic group. These he believed would be potential areas of conflict involving countries dissatisfied with current borders and seeking excuses for war: the German Sudetenland in Czechoslovakia, Hungarian Transylvania in Romania, German-speaking areas in Eastern Europe. The list seemed endless.

In his journal he recorded events which pointed either towards a war or to a reduction in international tension. The general pattern was that the Fascist powers made demands and the Western powers acceded. Meanwhile, Russia stood on the sidelines waiting for France or Britain to step in, which they failed to do as Austria and Czechoslovakia disappeared off the map. William watched the newsreel of Chamberlain waving his piece of paper with his cry of 'Peace in Our Time' and wondered how far Hitler would have to go before anyone stood up to him. The loudest Conservative voice in favour of active resistance to the Fascist powers was Churchill and he was not in the government.

Soon after the Germans began their piecemeal annexation of Czechoslovakia, William received a call from Fred

Sweetman, asking him round to dinner. He was pleased to go; he hadn't seen too much of him lately. It was, as usual, a very pleasant evening; Joyce was a good cook and was excellent company while her two young sons were amusing and conscientious, going off to play upstairs when told to do so. While Joyce cleared away after dinner, Fred and William sat in the living room with a couple of beers. They chatted about the world situation and how things were going in the group. Fred hadn't heard from David Harris for a while and nothing was known about most of the group members who had gone to Spain, except that two were killed at the Battle of the Ebro, one of them the artist Henry Brisk.

"The situation in Spain is becoming pretty hopeless," said Fred, pouring out two more beers. "The situation in Germany is getting worse, too."

"You mean about them taking over the Sudetenland?"

"Well, there *is* that. All the Czech defensive positions have been effectively removed, so the country is virtually helpless now if Germany wants to take the rest. But I was actually thinking of the treatment of the Jews. Every year their civil rights get eroded that much more and it can't be long before their lives won't be worth living."

William shook his head. "I remember you telling me they lost their citizenship rights some time ago. If I was Jewish I would leave."

"It's not as easy as it used to be, but you're right. That's why I want to ask you a favour, a very big favour."

"If I can help I'd be glad to. What did you have in mind?"

"It's my cousin, Karl; I have to get him out of Germany before it's too late."

"I didn't realise you had a cousin in Germany."

"My family came from Germany and my grandfather anglicised the family name, Suessmann, to Sweetman. My aunt, my mother's sister, married a distant relative, a German, and went to live there in the 1890s. She's dead now, and so is her husband. Karl is on his own; he never married and his brother died in the Great War."

"I suppose his position now is pretty difficult?"

"Yes. He had his own business, a small printing firm, and he decided to sell up because there's a constant fear of confiscation and the taxes are so high on Jews. At the moment he has enough money to get by and he would like to come to England."

"Can't he?"

"Well, Jews are no longer entitled to have a passport. They have a travel document with 'J' stamped on it and they are not allowed to take their money out of the country. So even if he does manage to get out he will be unable to support himself unless and until he gets a job. In those circumstances I'm not sure he would be welcome here."

"What can I do to help? Would you like me to try to find a job for him?"

Fred smiled. "I had something a bit trickier in mind. I want to make sure he can get out of the country first, hopefully with some of his savings."

"So where do I come in?"

"Do you have a passport?"

"Yes, I got one some years ago. I've only used it once, but I'm sure it's up to date."

"Well, the idea I have is that the two of us go over to Germany and you bring him back using my passport while I find another way to get home. I know I have a nerve to ask you, but most of my other friends are Jewish and their names might raise suspicion and put them at risk. He looks a bit like me so I think it might work."

William was aghast. "That's a completely crazy idea. If you

were caught and they discovered your relationship to Karl, God knows what would happen to you, let alone Karl. It's too dangerous."

"I promised my mother I would try."

William puffed out his cheeks. "Have you got a picture of Karl?"

Fred nodded. He walked over to a sideboard and produced a photo album, turning to the back and showing the page to William.

William looked at a sepia-tinted photograph of a young man in a German-style suit and large bow tie. There was a certain similarity to Fred in the face, around the mouth especially, but they would not immediately be recognised as relatives. "When was this taken?"

"A few years ago. He is thirty-seven now; five years younger than me."

"Has he still got his hair?"

"Yes. He has a good head of hair."

"If he tries to pass himself off as you, he will have to explain how he has more hair now than he did when the passport photo was taken. Sorry, Fred, but your hairline has receded a bit too much."

Fred ran his hand through his hair as if checking for himself and smiled sheepishly.

William looked at the photo again. "Actually, I think I look more like him than you do. How tall is he?"

"Five foot nine or ten."

"About the same as me. You know what I think?"

Fred shook his head. "Yes, but I couldn't ask you to do that."

William thought for a moment or two. "Look, there's a lot to think about. Let's leave it for now and give ourselves time to mull it over and try to come up with some ideas. Perhaps I could come round again early next week and we'll see if we can sort something out."

The following Tuesday, William called round after the children were in bed, and he and Fred resumed their discussions about an escape plan for Karl.

William took the lead. "If we do this, it has to work. There won't be a second chance. I have given it a lot of thought and I think our best hope is that we go to Germany together and I take spare clothes which Karl wears when he comes back with you."

"But how will you get out? Do you speak any German?"

"No, but I don't have to. I shall report my passport is missing at the nearest British consulate and they'll give me a duplicate, or whatever they do. Then I'll make my way home."

"But the risk—"

"I suppose if the Gestapo get hold of me there is a problem, but why should they be interested in a foolish Englishman?"

"It's still a lot for me to expect of you."

William ignored his friend's reservations. "What I don't understand is why Karl left it so long when the writing was on the wall?"

"Like all the others, he couldn't believe that a civilised people like the Germans would go this far. There has always been anti-Semitism in Germany, like everywhere else, but it was always manageable, until now. The Nazis might be without principle, but they are cunning. Little by little, they remove one right then another and a new norm is established. Then the next step is taken and the next until eventually you wake up one morning and discover you are no longer regarded as even a human being in your own country. And of course, the Jews are useful for their money; the Nazis can bleed them dry until they have nothing left. After that they'll presumably deport them to God knows where and not one German will try to stop them." He broke off and topped up their drinks; it was obvious he was holding back his emotions.

"Shall we try my plan?" asked William.

Fred sat down. "Yes, if you are sure. I don't know how to thank you," he said, his voice breaking a little.

William and Fred arranged a week's leave with their respective employers and a fortnight later the plan was put into operation. As a first step, Fred sent a letter to Karl, advising that he could expect a visit from his cousin and to make 'all arrangements', the signal to get packed.

William had planned the trip meticulously. To avoid any possibility of a trail from Karl leading to Fred and then perhaps to William, he had suggested that he and Fred travel independently to France and meet in Paris. Accordingly, Fred booked his passage with his car on the ferry from Dover to Calais while William travelled by the boat train. They would spend the first few days like genuine holidaymakers, gradually driving south and east until they were near the German border. Karl lived in Baden-Baden, less than ten miles from the French border, and they would use the pretext of spending a day in that city to effect the changeover. They had hired dinner suits to wear in the evening, and William's luggage would have an extra shirt, suit and tie so that Karl would be able to look like an Englishman when he arrived at the border.

On the first day, Fred and William arrived in Paris, each by his own route, and registered separately at a hotel in the Place de la République. They spent a couple of days sightseeing in the well-established pattern for Paris: the Eiffel Tower, the Louvre, Notre Dame, Montmartre and a boat trip on the Seine. After three nights in Paris, they drove down to Nancy, spent another night there, and then continued through Haguenau to Roppenheim where they crossed the Rhine into Germany.

Fred's Austin Twelve-Four was not old and performed perfectly on its first visit to the Continent. Now, at one o'clock on a dull afternoon, it rolled gently to the striped pole at the German border crossing and the guard came out of his office. Despite this part of the expedition being perfectly above board, they could both feel a quickening of the pulse.

The guard looked impassively at the number plate of the car and knocked on the left-hand window where William was sitting.

"*Reisspassen.*"

Fred was holding both their passports and handed them over to William, who gave them to the guard. William found himself unable to stop staring at the red armband with its black swastika in a white circle. Somehow it seemed more menacing in real life rather than in pictures.

"*Zweck Ihrer Reise?*"

"I'm sorry, we don't speak German," said William. Fred said nothing.

"What is the purpose of your journey?" asked the guard.

"We would like to see Baden-Baden and perhaps go to the casino."

The guard smiled. "You hope to win lots of money?"

"Well, not lose too much," said William, reciprocating the smile.

"How long will you stay in Germany?"

"Just today and tomorrow, probably."

The guard nodded and took the passports into the office. William and Fred looked at each other but neither spoke. A couple of minutes later he returned with their passports, duly stamped. He handed them over, saluted and raised the barrier, and Fred drove the car slowly away and into Germany.

Twenty minutes later they parked in the centre of the serene and charming spa town of Baden-Baden and booked into a hotel for one night, Fred speaking very passable German to the receptionist. Their passports were retained for registration, but the concierge said they would be returned to them that evening. From a public phone box, Fred telephoned Karl and said they would be round to see him at about four o'clock. After a light lunch they unpacked their luggage and transferred a set of clothes for Karl into an attaché case. With the aid of a map from the hotel, they spent an hour in the city centre, ostentatiously acting like keen tourists, finally following the map through the old town to Karl's house. They walked round to the back of the house and came in through the open gate into the neat, pretty garden. Fred knocked gently on the back door and led William in. A man, whom William instantly recognised from his photograph, was waiting for them in the large stone-floored kitchen. He looked thinner than in the photograph and his features were drawn, but he smiled broadly.

"Fred, it's good to see you," he said, shaking hands vigorously with his cousin. "William, welcome to my home. What you are prepared to do for a stranger has restored my faith in humanity. I shall always be beholden to you." He took William's hand in his and bowed a little. He spoke perfect English with no trace of an accent, better even than Fred had promised. William thought Karl would have little difficulty impersonating an Englishman and his belief in the expedition's success rose considerably.

Karl showed them into a parlour and invited them to sit on Bauhaus-style armchairs while he fetched a tray with glasses and some brandy. William admired the stylish furniture and expensive decor and thought how sad it was that this man was about to lose everything precious to him. They toasted each other and the success of the mission and then went through the plan for the next twenty-four hours.

William opened the attaché case and unfolded the carefully wrapped suit with the shirt and tie. "Try these on for size and if they are no good you can try what I am wearing now."

Karl took the clothes and went into the room next door to try them on. When he returned, he looked very different. *Clothes maketh the man*, thought William. "How does it fit? It looks pretty good to me."

Karl looked in the mirror. "An English gentleman," he said. "I think it would be better if you tied my tie; to make sure it looks right for an Englishman. Otherwise, it fits well; perhaps a little big round the waist, but my braces will deal with that." He pulled the waistband to illustrate the gap between trousers and waist.

"What about your shoes?"

"They're English. I bought them some years ago, from Church's in Bond Street."

"Excellent. What are you hoping to take with you?" asked Fred.

"Nothing, except some money if that's at all possible."

"I have been thinking about that," said William. "If you leave Germany with a considerable sum in reichsmarks it might lead to some awkward questions. I know it's not very likely, but it could happen. If you are willing to trust me, I believe I have a way of getting the money out more safely."

"Of course," said Karl. He went over to a desk and pulled out a thick bundle of bank notes. "This is what is left of my savings. It is about 115,000 reichsmarks, just over nine thousand pounds sterling, I believe."

"That's a lot of money," said Fred.

Karl smiled ruefully. "Yes, but not quite so much when you consider it is all that is left of my family business and the other interests we once had."

"What will happen to the house?" asked William.

"I dared not try to sell it; there are ears everywhere. It will be confiscated, no doubt. I would like to have given it to a Jewish family, but it would probably heap more trouble on them." He looked at something in the drawer then picked it up and threw it in a bin under the desk. It made a clang as metal hit metal.

"What was that?" asked Fred.

"My brother's Iron Cross. He would have done the same if he were still here."

"I think it best you take no luggage, nothing of your own," said Fred.

Karl nodded. "I thought that might be the case so I have purposely not looked around for mementos or nostalgic reminders."

"I'm sorry," said William.

"No matter, just possessions, they can be replaced and I have my memories."

They had another drink and arranged to pick Karl up at nine o'clock the following morning at the back of his house.

William and Fred returned to their hotel, changed into their dinner suits and dined in the restaurant. Afterwards, at about eight o'clock, they went to the casino at the Kurhaus, a fine old building with Corinthian columns that had begun as a spa resort before developing into one of the great casinos of Europe. They had divided Karl's money between them and William bought forty thousand reichsmarks' worth of chips while Fred had sixty-five thousand's worth, inevitably many of them in large denominations. The cashier showed no surprise at the large sums but did advise them that bets above a certain level might need managerial approval.

They walked into the red and gold playing salon and looked around at their fellow guests. All were extremely well dressed, the women draped in furs and jewels, some of the men in white tie and tails, the rest in dinner suits, the odd monocle or two. They could hear conversations in German and French, Italian and English, and they tried to keep away from the tables where they could hear English spoken. Fred played one table and William another.

As soon as he produced one of the large plaques worth a thousand marks, William attracted some attention. But his request for them to be changed into chips of twenty reichsmarks or lower soon dissipated the interest of his fellow players, except for one young woman. She seemed to have exhausted most of her funds and stood close to him, perhaps hoping he might bring her a change of fortune. The other players were equally interesting. Some had notepads, recording each spin of the wheel and seeking patterns in a random world, others grey-faced and sick of losing but having no choice but to go on in the hope the tide may turn. There were also the addicts; sometimes able to win but never truly satisfied until they lost. Finally, there were a few laughing and devil-may-care players, making a few wagers but for them mere distractions from the more important plans for the evening, especially the older men with attentive young women and the occasional lady of mature years with a young man who was apparently unaware that he was not much more than half her age.

To avoid suspicion, William played the table for some time, using a simple system of fifty on red. If that won, he would go to black with the same stake; if it lost he would double and redouble his stake on red until it finally came up. Then he would repeat the pattern. This meant small wins, or at worst small losses, for lots of playing time. The young woman next to him copied his style of play for a while but soon tired of its lack of excitement and went off to lose her money elsewhere. After about forty minutes, William and Fred stopped playing and had a break and a cocktail. At this point, William was up thirty reichsmarks and Fred was up fifty. Another hour and William was up sixty and Fred eighty and they called it a day.

They went back to the cashier to convert their winnings and asked if it were possible to have mostly francs as they were leaving for France the next morning. The cashier again showed no reaction, presumably because the casino made a profit on the exchange rate offered. The 105,000 reichsmarks were replaced with nearly four million francs and two thousand reichsmarks, and he gave receipts in both currencies to each of them, as requested. They took a taxi back to the hotel, collected their passports and put their money in the hotel safe before heading for the bar. After one drink, however, the need to celebrate more freely drove them to retire to one of their rooms before their excitement got the better of them. In Fred's room they ordered a bottle of champagne from room service and toasted their success in completing phase one of the operation.

As the euphoria faded and they talked about the next morning, their concerns began to surface. Fred was worried about Karl passing as William and William suggested he make sure that the border guard went to the driver's side when talking to them. William's concern was the money and what to say if they were searched.

"A huge win on the casino doesn't sound very likely," he said.

"But that's why we went to the casino; it's our alibi." Fred was clearly exasperated.

"I know. Just a touch of cold feet, I suppose."

"We've got two receipts each. We can play it by ear how much we use that excuse for having so much money. I don't think they'll be too bothered about us bringing a large sum into Britain. Getting it out of Germany is the big challenge; they have foreign exchange controls."

"I think I'll put most of the francs in my case and hope for the best," said William.

Fred nodded. "I've got a couple of cubby holes in the car where nobody would look, unless they take the whole thing to pieces."

William went back to his room and slept fitfully, dark dreams interrupted by periods when he could not get comfortable and he lay awake, going through the next day again and again.

XXX

WILLIAM WOKE EARLY AND WAITED FOR THE knock on the door from Fred. After breakfast, they collected their money from the safe, paid the bill and were given separate receipts, as they had requested. Then they loaded up the car with Fred's luggage, William keeping his few things in the attaché case. Fred took two thirds of the money and William's passport, while William kept the rest of the money. They parted without ceremony. William watched as Fred's car disappeared at the end of the road then went back to the casino. This time he did not play the tables but had a coffee in the restaurant and waited. He killed the time reading a novel he'd bought at the ferry terminal.

Fred drove to Karl's house, parking outside the rear gate. Karl was waiting for him at the back door and, over a cup of coffee, they went through the plan of the day one more time. Then Fred tied Karl's tie for him and sent him off to brush his hair to look as much as possible like it did in William's passport photo. Meanwhile he put most of the francs in with his tools in an oilskin bag behind the spare wheel in the boot and the rest of them he clipped under the dashboard. He kept looking around from time to time, but he saw no one. When everything was ready, Karl came out of the house quickly, locking the door but not the gate, and slipped into the car. Fred looked round once more and saw a curtain move in the house opposite.

They drove out of Baden-Baden as quickly as they could, without attracting attention. Having decided it was too risky to use the same border crossing as the previous night, they drove south to Kehl to cross the Rhine into Strasbourg, a journey of less than an hour. The trip was uneventful until they drove through Renchen. At the outskirts of the town the car backfired once, stuttered a few times and came to a halt. They got out of the car and Fred lifted the bonnet.

"What do you think it is?" asked Karl.

"Not sure. There's no smoke and it's not too hot; could be the coil or the carburettor. We may have to try to get help. Luckily, it's not far to town, but what a bugger!"

"Try not to look startled, but here comes a police car," whispered Karl as Fred fiddled with cables and wires.

"Let me do the talking," said Fred.

They heard the car stop and the sound of boots on the road surface.

"*Guten Morgen, darf ich ihnen helfen meine Herren?*"

They turned round to see a middle-aged policeman in a green uniform and high, crested cap. He was smiling, his hands behind his back.

"*Guten Morgen, sprechen sie Englisch?*" replied Fred.

"A little."

"The engine just stopped without warning," said Fred slowly.

The policeman smiled and went over to his car and came back with a toolbox. He opened it and revealed the meticulously packed tools and repair items. Having checked the distributor, he removed the top from the carburettor. With his screwdriver and a piece of wire he probed and prodded around and blew once as he checked all parts were clear. He replaced the cap with a look of satisfaction. "*Streugut*," he said. "Try to start, please."

Fred got behind the wheel and turned the ignition, praying for it to start. It did, first time. "Thank you so much," he said, jumping out and shaking the policeman's hand.

The policeman smiled cheerfully. "It is good I can help. *Gute Reise*."

The two cousins took their seats in the car and opened their windows. "Thank you," said Karl.

"*Danke schön*," called Fred.

"*Bitte schön*," said the policeman, saluting as they drove off with a wave, their hearts pounding.

"What did he mean, '*Streugut*'?" asked Fred.

"Grit."

Fred nodded. "Next stop France!"

Half an hour later, they had driven through Kehl and approached the border. The striped pole of the German border barrier came down gently after the previous vehicle and a guard approached the car. After looking at the number plate, he went round to the driver's side and Fred opened the window.

"Papers, please," he said in English.

Fred offered him the two passports and he examined the pictures cursorily before he flicked through to the page with the visa stamps. "You stayed only one day? You do not like Germany?"

Fred was already nervous and he kept his hands on the wheel in case they were starting to shake. He smiled. "We are travelling through France on holiday but wanted to play at the casino in Baden-Baden. Now we are resuming our journey to Strasbourg." He pronounced the city in the German way.

The guard nodded and looked over at Karl, whose face was in shadow. "Next time you come for a longer stay, perhaps."

"We will," said Karl.

Then the guard waved them on; a French van behind them had attracted his interest.

They drove the twenty yards to the French border and a customs officer approached the car. "*Bonjour, messieurs,*" he said in that Alsatian accent which sounded to Fred like a German speaking French. "*Passeports s'il vous plait.*" He looked at the passports and handed them back. "Have you anything to declare?" he asked in English.

"No, we did no shopping in Germany, just a trip to the casino."

"Welcome back to France," he said, and returned the passports.

The barrier went up and they were back in France. They sat silent in the car as they drove for a mile through the streets of Strasbourg, still not quite sure they were safe, before they stopped near a telephone box. Then they hugged each other and Karl buried his head in his hands for a few moments while Fred put an arm round his shoulder.

Fred went to the telephone box and asked the operator for an international call to the Kurhaus restaurant in Baden-Baden. He had built up a supply of French coins for this moment and put franc after franc in the slot as the operator made the connection.

William was still seated in the casino restaurant, now on his second coffee with a slice of Donauwelle. He felt strangely untroubled here in this beautiful building, radiating the charm and grandeur of a kinder age and somehow blanking out the nightmare that was the real background to life in Germany. He looked at his watch again and the first pang of fear that things were going wrong gripped him. He imagined Karl being hauled out of the car and challenged as to his identity, the border guards finding the money and then strip-searching Karl to reveal that he was wearing German underwear. It would be all up and the two of them would be arrested and neither would get out. Then he heard a male voice calling, "*Telefon fur Herrn Lyus,*" and he raised his hand and called, "Here!" He was taken to reception and handed a telephone receiver.

"Hello, William Lyus."

"It's Fred. We are in Strasbourg; all's well. We shall head for Calais after a break."

"Yes, make sure you go home today."

"Will do. Good luck."

William returned the receiver and settled his bill, then went back to the hotel.

"You are back, Mr Lyus?" asked the surprised concierge.

"Just about to set off, but would you know where the nearest British consulate is?"

"One moment," he said, and took a book from under the counter. He flicked through the pages. "There is a consulate-general in Munich and also in Frankfurt; that one would be nearer, perhaps. Is there a problem? Can I be of service?"

William smiled. "Nothing to worry about; all's well, thank you very much. Goodbye."

He had wanted to ask about trains but thought it better not to as he had arrived by car. Instead, he took a taxi to the main station and found there was a regular and frequent service to Frankfurt. He was not asked for his passport when he bought a ticket and he arrived in Frankfurt in time for a late lunch. He was not hungry; sorting out his passport was the imperative. He asked for directions at a travel bureau and noticed it had a photo booth. The travel agent helped him to operate it and he left twenty minutes later with a decent set of passport photographs.

As he came out of the travel bureau he saw a couple coming towards him with the yellow Star of David on their coats. They seemed happy and were chatting and smiling to each other. As they passed a group of Brownshirts, one of the troopers barged into them and the young woman fell over. The Brownshirt grabbed the young man by the shoulder and said something which sounded threatening. William stopped and went to help the young woman up, but another trooper waved him away, shouting at him; the only words he understood were 'nein' and 'Jüdin'. The young woman got up on her own and whispered, "Vielen danke," to William as she waited for her friend to be dismissed and they walked on. One or two of the troopers were now staring at William, but he looked straight ahead and walked briskly on. He shuddered as he thought of the plight of those who were forced to wear the star.

A few minutes later he arrived at the consulate-general. The office was large and quite grand, and he pushed the large swing door into the foyer, where several people were being attended to at the reception desk. After waiting for five minutes he was greeted by one of the staff.

"Good morning," William replied. "I am a British subject. I have lost my passport."

The receptionist took some details and asked if he had any proof of identity.

"Yes, I have my driving licence and my business card from the Amalgamated Engineering Union."

"Thank you. They will be very helpful," the receptionist said. "I won't be long; please take a seat." He disappeared into an office briefly and then asked William to come through.

William was shown into an office and greeted by a fair-haired man of about his own age.

"Mr Lyus, so sorry to hear about your difficulty. I'm Robert Harwood of the consulate staff. Take a chair, won't you? How long have you been in Germany?" He spoke with that upper-class drawl William had got used to when working at Bertram Drogo Motors.

"I arrived yesterday and stayed in Baden-Baden to play at the casino." He produced the receipt he'd been given at the hotel and passed it across the desk.

Harwood nodded and returned the receipt. "You are travelling alone?"

"Yes."

"You obviously arrived with a passport. What happened to it?"

William had been rehearsing an answer to this question ever since he hatched Karl's escape plan with Fred. "I'm not absolutely sure. After breakfast this morning I took a walk through the town and stood on the bridge over the river, the Oos, I think it's called. I was quite warm so I had removed my jacket and I lay it briefly on the bridge when I was asked to take the photograph of a young couple. I think the passport must have fallen out of my inside pocket as I couldn't find it later. I went back to the bridge and looked all round it, but my passport was gone."

"I see. That's rather bad luck after just one day here."

William smiled. He couldn't tell whether the man was sceptical of his explanation or not.

Harwood continued, "The normal procedure in this case is to give you an emergency passport, a travel document, so that you can get home. I'm afraid there is a fee involved and the passport will be impounded when you arrive back in Britain. It's quite straightforward; you complete an application form, pay the fee and 'Bob's Your Uncle'. Oh, you will need to supply a recent photo, one that can be cut up and stuck in the document."

William produced his photo booth passport photographs. "I had these taken at a travel bureau on the way here."

"Excellent! Those photo machines are marvellous things, aren't they? That'll be perfect."

"Can I pay the fee in sterling as I have very little German currency left?"

"Sterling will be fine."

William completed the form and an assistant took everything away, returning a quarter of an hour later with a beige-coloured travel document bearing the royal crest. Harwood signed the document before handing it over.

"You can use this to pass through several countries, but it is not advisable to use it as if it were an ordinary passport. I suggest you complete your holiday in Germany and then go home. Had you planned a long vacation?"

"No, just a few days more. I shan't outstay my welcome. Sorry to have put you to all this trouble."

"Not at all, not at all. That's what we're here for, getting people out of a jam. You'd be surprised how many people lose their passports every year – often they are stolen, of course. Yours will probably end up in the Rhine. Well, enjoy the rest of your break and if I were you I shouldn't be in too much of a hurry to holiday here again."

William wasn't keen on staying in Germany another day, but it was unlikely that Karl was missed in Baden-Baden yet and even if he was, they wouldn't be looking for an Englishman in Frankfurt; there was nothing to tie them up. He went into a gentlemen's outfitters to buy a change of shirt and underwear and replace his depleted travel clothes. The shop assistant was very courteous and helpful, and William began to relax a little.

He considered the possibility of a look around the city, but he didn't want to spend too much time on the streets as he found the atmosphere slightly menacing, especially as there were lots of police and Brownshirts about. He contented himself with a visit to the cathedral and had a coffee while he decided what to do next. He thought about travelling to Paris immediately, but he would arrive after nine and then there would be the business of finding a hotel. Deciding to spend the night in Frankfurt, he registered at a good hotel, enjoyed an excellent dinner, talked in the lounge to a very pleasant couple from Hanover who spoke fluent English and slept for ten hours. The following morning he settled his bill in cash and put most of his francs in the pockets of his dress suit in the attaché case. He took the train from Frankfurt to Paris and then the Fleche d'Or boat train to Calais and onto London, for which he still had a return ticket. He was relaxed as he walked into the Customs and Immigration Hall at Dover. The customs officer asked the usual questions then scrawled the white chalk cross on his attaché case. Porters were waiting to take luggage to the train and William gave his case to one of them along with his seat reservation ticket. Next, he smilingly presented his emergency passport to the immigration officer.

The immigration officer looked at the passport and then at William. "I won't keep you a moment, Mr Lyus." He walked over to an office and came back a couple of minutes later with another officer.

"Would you come with me, Mr Lyus?" said the man who had inspected his passport. The other officer took over the desk.

William followed the man to the office with 'Senior Immigration Officer' on the door. It was occupied by an older, stocky man, sitting behind a desk, smoking a cigarette. "Take a seat, Mr Lyus," he said. "Would you mind telling me about this emergency passport?"

William did his best to come over as a nonchalant, slightly bemused, innocent traveller. "There's not much to say. I lost my passport in Baden-Baden; I think it may have fallen out of my jacket. So, after giving up searching for it, I went to Frankfurt to get a new passport. I came home with it today."

"I see. Do you have any other proof of identity?"

"Yes." William produced his driving licence and business card.

"How did you travel to and from Germany?"

"By train."

"So why did you take your driving licence with you?"

"I thought I might want to hire a car at some point; just a whim on my part."

"Mm. Tell Mr Lyus what happened yesterday, Gough."

The immigration officer looked at William. "Yesterday a man came through Immigration whom I thought didn't look very much like his passport photograph. When I commented on the fact, he replied that he had been ill for some time and had lost weight. I remembered the surname because it is unusual and I have never come across it before. It was Lyus. When I saw you just now I recognised you from the long look I took at the photograph. The entry visa stamp in the passport was from near Baden-Baden."

"Mr Gough never forgets a face and he is very experienced in such matters. What do you say to that?"

William shrugged and tried to keep a calm expression. "Perhaps he found my passport and made use of it."

"Rather a coincidence that he should have travelled out of Germany the same day you lost it; almost as if he was ready to go."

William didn't answer.

"Then the very next day, you return from Germany as if you had no other reason to stay there." He stared hard at William, waiting for a reply but none came. "What was the purpose of your visit to Germany?"

"I had taken a short holiday to France and while in Nancy

I found time to spend a day in Baden-Baden to go to the casino. I only took a week's leave so couldn't stay too long."

"You went to Baden-Baden specifically to go to the casino?"

"Yes, a friend of mine had told me about it and I thought it might be worth a go."

"Do you have any evidence of that?"

"Yes. I have a receipt for the chips I cashed in." He produced it from his wallet.

"A thousand reichsmarks, eighty pounds. A lot of money."

"Yes, I started with about twenty pounds and had quite a big win." He smiled at the man, trying to look relaxed but aware he was sweating a little. He kept telling himself that however suspicious this man was, he was running out of ideas.

"I find your story frankly outlandish and difficult to believe. Why don't you own up and admit that you made some arrangement to give your passport to someone else?"

William did his best to look puzzled. "Why would I do that?"

"Who knows? Perhaps for money?"

"But I don't know anyone in Germany. I have never been to Germany until this trip. I've only once been to France before."

The senior immigration officer looked up at his colleague. "Gough?"

Gough nodded. "The passport was a couple of years old, but there were only two stamps in it, as Mr Lyus indicated."

His superior turned back to William. "You came by train and ferry, so I presume you are travelling back the same way?"

"Yes."

"Do you have the tickets you used travelling around France?"

"No, I don't tend to keep tickets I have used. All I have is this." He showed the man his return ticket for the Golden Arrow. "Look, I'm sorry that my passport was mislaid and may have been used by someone else, but the British Consulate in Frankfurt told me that many passports are reported lost every year. I fail to see why I should be singled out for interrogation after such a common mishap."

The senior immigration officer stared at William for a moment and the ordeal was ended. "You understand that the emergency passport has now to be surrendered and you will have to apply for a new full passport if you wish to travel abroad again. I can't stress enough how important it is to look after one's passport when overseas. The person who used your passport to gain entry to Britain illegally may well be a criminal or have other illicit intentions and he will disappear into society with no one knowing his whereabouts or intentions." He shook his head. "That will be all, Mr Lyus."

William was escorted back to the customs hall and set off on his journey home, feeling uneasy, even a little guilty, though he knew he had done the right thing. When he arrived in London, he telephoned Fred to check that he and Karl had arrived safely.

"Yes, everything went like clockwork. We are safely home. I won't go into detail until we meet. How about you?"

"Yes, no problems, just a slight hold-up at Dover."

"Will you come round for dinner on Saturday evening?"

"Yes, I'd like to. See you at about seven?"

The small dinner party included Fred's mother, Amelia, as well as Fred's wife and children. Karl's complexion looked better than when William had last seen him, and he appeared relaxed and years younger. He shook hands warmly with William and thanked him again for all he had done.

"It was nothing, really," said William. "I was glad to help."

"It may not seem much to you because everything went well, but you were in real danger, both you and Fred," said Fred's mother. "I am so grateful to have my nephew safe and sound. I'm sure Fred won't mind my saying that yours was the greater act of generosity, as you are not of our family, though I regard you as such after this." She clasped William's hand and kissed him.

Over dinner they recounted their adventures, which Fred's sons found exciting and they likened their father to Richard Hannay of *The Thirty-Nine Steps* or Carruthers in *The Riddle of the Sands*. Their father and his fellow accomplices had not enjoyed it so much at the time.

"Obviously the car breakdown and the German policeman helping us out gave us the best smile afterwards," Fred said, "but Karl found British Immigration the most difficult."

"Yes, the immigration officer was very concerned that it wasn't my photograph and I had no other proof of identity. It was only afterwards I remembered your name was on the label inside the jacket pocket of the suit. That would have proved my story."

William whistled. "Thank goodness you didn't remember. The immigration officer at Dover gave *me* a lot of trouble too. He remembered my passport from the day before and if he'd known you were wearing my suit I'd have had a lot of explaining to do. It was just bad luck that he checked us both, but I had to undergo quite an interrogation. I think they suspected I had sold my passport to someone trying to get out of Germany. I was really worried they would ask to see my luggage, as I didn't have enough for a week's holiday, but I did have a large amount of money. On the train home I remember thinking that however much you plan something there are always things you forget or would have done a different way. We should have tried to get the money into a bank before we left France or even Germany; we took such a risk."

After dinner they discussed Karl's plans for the future, which as yet were pretty vague. "I have been staying with Fred and Joyce, but I shall be moving in with Aunt Amelia next week. I have no other plans at the moment except sorting out my finances. I can't live off my family indefinitely."

His aunt smiled. "I am on my own in a big house, so it will be welcome company for me."

"That reminds me, I mustn't forget to give you your money," said William. He took the francs and the remaining reichsmarks he'd brought from Germany from his overcoat and put them on the table.

Karl, Fred and William went into the sitting room for a drink and to discuss the future.

"I must open a bank account," said Karl. "Will that be difficult?"

"Not in Britain. There are usually no questions asked if you are depositing money, especially with a merchant bank," said William.

"I know from Fred that your politics would not normally put you on the side of the capitalists, so I appreciate all the more you helping me."

William smiled. "But I didn't help you *because* you are a capitalist but because you were in danger. Your economic circumstances are irrelevant. In any case, from what I gather you didn't make your money exploiting the poor or less advantaged. Don't worry, if a government comes into power which taxes you to the hilt I won't stand up for you then."

Karl laughed. "Fair enough. Turning to another matter, I have converted some of the francs we brought over into pounds and I want to make you both a gift for what you did for me. I would like to give you each five hundred pounds."

William and Fred both protested and refused to take anything.

Karl waved their refusal away. "Without you both I would eventually have nothing, so all I have is yours by right."

"But five hundred pounds," said Fred. "You could buy a house in the suburbs with that."

"I'll have enough to buy that and much else besides with what I have left."

William shook his head. "Fred's right; I don't want to be paid for what I did."

Karl smiled. "I understand that, but saving a life is above any value one could place on it. I merely wish to say thank you. At least let me pay your expenses for the holiday you took purely on my account." He turned his back as he placed some money in two envelopes and sealed them. "That should cover it." He gave them an envelope each.

"Thank you, Karl," said William, putting the envelope in his pocket.

"There is something else I should like to give you, William. I shan't be a moment." He disappeared upstairs and returned with a neatly wrapped brown parcel which he handed to William.

William smiled and opened the package. It contained a gun and some ammunition. William gasped.

"I know you said I must bring nothing personal with me, but I was not going back. If I had been held at the border I would have shot myself rather than stay in Germany a day longer. I have no need of it now and I want you to have it as a souvenir."

"I don't know what to say," said William, staring at the PO8 Luger. He carefully wrapped it up again.

Later that night William opened the envelope – it contained £300. He thought it too generous but decided to accept the gift; it would be churlish not to do so. A few days later he bought a two-year old car, a Ford V8, and gave a considerable part of what he had left to help the work of the British Committee for Refugees from Czechoslovakia.

XXXI

THE EXPEDITION TO RESCUE KARL HAD BEEN carried out not a moment too soon. A couple of weeks later William read in the newspaper about the events of Kristallnacht, when the SA paramilitary and civilians attacked Jewish businesses, homes, hospitals and synagogues throughout Germany, Austria and the Sudetenland. He telephoned Karl to say how horrified he had been by the news and Karl said that he had been in contact with an old non-Jewish friend in Baden-Baden.

"It was as bad there as everywhere else. The Jewish men were rounded up by the SS and paraded through the streets to the synagogue, where they were forced to read anti-Semitic writings from the pulpit before the building was destroyed. Then they were taken away to a labour camp."

"My God, the whole male Jewish population."

"Yes, that would have been my fate too."

"How are you settling in now?"

"Very well. My aunt is kind and, of course, Fred and Joyce too. I am a little worried about being an illegal immigrant, but I had no trouble opening a bank account and have joined a bridge club to help me meet people. I am contented and things will get better from now on."

William wished Karl well for the future and put the telephone down.

He had told nobody about Karl's rescue and had no intention of ever doing so. In part, this was due to an excessive fear that should it ever get back to Germany, Karl might be harmed in some way. But mainly it was because he had no wish to talk as if he had done something special when any decent person would surely have done the same, especially knowing now what was being done to the Jews in Germany. The latest deprivations experienced by the Jews caused him to wonder if there might be a way to rescue others before it became impossible. These thoughts were still on his mind when next he met Stanley for a drink.

"You mean a kind of Scarlet Pimpernel organisation, smuggling people to safety out of Germany? It sounds a great idea, but I can't see how it would work. It's a police state. Isn't it?"

"I suppose it is, but it's not as if they have curfews every night and no one's allowed out."

Stanley was, unusually for him, still cautious. "I just don't think you'd have a chance."

"Well, I've done it once," said William, without thinking.

"How d'you mean?"

William found himself telling his friend the bare bones of his rescue of Karl, using no names or places.

"Are you pulling my leg?" Stanley was intrigued but still sceptical.

"No."

Stanley asked lots of questions starting 'What about' or 'What if' and William answered them without giving away too much. Stanley's early scepticism was replaced with admiration. He told William he thought it was a noble act on his part but warned him not to assume he could be sure of getting away with it a second time.

Any hopes that William might explore the idea further were soon overtaken by events. After further months of prevarication when Germany took over the rest of Czechoslovakia, Britain and a reluctant France finally declared war when Germany invaded Poland in September 1939.

William was pleased that war had come. Not because of a lurid desire for war but because he believed, like Churchill and others, that Fascism, and especially Nazism, represented a victory for the barbarians and must be destroyed before it became so powerful that it came to be the dominant force in human society. This would result in a return to a view of the world in which the 'other', whether it be those of another nation, race or religion, were not worthy of consideration as truly human and therefore deserved no dignity, no respect, not even mercy. Neither would it countenance the right of different philosophies to exist or for other points of view to be worthy of respect. It was as if the Age of the Enlightenment and all that had flowed from it had never existed. All those philosophers whom William had read and 'listened to', many of them German, were of no consequence, since Nazi philosophy, such as it was, had no interest in reason or scientific principles; it was merely the exercise of power.

At first, William was shocked by the Soviet government entering a non-aggression pact with Germany in August 1939. But on reflection he came to believe it was a defensive reaction to the failure of the Western powers to stand up to Germany over Czechoslovakia. Similarly, the decision by the Soviets to invade Poland and the Baltic states after war broke out was surely a defensive measure to provide a barrier to German expansionism at a future date. Who could blame them with the war in the west of Europe going disastrously, especially after the collapse of France and the Dunkirk evacuation? Despite his reservations about Churchill's views on almost everything else, William hoped he would not be dissuaded from continuing the war in the face of defeatism and pessimism among some members of the government. For William, like Churchill, this was a moral war against the forces of darkness. For now, he rolled up his map of Europe and considered how he might contribute to the fight.

At the age of thirty-five and working in an area with reserved occupation status, William would not be conscripted into the armed forces but would be expected to make a contribution to the war effort and he was pleased to do so. The trade unions were key in helping to address labour shortages during the war and William often worked long hours helping to streamline the process of matching essential engineering workers to where they were most needed. He liaised not only with companies but also with civil servants in the planning and executing of projects to provide much-needed skilled engineering workers for the war effort. He also joined the Air Raid Precautions (ARP) service as a way of making a direct contribution. It enabled him to expose himself to danger, especially at the height of the Blitz, though he considered it a pale reflection of the risks taken by fire fighters in London, let alone those who faced danger in the armed forces.

By the end of 1940 he was leading a team of firewatchers who were stationed on key buildings in the City of London. Their role was to watch for incendiary bombs landing on the buildings and any other fires which broke out. They would attempt to keep a fire under control, or even put it out with their limited equipment, until the fire brigade arrived. Their numbers had been greatly enhanced after the heavy and destructive use of incendiary bombs in the City in December 1940 when St Paul's

Cathedral was saved from destruction by the quick action of firewatchers on its roof. William's team included a number of new, young volunteers and he made a point of supporting them through the first week or two while they gained experience. One night in mid-December, he went up to the roof of one of the bank buildings on Lombard Street being watched over by Marjorie Allard, a young woman of about twenty. He had spoken to her a few times and she seemed friendly and keen to do a good job. He also thought her very attractive with her long, auburn hair, large, pale blue eyes and a curvaceous figure, which her siren suit failed to obscure entirely.

From the street, the roof of the building appeared flat and only the pediment was visible. In fact, hidden behind the pediment were two shallow gables which took rainwater into gullies and then down the drainpipes. There were also four large skylights standing proud of the flat parts of the roof. Marjorie was sitting in the corner of the roof, her tin hat pushed back off her forehead, looking through her binoculars. She glanced over at him as he approached and smiled. "Evening, Mr Lyus. All quiet so far."

She had all her equipment, stirrup pump, shovel and bucket, at the ready, and he noted that she was suitably alert, which impressed him. She was always very polite and proper, but he thought it was time they dropped the formalities. "Just call me William, Marjorie." He sat down beside her and took his flask of tea from his canvas bag. "Have you got a drink?" he asked, offering his spare cup to her.

"Thank very much; I've used mine up. I haven't got used to rationing it yet." She took the cup and William filled it for her.

"Would you like a sandwich? They're only fish paste, I'm afraid."

She smiled and took one. "I don't mind. I like salmon and shrimp," she said after a bite.

They had never really spoken to each other for any length of time and they chatted for a few minutes about where they lived and how much their own areas had been affected by the war. Marjorie asked him what he did in 'civvy street' and he told her about the union and the importance of engineering work for the war effort. "What about you?" he asked.

"I work in a munitions factory in Shoreditch and I've seen how much the engineers put in. I used to work in a sweet factory, so it is quite a change. I do like doing something that's important for the war effort, but it's very hard on my hands; sometimes they are bleeding at the end of the day." She showed them to him, but he couldn't see much in the dark. "Still, they give us extra milk and things to keep our strength up. They say the hard physical work means we have to have more than the basic rations."

William thought her quite sweet in her way, and very responsible and trustworthy, though so young. Suddenly he was aware that this was the first time he'd taken any real interest in a woman since Felicity.

Their conversation was interrupted by the plaintive cry of the sirens and soon after that they could see the Ack Ack tracer fire as the batteries swung into action. Then came the dull grinding sound of the German bombers overhead and the ground-shaking thuds as the heavy bombs wrought their havoc. Every two minutes a new wave of planes came over and fires were springing up everywhere as masses of incendiary bombs were released over the city. They heard a stick of them falling close by and took cover. When they looked up, three incendiary bombs had landed on the roof. At first, the bombs flashed, but they quickly settled down into pinpoints of brilliant white as each began gnawing at its surroundings.

They both jumped up and Marjorie gave an involuntary cry. Already one of the bombs was melting the lead on which it had fallen and another had set light to the wooden frame of one of the skylights. "We can deal with this," said William. "We must put out the one by the skylight. You man the pump and I'll take the hose."

Marjorie put the pump in one of the filled water buckets and was soon pumping to start a flow of water while William took the hose over to the skylight. One corner of the frame was burning ferociously and two small panes of glass had already crashed into the building below. Worried about the bomb falling into the building and starting a fire on the floor beneath, he played the jet of water onto the frame furthest from the bomb and then switched to a spray to try to put the flames out. He was careful not to aim a jet of water on the bomb itself as this might well cause the bomb to explode. Then he switched back to a jet to extinguish the flames on the skylight. Alternating between the two settings on the hose, William had the flames out on both bomb and fire in a few minutes, though it seemed like an age. After looking down into the gloom of the building to make sure a fire hadn't started beneath them, William turned his attention to the other two incendiary bombs. Both were now doing considerable damage to the lead and there was a risk they could burn their way into the roof.

From the sand bucket brought over by Marjorie, William took a shovel-load of sand and covered the second bomb. Then he scooped the bomb into the upright sand bucket and Marjorie took it to a safe place. The third bomb was dealt with by using the stirrup pump again.

There were fires burning in the street and a building not far away was alight, but the raid had finished and the guns had fallen silent. They could relax, but they were elated rather than tired.

"Well done, William. You were marvellous," shouted

Marjorie, and she threw her arms round him exultantly. He could feel her warm breath on his neck and her soft cheek against his and he could smell her perfume.

"Well done, Marjorie. We did it!" said William, putting his arms round her. He felt so alive, the most intense feeling he'd experienced since the rescue operation for Karl, and he was so pleased that he had shared this with Marjorie. Their faces separated and he looked at her smiling broadly, and on an impulse he kissed her on the mouth. It was only a brief kiss, more of joy than of desire, but he immediately apologised. "I am so sorry, Marjorie. I don't know what came over me. It must have been the thrill of it all."

She touched his arm. "I didn't mind. I am happy too." She kissed him on the cheek and then started tidying up the debris and getting the equipment back together. He could see her hands were shaking.

After the all-clear and when William was sure they would not be needed any longer on the roof he said, "I think we could both do with a drink." He took her to a small pub nearby and bought them both a Scotch, and they got to know each other better as they sat at a table in the corner of the bar.

"You were brilliant this evening, Marjorie. Thanks for all you did. Bottoms up!" he said.

She raised her glass. "Bottoms up. Crumbs! That's strong," she said as she took a swig of the drink.

William smiled. "Sorry, I should have added soda. Would you like something else?"

"No thanks, I'm just not used to it. We never drink in our family; my parents took the pledge when they were young so we've never had any in the house. The only time I had a drink when I was young was when I went to my Aunt Annie's and she would offer me a glass of port, if my parents weren't there. I thought it was so exciting and a bit naughty, like when you stay at someone else's house and you are allowed to stay up later than usual. But I don't drink generally."

William smiled inwardly at the suggestion she was no longer young but said nothing. They were still technically on duty, but the predictable patterns of the German bombing raids encouraged him to think they could relax for a while. They had another drink, a soft one for Marjorie this time, then he escorted her back to her post before he went on his tour of the other sites on his watch. Having called in on the rest of his team and checked all was well, he was drawn towards St Paul's. The cathedral looked the same as always, though a closer inspection revealed the damage to the dome which had been pierced by a bomb the previous October. Around the cathedral was pure devastation where Paternoster Row and the narrow lanes had been flattened, making the survival of the cathedral in open ground look the more remarkable, and the sight it presented more magnificent, perhaps nearer to the vision that Wren had intended.

He saw Marjorie from time to time after that and more than once he nearly asked her out, but he could never quite bring himself to do it. In part it was because he considered he was too old, at nearly twice her age, but more than that, he didn't want to care for anyone; this was not the time.

XXXII

THE WAR DID NOT GO WELL IN 1941, WITH THE
Blitz continuing and defeat after defeat in North Africa, yet by
the time the year was halfway through William was becoming
more optimistic about the outcome, as also was Churchill,
though he refrained from saying so publicly. The Blitz on
London and other cities, terrible though it was, virtually came
to a halt by the summer of 1941 as Hitler turned towards
Russia and launched an offensive on the Soviet Union in
June. William knew that history had frequently shown that
unless Russia was defeated quickly it would slowly drain the
life-blood from the invading army. Each month that Russia
resisted convinced him that the war was turning away from
Germany. Then in December, following the attack on Pearl
Harbor, Germany declared war on the United States and
William was certain that this act of madness would ensure
the war would be won by the allies.

He said as much to Stanley when they managed to find
time for a drink a week or so later.

"Well, I wish I was as optimistic as you," said Stanley, "what
with Rommel in North Africa and the Germans making huge
gains in Russia. We've got the Japs to worry about as well now."

William smiled. "Do you think the Germans will still try an invasion of Britain as we thought they would in 1940?"

"No," said Stanley.

"Why not?"

"Because they've got too much on their plate; the Russian offensive on top of the war in North Africa."

"There you are. The likelihood of an invasion has diminished for the foreseeable future and therefore we are in a better position than we were."

Stanley nodded. "For now, anyway."

"Yes, but looking ahead, it's a simple matter of resources; the total manpower of America, the Soviet Union and the British Empire far outnumber those of Germany and its allies."

"But the Germans may have better troops and better strategies to fight a war."

"Taking on three of the most powerful countries in the world simultaneously doesn't seem to be a particularly good strategy, but even if you are right it only counts if it's a short war. Over a long war, far superior forces will win because they can afford to take higher casualties in men and materials. The Confederacy had the best generals and they might have won the American Civil War if they got it over within a year or so but as the war went on there was only going to be one winner. As long as Russia keeps fighting it's only a matter of time before the Americans deliver the knockout blow like they did last time."

Stanley laughed. "You've got it all worked out. The situation in Russia is tough, though, and they are dependent on our supplies. Dick, you know, Lucy's husband, is on the Arctic convoys. He's a chief officer now, but I don't know on what ship, for obvious reasons."

"How's Lucy?"

"She's all right; keeps busy working in one of the war

GRAHAM DONNELLY

ministries now as she's alone a lot of the time and worries about Dick. Mum would like her to move in with her and Dad for the duration, but she likes her independence."

William found himself worrying about Dick too, for Lucy's sake, vaguely conscious of Stanley still talking in the background.

"Our generation's been lucky, really," continued Stanley, "too young for the last war and too old for this one. After Dunkirk I thought they might call up everyone, even my old man, to fight a possible invasion."

"You watch, it'll be the Germans fighting on the beaches and the landing grounds in the end, not us," replied William.

He believed what he said and worked hard to do whatever he could to help that happen. Earlier in the year, he had considered the possibility of volunteering for the army and told his boss as much, but he was assured that he was far more useful where he was than in the armed services. Any further thoughts on the subject were ended when, just after Christmas, he came home to find his mother collapsed on the floor and apparently unconscious.

He carried her into the front room and lay her on the sofa, where she began to come to. "What happened, Mum?"

"I don't know. I must have fainted."

William rang the doctor, who agreed to come round later that evening. He made his mother a cup of tea and she drank it but refused to eat anything, taking to her bed. The doctor came and gave her a full examination and left her upstairs while he spoke to William.

"I'm sorry, but I can't find anything wrong with her. It may be nervous exhaustion or something of that nature; the war affects different people in different ways. I'm prescribing a tonic and some tablets which may do the trick, we'll see."

"Can she be left alone?"

381

"Well, you might want to make some arrangement for someone to call in if you are out all day, I realise it must be difficult with your work." He took out his prescription pad and wrote two items on it which William found indecipherable. "I'll call in and see how she is in a couple of days. Let me know if she takes a turn for the worse."

William saw the doctor out and went up to see his mother again.

Lying on the bed, she smiled weakly when she saw him. "What did the doctor say?"

"He's not sure what the problem is. He thinks it may be your nerves."

"I have no memory of what happened."

"I can't not go into work; we are so busy at the moment. I'll ask Mrs Watson to check on you until I get home."

His mother gave a faint smile of resignation. "I shall be all right. You don't need to worry about me."

The next few days William gave his mother her breakfast before he left for work. Mrs Watson came in at lunchtime with some soup and made Alice a cup of tea in the afternoon. In the evening William would cook a meal, spend some time with his mother, and go downstairs to listen to the radio and read, unless summoned by a knock on the ceiling.

At the weekend he went to see his Aunt Agnes, his mother's younger and only surviving sister. She lived near Clapton Pond and he was conscious that he had rarely been to see her, especially as he was seeking a favour.

"Well, this is a surprise, young Billy," she exclaimed as she opened the front door. "Come in and I'll put the kettle on. Uncle Alf's on nights at the moment so he's in bed."

William was shown into the front room, decorated and furnished still in the Edwardian style, and a few minutes later his aunt appeared with tea and digestive biscuits and sat opposite him. Physically she was almost a polar opposite of her sister: a large, round face, topped by curly hair in the style of Queen Mary, arms that would not embarrass a navvy and a voluminous bosom that, if one was clasped to it, could bring rapid suffocation.

"Well, to what do I owe this visit?" she asked, forestalling William's plan of building up gently to his request.

"Well, it's Mum, she's not very well. The doctor thinks it might be some kind of nervous problem. She hasn't been up for three days and I have been asking one of the neighbours to look in, but I can't expect that to go on indefinitely. I was wondering whether you might be able to help out a bit for a little while."

Aunt Agnes's expression changed immediately from that of indulgent curiosity to unsympathetic dismissal. "That's *right*, I should cocoa! If you think I'm going to nurse your mother when she left everything to me and your Aunt Amy when our mother was ill and on the way out. And where was she when Amy was very poorly? Nowhere to be seen." She paused for breath but carried on before William could respond. "Your mother always plays the martyr without actually bearing the cross. I know she lost little Kitty, but that was a long time ago, and Jack too, but she thinks she's the only one that bad things ever happen to. It's always 'Poor Alice.'"

"But her illness could be real this time."

Agnes was not swayed by William's plaintive interruption. "I'm sorry you are lumbered again, seeing to her. You do too much; it's time you had your own wife and family instead of running round after her. She'll get better if she doesn't have too much attention, you mark my words."

William had expected his aunt to be less than enthusiastic towards his request and knew she could be relied upon to be forthright, but he was surprised by the vehemence of her response, not to mention the comment she had made about his personal life.

The heightened atmosphere was broken by the emergence of Uncle Alf, who came into the room in his belted-up trousers and a vest. "Hello, Billy. Fancy seeing you." He held out a hand.

"Don't you come into my best room with no shirt on," said Agnes. "Get dressed properly or go into the kitchen."

Alf smiled at Billy. "The nonsense she comes out with, still, best do as I'm told. She's got a fierce right hook." He stomped back upstairs.

She made a fresh pot of tea and a bacon sandwich for her husband, which he ate in the kitchen, despite now having a shirt on. After Alf joined the others in the front room William had an enjoyable afternoon with them both, reminiscing about past times and the retelling of amusing stories about the family which had them all laughing till they cried. When he took his leave, Agnes saw him to the door. "Goodbye, Billy. It's been lovely to see you again after all this time. I do feel for you and I'm sure you are worried about your mother. Keep me informed; if things get worse, I'll help," she said, relenting as she kissed him on the cheek.

Over the next few weeks, William managed through controlled negligence, as in calling on his neighbours less frequently and going out himself more often, to get his mother out of bed and functioning semi-independently. Aunt Agnes did her bit by inviting them both round for high tea one afternoon and this finally got Alice out of the house. After that, there was a slow journey back to normality, assisted by the two sisters seeing more of each other than they had done for years. William liked to believe that Alice had truly recovered from an undefined condition but had a lingering thought that there had not really been anything to recover from in the first place. Either way, despite the advice from Aunt Agnes, he could not help but always have a scintilla of concern for her when he was away from her and could not stop himself hating her for it.

The impact of America's entry into the war in December 1941 was not immediately apparent. But, as he pored over his maps of the war situation, William had no doubt that the balance would soon shift provided Soviet Russia hung on and the Americans entered the European theatre of war. Russia had even managed to recapture some territory early in 1942 but was dependent on support from the British and Americans. This help in armaments and other resources came via the Arctic convoys which were constantly under threat from German U-boats, surface ships and bombers. In June 1942 Convoy PQ 17 suffered the most severe losses of any convoy during these operations with twenty-four of thirty-five merchant ships sunk and the loss of 153 merchant mariners. Among those lost was Chief Officer Richard Stone, the husband of Lucy and brother-in-law of Stanley.

Stanley broke the news to him over the phone. "I don't have the full details, but he went down with the ship. That's what makes it even worse for Lucy; there'll be no funeral for him."

"I'd like to write to Lucy. Is she at the same address?"

"Well, you can reach her there, but not for long. She's decided to join the Wrens."

"The Wrens?"

"Yes, it's her way of getting back at them, I suppose. There's nothing to keep her in London; Mum and Dad are both doing all right."

After several attempts, William did write a letter of condolence to Lucy that he was almost satisfied with. He felt a strong impulse to see her and support her in her grief, but a combination of reticence lest she misunderstand his intentions and regret that it was all too late for their friendship to be rekindled led him to leave it at that.

His faith that the direction of the war would soon change was repaid when the victory at El Alamein and the prolonged siege of Stalingrad turned the tide against the Germans. The mood was sufficiently lightened in Britain for the serious war films of bravery to be augmented by comedies like *The Goose Steps Out* starring Will Hay, that ridiculed the Nazis, which William enjoyed seeing. In 1943 the war shifted more and more towards the Allies with the Axis powers forced to give up in North Africa, the Italians defeated and the Russians advancing in the East. William was not concerned with the Far East, which he felt could wait. He cared only for the destruction of Nazism and an end to its pogroms in central Europe.

Yet his belief in a final victory was always clouded by uncertainty of what would happen afterwards. He believed that Germany, like the Austrian and Ottoman Empires at the end of the First World War, should cease to exist once the war was over as Germany had forfeited its right to be considered a civilised major power. It had to be diminished in some way so that it could no longer be a threat to the rest of Europe. His view was reinforced by the growing evidence that Hitler's Reich had become totally committed to the extermination of the Jews, the Gypsies and various other groups. The fact that the Allies did not yet see saving the oppressed races as a primary reason for their conduct of the war made him doubt whether Germany would be made to pay for its infamy.

XXXII

In February 1944 William went to an engineering conference, as a trade union observer. He knew some of the other delegates and, after the last plenary session, four of them had a few drinks which carried on to dinner and eventually into a rather late evening. By this time they had been joined by two other delegates William didn't know. One of them, Desmond Mortain, was a design engineer with a large civil engineering company. Initially, he was very guarded about the project he was working on. However, in the hotel bar towards the end of the evening, he mentioned that he'd been working with a team including Hugh Iorys Hughes on a temporary harbour project. Neither William nor any of the others probed for further information but guessed it must be connected with the invasion of Europe, whenever that would come.

"Very interesting character, Hugh," said Mortain. "Brilliant conceptualist and designer; it's been great working with him. He's a very keen sailor too; I suppose that's why he's got a place on Mersea Island."

"Mersea Island? Where's that?" asked one of his listeners, a ship engineer from the Clyde.

"East coast, near Colchester. I've been to see him there a couple of times. His house is on the Coast Road with lovely views out onto the estuary. Very convenient too; just across the road from a good pub, the Victory." He paused for a moment then could not contain himself. "Guess who was there when I arrived the second time?" With no response, he half-whispered, "Winston Churchill," and smiled at the reaction.

"Really?" said one of them.

"Yes, and it wasn't a one-off event. He's been there several times, apparently. He likes the food at one of the local restaurants in West Mersea and enjoys a drink or two at some watering hole or other."

"What's he like, I mean, when he's not performing in public?" asked William.

"Well, I only spent an hour or so with him, but he was jovial and upbeat, told a couple of amusing stories after we'd finished dealing with the business at hand. Whether that's the real him or just another act he puts on, I couldn't say."

His social circle having dwindled over the years, William was pleased to accept an invitation to go out for another drink with Desmond a couple of weeks later. This was followed by a tour of Desmond's design office in Victoria and lunch in the company board room a fortnight after that. Like William, Desmond was not married and, from what he said when they talked about life outside work, appeared never to have had a serious relationship with a woman. After their lunch in the board room, Desmond said how much he enjoyed William's company and William picked up just a hint that Desmond might be interested in a more intimate relationship than pure friendship. William chose to ignore this as he might have been imagining it and anyway could always deal with any misunderstandings should the matter become more obvious.

On the fourth time they met up, in April, they went out to dinner and William was persuaded to go back to Desmond's flat for another drink or two. Without being asked, Desmond told William the details of the 'Mulberry Harbours' and that a European invasion was likely to happen at the end of May or early June. It was as if he wanted to share his secrets with William, to show he trusted him.

William looked at his watch; it was after eleven. "It's late. I think I ought to get going."

Desmond had been lolling on the sofa but sat up. "Oh, I thought you might stay longer."

"Sorry, I'm so busy at work."

Desmond's expression could not hide his disappointment. "Perhaps next time."

William gave a non-committal smile.

"If you fancy a drink or something next week, give me a ring," said Desmond as William stood up. "Not Thursday or Friday, I might be required for a trip to the island, for a final meeting before the balloon goes up."

William nodded. "I'll be in touch."

The following Wednesday he went home after a very stressful day at the office. His mother had recently returned home from having tea with her sister Agnes.

"Jimmy's wife is having her second," she said as she scuttled around in the kitchen. "Agnes said he's done so well, another promotion, and she thinks the world of Jimmy's wife: a really lovely girl. It's a pity you can't meet someone like that and settle down. I'm beginning to think I'll never have a grandchild."

She sighed in that special way of hers, the way that ground into his brain every time like a drill. He didn't answer but waited for the next salvo.

"I really don't know what's come over you. You're stuck in a dead-end job, earning no more than ten years ago and you haven't brought home a girl or even mentioned one for God knows how long. You want to wake your ideas up." She placed a plate of spam fritters and baked beans in front of him. "Not much at the butchers today."

William ate silently, ignoring his mother's tirade of vitriol, diluted with a dash of self-pity. "I'm going out," he said, pushing aside his half-eaten meal.

"Aren't you going to finish your tea?"

"I'm not hungry."

"Where are you going?"

"For a drink. Perhaps I'll meet a nice young lady and bring her back with me. Then you can tell me she's not good enough, like all the others I brought home."

He didn't look back, Alice's protestations ringing in his one good ear as he closed the front door and walked over to his car. He just drove, aiming nowhere in particular, in pretty much a straight line, first to Hackney then along Graham Road, Dalston Lane and Ball's Pond Road until he turned left down the Essex Road. He was in Islington, a place he hadn't been since he stopped going to meetings of the JM Group. He felt a pang of sadness as he remembered Felicity and what might have been, and he thought of turning back. Then, on a whim, he parked his car and walked into the saloon bar of the nearest pub, realising it was one he'd been in before. At the bar were two men and as he approached them he recognised David Harris, his old friend from the JM Group.

"Hello, David." he said.

David turned round and grinned. "William! Fancy seeing you in our old haunt, after all this time. It must be over five years." He hadn't changed much, a little less hair and a little more weight, and the scar down the side of his face which he'd picked up in Spain a little fainter. They shook hands and David introduced his companion. "This is Frank, we work together."

William shook hands with Frank and asked if he could buy them both a drink.

"Not for me, thanks. I only popped in for a quick one. I've got a darts match on tonight. Nice to meet you, William. See you tomorrow, Dave," said Frank, putting on his cap and heading for the door.

William bought two pints and they took a table in the corner.

"Well, this is a nice surprise, William. How have you been keeping? I haven't seen you since we had that drink with Fred just after I got back from Spain."

"I'm fine, thanks. Same job, same address, same everything, really. I have a reserved occupation, so not much action in the war, I'm afraid."

"I volunteered but that blast in Spain that gave me this," he pointed to his scar, "affected my lungs, so I wasn't accepted." He shrugged and took a sip of his drink. "Well, we lost Spain, but we'll win this one."

"I'll drink to that," said William, raising his glass.

"It's not the war that worries me; it's the peace," said David quietly.

"In what way?"

"I don't trust the Western allies to see it through. The Americans are paranoid about socialists, let alone communists, so will they let the Russians take over Germany? Churchill's no different; he's still the same old imperialist and warmonger. He would be up for taking on the Soviets if he thought they might become too powerful."

William nodded. "I must admit I have been worried that the allies won't really want to see Germany neutralised. They'll be looking to keep it strong as a balance to Russia."

"It makes me sick," said David. "The only chance of a just outcome to the war is that the Russians flatten Germany and socialism gets its chance in Europe, but they won't let it happen. Churchill and Roosevelt will make sure of that. There'll be some phoney occupation and then Germany will be allowed to build up again."

William shrugged. "There's nothing the Russians or anyone else can do about it. The peace treaty will be a compromise between the victors. They won't want to start another war now."

"You're right. Forget the war for now. Do you see much of the old JM crowd anymore?"

"No, I keep up with Fred and that's about it, really. How about you?"

David shook his head. "No. The group didn't exactly fold, but what with Spain and then the younger ones being called up it just sort of withered. Not much point in discussing political hypotheses when there's a real battle for civilisation going on. Anyway, I got married at the end of 1940 and I've got a young family too. It changes your perspective, I guess."

"I'm pleased for you," said William.

"I'm very lucky." He pointed at his chest. "I'm not a pretty sight under this, but it doesn't seem to matter to Stella. You never...?"

"No, it just didn't happen. Too late now, I think."

David shook his head encouragingly but stopped short of delivering a platitude. "Is your mother keeping well?"

William nodded.

"You've been a good son to your mother since she lost your father," David said, trying to find words of encouragement for his old friend whom he couldn't help seeing as a slightly sad, middle-aged bachelor.

William smiled weakly and changed the subject.

They had a couple of pints each, drunk slowly over two hours, while they talked about the group and their memories of their times together. Neither mentioned Felicity. David spoke of his hopes for the future and William realised he had none himself so made up a couple to avoid disappointing his friend. Then they parted, David waving cheerily and promising to keep in touch as he set off to walk home while William was left to his own thoughts on the drive back to Homerton. Passing an off licence, he stopped and bought a bottle of whisky to take home him; perhaps a few more drinks might lift his mood.

When he got home his mother was in bed. He sat in the front room with the bottle of 'Black and White' and a reflection on the events of the evening turned into a reflection of his whole life. Much as he hated to admit it, his mother was right; his life had reached a dead end. Every job he had held had ended in failure of one kind or another and this current one would lead nowhere except retirement, without even reaching the milestone necessary to earn a gold watch. He smiled and poured himself another glass to prepare for the even more painful reflection of his relationships with women, all of which had come to nothing. He skipped quickly through the minor entanglements, a few short-term friendships that had ultimately led nowhere. Then he faced the anguish of never being able to tell Lucy of his love for her and the consequent regret that was a hundred times worse than any pain he would have felt had she turned him down. Different, but equally hard to bear, was the brief joy of his shared love with Felicity and its guillotined end. Finally, there was Sylvia. His noble rejection of the illicit relationship she had offered him no longer seemed a sacrifice worth making. He couldn't see himself marrying now; he was too old for young single women and probably too set in his ways for the older ones. Then William recalled the passing expression of pity on David's face when he had admitted that he had no one now.

That thought seemed to open the floodgates to all his painful memories: the loss of little Kitty, his father's death when he had all to live for, the steady drip of failings and regrets which seemed to blot out all those happy times of his younger days which he could no longer bring clearly to mind. He stopped drinking; it neither brought a change in his mood nor deadened his sense of utter failure. He went over to the cabinet in which he kept Karl's pistol in a locked box and, taking out the gun, idly loaded it. He sat in his chair, staring at the Luger and considering the way out it offered.

Yes, ultimately his life had been a failure for which even his mother despised him. His father would probably have contempt for him too, if he were still alive. He had not lived up to his father's hopes and expectations. The only time he had participated in Jack's political activity had ended in his father's death, which he'd been impotent to prevent. His father had predicted that there would be a moment in William's life when he was called upon to do something of great importance and he would know when that time came. That would be when he fulfilled his destiny. But that moment had never come or perhaps he had not recognised it or had missed the opportunity. The details were unimportant: he had failed in this as in everything else and let his father down.

Yet, as he held the gun, his hands almost caressing the cold metal and stiff trigger, another thought pushed its way through the heavy clouds of gloom. Perhaps it was now: this was the moment of destiny. He thought back to David's words on Churchill and how he was the main block to the war ending honourably and the kind of peace that should follow. Just as he had caused countless deaths at Gallipoli, just as he had vilified the working classes in the general strike, how every fibre of his body opposed the reform of the Empire and hated socialism. Or was it that William's thoughts were deluded, the memory of those events distorted by time and his own disappointments? He searched for and found his journal and, turning to the pages on the general strike, read through it again. No, his memories were accurate; in fact, reading the journal once more made him even angrier. He read again of Churchill in 1926 whipping up tensions during the general strike in his newspaper and encouraging the middle classes into strike-breaking and how his father died trying to stop it.

Yes, this was the time his father had spoken of. Churchill had to be stopped and the course of the war set on the path of justice and he was the one to do it. As the thought began to develop in his mind, he was shocked by the enormity of it. Even if it were true that it should be done, what right had he to be the one to do it?

The only answer that made any sense to him was that he had been given a series of signs pointing him to this moment. Karl had inadvertently given him the means with this gun. Desmond Mortain had chosen him as the one to whom he would reveal Churchill's whereabouts. David Harris had been in the pub which he chanced to go in and had expressed the same worries about Churchill and his policies that William had harboured for years. Why should all these coincidences come together now unless they were guiding him to a purpose: a moment of destiny when he could change the course of history? His own view as to whether it should be done was irrelevant. It must be done and he hoped his father would have been proud of him.

Settled on his resolve and clinging to this newfound belief that his life might have some meaning, he crept up to his bedroom, kicked off his shoes and lay on the bed, intending to rest for a while before he set off. He was tired and a little drunk and he fell into a broken sleep. When he looked at the clock it was half-past six. Still resolute in his purpose, he went to the bathroom, shaved, and washed. Then he packed an overnight case, changed into a new sports jacket and light grey trousers and, collecting the gun, made his way out to the car. His watch showed seven fifteen as he set off quietly and headed for the North Essex coast. As he drove, his assignment seemed to make more and more sense. If Churchill was removed there was bound to be a delay in the launch of an attack on France. The government would lose impetus and perhaps the new leader might be less willing to accept the large casualties in British, American, Canadian and other troops which would follow, especially as the British General Staff had reservations about such an operation. If the second front were delayed by even three months, the Russians, already in the Ukraine, would be at least in Poland, and perhaps into Germany. The Russians would be in the ascendancy.

Though there was much to blame Churchill for, William bore him no great personal ill will. After all he had ensured that Britain, and later America, had stood up to Germany and made victory a probability. It was not a matter of his own feelings; it was a political assassination to remove from power the personification of a world view that should not be allowed to triumph. Only under these circumstances would it be possible to justify the objectively immoral act of taking a life, which he found abhorrent. If he lived, he would bear the guilt and suffer the consequences of his actions because he was impelled to do so for the greater good of humanity and of civilisation. Philosophically, his justification would be found in the writings of Jeremy Bentham and utilitarianism: 'The greatest happiness of the greatest number'.

En route he stopped at a workers' café for breakfast, enjoying a cup of tea but unable to finish his food. Then he drove to Epping Forest and practised his shooting, the first time he had ever fired any gun, let alone the Luger. He

would do what had to be done at close range so there was
no concern about accuracy; he just wanted to make sure he
could fire the gun without delay when the time came. As his
journey progressed he still experienced twinges of conscience
which he had to analyse and dismiss. Had it been Hitler, he
would have had no hesitation, but Churchill could not be cast
in the role of unpardonable monster, at least not by him. He
remembered a question posed by a theologian he had read
some years before: 'Can a morally wrong act be justified on
the basis of the lesser of two evils?'. The example given was of
a group of explorers in a cave who are suddenly threatened by
the water level rising quickly. As they make their way out of the
cave one of their number gets wedged in the narrow opening
and cannot be shifted. The explorers have some dynamite and
could blast their way out of the cave, but the person stuck in
the exit would die. If they don't use the dynamite, they will
all drown. Is it morally justifiable to kill the person who is
trapped to save the others or not? Despite the theologian
saying that morally the answer was no, William had taken
the opposite view in that particular case. In extremis, it was
acceptable to kill an innocent person to save the many and
he hoped he could stand by this principle even if he were the
one who had to lose his life to save others. Innocent or not,
Churchill was the one who would die for the greater good; he
clung to this justification.

After driving through the Essex countryside, he reached
Mersea Island still quite early in the morning. He crossed
the causeway, known as the Strood, and booked into the
Fountains Hotel for one night, picking up a local area map.
He spent the rest of the morning getting his bearings. First,
he drove out to East Mersea, parking near the closed golf
course. This part of his journey was not made out of necessity
or even from curiosity. Rather it was a reminder of fond

memories of Lucy, whom he missed and who he knew had spent happy times here. He took the path, past the clubhouse and out to the ferry point where the River Colne merges with the Blackwater as they flow out to the sea. He stood on the sand and looked across the water at Brightlingsea and Point Clear, where Lucy had a holiday home. To his right, across the estuary, was Bradwell, the ancient Saxon chapel clearly visible. While he was quietly thinking about the past and the immediate future, a couple of dog walkers greeted him and he spoke a few words before going back the way he'd come. Driving back to West Mersea, he stopped at St Edmund's, the parish church of East Mersea, and sat in a pew, reflecting on what was to come and vaguely hoping for just one more sign, to be sure. He must have sat there for nearly an hour, but no one came in to disturb his thoughts. When he went back to his car he remembered passing a pub on the road, the Dog and Pheasant, and returned there for a double brandy.

Returning to the hotel, he parked his car and walked through the small town, past the church of Saints Peter and Paul and down to the Coast Road, where he could look out over the estuary of the River Blackwater. There had been some bomb damage along the Coast Road and several houses flattened. He stared for a while at the coastal defences on the beach before strolling further along the road in search of the Victory pub, mentioned by Desmond Mortain. As he rounded the slight bend he could see the Victory on the right, a fine Edwardian, wide-fronted building looking out on the estuary. He stopped outside the Victory and looked over at the house on the opposite corner, assuming this must be the home of Hugh Iorys Hughes. Looking up Victory Road, he saw two army officers come out of a modern white house with a green-tiled roof and walk down the road towards him. The sight of them making him uneasy, he turned and continued on his way along the Coast Road, past the oyster sheds, the Sailing and Social Club, the boatyards and Yacht Club towards the 'Old City'. There the former Victory Inn stood among the oldest houses of the town. As he walked on he realised he had rounded the point of the island and was heading north. He strode a little longer, enjoying the bracing air and fresh breeze, past the fishermen's cottages until he could see, but not hear, the traffic crossing the Strood. He stood there for a while, a few moments of peace and calm, before he thought again about his purpose here and began the walk back to his chosen position near the Victory.

Now, here he was, waiting and watching for the great man to arrive. He was trying not to think anymore about what was to be done. He concentrated on the one thought, over and over: *Just do it!* It was getting warmer and he was very thirsty. The Luger was in his jacket and he planned to fire through his pocket like he'd seen James Cagney do in a gangster film. He checked the safety catch was off so he would be ready when it was needed. He hoped, he hoped with all his heart, it would be today rather than having to go through this all again the next day, if Churchill hadn't arrived yet. His throat was so dry and the the Victory looked invitingly at him from across the street. But he couldn't leave his position, not for a second: he didn't know when the moment would come. He wanted to check the gun: that it was definitely loaded, that it was still pointing the right way, but he couldn't do that in public and he knew he didn't need to. One or two passers-by said hello or smiled, but it was quiet along the front. It was too early in the season for many day-trippers and it was a dull day anyway.

"Billy," a voice called out. "Fancy seeing you here!"

He recognised the voice immediately and turned to see Lucy, walking towards him from the town. She was dressed in her Wrens uniform and had a dazzling smile on her face.

"Hello, Lucy," he replied, unable to say more than that.

"How lovely it is to see you. You look well." She looked him up and down. "And very smart." She put her arm round him and kissed him on the cheek.

They stood back from each other. "And you are in the Wrens; the uniform suits you."

She laughed. "So what are you doing here?"

"A couple of days off; thought I'd take a trip down here."

"Any particular reason?"

"It's a long story. What about you? How have you been?"

"Well, I'm glad I joined up; it's given me a purpose and it's broadened my horizons. I kept the place at Point Clear and I've finally been able to go there again. I'm only down for the day. Mum and Dad are staying there, and I just popped over on the ferry. Someone saw my uniform and gave me a lift to the town to collect some of Dick's things from the Yacht Club; I've left it long enough. I have to go back to London this evening, hence the uniform." She spoke quickly and paused to take a breath.

William thought how lovely she still was and hung on her every word, but he knew he must be ready. He had to get her to move on; she mustn't be here when it happens. But he was struck dumb, mesmerised as she spoke.

"Stanley told me about the time you rescued that poor man from Germany. What a wonderful thing to do, to save a life, and so brave. You should have got a medal for it."

"It wasn't that brave," he muttered.

She smiled at his modesty and shook her head. "I must get going, I have that appointment to keep," she said. "Oh, Billy, it's so lovely to see you. You know, I always loved you better than anyone, but I couldn't bring myself to say it. I hoped you knew. There, now I've said it when it's too late." She smiled tenderly. "When you've done what you have to do will you come and have a cup of tea with me at the Yacht Club, just for old times' sake? You might as well, it's a high tide this afternoon so you won't be able get off the island; the Strood will be under water." She laughed.

He couldn't speak but nodded.

She nodded too, kissed him on the cheek again and went off down the road towards the Yacht Club.

He was transfixed, staring after her, unable to think clearly, wanting a re-run of the last few minutes. He needed time to get things straight in his head, to reset the button for what he was here to do, but it was too late. He heard a cheer and there was Churchill coming up the road from the Sailing and Social Club, accompanied by a couple of army officers and three other men. He was wearing a topcoat and that rather odd hat of his, half-topper and half-bowler. He swung his stick as he walked. A woman with a small child spoke to him and he raised his hat and responded. Then he bent down to speak to the little boy and, taking off his hat, put it on the end of his stick and spun it in the air. All three of them laughed and he replaced his hat and resumed his walk.

The cluster of men was still thirty yards away, and William stood up and crossed the road, almost in slow motion, to stand on the corner of Victory Road outside Hughes's house. From here he could cover the approach to the house and be ready should Churchill decide to walk up Victory Road with the army officers.

He was trying to concentrate on the business at hand, but he kept thinking about Lucy and what she had said. Churchill was only five yards away now; he was shorter than William expected and his features were relaxed in a smile, with nothing of his famous bulldog expression. William's hand reached down into the pocket with the gun. *Now is the time; fire the gun, now, now!* an inner voice shouted at him.

"Hello, William! What on earth are you doing here?"

William saw behind Churchill the smiling face of Desmond Mortain.

"Prime Minister, may I introduce you to my friend William Lyus, who has done so much to help maintain the supply of skilled engineers during the war."

"Hello, Mr Lyus," said Churchill. "One of the unsung heroes who have backed up our front-line forces through this long campaign. Permit me to shake you by the hand." He offered his hand and William was unable to stop himself letting go of the gun and reciprocating the gesture. "Your efforts will reap their reward, now the war is almost won. Thank you." He doffed his hat and followed the waiting army major into the garden of the house.

There's still time, thought William, looking at Churchill's back. *There's still the coward's way*, but he hesitated and now it was too late; a hand was firmly on his arm.

Desmond was smiling broadly now. "William, so lovely to see you. Why are you here?"

"I er, I just met an old friend."

"Funny we should bump into each other here. Wish I'd known you were coming down; we could have travelled together." He looked slightly puzzled for a moment. "Ah well, back to work. Let's have lunch next week."

"Yes. I'll see you," said William as Desmond hastened off to catch up with the others.

He stood still for a few moments, watching the party disappear into the house. Then he turned and walked across the road and stood on the foreshore, staring at the gently bobbing boats moored further out. He had hesitated and failed in his mission. Now all those lives would be lost and the war would follow its inevitable path. Perhaps it wouldn't have made any difference anyway; the die was cast and

Churchill's instructions would have been carried out whoever took over. *The excuses are starting already,* he thought. Then he remembered his time in the church this morning, hoping for guidance. *But Lucy, wasn't she a sign too?* Going to the edge of the water, he took the pistol from his pocket and looked at it for a moment. He briefly turned the barrel towards his face and placed his finger on the trigger. Then he lowered the pistol and hurled it with all his might towards the river. As he watched it go, he thought of Sir Bedivere throwing the dying King Arthur's sword into the lake, but no hand appeared to take the pistol, only a gentle splash as it sailed into the water.

He heard a voice behind him. "Hey, mister, did you just throw your gun into the water?"

He looked round to see two boys of about ten, one dark-haired, the other fair, both in crewneck cable-stitch jumpers. One was looking at him, the other at the water.

"Yes."

"But we're at war, you might need it. Why did you do that?" asked the fair-headed boy.

"Because my war is over, son." He smiled and walked off towards the Yacht Club.

About the Author

Graham Donnelly was born in Homerton, East London, but now lives on Mersea Island off the Essex coast. His professional background includes government service, merchant banking and lecturing on economics. Following his success as a writer of books on business economics, Graham took to novel-writing. Take One Life is his third novel, following *Mussolini's Chest* and *Unwritten Rules*. All of Graham's books draw on his own background and his interest in political and socio-economic history.